THREE MEN IN THE DARK

COLLINS ✦ CHILLERS

·THREE·MEN· ·IN·THE·DARK·

TALES OF TERROR BY

JEROME K. JEROME
BARRY PAIN & ROBERT BARR

Edited, with an Introduction, by
HUGH LAMB

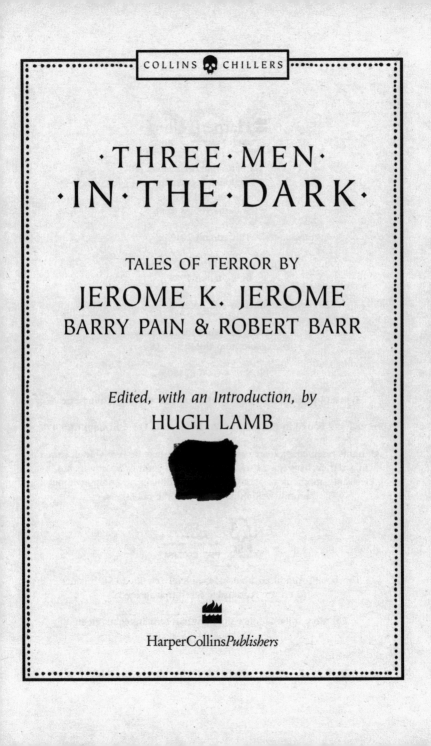

HarperCollins*Publishers*

HarperCollins*Publishers*
1 London Bridge Street
London SE1 9GF
www.harpercollins.co.uk

This edition 2017

First published in Great Britain
by Equation 1989

Selection, introduction and notes © Hugh Lamb 2017

A catalogue record for this book
is available from the British Library

ISBN 978-0-00-824905-2

Typeset by Palimpsest Book Production Ltd, Falkirk, Stirlingshire

Printed and bound in the UK by CPI Group (UK) Ltd, Croydon, CR0 4YY

MIX
Paper from
responsible sources
FSC™ C007454

This book is produced from independently certified FSC™ paper
to ensure responsible forest management.

For more information visit: www.harpercollins.co.uk/green

CONTENTS

*For two friends of mine, Mike Ashley and the late
Richard Dalby.*

INTRODUCTION

Say 'Jerome K. Jerome' to anyone reasonably well read and back comes *Three Men in a Boat*, every time. Press further and one in a hundred might say 'plays'. One in a thousand, if that, would say ghost stories. This is the price Jerome K. Jerome has paid for having one big literary hit – his other works have faded into undeserved obscurity.

Three Men in a Boat first appeared 128 years ago and it is still in print. There is even a Jerome Society, based in his home town of Walsall. Yet few people have read or know of his tales of terror. This is ironic, for he rubbed literary shoulders with such personal friends as H. Rider Haggard, Conan Doyle, Arthur Machen and H.G. Wells, whose works in this vein have all survived in print with no trouble.

My original idea was to compile a book of Jerome's tales of terror alone. However, I soon found that, good as they are, there just aren't enough of them to make up a decent sized book. So, and I hope even better, I have edited a book of stories by Jerome and two of his friends and contemporaries, Robert Barr and Barry Pain, both of whom wrote stories in this vein as good as Jerome's but whose work has suffered the same neglect as Jerome's stories. All three are connected by magazine work – Jerome and Barr founded one, and Jerome and Pain both edited another. Pain and Jerome were old friends; Barr and Jerome worked closely together. There was only 14 years' age difference between them and they all died in their sixties. Together they make fascinating reading.

Jerome Klapka Jerome was born in Walsall on 2 May 1859, the son of Jerome Clapp Jerome, a coal-mine owner on Cannock Chase. The two middle names of father and son, peculiar as they are, are not connected. Clapp comes from Clapa, a tenth-century Dane reputed to have founded the house of Jerome; Klapka was the name of an exiled Hungarian general, a friend of the family.

Jerome senior ran into bad luck when his mine flooded and he moved his family to London, where (for reasons unknown) he set up an ironmongery business in Limehouse. Jerome junior grew up in Poplar and was educated at Marylebone grammar school. After leaving school at 14, he wandered from job to job, trying his hand at work in a solicitor's office, a railway clerk and teaching. He also tried acting and, while he was no roaring success, it did give him the background for his first book *On the Stage and Off* (1888). This was a success and led to his next two books, *The Idle Thoughts of an Idle Fellow* and *Three Men in a Boat* (1889).

Three Men in a Boat was largely autobiographical, being based on Jerome's much-loved pleasure boating on the Thames and the three men were based on Jerome and his friends. As he put it: 'I did not intend to write a funny book at first. I did not know I was a humorist. [It] was really a history, I did not have to imagine or invent. Boating up and down the Thames has been my favourite sport ever since I could afford it. I just put down the things that happened.' *Idle Thoughts* was published by Andrew Tuer's Leadenhall Press (then known as Field and Tuer). Tuer himself had as good a sense of humour as Jerome: he called each 1,000 copies of the book an 'edition' and was able to advertise the book's 23rd edition in a matter of months.

As well as his books, Jerome turned to journalism. He

rapidly established a reputation as a writer, so much so that it led to an important meeting with Robert Barr.

Robert Barr was born in Glasgow on 16 September 1850 and his family emigrated to Canada when he was four years old. He was educated in Toronto and he started work as a teacher. It is reported that he was the headmaster of a public school at Windsor, Canada until 1876 (which meant he was a young headmaster indeed). In 1876 he married, and around this time, moved over the border into America, taking up a job as a reporter on the *Detroit Free Press*. He made such a success of it that the proprietors sent him to Britain in 1881 to set up a British edition. It is hard to believe that, even in the 1880s when papers were avidly read in all kinds of forms, a newspaper called the *Detroit Free Press* would be a major success in the Home Counties but it does seem that Barr made a go of it.

Barr used the pseudonym Luke Sharp for much of his journalism, as well as a splendid send-up of a famous detective, in *The Adventures of Sherlaw Kombs* (1892), and it was under this *nom de plume* that he published his first book *Strange Happenings* (1883). He mainly used his own name thereafter and quickly built up a reputation for his writing, generally in magazines but also in an interestingly long list of books.

It was nine years before he published another book under his own name, the skilled collection of stories *From a Steamer Chair* (1892). He is now mainly remembered, by crime fiction enthusiasts, for his crime novels and detective stories. He invented the renowned sleuth Eugene Valmont, claimed to have been the model for Agatha Christie's Hercule Poirot. He kept up his output of books right up to his somewhat early death on 21 October 1912.

Barr's meeting with Jerome in 1892 resulted in *The Idler*, one of the most notable magazines of the era, first appearing in February 1892. Jerome recounts the circumstances: '*The Idler* was Barr's idea. But the title was mine. Barr had made the English edition of the *Detroit Free Press* quite a good property, and was keen to start something of his own. He wanted a popular name and, at first, was undecided between Kipling and myself. He chose me – as, speaking somewhat bitterly, he later on confessed to me – thinking I should be the easier to "manage". He had not liked the look of Kipling's jaw.'

Kipling was obviously not offended for he contributed to *The Idler* in company with the major literary names of the day. This illustrated monthly magazine attracted names like Marie Corelli, George Bernard Shaw, Hall Caine, Eden Phillpotts, G.R. Sims and Conan Doyle. The division of editorial responsibility between Jerome and Barr is not clear but Jerome seems to have spent a lot of time on his other love, drama (and here he made an even bigger reputation).

Jerome's autobiography *My Life and Times* (1926) reveals him to be the most dreadful name dropper, but it is full of little snippets for the ghost story enthusiast. He knew Arthur Machen: 'he has developed into a benevolent looking white haired gentleman. He might be one of the brothers Cheeryble stepped out of *Nicholas Nickleby* . . . for ability to create an atmosphere of nameless terror, I can think of no author living or dead who comes near him.'

H. Rider Haggard, meanwhile, was 'a somewhat solemn gentleman, taking himself always very seriously. Mrs Barry Pain was the only one of us who would venture to chaff him.'

The Idler started a ritual which still goes on today among contributors to *Private Eye:* all those involved used to gather for a monthly lunch with whoever cared to attend, to swop ideas and gossip and plan future issues.

Mrs Barry Pain, the chaffer of Rider Haggard, shared her husband's renown as a playwright. Barry Pain himself, the youngest of the trio and the most prolific, was born in Cambridge either on 28 September or 22 October 1864 (he is reliably listed as being born on both dates), the son of a draper. He was educated at Sedbergh school, where he edited the school magazine, and went on to Cambridge. A fellow student of Pain, E.F. Benson recalls in his *Our Family Affairs* (1920) that when Benson started up a college magazine, Pain 'sent us one of the best parodies in the language, called "The Poets at Tea", in which Wordsworth, Tennyson, Christina Rossetti, Swinburne and others were ludicrously characteristic of themselves. He also tried to galvanize the *Cambridge Fortnightly* into life by one or more admirable short stories.' We shall hear more of Pain's stories later.

When he graduated in 1886, Pain spent four years rather surprisingly as an army coach at Guildford. He moved to London in 1890 and started writing seriously for a living, making regular contributions to magazines. His first book, *In a Canadian Canoe*, appeared in 1891; this was a selection of revised stories he had first published in, among others, Benson's *Cambridge Fortnightly*.

Short stories were Pain's forte; he was to publish over a dozen books of them, including the noted *Stories in the Dark* (1901).

Pain and Jerome met and became friends. This friendship was to aid Jerome considerably in the troubled circumstances in which he was to find himself.

In 1892, Jerome, ever active, founded a weekly paper called *Today*, which was to be different from *The Idler* but carried fine illustrations from the likes of Sidney Sime and Aubrey Beardsley. It was by all accounts a fine work but one of the most troubled of the day.

The very first issue, February 1892, caused Jerome to sue his printer for bad workmanship. Jerome won his case but was awarded damages of one farthing. This sum was to prove grotesquely ironic for Jerome.

Four years later Jerome himself was sued over an article in *Today* concerning a process claiming to make domestic gas out of water. The inventor of the process, Samson Fox, took Jerome to court for libel. Fox won his case and was awarded damages – of one farthing. Far more serious, however, was the matter of costs which fell on both parties. Fox had to find £11,000 and Jerome was obliged to pay £9,000. In those days such a sum could mean financial ruin (today's equivalent is probably over half a million pounds).

The expense meant that Jerome had to sell his interests in both *The Idler* and *Today*, and his old friend Barry Pain took over as editor of *Today*.

Jerome's literary career continued apace, however, proving his financial saviour. He found fame as a dramatist with his 1908 play *The Passing of the Third Floor Back*, and wrote other successes including *The Master of Mrs Chilvers* (1911) and *The Great Gamble* (1914). He encountered Bram Stoker, then manager of the Lyceum theatre, who Jerome recalls sending out complimentary invitations to opening nights by going through Burke's Peerage, thus ensuring the stalls would be filled with enough important people to warrant a good report in the next day's papers.

He was a great traveller, all over Europe and Russia, and lived abroad for many years. He was particularly fond of Germany. The First World War put both he and Pain on the spot.

Jerome liked the Germans but detested German militarism. For that reason he volunteered to fight but was turned down. He got round this by driving an ambulance for the French army (the French not being too bothered about employing a 55-year-old for war service), returning home in early 1917. Jerome was also one of the few voices brave enough to speak out in disbelief over the atrocities reportedly committed by the Germans, earning himself much vilification: 'It was these stories of German atrocities that first caused me to doubt whether this really was a Holy War.' Brave words in the hysterical, patriotic fever of 1914 Britain.

Pain, meanwhile, was just as keen as Jerome to do his bit, but no less disqualified through his age. He managed to join the Royal Naval Volunteer Reserve's anti-aircraft section in April 1915 and found himself operating a searchlight on Parliament Hill. His eyes failed him and he had to abandon this, becoming in 1917 a member of the London Appeal Tribunal, adjudicating on claims for exemption from military service.

Robert Barr had died in 1912. Pain and Jerome both got through the war unscathed, and returned to writing. Pain produced some less humorous works, like his rather offbeat novel, *The Later Years* (1927). Jerome worked on his autobiography and some more plays.

Jerome went on a motoring tour in May 1927. He suffered a brain haemorrhage and was rushed to Northampton hospital where he died on 14 June. He is buried at Ewelm churchyard, near Oxford, with his sister and stepdaughter, near the place in which he lived for many years. Funeral services were held at Golders Green and Walsall.

Jerome would have probably borrowed, for one of his comic characters, the name of the officiating clergyman at Golders Green: the Reverend Herbert Trundle.

Barry Pain, the last survivor of the trio, died within the year, at Watford on 5 May 1928.

Jerome, Pain and Barr all turned their hand to writing tales of terror. I use the expression 'tales of terror' in preference to 'ghost story', for unlike the bulk of their Victorian contemporaries, not one of them seemed to be interested in ghost stories *per se*.

Jerome's only book of ghost stories *Told After Supper* (1891) was an alarmingly accurate send-up of the Dickens school of supernatural fiction.

Robert Barr wrote few ghost stories, being more interested in what could loosely be termed crime fiction; Barry Pain's stories were just plain odd.

Rather than group each author's stories together in a stodgy lump, I have arranged them in the best order I can find. It gives them extra reading value to compare them with each other.

Jerome proves to be surprisingly versatile in his choice of material. 'The Dancing Partner', from *Novel Notes* (1893), is probably his most widely known work in this vein, yet has not lost its appeal through over-exposure. Oddly neglected but from the same source as 'The Dancing Partner' are 'The

Skeleton' and 'The Snake', two short but sharp pieces. 'Silhouettes' (from the very first issue of *The Idler*) and 'The Woman of the Saeter' are strange stories indeed. Jerome wrote of these two: '[They] are not intended to be amusing. I should be glad if they were judged from some other standpoint than humour.' You'll see what he meant. 'The Woman of the Saeter' is straightforward enough, but what on earth he was trying to achieve in 'Silhouettes' is another matter altogether. What sort of humorist could write the paragraph starting 'From these sea-scented scenes, my memory travels . . .'? The story could hardly be an incident from his father's coal mining days – if so, it is not recorded anywhere else – and is probably the most unfunny thing he ever wrote.

Jerome himself may have given us a clue. He said in his autobiography: 'I can see the humorous side of things and enjoy the fun when it comes; but look where I will, there always seems to me more sadness than joy in life . . . having won success as a humorist, I immediately became serious. I have a kink in my brain, I suppose. I can't help it.' Quite frankly, 'Silhouettes' reads like the writing of a manic-depressive on a downward spell. If Jerome could lose his sense of humour, or even doubt if he had one to start with, then his humorous writing takes on a whole new slant.

Barry Pain, on the other hand, seemed to have no such worries. His main claim to fame was the Eliza series of books, the musings and adventures of a London housewife. Other works for which he may be remembered are *De Omnibus* (1901), the ramblings of a bus driver; and the creation of the likeable criminal Constantine Dix.

His weird stories range widely in their themes. 'The Undying Thing' deals with what seems to be a werewolf survival; 'The Green Light' with the conscience of a murderer; 'Smeath' is a harsh tale of a hunchback and a conman; 'The Glass of Supreme Moments' tells of a mirror that lures men to their deaths.

Pain seems most at home in the genre and is probably the writer out of the three with the most modern appeal.

Robert Barr, on the other hand, was somewhat ahead of his time in the stories included here. He produced a book called *Revenge!* (1896) which both employed the plot devices of the conte cruel and pre-dated the neat, twist endings of so many of the crime pulp stories of the 1930s and 1940s. Perhaps the best example is 'An Alpine Divorce' which would not be out of place in TV's *Tales of the Unexpected*.

All three enjoyed a good story. The neglect of the stories in here is surprising but I think it makes for an interesting and enjoyable collection. They've been forgotten for far too long; I hope you enjoy them.

Hugh Lamb
Sutton, Surrey
May 2017

THE SKELETON

Jerome K. Jerome

One evening Jephson asked me if I believed in spiritualism to its fullest extent.

'That is rather a large question,' I answered. 'What do you mean by "spiritualism to its fullest extent"?'

'Well, do you believe that the spirits of the dead have not only the power of revisiting this earth at their will, but that, when here, they have the power of action, or rather, of exciting to action? Let me put a definite case. A spiritualist friend of mine, a sensible and by no means imaginative man, once told me that a table, through the medium of which the spirit of a friend had been in the habit of communicating with him, came slowly across the room towards him, of its own accord, one night as he sat alone, and pinioned him against the wall. Now can any of you believe that, or can't you?'

'I could,' Brown took it upon himself to reply; 'but, before doing so, I should wish for an introduction to the friend who told you the story. Speaking generally,' he continued, 'it seems to me that the difference between what we call the natural and the supernatural is merely the difference between frequency and rarity of occurrence. Having regard to the phenomena we are compelled to admit, I think it illogical to disbelieve anything we are unable to disprove.'

'For my part,' remarked MacShaughnassy, 'I can believe in the ability of our spirit friends to give the quaint entertainments credited to them much easier than I can in their desire to do so.'

'You mean,' added Jephson, 'that you cannot understand why a spirit, not compelled as we are by the exigencies of society, should care to spend its evenings on a laboured and childish conversation with a room full of abnormally uninteresting people.'

'That is precisely what I cannot understand,' MacShaughnassy agreed.

'Nor I, either,' said Jephson. 'But I was thinking of something very different altogether. Suppose a man died with the dearest wish of his heart unfulfilled, do you believe that his spirit might have power to return to earth and complete the interrupted work?'

'Well,' answered MacShaughnassy, 'if one admits the possibility of spirits retaining any interest in the affairs of this world at all, it is certainly more reasonable to imagine them engaged upon a task such as you suggest, than to believe that they occupy themselves with the performance of mere drawing-room tricks. But what are you leading up to?'

'Why, to this,' replied Jephson, seating himself straddle-legged across his chair, and leaning his arms upon the back. 'I was told a story this morning at the hospital by an old French doctor. The actual facts are few and simple; all that is known can be read in the Paris police records of sixty-two years ago.

'The most important part of the case, however, is the part that is not known, and that never will be known.

'The story begins with a great wrong done by one man unto another man. What the wrong was I do not know. I am inclined to think, however, it was connected with a woman. I think that, because he who had been wronged hated him who had wronged him with a hate such as does not often burn in a man's brain, unless it be fanned by the memory of a woman's breath.

'Still that is only conjecture, and the point is immaterial. The man who had done the wrong fled, and the other man followed him. It became a point-to-point race, the first man having the advantage of a day's start. The course was the whole world, and the stakes were the first man's life.

'Travellers were few and far between in those days, and this made the trail easy to follow. The first man, never knowing how far or how near the other was behind him, and hoping now and again that he might have baffled him, would rest for a while. The second man, knowing always just how far the first one was before him, never paused, and thus each day the man who was spurred by Hate drew nearer to the man who was spurred by Fear.

'At this town the answer to the never-varied question would be:

'"At seven o'clock last evening, Monsieur."

'"Seven – ah; eighteen hours. Give me something to eat, quick, while the horses are being put to."

'At the next the calculation would be sixteen hours.

'Passing a lonely châlet, Monsieur puts his head out of the window:

'"How long since a carriage passed this way, with a tall, fair man inside?"

'"Such a one passed early this morning, Monsieur."

'"Thanks, drive on, a hundred francs apiece if you are through the pass before daybreak."

'"And what for dead horses, Monsieur?"

'"Twice their value when living."

'One day the man who was ridden by Fear looked up, and saw before him the open door of a cathedral, and passing in, knelt down and prayed. He prayed long and fervently, for men, when they are in sore straits, clutch eagerly at the straws of faith. He prayed that he might be forgiven his sin, and, more important still, that he might be pardoned the consequences of his sin, and be delivered from his adversary; and a few chairs from him, facing him, knelt his enemy, praying also.

'But the second man's prayer, being a thanksgiving merely, was short, so that when the first man raised his eyes, he saw the face of his enemy gazing at him across the chair-tops, with a mocking smile upon it.

'He made no attempt to rise, but remained kneeling, fascinated by the look of joy that shone out of the other man's eyes. And the other man moved the high-backed chairs one by one, and came towards him softly.

'Then, just as the man who had been wronged stood beside the man who had wronged him, full of gladness that his opportunity had come, there burst from the cathedral tower a sudden clash of bells, and the man, whose opportunity had come, broke his heart and fell back dead, with that mocking smile still playing round his mouth.

'And so he lay there.

'Then the man who had done the wrong rose up and passed out, praising God.

'What became of the body of the other man is not known. It was the body of a stranger who had died suddenly in the cathedral. There was none to identify it, none to claim it.

'Years passed away, and the survivor in the tragedy became a worthy and useful citizen, and a noted man of science.

'In his laboratory were many objects necessary to him in his researches, and, prominent among them, stood in a certain corner a human skeleton. It was a very old and much-mended skeleton, and one day the long-expected end arrived, and it tumbled to pieces.

'Thus it became necessary to purchase another.

'The man of science visited a dealer he well knew – a little parchment-faced old man who kept a dingy shop, where nothing was ever sold, within the shadow of the towers of Notre Dame.

'The little parchment-faced old man had just the very thing that Monsieur wanted – a singularly fine and well-proportioned "study". It should be sent round and set up in Monsieur's laboratory that very afternoon.

'The dealer was as good as his word. When Monsieur entered his laboratory that evening, the thing was in its place.

'Monsieur seated himself in his high-backed chair, and tried to collect his thoughts. But Monsieur's thoughts were unruly, and inclined to wander, and to wander always in one direction.

'Monsieur opened a large volume and commenced to read. He read of a man who had wronged another and fled from him, the other man following. Finding himself reading this, he closed the book angrily, and went and stood by the window and looked out. He saw before him the sun-pierced nave of a great cathedral, and on the stones lay a dead man with a mocking smile upon his face.

'Cursing himself for a fool, he turned away with a laugh. But his laugh was short-lived, for it seemed to him that something else in the room was laughing also. Struck suddenly still, with his feet glued to the ground, he stood listening for a while: then sought with starting eyes the corner from where the sound had seemed to come. But the white thing standing there was only grinning.

'Monsieur wiped the damp sweat from his head and hands, and stole out.

'For a couple of days he did not enter the room again. On the third, telling himself that his fears were those of a hysterical girl, he opened the door and went in. To shame himself, he took his lamp in his hand, and crossing over to the far corner where the skeleton stood, examined it. A set of bones bought for three hundred francs. Was he a child, to be scared by such a bogey!

'He held his lamp up by the front of the thing's grinning head. The flame of the lamp flickered as though a faint breath had passed over it.

'The man explained this to himself by saying that the walls of the house were old and cracked, and that the wind might creep in anywhere. He repeated this explanation to himself as he re-crossed the room, walking backwards, with his eyes fixed on the thing. When he reached his desk, he sat down and gripped the arms of his chair till his fingers turned white.

'He tried to work, but the empty sockets in that grinning head seemed to be drawing him towards them. He rose and battled with his inclination to fly screaming from the room. Glancing fearfully about him, his eye fell upon a high screen, standing before the door. He dragged it forward, and placed it between himself and the thing, so that he could not see it – nor it see him. Then he sat down again to his work. For a while he forced himself to look at the book in front of him, but at last, unable to control himself any longer, he suffered his eyes to follow their own bent.

'It may have been an hallucination. He may have accidentally placed the screen so as to favour such an illusion. But what he saw was a bony hand coming round the corner of the screen, and, with a cry, he fell to the floor in a swoon.

'The people of the house came running in, and lifting him up, carried him out, and laid him upon his bed. As soon as he recovered, his first question was, where had they found the thing – where was it when they entered the room? When they told him they had seen it standing where it always stood, and had gone down into the room to look again, because of his frenzied entreaties, and returned trying to hide their smiles, he listened to their talk about overwork, and the necessity for change and rest, and said they might do with him as they would.

'So for many months the laboratory door remained locked. Then there came a chill autumn evening when the man of science opened it again, and closed it behind him.

'He lighted his lamp, and gathered his instruments and books around him, and sat down before them in his high-backed chair. And the old terror returned to him.

'But this time he meant to conquer himself. His nerves were stronger now, and his brain clearer; he would fight his unreasoning fear. He crossed to the door and locked himself in, and flung the key to the other end of the room, where it fell among jars and bottles with an echoing clatter.

'Later on, his old housekeeper, going her final round, tapped at his door and wished him good-night, as was her custom. She received no response, at first, and, growing nervous, tapped louder and called again; and at length an answering "good-night" came back to her.

'She thought little about it at the time, but afterwards she remembered that the voice that had replied to her had been strangely grating and mechanical. Trying to describe it, she likened it to such a voice as she would imagine coming from a statue.

'Next morning his door remained still locked. It was no unusual thing for him to work all night and far into the next day, so no one thought to be surprised. When, however, evening came, and yet he did not appear, his servants gathered outside the room and whispered, remembering what had happened once before.

'They listened, but could hear no sound. They shook the door and called to him, then beat with their fists upon the wooden panels. But still no sound came from the room.

'Becoming alarmed, they decided to burst open the door, and, after many blows, it gave way, and they crowded in.

'He sat bolt upright in his high-backed chair. They thought at first he had died in his sleep. But when they drew nearer and the light fell upon him, they saw the livid marks of bony fingers round his throat; and in his eyes there was a terror such as is not often seen in human eyes.'

THE MOON-SLAVE

Barry Pain

The Princess Viola had, even in her childhood, an inevitable submission to the dance; a rhythmical madness in her blood answered hotly to the dance music, swaying her, as the wind sways trees, to movements of perfect sympathy and grace.

For the rest, she had her beauty and her long hair, that reached to her knees, and was thought lovable; but she was never very fervent and vivid unless she was dancing; at other times there almost seemed to be a touch of lethargy upon her. Now, when she was sixteen years old, she was betrothed to the Prince Hugo. With others the betrothal was merely a question of state. With her it was merely a question of obedience, to the wishes of authority; it had been arranged; Hugo was *comme ci, comme ça* – no good in her eyes; it did not matter. But with Hugo it was quite different – he loved her.

The betrothal was celebrated by a banquet, and afterwards by a dance in the great hall of the palace. From this dance the Princess soon made her escape, quite discontented, and went to the furthest part of the palace gardens, where she could no longer hear the music calling her.

'They are all right,' she said to herself as she thought of the men she had left, 'but they cannot dance. Mechanically they are all right; they have learned it and don't make childish mistakes; but they are only one-two-three machines. They haven't the inspiration of dancing. It is so different when I dance alone.'

She wandered on until she reached an old forsaken maze. It had been planned by a former king. All round it was a high crumbling wall with foxgloves growing on it. The maze itself had all its paths bordered with high opaque hedges; in the very centre was a circular open space with tall pine trees growing round it. Many years ago the clue to the maze had been lost; it was but rarely now that anyone entered it. Its gravel paths were green with weeds, and in some places the hedges, spreading beyond their borders, had made the way almost impassable.

For a moment or two Viola stood peering in at the gate – a narrow gate with curiously twisted bars of wrought iron surmounted by a heraldic device. Then the whim seized her to enter the maze and try to find the space in the centre. She opened the gate and went in.

Outside everything was uncannily visible in the light of the full moon, but here in the dark shaded alleys the night was conscious of itself. She soon forgot her purpose, and wandered about quite aimlessly, sometimes forcing her way where the brambles had flung a laced barrier across her path, and a dragging mass of convolvulus struck wet and cool upon her cheek. As chance would have it she suddenly found herself standing under the tall pines, and looking at the open space that formed the goal of the maze. She was pleased that she had got there. Here the ground was carpeted with sand, fine and, as it seemed, beaten hard. From the summer night sky immediately above, the moonlight, unobstructed here, streamed straight down upon the scene.

Viola began to think about dancing. Over the dry, smooth sand her little satin shoes moved easily, stepping and gliding, circling and stepping, as she hummed the tune to which they moved. In the centre of the space she paused, looked at the wall of dark trees all round, at the shining stretches of silvery sand and at the moon above.

'My beautiful, moonlit, lonely, old dancing-room, why did I never find you before?' she cried; 'but,' she added, 'you need music – there must be music here.'

In her fantastic mood she stretched her soft, clasped hands upwards towards the moon.

'Sweet moon,' she said in a kind of mock prayer, 'make your white light come down in music into my dancing-room here, and I will dance most deliciously for you to see.' She flung her head backward and let her hands fall; her eyes were half closed, and her mouth was a kissing mouth. 'Ah! sweet moon,' she whispered, 'do this for me, and I will be your slave; I will be what you will.'

Quite suddenly the air was filled with the sound of a grand invisible orchestra. Viola did not stop to wonder. To the music of a slow saraband she swayed and postured. In the music there was the regular beat of small drums and a perpetual drone. The air seemed to be filled with the perfume of some bitter spice. Viola could fancy almost that she saw a smouldering camp fire and heard far off the roar of some desolate wild beast. She let her long hair fall, raising the heavy strands of it in either hand as she moved slowly to the laden music. Slowly her body swayed with drowsy grace, slowly her satin shoes slid over the silver sand.

The music ceased with a clash of cymbals. Viola rubbed her eyes. She fastened her hair up carefully again. Suddenly she looked up, almost imperiously.

'Music! more music!' she cried.

Once more the music came. This time it was a dance of caprice, pelting along the violin strings, leaping, laughing, wanton. Again an illusion seemed to cross her eyes. An old king was watching her, a king with the sordid history of the exhaustion of pleasure written on his flaccid face. A hook-nosed courtier by his side settled the ruffles at his wrists and mumbled *Ravaissant! Quel malheur que la vieillesse!* It was a strange illusion. Faster and faster she sped to the music, stepping, spinning, pirouetting; the dance was light as thistle-down, fierce as fire, smooth as a rapid stream.

The moment that the music ceased Viola became horribly afraid. She turned and fled away from the moonlit space, through the trees, down the dark alleys of the maze, not heeding in the least which turn she took, and yet she found herself soon at the outside iron gate. From thence she ran through the palace garden, hardly ever pausing to take breath, until she reached the palace itself. In the eastern sky the first signs of dawn were showing; in the palace the festivities were drawing to an end. As she stood alone in the outer hall Prince Hugo came towards her.

'Where have you been, Viola?' he said sternly. 'What have you been doing?'

She stamped her little foot.

'I will not be questioned,' she replied angrily.

'I have some right to question,' he said.

She laughed a little.

'For the first time in my life,' she said, 'I have been dancing.'

He turned away in hopeless silence.

The months passed away. Slowly a great fear came over Viola, a fear that would hardly ever leave her. For every month at the full moon, whether she would or no, she found herself driven to the maze, through its mysterious walks into that strange dancing-room. And when she was there the music began once more, and once more she danced most deliciously for the moon to see. The second time that this happened she had merely thought that it was a recurrence of her own whim, and that the music was but a trick that the imagination had chosen to repeat. The third time frightened her, and she knew that the force that sways the tides had strange power over her. The fear grew as the year fell, for each month the music went on for a longer time – each month some of the pleasure had gone from the dance. On bitter nights in winter the moon called her and she came, when the breath was vapour, and the trees that circled her dancing-room were black bare skeletons, and the frost was cruel. She dared not tell anyone, and yet it was with difficulty that she kept her secret. Somehow chance seemed to favour her, and she always found a way to return from her midnight dance to her own room without being observed. Each month the summons seemed to be more imperious and urgent. Once when she was alone on her knees before the lighted altar in the private chapel of the palace she suddenly felt that the words of the familiar Latin prayer had gone from her memory. She rose to her feet, she sobbed bitterly, but the call had come and she could not resist it. She passed out of the chapel and down the palace gardens. How madly she danced that night!

She was to be married in the spring. She began to be more gentle with Hugo now. She had a blind hope that when they were married she might be able to tell him about it, and he might be able to protect her, for she had always known him to be fearless. She could not love him, but she tried to be good to him. One day he mentioned to her that he had tried to find his way to the centre of the maze, and had failed. She smiled faintly. If only she could fail! But she never did.

On the night before the wedding day she had gone to bed and slept peacefully, thinking with her last waking moments of Hugo. Overhead the full moon came up the sky. Quite suddenly Viola was wakened with the impulse to fly to the dancing-room. It seemed to bid her hasten with breathless speed. She flung a cloak around her, slipped her naked feet into her dancing-shoes and hurried forth. No one saw her or heard her – on the marble staircase of the palace, on down the terraces of the garden, she ran as fast as she could. A thorn plant caught in her cloak, but she sped on, tearing it free; a sharp stone cut through the satin of one shoe, and her foot was wounded and bleeding, but she sped on. As the pebble that is flung from a cliff must fall until it reaches the sea, as the white ghost-moth must come in from cool hedges and scented darkness to a burning death in the lamp by which you sit so late – so Viola had no choice. The moon called her. The moon drew her to that circle of hard, bright sand and the pitiless music.

It was brilliant, rapid music tonight. Viola threw off her cloak and danced. As she did so, she saw that a shadow lay over a fragment of the moon's edge. It was the night of a total eclipse. She heeded it not. The intoxication of the dance was on her. She was all in white; even her face was pale in the moonlight. Every movement was full of poetry and grace.

The music would not stop. She had grown deathly weary. It seemed to her that she had been dancing for hours, and the shadow had nearly covered the moon's face, so that it was almost dark. She could barely see the trees around her. She went on dancing, stepping, spinning, pirouetting, held by the merciless music.

It stopped at last, just when the shadow had quite covered the moon's face, and all was dark. But it stopped only for a moment, and then began again. This time it was a slow, passionate waltz. It was useless to resist; she began to dance once more. As she did so she uttered a sudden shrill scream of horror, for in the dead darkness a hot hand had caught her own and whirled her round, *and she was no longer dancing alone*.

The search for the missing Princess lasted during the whole of the following day. In the evening Prince Hugo, his face anxious and firmly set, passed in his search the iron gate of the maze, and noticed on the stones beside it the stain of a drop of blood. Within the gate was another stain. He followed this clue, which had been left by Viola's wounded foot, until he reached that open space in the centre that had served Viola for her dancing-room. It was quite empty. He noticed that the sand round the edges was all worn down, as though someone had danced there, round and round, for a long time. But no separate footprint was distinguishable there. Just outside this track, however, he saw two footprints clearly defined close together: one was the print of a tiny satin shoe; the other was the print of a large naked foot – a cloven foot.

THE UNDYING THING

Barry Pain

I

Up and down the oak-panelled dining-hall of Mansteth the master of the house walked restlessly. At formal intervals down the long severe table were placed four silver candlesticks, but the light from these did not serve to illuminate the whole of the surroundings. It just touched the portrait of a fair-haired boy with a sad and wistful expression that hung at one end of the room; it sparkled on the lid of a silver tankard. As Sir Edric passed to and fro it lit up his face and figure. It was a bold and resolute face with a firm chin and passionate, dominant eyes. A bad past was written in the lines of it. And yet every now and then there came over it a strange look of very anxious gentleness that gave it some resemblance to the portrait of the fair-haired boy. Sir Edric paused a moment before the portrait and surveyed it carefully, his strong brown hands locked behind him, his gigantic shoulders thrust a little forward.

'Ah, what I was!' he murmured to himself – 'what I was!'

Once more he commenced pacing up and down. The candles, mirrored in the polished wood of the table, had burnt low. For hours Sir Edric had been waiting, listening intently for some sound from the room above or from the broad staircase outside. There had been sounds – the wailing of a woman, a quick abrupt voice, the moving of rapid feet. But for the last hour he had heard nothing. Quite suddenly he stopped and dropped on his knees against the table:

'God, I have never thought of Thee. Thou knowest that – Thou knowest that by my devilish behaviour and cruelty I did veritably murder Alice, my first wife, albeit the physicians did maintain that she died of a decline – a wasting sickness. Thou knowest that all here in Mansteth do hate me, and that rightly. They say, too, that I am mad; but that they say not rightly, seeing that I know how wicked I am. I always knew it, but I never cared until I loved – oh, God, I never cared!'

His fierce eyes opened for a minute, glared round the room, and closed again tightly. He went on:

'God, for myself I ask nothing; I make no bargaining with Thee. Whatsoever punishment Thou givest me to bear I will bear it; whatsoever Thou givest me to do I will do it. Whether Thou killest Eve or whether Thou keepest her in life – and never have I loved but her – I will from this night be good. In due penitence will I receive the holy Sacrament of Thy Body and Blood. And my son, the one child that I had by Alice, I will fetch back again from Challonsea, where I kept him in order that I might not look upon him, and I will be to him a father in deed and very truth. And in all things, so far as in me lieth, I will make restitution and atonement. Whether Thou hearest me or whether Thou hearest me not, these things shall be. And for my prayer, it is but this: of Thy loving kindness, most merciful God, be Thou with Eve and make her happy; and after these great pains and perils of childbirth send her Thy peace. Of Thy loving-kindness, Thy merciful loving-kindness, O God!'

Perhaps the prayer that is offered when the time for praying is over is more terribly pathetic than any other. Yet one might hesitate to say that this prayer was unanswered.

Sir Edric rose to his feet. Once more he paced the room. There was a strange simplicity about him, the simplicity that scorns an incongruity. He felt that his lips and throat were parched and dry. He lifted the heavy silver tankard from the table and raised the lid; there was still a good draught of mulled wine in it with the burnt toast, cut heart-shaped, floating on the top.

'To the health of Eve and her child,' he said aloud, and drained it to the last drop.

Click, click! As he put the tankard down he heard distinctly two doors opened and shut quickly, one after the other. And then slowly down the stairs came a hesitating step. Sir Edric could bear the suspense no longer. He opened the dining-room door, and the dim light strayed out into the dark hall beyond.

'Dennison,' he said, in a low, sharp whisper, 'is that you?'

'Yes, yes. I am coming, Sir Edric.'

A moment afterwards Dr Dennison entered the room. He was very pale; perspiration streamed from his forehead; his cravat was disarranged. He was an old man, thin, with the air of proud humility. Sir Edric watched him narrowly.

'Then she is dead,' he said, with a quiet that Dr Dennison had not expected.

'Twenty physicians – a hundred physicians could not have saved her, Sir Edric. She was—' He gave some details of medical interest.

'Dennison,' said Sir Edric, still speaking with calm and restraint, 'why do you seem thus indisposed and panic-stricken? You are a physician; have you never looked upon the face of death before? The soul of my wife is with God—'

'Yes,' murmured Dennison, 'a good woman, a perfect, saintly woman.'

'And,' Sir Edric went on, raising his eyes to the ceiling as though he could see through it, 'her body lies in great dignity and beauty upon the bed, and there is no horror in it. Why are you afraid?'

'I do not fear death, Sir Edric.'

'But your hands – they are not steady. You are evidently overcome. Does the child live?'

'Yes, it lives.'

'Another boy – a brother for young Edric, the child that Alice bore me?'

'There – there is something wrong. I do not know what to do. I want you to come upstairs. And, Sir Edric, I must tell you, you will need your self-command.'

'Dennison, the hand of God is heavy upon me; but from this time forth until the day of my death I am submissive to it, and God send that that day may come quickly! I will follow you and I will endure.'

He took one of the high silver candlesticks from the table and stepped towards the door. He strode quickly up the staircase, Dr Dennison following a little way behind him.

As Sir Edric waited at the top of the staircase he heard suddenly from the room before him a low cry. He put down the candlestick on the floor and leaned back against the wall listening. The cry came again, a vibrating monotone ending in a growl.

'Dennison, Dennison!'

His voice choked; he could not go on.

'Yes,' said the doctor, 'it is in there. I had the two women out of the room, and got it here. No one but myself has seen it. But you must see it, too.'

He raised the candle and the two men entered the room – one of the spare bedrooms. On the bed there was something moving under cover of a blanket. Dr Dennison paused for a moment and then flung the blanket partially back.

They did not remain in the room for more than a few seconds. The moment they got outside, Dr Dennison began to speak.

'Sir Edric, I would fain suggest somewhat to you. There is no evil, as Sophocles hath it in his "Antigone", for which man hath not found a remedy, except it be death, and here—'

Sir Edric interrupted him in a husky voice.

'Downstairs, Dennison. This is too near.'

It was, indeed, passing strange. When once the novelty of this – this occurrence had worn off, Dr Dennison seemed no longer frightened. He was calm, academic, interested in an unusual phenomenon. But Sir Edric, who was said in the village to fear nothing in earth, or heaven, or hell, was obviously much moved.

When they had got back to the dining-room, Sir Edric motioned the doctor to a seat.

'Now, then,' he said, 'I will hear you. Something must be done – and tonight.'

'Exceptional cases,' said Dr Dennison, 'demand exceptional remedies. Well, it lies there upstairs and is at our mercy. We can let it live, or, placing one hand over the mouth and nostrils, we can—'

'Stop,' said Sir Edric. 'This thing has so crushed and humiliated me that I can scarcely think. But I recall that while I waited for you I fell upon my knees and prayed that God would save Eve. And, as I confessed unto Him more than I will ever confess unto man, it seemed to me that it were ignoble to offer a price for His favour. And I said that whatsoever punishment I had to bear, I would bear it; and whatsoever He called upon me to do, I would do it; and I made no conditions.'

'Well?'

'Now my punishment is of two kinds. Firstly my wife, Eve, is dead. And this I bear more easily because I know that she is numbered with the company of God's saints, and with them her pure spirit finds happier communion than with me; I was not worthy of her. And yet she would call my roughness by gentle, pretty names. She gloried, Dennison, in the mere strength of my body, and in the greatness of my stature. And I am thankful that she never saw this – this shame that has come upon the house. For she was a proud woman, with all her gentleness, even as I was proud and bad until it pleased

God this night to break me even to the dust. And for my second punishment, that, too, I must bear. This thing that lies upstairs, I will take and rear; it is bone of my bone and flesh of my flesh; only, if it be possible, I will hide my shame so that no man but you shall know of it.'

'This is not possible. You cannot keep a living being in this house unless it be known. Will not these women say, "Where is the child?"'

Sir Edric stood upright, his powerful hands linked before him, his face working in agony; but he was still resolute.

'Then if it must be known, it shall be known. The fault is mine. If I had but done sooner what Eve asked, this would not have happened. I will bear it.'

'Sir Edric, do not be angry with me, for if I did not say this, then I should be but an ill counsellor. And, firstly, do not use the word shame. The ways of nature are past all explaining; if a woman be frail and easily impressed, and other circumstances concur, then in some few rare cases a thing of this sort does happen. If there be shame, it is not upon you but upon nature – to whom one would not lightly impute shame. Yet it is true that common and uninformed people might think that this shame was yours. And herein lies the great trouble – the shame would rest also on her memory.'

'Then,' said Sir Edric, in a low, unfaltering voice, 'this night for the sake of Eve I will break my word, and lose my own soul eternally.'

About an hour afterwards Sir Edric and Dr Dennison left the house together. The doctor carried a stable lantern in his hand. Sir Edric bore in his arms something wrapped in a blanket. They went through the long garden, out into the orchard that skirts the north side of the park, and then across a field to a small dark plantation known as Hal's Planting. In the very heart of Hal's Planting there are some curious caves: access to the innermost chamber of them is exceedingly difficult and dangerous, and only possible to a climber of exceptional skill and courage. As they returned from these caves, Sir Edric no longer carried his burden. The dawn was breaking and the birds began to sing.

'Could not they be quiet just for this morning?' said Sir Edric wearily.

There were but few people who were asked to attend the funeral of Lady Vanquerest and of the baby which, it was said, had only survived her by a few hours. There were but three people who knew that only one body – the body of Lady Vanquerest – was really interred on that occasion. These three were Sir Edric Vanquerest, Dr Dennison, and a nurse whom it had been found expedient to take into their confidence.

During the next six years Sir Edric lived, almost in solitude, a life of great sanctity, devoting much of his time to the education of the younger Edric, the child that he had by his first wife. In the course of this time some strange stories began to be told and believed in the neighbourhood with reference to Hal's Planting, and the place was generally avoided.

When Sir Edric lay on his deathbed the windows of the chamber were open, and suddenly through them came a low cry. The doctor in attendance hardly regarded it, supposing that it came from one of the owls in the trees outside. But Sir Edric, at the sound of it, rose right up in bed before anyone could stay him, and flinging up his arms cried, 'Wolves! wolves! wolves!' Then he fell forward on his face, dead.

And four generations passed away.

II

Towards the latter end of the nineteenth century, John Marsh, who was the oldest man in the village of Mansteth, could be prevailed upon to state what he recollected. His two sons supported him in his old age; he never felt the pinch of poverty, and he always had money in his pocket; but it was a settled principle with him that he would not pay for the pint of beer which he drank occasionally in the parlour of The Stag. Sometimes Farmer Wynthwaite paid for the beer; sometimes it was Mr Spicer from the post office; sometimes the landlord of The Stag himself would finance the old man's evening dissipation. In return, John Marsh was prevailed upon to state what he recollected; this he would do with great heartiness and strict impartiality, recalling the intemperance of a former Wynthwaite and the dishonesty of some ancestral Spicer, while he drank the beer of their direct descendants. He would tell you, with two tough old fingers crooked round the handle of the pewter that you had provided, how your grandfather was a poor thing, 'fit for nowt but to brak steeans by ta rord-side.' He was so disrespectful that it was believed that he spoke truth. He was particularly disrespectful when he spoke of that most devilish family, the Vanquerests; and he never tired of recounting the stories that from generation to generation had grown up about them. It would be objected, sometimes, that the present Sir Edric, the last surviving member of the race, was a pleasant-spoken young man, with none of the family wildness and hot temper. It was for no sin of his that Hal's Planting was haunted – a thing which everyone in Mansteth, and many beyond it, most devoutly believed. John Marsh would hear no apology for him, nor for any of his ancestors; he recounted the prophecy that an old mad woman had made of the family before her strange death, and hoped, fervently, that he might live to see it fulfilled.

The third baronet, as has already been told, had lived the latter part of his life, after his second wife's death, in peace and quietness. Of him John Marsh remembered nothing, of course, and could only recall the few fragments of information that had been handed down to him. He had been told that this Sir Edric, who had travelled a good deal, at one time kept wolves, intending to train them to serve as dogs; these wolves were not kept under proper restraint, and became a kind of terror to the neighbourhood. Lady Vanquerest, his second wife, had asked him frequently to destroy these beasts, but Sir Edric, although it was said that he loved his second wife even more than he hated the first, was obstinate when any of his whims were crossed, and put her off with promises. Then one day Lady Vanquerest herself was attacked by the wolves; she was not bitten, but she was badly frightened. That filled Sir Edric with remorse, and, when it was too late, he went out into the yard where the wolves were kept and shot them all. A few months afterwards Lady Vanquerest died in childbirth. It was a queer thing, John Marsh noted, that it was just at this time that Hal's Planting began to get such a bad name. The fourth baronet was, John Marsh considered, the worst of the race; it was to him that the old mad woman had made her prophecy, an incident that Marsh himself had witnessed in his childhood and still vividly remembered.

The baronet, in his old age, had been cast up by his vices on the shores of melancholy; heavy-eyed, grey-haired, bent, he seemed to pass through life as in a dream. Every day he would go out on horseback, always at a walking pace, as though he were following the funeral of his past self. One night he was riding up the village street as this old woman came down it. Her name was Ann Ruthers; she had a kind of reputation in the village, and although all said that she was mad, many of her utterances were remembered, and she was treated with respect. It was growing dark, and the village street was almost empty; but just at the lower end was the usual group of men by the door of The Stag, dimly illuminated by the light that came through the quaint windows of the old inn. They glanced at Sir Edric as he rode slowly past them, taking no notice of their respectful salutes. At the upper end of the street there were two persons. One was Ann Ruthers, a tall, gaunt old woman, her head wrapped in a shawl; the other was John Marsh. He was then a boy of eight, and he was feeling somewhat frightened. He had been on an expedition to a distant and foetid pond, and in the black mud and clay about its borders he had discovered live newts; he had three of them in his pocket, and this was to some extent a joy to him, but his joy was damped by his knowledge that he was coming home much too late, and would probably be chastised in consequence. He was unable to walk fast or to run, because Ann Ruthers was immediately in front of him, and he dared not pass her, especially at night. She walked on until she met Sir Edric, and then, standing still, she called him by name. He pulled in his horse and raised his heavy eyes to look at her. Then in loud clear tones she spoke to him, and John Marsh heard and remembered every word that she said; it was her prophecy of the end of the Vanquerests. Sir Edric never answered a word. When she had finished, he rode on, while she remained standing there, her eyes fixed on the stars above her. John Marsh dared not pass the mad woman; he turned round and walked back, keeping close to Sir Edric's horse. Quite suddenly, without a word of warning, as if in a moment of ungovernable irritation, Sir Edric wheeled his horse round and struck the boy across the face with his switch.

On the following morning John Marsh – or rather, his parents – received a handsome solatium in coin of the realm; but sixty-five years afterwards he had not forgiven that blow, and still spoke of the Vanquerests as a most devilish family, still hoped and prayed that he might see the prophecy fulfilled. He would relate, too, the death of Ann Ruthers, which occurred either later on the night of her prophecy or early on the following day. She would often roam about the country all night, and on this particular night she left the main road to wander over the Vanquerest lands, where trespassers, especially at night, were not welcomed. But no one saw her, and it seemed that she had made her way to a part where no one was likely to see her; for none of the keepers would have entered Hal's Planting by night. Her body was found there at noon on the following day, lying under the tall bracken, dead, but without any mark of violence upon it. It was considered that she had died in a fit. This naturally added to the ill-repute of Hal's Planting. The woman's death caused considerable sensation in the village. Sir Edric sent a messenger to the married sister with whom she had lived, saying that he wished to pay all the funeral expenses. This offer, as John Marsh recalled with satisfaction, was refused.

Of the last two baronets he had but little to tell. The fifth baronet was credited with the family temper, but he conducted himself in a perfectly conventional way, and did not seem in the least to belong to romance. He was a good man of business, and devoted himself to making up, as far as he could, for the very extravagant expenditure of his predecessors. His son, the present Sir Edric, was a fine young fellow and popular in the village. Even John Marsh could find nothing to say against him; other people in the village were interested in him. It was said that he had chosen a wife in London – a Miss Guerdon – and would shortly be back to see that Mansteth Hall was put in proper order for her before his marriage at the close of the season. Modernity kills ghostly romance. It was difficult to associate this modern and handsome Sir Edric, bright and spirited, a good sportsman and a good fellow, with the doom that had been foretold for the Vanquerest family. He himself knew the tradition and laughed at it. He wore clothes made by a London tailor, looked healthy, smiled cheerfully, and, in a vain attempt to shame his own head keeper, had himself spent a night alone in Hal's Planting. This last was used by Mr Spicer in argument, who would ask John Marsh what he made of it. John Marsh replied, contemptuously, that it was 'nowt'. It was not so that the Vanquerest family was to end; but when the thing, whatever it was, that lived in Hal's Planting, left it and came up to the house, to Mansteth Hall itself, then one would see the end of the Vanquerests. So Ann Ruthers had prophesied. Sometimes Mr Spicer would ask the pertinent question, how did John Marsh know that there really was anything in Hal's Planting? This he asked, less because he disbelieved, than because he wished to draw forth an account of John's personal experiences. These were given in great detail, but they did not amount to very much. One night John Marsh had been taken by business – Sir Edric's keepers would have called the business by hard names – into the neighbourhood of Hal's Planting. He had been suddenly startled by a cry, and had run away as though he were running for his life. That was all he could tell about the cry – it was the kind of cry to make a man lose his head and run. And then it always happened that John Marsh was urged by his companions to enter Hal's Planting himself, and discover what was there. John pursed his thin lips together, and hinted that that also might be done one of these days. Whereupon Mr Spicer looked across his pipe to Farmer Wynthwaite, and smiled significantly.

Shortly before Sir Edric's return from London, the attention of Mansteth was once more directed to Hal's Planting, but not by any supernatural occurrence. Quite suddenly, on a calm day, two trees there fell with a crash; there were caves in the centre of the plantation, and it seemed as if the roof of some big chamber in these caves had given way.

They talked it over one night in the parlour of The Stag. There was water in these caves, Farmer Wynthwaite knew it; and he expected a further subsidence. If the whole thing collapsed, what then?

'Ay,' said John Marsh. He rose from his chair, and pointed in the direction of the Hall with his thumb. 'What then?'

He walked across to the fire, looked at it meditatively for a moment, and then spat in it.

'A trewly wun'ful owd mon,' said Farmer Wynthwaite as he watched him.

III

In the smoking-room at Mansteth Hall sat Sir Edric with his friend and intended brother-in-law, Dr Andrew Guerdon. Both men were on the verge of middle-age; there was hardly a year's difference between them. Yet Guerdon looked much the older man; that was, perhaps, because he wore a short, black beard, while Sir Edric was clean shaven. Guerdon was thought to be an enviable man. His father had made a fortune in the firm of Guerdon, Guerdon, and Bird; the old style was still retained at the bank, although there was no longer a Guerdon in the firm. Andrew Guerdon had a handsome allowance from his father, and had also inherited money through his mother. He had taken the degree of Doctor of Medicine; he did not practise, but he was still interested in science, especially in out-of-the-way science. He was unmarried, gifted with perpetually good health, interested in life, popular. His friendship with Sir Edric dated from their college days. It had for some years been almost certain that Sir Edric would marry his friend's sister, Ray Guerdon, although the actual betrothal had only been announced that season.

On a bureau in one corner of the room were spread a couple of plans and various slips of paper. Sir Edric was wrinkling his brows over them, dropping cigar-ash over them, and finally getting angry over them. He pushed back his chair irritably, and turned towards Guerdon.

'Look here, old man!' he said. 'I desire to curse the original architect of this house – to curse him in his down-sitting and his uprising.'

'Seeing that the original architect has gone to where beyond these voices there is peace, he won't be offended. Neither shall I. But why worry yourself? You've been rooted to that blessed bureau all day, and now, after dinner, when every self-respecting man chucks business, you return to it again – even as a sow returns to her wallowing in the mire.'

'Now, my good Andrew, do be reasonable. How on earth can I bring Ray to such a place as this? And it's built with such ingrained malice and vexatiousness that one can't live in it as it is, and can't alter it without having the whole shanty tumble down about one's ears. Look at this plan now. That thing's what they're pleased to call a morning-room. If the window had been *here* there would have been an uninterrupted view of open country. So what does this forsaken fool of an architect do? He sticks it *there*, where you see it on the plan, looking straight on to a blank wall with a stable yard on the other side of it. But that's a trifle. Look here again—'

'I won't look any more. This place is all right. It was good enough for your father and mother and several generations before them until you arose to improve the world; it was good enough for you until you started to get married. It's a picturesque place, and if you begin to alter it you'll spoil it.' Guerdon looked round the room critically. 'Upon my word,' he said, 'I don't know of any house where I like the smoking-room as well as I like this. It's not too big, and yet it's fairly lofty; it's got those comfortable-looking oak-panelled walls. That's the right kind of fireplace, too, and these corner cupboards are handy.'

'Of course this won't *remain* the smoking-room. It has the morning sun, and Ray likes that, so I shall make it into her boudoir. It *is* a nice room, as you say.'

'That's it, Ted, my boy,' said Guerdon bitterly; 'take a room which is designed by nature and art to be a smoking-room and turn it into a boudoir. Turn it into the very deuce of a boudoir with the morning sun laid on for ever and ever. Waste the twelfth of August by getting married on it. Spend the winter in foreign parts, and write letters that you can breakfast out of doors, just as if you'd created the mildness of the climate yourself. Come back in the spring and spend the London season in the country in order to avoid seeing anybody who wants to see you. That's the way to do it; that's the way to get yourself generally loved and admired!'

'That's chiefly imagination,' said Sir Edric. 'I'm blest if I can see why I should not make this house fit for Ray to live in.'

'It's a queer thing: Ray was a good girl, and you weren't a bad sort yourself. You prepare to go into partnership, and you both straightaway turn into despicable lunatics. I'll have a word or two with Ray. But I'm serious about this house. Don't go tinkering it; it's got a character of its own, and you'd better leave it. Turn half Tottenham Court Road and the culture thereof – Heaven help it! – into your town house if you like, but leave this alone.'

'Haven't got a town house – yet. Anyway I'm not going to be unsuitable; I'm not going to feel myself at the mercy of a big firm. I shall supervise the whole thing myself. I shall drive over to Challonsea tomorrow afternoon and see if I can't find some intelligent and fairly conscientious workmen.'

'That's all right; you supervise them and I'll supervise you. You'll be much too new if I don't look after you. You've got an old legend, I believe, that the family's coming to a bad end; you must be consistent with it. As you are bad, be beautiful. By the way, what do you yourself think of the legend?'

'It's nothing,' said Sir Edric, speaking, however, rather seriously. 'They say that Hal's Planting is haunted by something that will not die. Certainly an old woman, who for some godless reason of her own made her way there by night, was found there dead on the following morning; but her death could be, and was, accounted for by natural causes. Certainly, too, I haven't a man in my employ who'll go there by night now.'

'Why not?'

'How should I know? I fancy that a few of the villagers sit boozing at The Stag in the evening, and like to scare themselves by swopping lies about Hal's Planting. I've done my best to stop it. I once, as you know, took a rug, a revolver and a flask of whisky and spent the night there myself. But even that didn't convince them.'

'Yes, you told me. By the way, did you hear or see anything?'

Sir Edric hesitated before he answered. Finally he said:

'Look here, old man, I wouldn't tell this to anyone but

yourself. I did think that I heard something. About the middle of the night I was awakened by a cry; I can only say that it was the kind of cry that frightened me. I sat up, and at that moment I heard some great, heavy thing go swishing through the bracken behind me at a great rate. Then all was still; I looked about, but I could find nothing. At last I argued as I would argue now that a man who is just awake is only half awake, and that his powers of observation, by hearing or any other sense, are not to be trusted. I even persuaded myself to go to sleep again, and there was no more disturbance. However, there's a real danger there now. In the heart of the plantation there are some caves and a subterranean spring; lately there has been some slight subsidence there, and the same sort of thing will happen again in all probability. I wired today to an expert to come and look at the place; he has replied that he will come on Monday. The legend says that when the thing that lives in Hal's Planting comes up to the Hall, the Vanquerests will be ended. If I cut down the trees and then break up the place with a charge of dynamite I shouldn't wonder if I spoiled that legend.'

Guerdon smiled.

'I'm inclined to agree with you all through. It's absurd to trust the immediate impressions of a man just awakened; what you heard was probably a stray cow.'

'No cow,' said Sir Edric impartially. 'There's a low wall all round the place – not much of a wall, but too much for a cow.'

'Well, something else – some equally obvious explanation. In dealing with such questions, never forget that you're in the nineteenth century. By the way, your man's coming on Monday. That reminds me today's Friday, and as an indisputable consequence tomorrow's Saturday, therefore, if you want to find your intelligent workmen it will be of no use to go in the afternoon.'

'True,' said Sir Edric, 'I'll go in the morning.' He walked to a tray on a side table and poured a little whisky into a tumbler.

'They don't seem to have brought any seltzer water,' he remarked in a grumbling voice.

He rang the bell impatiently.

'Now why don't you use those corner cupboards for that kind of thing? If you kept a supply there, it would be handy in case of accidents.'

'They're full up already.'

He opened one of them and showed that it was filled with old account books and yellow documents tied up in bundles. The servant entered.

'Oh, I say, there isn't any seltzer. Bring it, please.'

He turned again to Guerdon.

'You might do me a favour when I'm away tomorrow, if there's nothing else that you want to do. I wish you'd look through all these papers for me. They're all old. Possibly some of them ought to go to my solicitor, and I know that a lot of them ought to be destroyed. Some few may be of family interest. It's not the kind of thing that I could ask a stranger or a servant to do for me, and I've so much on hand just now before my marriage—'

'But of course, my dear fellow, I'll do it with pleasure.'

'I'm ashamed to give you all this bother. However, you said that you were coming here to help me, and I take you at your word. By the way, I think you'd better not say anything to Ray about the Hal's Planting story.'

'I may be some of the things that you take me for, but really I am not a common ass. Of course I shouldn't tell her.'

'I'll tell her myself, and I'd sooner do it when I've got the whole thing cleared up. Well, I'm really obliged to you.'

'I needn't remind you that I hope to receive as much again. I believe in compensation. Nature always gives it and always requires it. One finds it everywhere, in philology and onwards.'

'I could mention omissions.'

'They are few, and make a belief in a hereafter to supply them logical.'

'Lunatics, for instance?'

'Their delusions are often their compensation. They argue correctly from false premises. A lunatic believing himself to be a millionaire has as much delight as money can give.'

'How about deformities or monstrosities?'

'The principle is there, although I don't pretend that the compensation is always adequate. A man who is deprived of one sense generally has another developed with unusual acuteness. As for monstrosities of at all a human type one sees none; the things exhibited in fairs are, almost without exception, frauds. They occur rarely, and one does not know enough about them. A really good textbook on the subject would be interesting. Still, such stories as I have heard would bear out my theory – stories of their superhuman strength and cunning, and of the extraordinary prolongation of life that has been noted, or is said to have been noted, in them. But it is hardly fair to test my principle by exceptional cases. Besides, anyone can prove anything except that anything's worth proving.'

'That's a cheerful thing to say. I wouldn't like to swear that I could prove how the Hal's Planting legend started; but I fancy, do you know, that I could make a very good shot at it.'

'Well?'

'My great-grandfather kept wolves – I can't say why. Do you remember the portrait of him? – not the one when he was a boy, the other. It hangs on the staircase. There's now a group of wolves in one corner of the picture. I was looking carefully at the picture one day and thought that I detected some over-painting in that corner; indeed, it was done so roughly that a child would have noticed it if the picture had been hung in a better light. I had the over-painting removed by a good man, and underneath there was a group of wolves depicted. Well, one of these wolves must have escaped, got into Hal's Planting, and scared an old woman or two; that would start a story, and human mendacity would do the rest.'

'Yes,' said Guerdon meditatively, 'that doesn't sound

improbable. But why did your great-grandfather have the wolves painted out?'

IV

Saturday morning was fine, but very hot and sultry. After breakfast, when Sir Edric had driven off to Challonsea, Andrew Guerdon settled himself in a comfortable chair in the smoking-room. The contents of the corner cupboard were piled up on a table by his side. He lit his pipe and began to go through the papers and put them in order. He had been at work about a quarter of an hour when the butler entered rather abruptly, looking pale and disturbed.

'In Sir Edric's absence, sir, it was thought that I had better come to you for advice. There's been an awful thing happened.'

'Well?'

'They've found a corpse in Hal's Planting about half an hour ago. It's the body of an old man, John Marsh, who used to live in the village. He seems to have died in some kind of a fit. They were bringing it here, but I had it taken down to the village where his cottage is. Then I sent for the police and a doctor.'

There was a moment or two's silence before Guerdon answered.

'This is a terrible thing. I don't know of anything else that you could do. Stop; if the police want to see the spot where the body was found, I think that Sir Edric would like them to have every facility.'

'Quite so, sir.'

'And no one else must be allowed there.'

'No, sir. Thank you.'

The butler withdrew.

Guerdon arose from his chair and began to pace up and down the room.

'What an impressive thing a coincidence is!' he thought to

himself. 'Last night the whole of Hal's Planting story seemed to be not worth consideration. But this second death there – it can be only coincidence. What else could it be?'

The question would not leave him. What else could it be? Had that dead man seen something there and died in sheer terror of it? Had Sir Edric really heard something when he spent that night there alone? He returned to his work, but he found that he got on with it but slowly. Every now and then his mind wandered back to the subject of Hal's Planting. His doubts annoyed him. It was unscientific and unmodern of him to feel any perplexity, because a natural and rational explanation was possible; he was annoyed with himself for being perplexed.

After luncheon he strolled round the grounds and smoked a cigar. He noticed that a thick bank of dark, slate-coloured clouds was gathering in the west. The air was very still. In a remote corner of the garden a big heap of weeds was burning; the smoke went up perfectly straight. On the top of the heap light flames danced; they were like the ghosts of flames in the strange light. A few big drops of rain fell. The small shower did not last for five seconds. Guerdon glanced at his watch. Sir Edric would be back in an hour, and he wanted to finish his work with the papers before Sir Edric's return, so he went back into the house once more.

He picked up the first document that came to hand. As he did so, another, smaller, and written on parchment, which had been folded in with it, dropped out. He began to read the parchment; it was written in faded ink, and the parchment itself was yellow and in many places stained. It was the confession of the third baronet – he could tell that by the date upon it. It told the story of that night when he and Dr Dennison went together carrying a burden through the long garden out into the orchard that skirts the north side of the park, and then across a field to a small, dark plantation. It told how he made a vow to God and did not keep it. These were the last words of the confession:

'Already upon me has the punishment fallen, and the

devil's wolves do seem to hunt me in my sleep nightly. But I know that there is worse to come. The thing that I took to Hal's Planting is dead. Yet it will come back again to the Hall, and then will the Vanquerests be at an end. This writing I have committed to chance, neither showing it nor hiding it, and leaving it to chance if any man shall read it.'

Underneath there was a line written in darker ink, and in quite a different handwriting. It was dated fifteen years later, and the initials R.D. were appended to it:

'It is not dead. I do not think that it will ever die.'

When Andrew Guerdon had finished reading this document, he looked slowly round the room. The subject had got on his nerves, and he was almost expecting to see something. Then he did his best to pull himself together. The first question he put to himself was this: 'Has Ted ever seen this?' Obviously he had not. If he had he could not have taken the tradition of Hal's Planting so lightly, nor have spoken of it so freely. Besides, he would either have mentioned the document to Guerdon, or he would have kept it carefully concealed. He would not have allowed him to come across it casually in that way. 'Ted must never see it,' thought Guerdon to himself. He then remembered the pile of weeds he had seen burning in the garden. He put the parchment in his pocket, and hurried out. There was no one about. He spread the parchment on the top of the pile, and waited until it was entirely consumed. Then he went back to the smoking-room; he felt easier now.

'Yes,' thought Guerdon, 'if Ted had first of all heard of the finding of that body, and then had read that document, I believe that he would have gone mad. Things that come near us affect us deeply.'

Guerdon himself was much moved. He clung steadily to reason; he felt himself able to give a natural explanation all through, and yet he was nervous. The net of coincidence had closed in around him; the mention in Sir Edric's confession of the prophecy which had subsequently become traditional in the village alarmed him. And what did that last line mean? He supposed that R.D. must be the initials of Dr Dennison. What did he mean by saying that the thing was not dead? Did he mean that it had not really been killed, that it had been gifted with some preternatural strength and vitality and had survived, though Sir Edric did not know it? He recalled what he had said about the prolongation of the lives of such things. If it still survived, why had it never been seen? Had it joined to the wild hardiness of the beast a cunning that was human – or more than human? How could it have lived? There was water in the caves, he reflected, and food could have been secured – a wild beast's food. Or did Dr Dennison mean that though the thing itself was dead, its wraith survived and haunted the place? He wondered how the doctor had found Sir Edric's confession, and why he had written that line at the end of it. As he sat thinking, a low rumble of thunder in the distance startled him. He felt a touch of panic – a sudden impulse to leave Mansteth at once and, if possible, to take Ted with him. Ray could never live there. He went over the whole thing in his mind again and again, at one time calm and argumentative about it, and at another shaken by blind horror.

Sir Edric, on his return from Challonsea a few minutes afterwards, came straight to the smoking-room where Guerdon was. He looked tired and depressed. He began to speak at once:

'You needn't tell me about it – about John Marsh. I heard about it in the village.'

'Did you? It's a painful occurrence, although, of course—'

'Stop. Don't go into it. Anything can be explained – I know that.'

'I went through those papers and account books while you were away. Most of them may just as well be destroyed; but there are a few – I put them aside there – which might be kept. There was nothing of any interest.'

'Thanks; I'm much obliged to you.'

'Oh, and look here, I've got an idea. I've been examining the plans of the house, and I'm coming round to your opinion. There are some alterations which should be made, and yet I'm afraid that they'd make the place look patched and renovated. It wouldn't be a bad thing to know what Ray thought about it.'

'That's impossible. The workmen come on Monday, and we can't consult her before then. Besides, I have a general notion what she would like.'

'We could catch the night express to town at Challonsea, and—'

Sir Edric rose from his seat angrily and hit the table.

'Good God! don't sit there hunting up excuses to cover my cowardice, and making it easy for me to bolt. What do you suppose the villagers would say, and what would my own servants say, if I ran away tonight? I am a coward – I know it. I'm horribly afraid. But I'm not going to act like a coward if I can help it.'

'Now, my dear chap, don't excite yourself. If you are going to care at all – to care as much as the conventional damn – for what people say, you'll have no peace in life. And I don't believe you're afraid. What are you afraid of?'

Sir Edric paced once or twice up and down the room, and then sat down again before replying.

'Look here, Andrew, I'll make a clean breast of it. I've always laughed at the tradition; I forced myself, as it seemed at least, to disprove it by spending a night in Hal's Planting; I took the pains even to make a theory which would account for its origin. All the time I had a sneaking, stifled belief in it. With the help of my reason I crushed that; but now my reason has thrown up the job, and I'm afraid. I'm afraid of the Undying Thing that is in Hal's Planting. I heard it that night. John Marsh saw it last night – they took me to see the body, and the face was awful; and I believe that one day it will come from Hal's Planting—'

'Yes,' interrupted Guerdon, 'I know. And at present I

believe as much. Last night we laughed at the whole thing, and we shall live to laugh at it again, and be ashamed of ourselves for a couple of superstitious old women. I fancy that beliefs are affected by weather – there's thunder in the air.'

'No,' said Sir Edric, 'my belief has come to stay.'

'And what are you going to do?'

'I'm going to test it. On Monday I can begin to get to work, and then I'll blow up Hal's Planting with dynamite. After that we shan't need to believe – we shall *know*. And now let's dismiss the subject. Come down into the billiard-room and have a game. Until Monday I won't think of the thing again.'

Long before dinner, Sir Edric's depression seemed to have completely vanished. At dinner he was boisterous and amused. Afterwards he told stories and was interesting.

It was late at night; the terrific storm that was raging outside had awoke Guerdon from sleep. Hopeless of getting to sleep again, he had arisen and dressed, and now sat in the window-seat watching the storm. He had never seen anything like it before; and every now and then the sky seemed to be torn across as if by hands of white fire. Suddenly he heard a tap at his door, and looked round. Sir Edric had already entered; he also had dressed. He spoke in a curious, subdued voice.

'I thought you wouldn't be able to sleep through this. Do you remember that I shut and fastened the dining-room window?'

'Yes, I remember it.'

'Well, come in here.'

Sir Edric led the way to his room, which was immediately over the dining-room. By leaning out of the window they could see that the dining-room window was open wide.

'Burglar,' said Guerdon meditatively.

'No,' Sir Edric answered, still speaking in a hushed voice. 'It is the Undying Thing – it has come for me.'

He snatched up the candle, and made towards the staircase;

Guerdon caught up the loaded revolver which always lay on the table beside Sir Edric's bed and followed him. Both men ran down the staircase as though there were not another moment to lose. Sir Edric rushed at the dining-room door, opened it a little, and looked in. Then he turned to Guerdon, who was just behind him.

'Go back to your room,' he said authoritatively.

'I won't,' said Guerdon. 'Why? What is it?'

Suddenly the corners of Sir Edric's mouth shot outward into the hideous grin of terror.

'It's there! It's there!' he gasped.

'Then I come in with you.'

'Go back!'

With a sudden movement, Sir Edric thrust Guerdon away from the door, and then, quick as light, darted in, and locked the door behind him.

Guerdon bent down and listened. He heard Sir Edric say in a firm voice:

'Who are you? What are you?'

Then followed a heavy, snorting breathing, a low, vibrating growl, an awful cry, a scuffle.

Then Guerdon flung himself at the door. He kicked at the lock, but it would not give way. At last he fired his revolver at it. Then he managed to force his way into the room. It was perfectly empty. Overhead he could hear footsteps; the noise had awakened the servants; they were standing, tremulous, on the upper landing.

Through the open window access to the garden was easy. Guerdon did not wait to get help; and in all probability none of the servants could have been persuaded to come with him. He climbed out alone, and, as if by some blind impulse, started to run as hard as he could in the direction of Hal's Planting. He knew that Sir Edric would be found there.

But when he got within a hundred yards of the plantation, he stopped. There had been a great flash of lightning, and he saw that it had struck one of the trees. Flames darted about the plantation as the dry bracken caught. Suddenly, in the light of another flash, he saw the whole of the trees fling their heads upwards; then came a deafening crash, and the ground slipped under him, and he was flung forward on his face. The plantation had collapsed, fallen through into the caves beneath it. Guerdon slowly regained his feet; he was surprised to find that he was unhurt. He walked on a few steps, and then fell again; this time he had fainted away.

PURIFICATION

Robert Barr

Eugène Caspilier sat at one of the metal tables of the Café Égalité, allowing the water from the carafe to filter slowly through a lump of sugar and a perforated spoon into his glass of absinthe. It was not an expression of discontent that was to be seen on the face of Caspilier, but rather a fleeting shade of unhappiness which showed he was a man to whom the world was being unkind. On the opposite side of the little round table sat his friend and sympathizing companion, Henri Lacour. He sipped his absinthe slowly, as absinthe should be sipped, and it was evident that he was deeply concerned with the problem that confronted his comrade.

'Why, in Heaven's name, did you marry her? That, surely, was not necessary.'

Eugène shrugged his shoulders. The shrug said plainly, 'Why indeed? Ask me an easier one.'

For some moments there was silence between the two. Absinthe is not a liquor to be drunk hastily, or even to be talked over too much in the drinking. Henri did not seem to expect any other reply than the expressive shrug, and each man consumed his beverage dreamily, while the absinthe, in return for this thoughtful consideration, spread over them its benign influence, gradually lifting from their minds all care and worry, dispersing the mental clouds that hover over all men at times, thinning the fog until it disappeared, rather than rolling the vapour away, as the warm sun dissipates into invisibility the opaque morning mists, leaving nothing but clear air all around and a blue sky overhead.

'A man must live,' said Caspilier at last; 'and the profession of decadent poet is not a lucrative one. Of course there is undying fame in the future, but then we must have our absinthe in the present. Why did I marry her, you ask? I was the victim of my environment. I must write poetry; to write poetry, I must live; to live, I must have money; to get money, I was forced to marry. Valdorème is one of the best pastry-cooks in Paris; is it my fault, then, that the Parisians have a greater love for pastry than for poetry? Am I to blame that her wares are more sought for at her shop than are mine at the booksellers'? I would willingly have shared the income of the shop with her without the folly of marriage, but Valdorème has strange, barbaric notions which were not overturnable by civilized reason. Still my action was not wholly mercenary, nor indeed mainly so. There was a rhythm about her name that pleased me. Then she is a Russian, and my country and hers were at that moment in each other's arms, so I proposed to Valdorème that we follow the national example. But, alas! Henri, my friend, I find that even ten years' residence in Paris will not eliminate the savage from the nature of a Russian. In spite of the name that sounds like the soft flow of a rich mellow wine, my wife is little better than a barbarian. When I told her about Tenise, she acted like a mad woman – drove me into the streets.'

'But why did you tell her about Tenise?'

'*Pourquoi*? How I hate that word! Why! Why!! Why!!! It dogs one's actions like a bloodhound, eternally yelping for a reason. It seems to me that all my life I have had to account to an enquiring why. I don't know why I told her; it did not appear to be a matter requiring any thought or consideration. I spoke merely because Tenise came into my mind at the moment. But after that, the deluge; I shudder when I think of it.'

'Again the why?' said the poet's friend. 'Why not cease to think of conciliating your wife? Russians are unreasoning aborigines. Why not take up life in a simple poetic way with Tenise, and avoid the Rue De Russie altogether?'

Caspilier sighed gently. Here fate struck him hard. 'Alas! my friend, it is impossible. Tenise is an artist's model, and those brutes of painters who get such prices for their daubs, pay her so little each week that her wages would hardly keep me in food and drink. My paper, pens, and ink I can get at the cafés, but how am I going to clothe myself? If Valdorème would but make us a small allowance, we could be so happy. Valdorème is madame, as I have so often told her, and she owes me something for that; but she actually thinks that because a man is married he should come dutifully home like a bourgeois grocer. She has no poetry, no sense of the needs of a literary man, in her nature.'

Lacour sorrowfully admitted that the situation had its embarrassments. The first glass of absinthe did not show clearly how they were to be met, but the second brought bravery with it, and he nobly offered to beard the Russian lioness in her den, explain the view Paris took of her unjustifiable conduct, and, if possible, bring her to reason.

Caspilier's emotion overcame him, and he wept silently, while his friend, in eloquent language, told how famous authors, whose names were France's proudest possession, had been forgiven by their wives for slight lapses from strict domesticity, and these instances, he said, he would recount to Madame Valdorème, and so induce her to follow such illustrious examples.

The two comrades embraced and separated; the friend to use his influence and powers of persuasion with Valdorème; the husband to tell Tenise how blessed they were for having such a friend to intercede for them; for Tenise, bright little Parisienne that she was, bore no malice against the unreasonable wife of her lover.

Henri Lacour paused opposite the pastry-shop on the Rue

de Russie that bore the name of 'Valdorème' over the temptingly filled windows. Madame Caspilier had not changed the title of her well-known shop when she gave up her own name. Lacour caught sight of her serving her customers, and he thought she looked more like a Russian princess than a shopkeeper. He wondered now at the preference of his friend for the petite black-haired model. Valdorème did not seem more than twenty; she was large, and strikingly handsome, with abundant auburn hair that was almost red. Her beautifully moulded chin denoted perhaps too much firmness, and was in striking contrast to the weakness of her husband's lower face. Lacour almost trembled as she seemed to flash one look directly at him, and, for a moment, he feared she had seen him loitering before the window. Her eyes were large, of a limpid amber colour, but deep within them smouldered a fire that Lacour felt he would not care to see blaze up. His task now wore a different aspect from what it had worn in front of the Café Egalité. Hesitating a moment, he passed the shop, and, stopping at a neighbouring café, ordered another glass of absinthe. It is astonishing how rapidly the genial influence of this stimulant departs!

Fortified once again, he resolved to act before his courage had time to evaporate, and so, goading himself on with the thought that no man should be afraid to meet any woman, be she Russian or civilized, he entered the shop, making his most polite bow to Madame Caspilier.

'I have come, madame,' he began, 'as the friend of your husband, to talk with you regarding his affairs.'

'Ah!' said Valdorème; and Henri saw with dismay the fires deep down in her eyes rekindle. But she merely gave some instructions to an assistant, and, turning to Lacour, asked him to be so good as to follow her.

She led him through the shop and up the stairs at the back, throwing open a door on the first floor. Lacour entered a neat drawing-room, with windows opening out upon the street. Madame Caspilier seated herself at a table, resting her elbow upon it, shading her eyes with her hand, and yet Lacour felt them searching his very soul.

'Sit down,' she said. 'You are my husband's friend. What have you to say?'

Now, it is a difficult thing for a man to tell a beautiful woman that her husband – for the moment – prefers someone else, so Lacour began on generalities. He said a poet might be likened to a butterfly, or perhaps to the more industrious bee, who sipped nectar from every flower, and so enriched the world. A poet was a law unto himself, and should not be judged harshly from what might be termed a shopkeeping point of view. Then Lacour, warming to his work, gave many instances where the wives of great men had condoned and even encouraged their husband's little idiosyncrasies, to the great augmenting of our most valued literature.

Now and then, as this eloquent man talked, Valdorème's eyes seemed to flame dangerously in the shadow, but the woman neither moved not interrupted him while he spoke When he had finished, her voice sounded cold and unimpassioned, and he felt with relief that the outbreak he had feared was at least postponed.

'You would advise me then,' she began, 'to do as the wife of that great novelist did, and invite my husband and the woman he admires to my table?'

'Oh, I don't say I could ask you to go so far as that,' said Lacour; 'but—'

'I'm no halfway woman. It is all or nothing with me. If I invited my husband to dine with me, I would also invite this creature— What is her name? Tenise, you say. Well, I would invite her too. Does she know he is a married man?'

'Yes,' cried Lacour eagerly; 'but I assure you, madame, she has nothing but the kindliest feelings towards you. There is no jealousy about Tenise.'

'How good of her! How very good of her!' said the Russian woman, with such bitterness that Lacour fancied uneasily that he had somehow made an injudicious remark, whereas all his efforts were concentrated in a desire to conciliate and please.

'Very well,' said Valdorème, rising. 'You may tell my husband that you have been successful in your mission. Tell him that I will provide for them both. Ask them to honour me with their presence at breakfast tomorrow morning at twelve o'clock. If he wants money, as you say, here are two hundred francs, which will perhaps be sufficient for his wants until midday tomorrow.'

Lacour thanked her with a profuse graciousness that would have delighted any ordinary giver, but Valdorème stood impassive like a tragedy queen, and seemed only anxious that he should speedily take his departure, now that his errand was done.

The heart of the poet was filled with joy when he heard from his friend that at last Valdorème had come to regard his union with Tenise in the light of reason. Caspilier, as he embraced Lacour, admitted that perhaps there was something to be said for his wife after all.

The poet dressed himself with more than usual care on the day of the feast, and Tenise, who accompanied him, put on some of the finery that had been bought with Valdorème's donation. She confessed that she thought Eugène's wife had acted with consideration towards them, but maintained that she did not wish to meet her, for, judging from Caspilier's account, his wife must be a somewhat formidable and terrifying person; still she went with him, she said, solely through good nature, and a desire to heal family differences. Tenise would do anything in the cause of domestic peace.

The shop assistant told the pair, when they had dismissed the cab, that madame was waiting for them upstairs. In the drawing-room Valdorème was standing with her back to the window like a low-browed goddess, her tawny hair loose over her shoulders, and the pallor of her face made more conspicuous by her costume of unrelieved black. Caspilier, with the grace characteristic of him, swept off his hat, and made a low, deferential bow; but when he straightened himself up, and began to say the complimentary things and poetical phrases he had put together for the occasion at the café the night before, the lurid look of the Russian made his tongue falter; and Tenise, who had never seen a woman of this sort before, laughed a nervous, half-frightened little laugh, and clung closer to her lover than before. The wife was even more forbidding than she had imagined. Valorème shuddered slightly when she saw this intimate movement on the part of her rival, and her hand clenched and unclenched convulsively.

'Come,' she said, cutting short her husband's halting harangue, and sweeping past them, drawing her skirts aside on nearing Tenise, she led the way up to the dining-room a floor higher.

'I'm afraid of her,' whimpered Tenise, holding back. 'She will poison us.'

'Nonsense,' said Caspilier, in a whisper. 'Come along. She is too fond of me to attempt anything of that kind, and you are safe when I am here.'

Valorème sat at the head of the table, with her husband at her right hand and Tenise on her left. The breakfast was the best either of them had ever tasted. The hostess sat silent, but no second talker was needed when the poet was present. Tenise laughed merrily now and then at his bright sayings, for the excellence of the meal had banished her fears of poison.

'What penetrating smell is this that fills the room? Better open the window,' said Caspilier.

'It is nothing,' replied Valorème, speaking for the first time since they had sat down. 'It is only naphtha. I have had this room cleaned with it. The window won't open, and if it would, we could not hear you talk with the noise from the street.'

The poet would suffer anything rather than have his

eloquence interfered with, so he said no more about the fumes of the naphtha. When the coffee was brought in, Valdorème dismissed the trim little maid who had waited on them.

'I have some of your favourite cigarettes here. I will get them.'

She arose, and, as she went to the table on which the boxes lay, she quietly and deftly locked the door, and, pulling out the key, slipped it into her pocket.

'Do you smoke, mademoiselle?' she asked, speaking to Tenise. She had not recognized her presence before.

'Sometimes, madame,' answered the girl, with a titter.

'You will find these cigarettes excellent. My husband's taste in cigarettes is better than in many things. He prefers the Russian to the French.'

Caspilier laughed loudly.

'That's a slap at you, Tenise,' he said.

'At me? Not so; she speaks of cigarettes, and I myself prefer the Russian, only they are so expensive.'

A look of strange eagerness came into Valdorème's expressive face, softened by a touch of supplication. Her eyes were on her husband, but she said rapidly to the girl—

'Stop a moment, mademoiselle. Do not light your cigarette until I give the word.'

Then to her husband she spoke beseechingly in Russian, a language she had taught him in the early months of their marriage.

'Yevgenii, Yevgenii! Don't you see the girl's a fool? How can you care for her? She would be as happy with the first man she met in the street. I – I think only of you. Come back to me, Yevgenii!'

She leaned over the table towards him, and in her vehemence clasped his wrist. The girl watched them both with a smile. It reminded her of a scene in an opera she had heard once in a strange language. The prima donna had looked and pleaded like Valdorème.

Caspilier shrugged his shoulders, but did not withdraw his wrist from her firm grasp.

'Why go over the whole weary ground again?' he said. 'If it were not Tenise, it would be somebody else. I was never meant for a constant husband, Val. I understood from Lacour that we were to have no more of this nonsense.'

She slowly relaxed her hold on his unresisting wrist. The old, hard look came into her face as she drew a deep breath. The fire in the depths of her amber eyes rekindled, as the softness went out of them.

'You may light your cigarette now, mademoiselle,' she said almost in a whisper to Tenise.

'I swear I could light mine in your eyes, Val,' cried her husband. 'You would make a name for yourself on the stage. I will write a tragedy for you, and we will—'

Tenise struck the match. A simultaneous flash of lightning and clap of thunder filled the room. The glass in the window fell clattering into the street. Valdorème was standing with her back against the door. Tenise, fluttering her helpless little hands before her, tottered shrieking to the broken window. Caspilier, staggering panting to his feet, gasped—

'You Russian devil! The key, the key!'

He tried to clutch her throat, but she pushed him back.

'Go to your Frenchwoman. She's calling for help.'

Tenise sank by the window, one burning arm hanging over the sill, and was silent. Caspilier, mechanically beating back the fire from his shaking head, whimpering and sobbing, fell against the table, and then went headlong in the floor.

Valdorème, a pillar of fire, swaying gently to and fro, before the door, whispered in a voice of agony—

'Oh, Eugène, Eugène!' and flung herself like a flaming angel – or fiend – on the prostrate form of the man.

THE END OF A SHOW

Barry Pain

It was a little village in the extreme north of Yorkshire, three miles from a railway station on a small branch line. It was not a progressive village; it just kept still and respected itself. The hills lay all round it, and seemed to shut it out from the rest of the world. Yet folk were born, and lived, and died, much as in the more important centres; and there were intervals which required to be filled with amusement. Entertainments were given by amateurs from time to time in the schoolroom; sometimes hand-bell ringers or a conjurer would visit the place, but their reception was not always encouraging. 'Conjurers is nowt, an' ringers is nowt,' said the sad native judiciously; 'ar dornt regard 'em.' But the native brightened up when in the summer months a few caravans found their way to a piece of waste land adjoining the churchyard. They formed the village fair, and for two days they were a popular resort. But it was understood that the fair had not the glories of old days; it had dwindled. Most things in connection with this village dwindled.

The first day of the fair was drawing to a close. It was half-past ten at night, and at eleven the fair would close until the following morning. This last half-hour was fruitful in business. The steam roundabout was crowded, the proprietor of the peep-show was taking pennies very fast, although not so fast as the proprietor of another, somewhat repulsive, show. A fair number patronized a canvas booth which bore the following inscription:

POPULAR SCIENCE LECTURES
Admission Free

At one end of this tent was a table covered with red baize; on it were bottles and boxes, a human skull, a retort, a large book, and some bundles of dried herbs. Behind it was the lecturer, an old man, grey and thin, wearing a bright-coloured dressing-gown. He lectured volubly and enthusiastically; his energy and the atmosphere of the tent made him very hot, and occasionally he mopped his forehead.

'I am about to exhibit to you,' he said, speaking clearly and correctly, 'a secret known to few, and believed to have come originally from those wise men of the East referred to in Holy Writ.' Here he filled two test-tubes with water, and placed some bluish-green crystals in one and some yellow crystals in the other. He went on talking, quoting scraps of Latin, telling stories, making local and personal allusions, finally coming back again to his two test-tubes, both of which now contained almost colourless solutions. He poured them both together into a flat glass vessel, and the mixture at once turned to a deep brownish purple. He threw a fragment of something on to the surface of the mixture, and that fragment at once caught fire. This favourite trick succeeded; the audience were undoubtedly impressed, and before they quite realized by what logical connection the old man had arrived at the subject, he was talking to them about the abdomen. He seemed to know the most unspeakable and intimate things about the abdomen. He had made pills which suited its peculiar needs, which he could and would sell in boxes at sixpence and one shilling, according to size. He sold four boxes at once, and was back in his classical and anecdotal stage, when a woman pressed forward. She was a very poor woman. Could she have a box of these pills at half-price? Her son was bad, very bad. It would be a kindness.

He interrupted her in a dry, distinct voice:

'Woman, I never yet did anyone a kindness, not even myself.'

However, a friend pushed some money into her hand, and she bought two boxes.

It was past twelve o'clock now. The flaring lights were out in the little group of caravans on the waste ground. The tired proprietors of the shows were asleep. The gravestones in the churchyard were glimmering white in the bright moonlight. But at the entrance to that little canvas booth the quack doctor sat on one of his boxes, smoking a clay pipe. He had taken off the dressing-gown, and was in his shirt-sleeves; his clothes were black, much worn. His attention was arrested – he thought that he heard the sound of sobbing.

'It's a God-forsaken world,' he said aloud. After a second's silence he spoke again. 'No, I never did a kindness even to myself, though I thought I did, or I shouldn't have come to this.'

He took his pipe from his mouth and spat. Once more he heard that strange wailing sound; this time he arose, and walked in the direction of it.

Yes, that was it. It came from that caravan standing alone where the trees made a dark spot. The caravan was gaudily painted, and there were steps from the door to the ground. He remembered having noticed it once during the day. It was evident that someone inside was in trouble – great trouble. The old man knocked gently at the door.

'Who's there? What's the matter?'

'Nothing,' said a broken voice from within.

'Are you a woman?'

There was a fearful laugh.

'Neither man nor woman – a show.'

'What do you mean?'

'Go round to the side, and you'll see.'

The old man went round, and by the light of two wax matches caught a glimpse of part of the rough painting on the side of the caravan. The matches dropped from his hand. He came back, and sat down on the step of the caravan.

'You are not like that,' he said.

'No, worse. I'm not dressed in pretty clothes, and lying on a crimson velvet couch. I'm half naked, in a corner of this cursed box, and crying because my owner beat me. Now go, or I'll open the door and show myself to you as I am now. It would frighten you; it would haunt your sleep.'

'Nothing frightens me. I was a fool once, but I have never been frightened. What right has this owner over you?'

'He is my father,' the voice screamed loudly; then there was more weeping; then it spoke again:

'It's awful; I could bear anything now – anything – if I thought it would ever be any better; but it won't. My mind's a woman's and my wants are a woman's, but I am not a woman. I am a show. The brutes stand round me, talk to me, touch me!'

'There's a way out,' said the old man quietly, after a pause. An idea had occurred to him.

'I know – and I daren't take it – I've got a thing here, but I daren't use it.'

'You could drink something – something that wouldn't hurt?'

'Yes.'

'You are quite alone?'

'Yes; my owner is in the village, at the inn.'

'Then wait a minute.'

The old man hastened back to the canvas booth, and fumbled about with his chemicals. He murmured something about doing someone a kindness at last. Then he returned to the caravan with a glass of colourless liquid in his hand.

'Open the door and take it,' he said.

The door was opened a very little way. A thin hand was thrust out and took the glass eagerly. The door closed, and the voice spoke again.

'It will be easy?'

'Yes.'

'Goodbye, then. To your health—'

The old man heard the glass crash on the wooden floor, then he went back to his seat in front of the booth, and carefully lit another pipe.

'I will not go,' he said aloud. 'I fear nothing – not even the results of my best action.'

He listened attentively.

No sound whatever came from the caravan. All was still. Far away the sky was growing lighter with the dawn of a fine summer day.

THE HAUNTED MILL

OR

THE RUINED HOME

Jerome K. Jerome

This tale comes from Told After Supper *and incorporates the introduction to the book, so that readers can better understand the literary motive behind it. I have selected only this story from the book as the introduction is probably the best thing in it and one tale will suffice to show what Jerome was driving at. I hope you agree he succeeded.*

INTRODUCTION

It was Christmas Eve.

I begin this way, because it is the proper, orthodox, respectable way to begin, and I have been brought up in a proper, orthodox, respectable way, and taught to always do the proper, orthodox, respectable thing; and the habit clings to me.

Of course, as a mere matter of information it is quite unnecessary to mention the date at all. The experienced reader knows it was Christmas Eve, without my telling him. It always is Christmas Eve, in a ghost story.

Christmas Eve is the ghosts' great gala night. On Christmas Eve they hold their annual fête. On Christmas Eve everybody in Ghostland who *is* anybody – or rather, speaking of ghosts, one should say, I suppose, every nobody who *is* any nobody – comes out to show himself or herself, to see and to be seen, to promenade about and display their winding-sheets and grave-clothes to each other, to criticize one another's style, and sneer at one another's complexion.

'Christmas Eve Parade,' as I expect they themselves term it, is a function, doubtless, eagerly prepared for and looked forward to throughout Ghostland, especially by the swagger set, such as the murdered Barons, the crime-stained

Countesses, and the Earls who came over with the Conqueror, and assassinated their relatives, and died raving mad.

Hollow moans and fiendish grins are, one may be sure, energetically practised up. Blood-curdling shrieks and marrow-freezing gestures are probably rehearsed for weeks beforehand. Rusty chains and gory daggers are overhauled, and put into good working order; and sheets and shrouds, laid carefully by from the previous year's show, are taken down and shaken out, and mended, and aired.

Oh, it is a stirring night in Ghostland, the night of December the twenty-fourth!

Ghosts never come out on Christmas night itself, you may have noticed. Christmas Eve, we suspect, has been too much for them; they are not used to excitement. For about a week after Christmas Eve, the gentlemen ghosts, no doubt, feel as if they were all head, and go about making solemn resolutions to themselves that they will stop in next Christmas Eve; while the lady spectres are contradictory and snappish, and liable to burst into tears and leave the room hurriedly on being spoken to, for no perceptible cause whatever.

Ghosts with no position to maintain – mere middle-class ghosts – occasionally, I believe, do a little haunting on off-nights: on All-hallows Eve, and at Midsummer; and some will even run up for a mere local event – to celebrate, for instance, the anniversary of the hanging of somebody's grandfather, or to prophesy a misfortune.

He does love prophesying a misfortune, does the average British ghost. Send him out to prognosticate trouble to somebody, and he is happy. Let him force his way into a peaceful home, and turn the whole house upside down by foretelling a funeral, or predicting a bankruptcy, or hinting at a coming disgrace, or some terrible disaster, about which nobody in their senses would want to know sooner than they could possibly help, and the prior knowledge of which can serve no useful purpose whatsoever, and he feels that he is combining duty with pleasure. He would never forgive himself if anybody in his family had a trouble and he had not been there for a couple of months beforehand, doing silly tricks on the lawn, or balancing himself on somebody's bed-rail.

Then there are, besides, the very young, or very conscientious ghosts with a lost will or an undiscovered number weighing heavy on their minds, who will haunt steadily all the year round; and also the fussy ghost, who is indignant at having been buried in the dustbin or in the village pond, and who never gives the parish a single night's quiet until somebody has paid for a first-class funeral for him.

But these are the exceptions. As I have said, the average orthodox ghost does his one turn a year, on Christmas Eve, and is satisfied.

Why on Christmas Eve, of all nights in the year, I never could myself understand. It is invariably one of the most dismal of nights to be out in – cold, muddy, and wet. And besides, at Christmas time, everybody has quite enough to put up with in the way of a houseful of living relations, without wanting the ghosts of any dead ones mooning about the place, I am sure.

There must be something ghostly in the air of Christmas – something about the close, muggy atmosphere that draws up the ghosts, like the dampness of the summer rains brings out the frogs and snails.

And not only do the ghosts themselves always walk on Christmas Eve, but live people always sit and talk about them on Christmas Eve. Whenever five or six English-speaking people meet round a fire on Christmas Eve, they start telling each other ghost stories. Nothing satisfies us on Christmas Eve but to hear each other tell authentic anecdotes about spectres. It is a genial, festive season, and we love to muse upon graves, and dead bodies, and murders, and blood.

There a good deal of similarity about our ghostly experiences; but this of course is not our fault but the fault of the ghosts, who never will try any new performances, but always will keep steadily to the old, safe business. The consequence is that, when you have been at one Christmas Eve party, and heard six people relate their adventures with spirits, you do not require to hear any more ghost stories. To listen to any further ghost stories after that would be like sitting out two farcical comedies, or taking in two comic journals; the repetition would become wearisome.

There is always the young man who was, one year, spending the Christmas at a country house, and, on Christmas Eve, they put him to sleep in the west wing. Then in the middle of the night, the room door quietly opens and somebody – generally a lady in her nightdress – walks slowly in, and comes and sits on the bed. The young man thinks it must be one of the visitors, or some relative of the family, though he does not remember having previously seen her, who, unable to go to sleep, and feeling lonesome, all by herself, has come into his room for a chat. He has no idea it is a ghost: he is so unsuspicious. She does not speak, however; and, when he looks again, she is gone!

The young man relates the circumstance at the breakfast table next morning, and asks each of the ladies present if it were she who was the visitor. But they all assure him that it was not, and the host, who has grown deadly pale, begs him to say no more about the matter, which strikes the young man as a singularly strange request.

After breakfast the host takes the young man into a corner, and explains to him that what he saw was the ghost of a lady who had been murdered in that very bed, or who had murdered somebody else there – it does not really matter which: you can be a ghost by murdering somebody else or by being murdered yourself, whichever you prefer. The murderer ghost is, perhaps, the more popular; but, on the other hand, you can frighten people better if you are the murdered one, because then you can show your wounds and do groans.

Then there is the sceptical guest – it is always 'the guest' who gets let in for this sort of thing, by-the-bye. A ghost never thinks much of his own family: it is 'the guest' he likes to haunt who after listening to the host's ghost story, on Christmas Eve, laughs at it, and says that he does not believe there are such things as ghosts at all; and that he will sleep in the haunted chamber that very night, if they will let him.

Everybody urges him not to be so reckless, but he persists in his foolhardiness, and goes up to the Yellow Chamber (or whatever colour the haunted room may be) with a light heart and a candle, and wishes them all good-night, and shuts the door.

Next morning he has got snow-white hair.

He does not tell anybody what he has seen: it is too awful.

There is also the plucky guest, who sees a ghost, and knows it is a ghost, and watches it, as it comes into the room and disappears through the wainscot, after which, as the ghost does not seem to be coming back, and there is nothing, consequently, to be gained by stopping awake, he goes to sleep.

He does not mention having seen the ghost to anybody, for fear of frightening them – some people are so nervous about ghosts, – but determines to wait for the next night, and see if the apparition appears again.

It does appear again, and, this time, he gets out of bed, dresses himself and does his hair, and follows it; and then discovers a secret passage leading from the bedroom down into the beer-cellar, – a passage which, no doubt, was not unfrequently made use of in the bad old days of yore.

After him comes the young man who woke up with a strange sensation in the middle of the night, and found his rich bachelor uncle standing by his bedside. The rich uncle smiled a weird sort of smile and vanished. The young man immediately got up and looked at his watch. It had stopped at half-past four, he having forgotten to wind it.

He made enquiries the next day, and found that, strangely enough, his rich uncle, whose only nephew he was, had married a widow with eleven children at exactly a quarter to twelve, only two days ago.

The young man does not attempt to explain the extraordinary circumstance. All he does is to vouch for the truth of his narrative.

And, to mention another case, there is the gentleman who is returning home late at night, from a Freemasons' dinner, and who, noticing a light issuing from a ruined abbey, creeps up, and looks through the keyhole. He sees the ghost of a 'grey sister' kissing the ghost of a brown monk, and is so inexpressibly shocked and frightened that he faints on the spot, and is discovered there the next morning, lying in a heap against the door, still speechless, and with his faithful latch-key clasped tightly in his hand.

All these things happen on Christmas Eve, they are all told of on Christmas Eve. For ghost stories to be told on any other evening than the evening of the twenty-fourth of December would be impossible in English society as at present regulated. Therefore, in introducing the sad but authentic ghost story that follows, I feel that it is unnecessary to inform the student of Anglo-Saxon literature that the date on which it was told and on which the incidents took place was – Christmas Eve.

Nevertheless, I do so.

THE HAUNTED MILL

Well, you all know my brother-in-law, Mr Parkins (began Mr Coombes, taking the long clay pipe from his mouth, and putting it behind his ear: we did not know his brother-in-law, but we said we did, so as to save time), and you know of course that he once took a lease on an old mill in Surrey, and went to live there.

Now you must know that, years ago, this very mill had been occupied by a wicked old miser, who died there, leaving – so it was rumoured – all his money hidden somewhere about the place. Naturally enough, everyone who had since come to live at the mill had tried to find the treasure; but none had ever succeeded, and the local wiseacres said that nobody ever would, unless the ghost of the miserly miller should, one day, take a fancy to one of the tenants, and disclose to him the secret of the hiding-place.

My brother-in-law did not attach much importance to the story, regarding it as an old woman's tale, and, unlike his predecessors, made no attempt whatever to discover the hidden gold.

'Unless business was very different then from what it is now,' said my brother-in-law, 'I don't see how a miller could very well have saved anything, however much of a miser he might have been: at all events, not enough to make it worth the trouble of looking for it.'

Still, he could not altogether get rid of the idea of that treasure.

One night he went to bed. There was nothing very extraordinary about that, I admit. He often did go to bed of a night. What *was* remarkable, however, was that exactly as the clock of the village church chimed the last stroke of twelve, my brother-in-law woke up with a start, and felt himself quite unable to go to sleep again.

Joe (his Christian name was Joe) sat up in bed, and looked around.

At the foot of the bed something stood very still, wrapped in shadow.

It moved into the moonlight, and then my brother-in-law saw that it was the figure of a wizened little old man, in knee-breeches and a pigtail.

In an instant the story of the hidden treasure and the old miser flashed across his mind.

'He's come to show me where it's hid,' thought my brother-in-law; and he resolved that he would not spend all this money on himself, but would devote a small percentage of it towards doing good to others.

The apparition moved towards the door: my brother-in-law put on his trousers and followed it. The ghost went downstairs into the kitchen, glided over and stood in front of the hearth, sighed and disappeared.

Next morning, Joe had a couple of bricklayers in, and made them haul out the stove and pull down the chimney, while he stood behind with a potato-sack in which to put the gold.

They knocked down half the wall, and never found so much as a fourpenny bit. My brother-in-law did not know what to think.

The next night the old man appeared again, and led the

way into the kitchen. This time, however, instead of going to the fireplace, it stood more in the middle of the room, and sighed there.

'Oh, I see what he means now,' said my brother-in-law to himself, 'it's under the floor. Why did the old idiot go and stand up against the stove, so as to make me think it was up the chimney?'

They spent the next day in taking up the kitchen floor; but the only thing they found was a three-pronged fork, and the handle of that was broken.

On the third night, the ghost reappeared, quite unabashed, and for a third time made for the kitchen. Arrived there, it looked up at the ceiling and vanished.

'Umph! he don't seem to have learned much sense where he's been to,' muttered Joe, as he trotted back to bed; 'I should have thought he might have done that at first.'

Still, there seemed no doubt now where the treasure lay, and the first thing after breakfast they started pulling down the ceiling. They got every inch of ceiling down, and they took up the boards of the room above.

They discovered about as much treasure as you would expect to find in an empty quart pot.

On the fourth night, when the ghost appeared, as usual, my brother-in-law was so wild that he threw his boots at it; and the boots passed through the body, and broke a looking-glass.

On the fifth night, when Joe awoke, as he always did now at twelve, the ghost was standing in a dejected attitude, looking very miserable. There was an appealing look in its large sad eyes that quite touched my brother-in-law.

'After all,' he thought, 'perhaps the silly chap's doing his best. Maybe he has forgotten where he really did put it, and is trying to remember. I'll give him another chance.'

The ghost appeared grateful and delighted at seeing Joe prepare to follow him, and led the way into the attic, pointed to the ceiling, and vanished.

'Well, he's hit it this time, I do hope,' said my brother-in-law; and next day they set to work to take the roof off the place.

It took them three days to get the roof thoroughly off, and all they found was a bird's nest; after securing which they covered up the house with tarpaulins, to keep it dry.

You might have thought that would have cured the poor fellow of looking for treasure. But it didn't.

He said there must be something in it all, or the ghost would never keep on coming as it did; and that, having gone so far, he would go on to the end, and solve the mystery, cost what it might.

Night after night, he would get out of his bed and follow that spectral old fraud about the house. Each night, the old man would indicate a different place; and, on each following day, my brother-in-law would proceed to break up the mill at the point indicated, and look for the treasure. At the end of three weeks, there was not a room in the mill fit to live in. Every wall had been pulled down, every floor had been taken up, every ceiling had had a hole knocked in it. And then, as suddenly as they had begun, the ghost's visits ceased; and my brother-in-law was left to rebuild the place at his leisure.

'What induced the old image to play such a silly trick upon a family man and a ratepayer?' Ah! that's just what I cannot tell you.

Some said that the ghost of the wicked old man had done it to punish my brother-in-law for not believing in him at first; while others held that the apparition was probably that of some deceased local plumber and glazier, who would naturally take an interest in seeing a house knocked about and spoilt. But nobody knew anything for certain.

THE UNFINISHED GAME

Barry Pain

At Tanslowe, which is on the Thames, I found just the place that I wanted. I had been born in the hotel business, brought up in it, and made my living at it for thirty years. For the last twenty I had been both proprietor and manager, and had worked uncommonly hard, for it is personal attention and plenty of it which makes a hotel pay. I might have retired altogether, for I was a bachelor with no claims on me and had made more money than enough; but that was not what I wanted. I wanted a nice, old-fashioned house, not too big, in a nice place with a longish slack season. I cared very little whether I made it pay or not. The Regency Hotel at Tanslowe was just the thing for me. It would give me a little to do and not too much. Tanslowe was a village, and though there were two or three public houses, there was no other hotel in the place, nor was any competition likely to come along. I was particular about that, because my nature is such that competition always sets me fighting, and I cannot rest until the other shop goes down. I had reached a time of life when I did want to rest and did not want any more fighting. It was a free house, and I have always had a partiality for being my own master. It had just the class of trade that I liked – principally gentlefolk taking their pleasure in a holiday on the river. It was very cheap, and I like value for money. The house was comfortable, and had a beautiful garden sloping down to the river. I meant to put in some time in that garden – I have a taste that way.

The place was so cheap that I had my doubts. I wondered if it was flooded when the river rose, if it was dropping to pieces with dry-rot, if the drainage had been condemned, if they were going to start a lunatic asylum next door, or what it was. I went into all these points and a hundred more. I found one or two trifling drawbacks, and one expects them in any house, however good – especially when it is an old place like the Regency. I found nothing whatever to stop me from taking the place.

I bought the whole thing, furniture and all, lock, stock and barrel, and moved in. I brought with me my own head-waiter and my man-cook, Englishmen both of them. I knew they would set the thing in the right key. The head-waiter, Silas Goodheart, was just over sixty, with grey hair and a wrinkled face. He was worth more to me than two younger men would have been. He was very precise and rather slow in his movements. He liked bright silver, clean table-linen, and polished glass. Artificial flowers in the vases on his tables would have given him a fit. He handled a decanter of old port as if he loved it – which, as a matter of fact, he did. His manner to visitors was a perfect mixture of dignity, respect and friendliness. If a man did not quite know what he wanted for dinner, Silas had sympathetic and very useful suggestions. He took, I am sure, a real pleasure in seeing people enjoy their luncheon or dinner. Americans loved him, and tipped him out of all proportion. I let him have his own way, even when he gave the thing away.

'Is the coffee all right here?' a customer asked after a good dinner.

'I cannot recommend it,' said Silas. 'If I might suggest, sir, we have the Chartreuse of the old French shipping.'

I overheard that, but I said nothing. The coffee was extract, for there was more work than profit in making it good. As it was, that customer went away pleased, and came back again and again, and brought his friends too. Silas was really the only permanent waiter. When we were busy I got one or two foreigners from London temporarily. Silas soon educated them. My cook, Timbs, was an honest chap, and understood English fare. He seemed hardly ever to eat, and never sat down to a meal; he lived principally on beer, drank enough of it to frighten you, and was apparently never the worse for it. And a butcher who tried to send him second-quality meat was certain of finding out his mistake.

The only other man I brought with me was young Harry Bryden. He always called me uncle, but as a matter of fact he was no relation of mine. He was the son of an old friend. His parents died when he was seven years old and left him to me. It was about all they had to leave. At this time he was twenty-two, and was making himself useful. There was nothing which he was not willing to do, and he could do most things. He would mark at billiards, and played a good game himself. He had run the kitchen when the cook was away on his holiday. He had driven the station-omnibus when the driver was drunk one night. He understood book-keeping, and when I got a clerk who was a wrong 'un, he was on to him at once and saved me money. It was my intention to make him take his proper place more when I got to the Regency; for he was to succeed me when I died. He was clever, and not bad-looking in a gipsy-faced kind of way. Nobody is perfect, and Harry was a cigarette maniac. He began when he was a boy, and I didn't spare the stick when I caught him at it. But nothing I could say or do made any difference; at twenty-two he was old enough and big enough to have his own way, and his own way was to smoke cigarettes eternally. He was a bundle of nerves, and got so jumpy sometimes that some people thought he drank, though he had never in his life tasted liquor. He inherited his nerves from his mother, but I daresay the cigarettes made them worse.

I took Harry down with me when I first thought of taking the place. He went over it with me and made a lot of useful suggestions. The old proprietor had died eighteen months before, and the widow had tried to run it for herself and made a mess of it. She had just sense enough to clear out before things got any worse. She was very anxious to go, and I thought that might have been the reason why the price was so low.

The billiard-room was an annexe to the house, with no rooms over it. We were told that it wasn't used once in a twelvemonth, but we took a look at it – we took a look at everything. The room had got a very neglected look about it. I sat down on the platform – tired with so much walking and standing – and Harry whipped the cover off the table. 'This was the one they had in the Ark,' he said.

There was not a straight cue in the rack, the balls were worn and untrue, the jigger was broken. Harry pointed to the board. 'Look at that, uncle,' he said. 'Noah had made forty-eight; Ham was doing nicely at sixty-six; and then the Flood came and they never finished.' From neatness and force of habit he moved over and turned the score back. 'You'll have to spend some money here. My word, if they put the whole lot in at a florin we're swindled.' As we came out Harry gave a shiver. 'I wouldn't spend a night in there,' he said, 'not for a five-pound note.'

His nerves always made me angry. 'That's a very silly thing to say,' I told him. 'Who's going to ask you to sleep in a billiard-room?'

Then he got a bit more practical, and began to calculate how much I should have to spend to make a bright, up-to-date billiard-room of it. But I was still angry.

'You needn't waste your time on that,' I said, 'because the place will stop as it is. You heard what Mrs Parker said – that it wasn't used once in a twelvemonth. I don't want to attract all the loafers in Tanslowe into my house. Their custom's worth nothing, and I'd sooner be without it. Time enough to put that room right if I find my staying visitors want it, and people who've been on the river all day are mostly too tired for a game after dinner.'

Harry pointed out that it sometimes rained, and there was the winter to think about. He had always got plenty to say, and what he said now had sense in it. But I never go chopping and changing about, and I had made my mind up. So I told him he had got to learn how to manage the house, and not waste half his time over the billiard-table. I had a good deal done to the rest of the house in the way of redecorating and improvements, but I never touched the annexe.

The next time I saw the room was the day after we moved in. I was alone, and I thought it certainly did look a dingy hole as compared with the rest of the house. Then my eye happened to fall on the board and it still showed sixty-six – forty-eight, as it had done when I entered the room with Harry three months before. I altered the board myself this time. To me it was only a funny coincidence; another game had been played there and had stopped exactly at the same point. But I was glad Harry was not with me, for it was the kind of thing that would have made him jumpier than ever.

It was the summer time and we soon had something to do. I had been told that motor cars had cut into the river trade a good deal; so I laid myself out for the motorist. Tanslowe was just a nice distance for a run from town before lunch. It was all in the old-fashioned style, but there was plenty of choice and the stuff was good; and my wine-list was worth consideration. Prices were high, but people will pay when they are pleased with the way they are treated. Motorists who had been once came again and sent their friends. Saturday to Monday we had as much as ever we could do, and more than I had ever meant to do. But I am built like that – once I am in a shop I have got to run it for all it's worth.

I had been there about a month, and it was about the height of our season, when one night, for no reason that I could make out, I couldn't get to sleep. I had turned in, tired enough, at half-past ten, leaving Harry to shut up and see the lights out, and at a quarter past twelve I was still awake. I thought to myself that a pint of stout and a biscuit might be the cure for that. So I lit my candle and went down to the bar. The gas was out on the staircase and in the passages, and all was quiet. The door into the bar was locked, but I had thought to bring my pass-key with me. I had just drawn my tankard of stout when I heard a sound that made me put the tankard down and listen again.

The billiard-room door was just outside in the passage, and there could not be the least doubt that a game was going on. I could hear the click-click of the balls as plainly as possible. It surprised me a little, but it did not startle me. We had several staying in the house, and I supposed two of them had fancied a game. All the time that I was drinking the stout and munching my biscuit the game went on – click, click-click, click. Everybody has heard the sound hundreds of times standing outside the glass-panelled door of a billiard-room and waiting for the stroke before entering. No other sound is quite like it.

Suddenly the sound ceased. The game was over. I had nothing on but my pyjamas and a pair of slippers, and I thought I would get upstairs again before the players came out. I did not want to stand there shivering and listening to complaints about the table. I locked the bar, and took a glance at the billiard-room door as I was about to pass it. What I saw made me stop short. The glass panels of the door were as black as my Sunday hat, except where they reflected the light of my candle. The room, then, was not lit up, and people do not play billiards in the dark. After a second or two I tried the handle. The door was locked. It was the only door to the room.

I said to myself: 'I'll go on back to bed. It must have been my fancy, and there was nobody playing billiards at all.' I moved a step away, and then I said to myself again: 'I know perfectly well that a game *was* being played. I'm only making excuses because I'm in a funk.'

That settled it. Having driven myself to it, I moved pretty quickly. I shoved in my pass-key, opened the door, and said 'Anybody there?' in a moderately loud voice that sounded somehow like another man's. I am very much afraid that I should have jumped if there had come any answer to my challenge, but all was silent. I took a look round. The cover was on the table. An old screen was leaning against it; it had been put there to be out of the way. As I moved my candle the shadows of things slithered across the floor and crept up the walls. I noticed that the windows were properly fastened, and then, as I held my candle high, the marking-board seemed to jump out of the darkness. The score recorded was sixty-six – forty-eight.

I shut the door, locked it again, and went up to my room. I did these things slowly and deliberately, but I was frightened and I was puzzled. One is not at one's best in the small hours.

The next morning I tackled Silas.

'Silas,' I said, 'what do you do when gentlemen ask for the billiard-room?'

'Well, sir,' said Silas, 'I put them off if I can. Mr Harry directed me to, the place being so much out of order.'

'Quite so,' I said. 'And when you can't put them off?'

'Then they just try it, sir, and the table puts them off. It's very bad. There's been no game played there since we came.'

'Curious,' I said. 'I thought I heard a game going on last night.'

'I've heard it myself, sir, several times. There being no light in the room, I've put it down to a loose ventilator. The wind moves it and it clicks.'

'That'll be it,' I said. Five minutes later I had made sure that there was no loose ventilator in the billiard-room. Besides, the sound of one ball striking another is not quite like any other sound. I also went up to the board and turned the score back, which I had omitted to do the night before. Just then Harry passed the door on his way from the bar, with a cigarette in his mouth as usual. I called him in.

'Harry,' I said, 'give me thirty, and I'll play you a hundred up for a sovereign. You can tell one of the girls to fetch our cues from upstairs.'

Harry took his cigarette out of his mouth and whistled. 'What, uncle!' he said. 'Well, you're going it, I don't think. What would you have said to me if I'd asked you for a game at ten in the morning?'

'Ah!' I said, 'but this is all in the way of business. I can't see much wrong with the table, and if I can play on it, then other people may. There's a chance to make a sovereign for you anyhow. You've given me forty-five and a beating before now.'

'No, uncle,' he said, 'I wouldn't give you thirty. I wouldn't give you one. The table's not playable. Luck would win against Roberts on it.'

He showed me the faults of the thing and said he was busy. So I told him if he liked to lose the chance of making a sovereign he could.

'I hate that room,' he said, as we came out. 'It's not too clean, and it smells like a vault.'

'It smells a lot better than your cigarettes,' I said. For the next six weeks we were all busy, and I gave little thought to the billiard-room. Once or twice I heard old Silas telling a customer that he could not recommend the table, and that the whole room was to be redecorated and refitted as soon as we got the estimates. 'You see, sir, we've only been here a little while, and there hasn't been time to get everything as we should like it quite yet.'

One day Mrs Parker, the woman who had the Regency before me, came down from town to see how we were getting on. I showed the old lady round, pointed out my improvements, and gave her a bit of lunch in my office.

'Well, now,' I said, as she sipped her glass of port afterwards, 'I'm not complaining of my bargain, but isn't the billiard-room a bit queer?'

'It surprises me,' she said, 'that you've left it as it is.

Especially with everything going ahead, and the yard half full of motors. I should have taken it all down myself if I'd stopped. That iron roof's nothing but an eyesore, and you might have a couple of beds of geraniums there and improve the look of your front.'

'Let's see,' I said. 'What was the story about that billiard-room?'

'What story do you mean?' she said, looking at me suspiciously.

'The same one you're thinking of,' I said.

'About that man, Josiah Ham?'

'That's it.'

'Well, I shouldn't worry about that if I were you. That was all thirty years ago, and I doubt if there's a soul in Tanslowe knows it now. Best forgotten, I say. Talk of that kind doesn't do a hotel any good. Why, how did you come to hear of it?'

'That's just it,' I said. 'The man who told me was none too clear. He gave me a hint of it. He was an old commercial passing through, and had known the place in the old days. Let's hear your story and see if it agrees with his.'

But I had told my fibs to no purpose. The old lady seemed a bit flustered. 'If you don't mind, Mr Sanderson, I'd rather not speak of it.'

I thought I knew what was troubling her. I filled her glass and my own. 'Look here,' I said. 'When you sold the place to me it was a fair deal. You weren't called upon to go thirty years back, and no reasonable man would expect it. I'm satisfied. Here I am, and here I mean to stop, and twenty billiard-rooms wouldn't drive me away. I'm not complaining. But just as a matter of curiosity, I'd like to hear your story.'

'What's your trouble with the room?'

'Nothing to signify. But there's a game played there and marked there – and I can't find the players, and I think it's never finished. It stops always at sixty-six – forty-eight.'

She gave a glance over her shoulder. 'Pull the place down,' she said. 'You can afford to do it, and I couldn't.' She finished her port. 'I must be going, Mr Sanderson. There's rain coming on, and I don't want to sit in the train in my wet things. I thought I would just run down to see how you were getting on, and I'm sure I'm glad to see the old place looking up again.'

I tried again to get the story out of her, but she ran away from it. She had not got the time, and it was better not to speak of such things. I did not worry her about it much, as she seemed upset over it.

I saw her across to the station, and just got back in time. The rain came down in torrents. I stood there and watched it, and thought it would do my garden a bit of good. I heard a step behind me and looked round. A fat chap with a surly face stood there, as if he had just come out of the coffee-room. He was the sort that might be a gentleman and might not.

'Afternoon, sir,' I said. 'Nasty weather for motoring.'

'It is,' he said. 'Not that I came in a motor. You the proprietor, Mr Sanderson?'

'I am,' I said. 'Came here recently.'

'I wonder if there's any chance of a game of billiards.'

'I'm afraid not,' I said. 'Table's shocking. I'm having it all done up afresh, and then—'

'What's it matter?' said he. 'I don't care. It's something to do, and one can't go out.'

'Well,' I said, 'if that's the case, I'll give you a game, sir. But I'm no flyer at it at the best of times, and I'm all out of practice now.'

'I'm no good myself. No good at all. And I'd be glad of the game.'

At the billiard-room door I told him I'd fetch a couple of decent cues. He nodded and went in.

When I came back with my cue and Harry's, I found the gas lit and the blinds drawn, and he was already knocking the balls about.

'You've been quick, sir,' I said, and offered him Harry's

cue. But he refused and said he would keep the one he had taken from the rack. Harry would have sworn if he had found that I had lent his cue to a stranger, so I thought that was just as well. Still, it seemed to me that a man who took a twisted cue by preference was not likely to be an expert.

The table was bad, but not so bad as Harry had made out. The luck was all my side. I was fairly ashamed of the flukes I made, one after the other. He said nothing, but gave a short, loud laugh once or twice – it was a nasty-sounding laugh. I was at thirty-seven when he was nine, and I put on eleven more at my next visit and thought I had left him nothing.

Then the fat man woke up. He got out of his first difficulty, and after that the balls ran right for him. He was a player, too, with plenty of variety and resource, and I could see that I was going to take a licking. When he had reached fifty-one, an unlucky kiss left him in an impossible position. But I miscued, and he got going again. He played very, very carefully now, taking a lot more time for consideration than he had done in his previous break. He seemed to have got excited over it, and breathed hard, as fat men do when they are worked up. He had kept his coat on, and his face shone with perspiration.

At sixty-six he was in trouble again; he walked round to see the exact position, and chalked his cue. I watched him rather eagerly, for I did not like the score. I hoped he would go on. His cue slid back to strike, and then dropped with a clatter from his hand. The fat man was gone – gone, as I looked at him, like a flame blown out, vanished into nothing.

I staggered away from the table. I began to back slowly towards the door, meaning to make a bolt for it. There was a click from the scoring-board, and I saw the thing marked up. And then – I am thankful to say – the billiard-room door opened, and I saw Harry standing there. He was very white and shaky. Somehow, the fact that he was frightened helped to steady me.

'Good heavens, uncle!' he gasped. 'I've been standing outside. What's the matter? What's happened?'

'Nothing's the matter.' I said sharply. 'What are you shivering about?' I swished back the curtain, and sent up the blind with a snap. The rain was over now, and the sun shone in through the wet glass – I was glad of it.

'I thought I heard voices – laughing – somebody called the score.'

I turned out the gas. 'Well,' I said, 'this table's enough to make any man laugh, when it don't make him swear. I've been trying your game of one hand against the other, and I daresay I called the score out loud. It's no catch – not even for a wet afternoon. I'm not both-handed, like the apes and Harry Bryden.'

Harry is as good with the left hand as the right, and a bit proud of it. I slid my own cue back into its case. Then, whistling a bit of a tune, I picked up the stranger's cue, which I did not like to touch. I nearly dropped it again when I saw the initials 'J.H.' on the butt. 'Been trying the cues,' I said, as I put it in the rack. He looked at me as if he were going to ask more questions. So I put him on to something else. 'We've not got enough cover for those motor cars,' I said. 'Lucky we hadn't got many here in this rain. There's plenty of room for another shed, and it needn't cost much. Go and see what you can make of it. I'll come out directly, but I've got to talk to that girl in the bar first.'

He went off, looking rather ashamed of his tremors.

I had not really very much to say to Miss Hesketh in the bar. I put three fingers of whisky in a glass and told her to put a dash of soda on top of it. That was all. It was a full-sized drink and did me good.

Then I found Harry in the yard. He was figuring with pencil on the back of an envelope. He was always pretty smart where there was anything practical to deal with. He had spotted where the shed was to go, and was finding what it would cost at a rough estimate.

'Well,' I said, 'if I went on with that idea of mine about the flower-beds it needn't cost much beyond the labour.'

'What idea?'

'You've got a head like a sieve. Why, carrying on the flower-beds round the front where the billiard-room now stands. If we pulled that down it would give us all the materials we want for the new motorshed. The roofing's sound enough, for I was up yesterday looking into it.'

'Well, I don't think you mentioned it to me, but it's a rare good idea.'

'I'll think about it,' I said.

That evening my cook, Timbs, told me he'd be sorry to leave me, but he was afraid he'd find the place too slow for him – not enough doing. Then old Silas informed me that he hadn't meant to retire so early, but he wasn't sure – the place was livelier than he had expected, and there would be more work than he could get through. I asked no questions. I knew the billiard-room was somehow or other at the bottom of it, and so it turned out. In three days' time the workmen were in the house and bricking up the billiard-room door; and after that Timbs and old Silas found the Regency suited them very well after all. And it was not just to oblige Harry, or Timbs, or Silas that I had the alteration made. That unfinished game was in my mind; I had played it, and wanted never to play it again. It was of no use for me to tell myself that it had all been a delusion, for I knew better. My health was good, and I had no delusions. I had played it with Josiah Ham – with the lost soul of Josiah Ham – and that thought filled me not with fear, but with a feeling of sickness and disgust.

It was two years later that I heard the story of Josiah Ham, and it was not from old Mrs Parker. An old tramp came into the saloon bar begging, and Miss Hesketh was giving him the rough side of her tongue.

'Nice treatment!' said the old chap. 'Thirty years ago I worked here, and made good money, and was respected, and now it's insults.'

And then I struck in. 'What did you do here?' I asked.

'Waited at table and marked at billiards.'

'Till you took to drink?' I said.

'Till I resigned from a strange circumstance.'

I sent him out of the bar, and took him down the garden, saying I'd find him an hour or two's work. 'Now, then,' I said, as soon as I had got him alone, 'what made you leave?'

He looked at me curiously. 'I expect you know, sir,' he said. 'Sixty-six. Unfinished.'

And then he told me of a game played in that old billiard-room on a wet summer afternoon thirty years before. He, the marker, was one of the players. The other man was a commercial traveller, who used the house pretty regularly. 'A fat man, ugly-looking, with a nasty laugh. Josiah Ham his name was. He was sixty-six when he got himself into a tight place. He moved his ball – did it when he thought I wasn't looking. But I saw it in the glass, and I told him of it. He got very angry. He said he wished he might be struck dead if he ever touched the ball.'

The old tramp stopped. 'I see,' I said.

'They said it was apoplexy. It's known to be dangerous for fat men to get very angry. But I'd had enough of it before long. I cleared out, and so did the rest of the servants.'

'Well,' I said, 'we're not so superstitious nowadays. And what brought you down in the world?'

'It would have driven any man to it,' he said. 'And once the habit is formed – well, it's there.'

'If you keep off it I can give you a job weeding for three days.'

He did not want the work. He wanted a shilling and he got it; and I saw to it that he did not spend it in my house.

We have got a very nice billiard-room upstairs now. Two new tables and everything ship-shape. You may find Harry there most evenings. It is all right. But I have never taken to billiards again myself.

And where the old billiard-room was there are flower beds. The pansies that grow there have got funny markings – like figures.

THE GLASS OF SUPREME MOMENTS

Barry Pain

Lucas Morne sat in his college rooms, when the winter afternoon met the evening, depressed and dull. There were various reasons for his depression. He was beginning to be a little nervous about his health. A week before he had run second in a mile race, the finish of which had been a terrible struggle; ever since then any violent exertion or excitement had brought on symptoms which were painful, and to one who had always been strong, astonishing. He had felt them early that afternoon, on coming from the river. Besides, he was discontented with himself. He had had several visitors in his rooms that afternoon, who were better than he was, men who had enthusiasms and had found them satisfying. Lucas had a moderate devotion to athletics, but no great enthusiasm. Neither had he the finer perceptions. Neither was he a scholar. He was just an ordinary man, and reputed to be a good fellow.

His visitors had drunk his tea, talked of their own enthusiasms, and were now gone. Nothing is so unclean as a used teacup; nothing is so cold as toast which has once been hot, and the concrete expression of dejection is crumbs. Even Lucas Morne, who had not the finer perceptions, was dimly conscious that his room had become horrible, and now flung open the window. One of the men – a large, clumsy man – had been smoking mitigated Latakia; and Latakia has a way of rolling itself all round the atmosphere and kicking. Lucas seated himself in his easiest chair.

His rooms were near the chapel, and he could hear the organ. The music and the soft fall of the darkness were soothing; he could hardly see the used teacups now; the light from the gas-lamp outside came just a little way into the room, shyly and obliquely.

Well, he had not noticed it before, but the fireplace had become a staircase. He felt too lazy to wonder much at this. He would, he thought, have the things all altered back again on the morrow. It would be worthwhile to sell the staircase, seeing that its steps were fashioned of silver and crystal. Unfortunately he could not see how much there was of it, or whither it led. The first five steps were clear enough; he felt convinced that the workmanship of them was Japanese. But the rest of the staircase was hidden from his sight by a grey veil of mist. He found himself a little angry, in a severe and strictly logical way, that in these days of boasted science we could not prevent a piece of fog, measuring ten feet by seven, from coming in at an open window and sitting down on a staircase which had only just begun to exist, and blotting out all but five steps of it in its very earliest moments. He allowed that it was a beautiful mist; its colour changed slowly from grey to rose, and then back again from rose to grey; fireflies of silver and gold shot through it at intervals; but it was a nuisance, because he wanted to see the rest of the staircase, and it prevented him. Every moment the desire to see more grew stronger. At last he determined to shake off his laziness, and go up the staircase and through the mist into the something beyond. He felt sure that the something beyond would be beautiful – sure with the certainty which was nothing to do with logical conviction.

It seemed to him that it was with an effort that he brought himself to rise from the chair and walk to the foot of that lovely staircase. He hesitated there for a moment or two, and as he did so he heard the sound of footsteps, high up, far away, yet coming nearer and nearer, with light music in the sound of them. Someone was coming down the staircase. He listened eagerly and excitedly. Then through the grey mist came a figure robed in grey.

It was the figure of a woman – young, with wonderful grace in her movements. Her face was veiled, and all that could be seen of her as she paused on the fifth step was the soft dark hair that reached to her waist, and her arms – white wonders of beauty. The rest was hidden by the grey veil and the long grey robe, that left, however, their suggestion of classical grace and slenderness. Lucas Morne stood looking at her tremulously. He felt sure, too, that she was looking at him, and that she could see through the folds of the thin grey veil that hid her face. She was the first to speak. Her voice in its gentleness and delicacy was like the voice of a child; it was only afterwards that he heard in it the under-thrill which told of more than childhood.

'Why have you not come? I have been waiting for you, you know, up there. And this is the only time,' she added.

'I am very sorry,' he stammered. 'You see – I never knew the staircase was there until today. In fact – it seems very stupid of me – but I always thought it was a fireplace. I must have been dreaming, of course. And then this afternoon I thought, or dreamed, that a lot of men came in to see me. Perhaps they really did come; and we got talking, you know—'

'Yes,' she said, with the gentlest possible interruption. 'I *do* know. There was one man, Fynsale, large, ugly, clumsy, a year your senior. He sat in that chair over there, and sulked, and smoked Latakia. I rather like the smell of Latakia. He especially loves to write or to say some good thing; and at times he can do it. Therefore you envy him. Then there was

Blake. Blake is an athlete, like yourself, but is just a little more successful. Yes, I know you are good, but Blake is very good. You were tried for the Varsity – Blake was selected. He and Fynsale both have delight in ability, and you envy both. There was that dissenting little Paul Reece. He is not exactly in your set, but you were at school with him, and so you tolerate him. How good he is, for all his insignificance and social defects! Blake knows that, and kept a guard on his talk this afternoon. He would not offend Paul Reece for worlds. Paul's belief gives him earnestness, his earnestness leads him to self-sacrifice, and self-sacrifice is deep delight to him. You have more ability than Paul Reece, but you cannot reach that kind of enthusiastic happiness, and therefore you envy him. I could say similar things of the other men. It was because they made you vaguely dissatisfied with yourself that they bored you. You take pleasure – a certain pleasure – in athletics, and that pleasure would become an enthusiastic delight if you were a little better at them. Some men could get the enthusiastic delight out of as much as you can do, but your temperament is different. I know you well. You are not easily satisfied. You are not clever, but you are—' She paused, but without any sign of embarrassment.

'What am I?' he asked eagerly. He felt sure that it would be something good, and he was not less vain than other men.

'I do not think I will say – not now.'

'But who are you?' His diffidence and stammering had vanished beneath her calm, quiet talk. 'You must let me at least ask that. Who are you? And how do you know all this?'

'I am a woman, but not an earth-woman. And the chief difference between us is that I know nearly all the things you do not know, and you do not know nearly all the things that I know. Sometimes I forget your ignorance – do not be angry for a word; there is no other for it, and it is not your fault. I forgot it just now when I asked you why you had not come to me up the staircase of silver and crystal, through the grey veil where the fireflies live, and into that quiet room beyond.

This is the only time; tomorrow it will not be possible. And I have—' Once more she paused. There was a charm for Lucas Morne in the things which she did not say. 'Your room is dark,' she continued, 'and I can hardly see you.'

'I will light the lamp,' said Lucas hurriedly, 'and – and won't you let me get you some tea?' He saw, as soon as he had said it, how unspeakably ludicrous this proffer of hospitality was. He almost fancied a smile, a moment's shimmer of little white teeth, beneath the long grey veil. 'Or shall I come now – at once,' he added.

'Come now; I will show you the mirror.'

'What is that?'

'You will understand when you see it. It is the glass of supreme moments. I shall tell you about it. But come.'

She looked graceful, and she suggested the most perfect beauty as she stood there, a slight figure against the background of grey mist, which had grown luminous as the room below grew darker. Lucas Morne went carefully up the five steps, and together they passed through the grey, misty curtain. He was wondering what the face was like which was hidden beneath that veil; would it be possible to induce her to remove the veil? He might perhaps, lead the conversation thither – delicately and subtly.

'A cousin of mine,' he began, 'who has travelled a good deal, once told me that the women of the East—'

'Yes,' she said, and her voice and way were so gentle that it hardly seemed like an interruption; 'and so do I.'

He felt very much anticipated; for a moment he was driven back into the shy and stammering state. There were only a few more steps now, and then they entered through a rosy curtain into a room, which he supposed to be 'that quiet room beyond', of which she had spoken.

It was a large room, square in shape. The floor was covered with black and white tiles, with the exception of a small square space in the centre, which looked like silver, and over which a ripple seemed occasionally to pass. She pointed it out

to him. 'That,' she said, 'is the glass of supreme moments.'
There were no windows, and the soft light that filled the
room seemed to come from that liquid silver mirror in the
centre of the floor. The walls, which were lofty, were hung
with curtains of different colours, all subdued, dreamy,
reposeful. These colours were repeated in the painting of the
ceiling. In a recess at the further end of the room there were
seats on which one could sleep. There was a faint smell of
syringa in the air, making it heavy and drowsy. Now and
then one heard faintly, as if afar off, the great music of an
organ. Could it, he found himself wondering, be the organ of
the college chapel? It was restful and pleasant to hear. She
drew him to one of the seats in the recess, and once more
pointed to the mirror.

'All the ecstasy in the world lies reflected there. The
supreme moments of each man's life – the scene, the spoken
words – all lie there. Past and present, and future – all are
there.'

'Shall I be able to see them?'

'If you will.'

'And how?'

'Bend over the mirror, and say the name of the man or
woman into whose life you wish to see. You only have to
want it, and it will appear before your eyes. But there are
some lives which have no supreme moments.'

'Commonplace lives?'

'Yes.'

Lucas Morne walked to the edge of the mirror and knelt
down looking into it. The ripple passed to and fro over the
surface. For a moment he hesitated, doubting for whom he
should ask; and then he said in a low voice: 'Are there
supreme moments in the life of Blake – Vincent Blake, the
athlete?' The surface of the mirror suddenly grew still, and in
it rose what seemed a living picture.

He could see once more the mile race in which he had
been defeated by Blake. It was the third and last lap; and he

himself was leading by some twenty yards, for Blake was waiting. There was a vast crowd of spectators, and he could hear every now and then the dull sound of their voices. He saw Vincent Blake slightly quicken his pace, and marked his own plucky attempt to answer it; he saw, too, that he had very little left in him. Gradually Blake drew up, until at a hundred yards from the finish there were not more than five yards between the two runners. Then he noticed his own fresh attempt. There were some fifty yards of desperate fighting, in which neither seemed to gain or lose an inch on the other. The voices of the excited crowd rose to a roar. And then – then Blake had it his own way. He saw himself passed a yard from the tape.

'Blake has always just beaten me,' he said savagely as he turned from the mirror.

He went back to his seat. 'Tell me,' he said: 'Does that picture really represent the supreme moments of Blake's life?'

'Yes' answered the veiled woman, 'he will have nothing quite like the ecstasy which he felt at winning that race. He will marry, and have children, and his married life will be happy, but the happiness will not be so intense. There is an emotion-meter outside this room, you know, which measures such things.'

'Now if one wanted to bet on a race,' he began. Then he stopped short. He had none of the finer perceptions, but it did not take these to show him that he was becoming a little inappropriate. 'I will look again at the mirror,' he added after a pause. 'I am afraid, though, that all this will make me more discontented with myself.'

Once more he looked into the glass of supreme moments. He murmured the name of Paul Reece, the good little dissenter, his old schoolfellow. It was not in the power of accomplishment that Paul Reece excelled Lucas Morne, but only in the goodness and spirituality of his nature. As he looked, once more a picture formed on the surface of the mirror. It was of the future this time.

It was a sombre picture of the interior of a church. Through the open door one saw the snow falling slowly into the dusk of a winter afternoon. Within, before the richly decorated altar, flickered the little ruby flames of hanging lamps. On the walls, dim in the dying light, were painted the stations of the Cross. The fragrance of the incense smoke still lingered in the air. He could see but one figure, bowed, black-robed, before the altar. 'And is this Paul Reece – who was a dissenter?' he asked himself, knowing that it was he. Someone was seated at the organ, and the cry of music was full of appeal, and yet full of peace; '*Agnus, Dei, qui tollis peccata mundi!*'

Then the picture died away, and once more the little ripple moved too and fro over the surface of the liquid silver mirror. Lucas went back again to his place. The veiled woman was leaning backward, her small white hands linked together. She did not speak, but he was sure that she was looking at him – looking at him intently. Slowly it came to him that there was in this woman a subtle, mastering attraction which he had never known before. And side by side with this thought there still remained the feeling which had filled him as he witnessed the supreme moments of Paul Reece, a paradoxical feeling which was half restlessness and half peace.

'I do not know if I envy Paul,' he said, 'but if so, it is not the envy which hurts. I shall never be like him. I can't feel as he does. It's not in me. But this picture did not make me angry as the other did.' He looked steadfastly at the graceful, veiled figure, and added in a lower tone: 'When I spoke of the travels of my cousin a little while ago – over Palestine, and Turkey, and thereabouts, you know – I had meant to lead up to the question, as you saw. I had meant to ask if you would put away your veil and let me see your face. And there are many things which I want to know about you. May I not stay here by your side and talk?'

'Soon, very soon I will talk with you, and after that you shall see me. What do you think, then, of the glass of supreme moments?'

'It is wonderful. I only feared the sight of the exquisite happiness in others would make me more discontented. At first you seemed to think that I was too dissatisfied.'

'Do not be deceived. Do not think that these supreme moments are everything; for that life is easiest which is gentle, level, placid, and has no supreme moments. There is a picture in the life of your friend Fynsale which I wish you to see. Look at it in the mirror, and then I shall have something to tell you.'

Lucas did as he was bidden. The mirror showed him a wretched, dingy room – sitting-room and bedroom combined – in a lodging house. At a little rickety table, pushed in front of a very small fire, Fynsale sat writing by lamplight. The lamp was out of order apparently. The combined smell of lamp and Latakia was poignant. There was a pile of manuscript before him, and on the top of it he was placing the sheet he had just written. Then he rose from his chair, folded his arms on the mantelpiece, and bent down, with his head on his hands, looking into the fire. It was an uncouth attitude of which, Lucas remembered, Fynsale had been particularly fond when he was at college.

When the picture had passed, Lucas looked round, and saw that the veiled woman had left the recess, and was now standing by his side. 'I do not understand this,' he said. 'How can those be the supreme moments in Fynsale's life? He looked poor and shabby, and the room was positively wretched. Where does the ecstasy come in?'

'He has just finished his novel; and he is quite madly in love with it. Some of it is very good, and some of it – from merely physical reasons – is very bad; he was half-starved when he was writing it, and it is not possible to write very well when one is half-starved. But he loves it. I am speaking of all this as if, like the picture of it, it was present; although, of course, it has not happened yet. But I will tell you more. I will show you, in this case at least, what these moments of ecstasy are worth. Some of Fynsale's book, I have said, is very good, and some of it is very bad; but none of it is what people want. He will take it to publisher after publisher, and they will refuse it. After three years it will at last be published, and it will not succeed in the least. And all through these years of failure he will recall from time to time the splendid joy he felt at finishing that book, and how glad he was that he had made it. The thought of that past ecstasy will make the torture all the worse.'

'Perhaps, then, after all, I should be glad that I am commonplace?' said Lucas.

'It does not always follow, though, that the commonplace people have commonplace lives. There have been men who have been so ordinary that it hurt one to have anything to do with them, and yet the gods have made them come into poetry.'

Once more Lucas fancied that a smile with magic in it might be fluttering under that grey veil. Every moment the fascination of this woman, whose face he had not seen, and with whom he had spoken for so short a time, grew stronger on him. He did not know from whence it came, whether it lay in the grace of her figure and her movements, or in the beauty of her long dark hair, or in the music of her voice, or in that subtle, indefinable way in which she seemed to show him that she cared for him deeply. The room itself, quiet, mystical, restful, dedicated to the ecstasy of the world, had its effect upon his senses. More than ever before he felt himself impressed, tremulous with emotion. He knew that she saw how, in spite of himself, the look of adoration would come into his eyes.

And suddenly, she, whom but a moment before he had imagined to be smiling at her own light thoughts, seemed swayed by a more serious impulse.

'You must be comforted, though, and be angry with yourself no longer. For you are *not* commonplace, because you know that you *are* commonplace. It is something to have wanted the right things, although the gods have given you no power to attain them, nor even the wit and words to make your want eloquent.' Her voice was deeper, touched with the under-thrill.

'This,' he said, 'is the second time you have spoken of the gods – and yet we are in the nineteenth century.'

'Are we? I am very old and very young. Time is nothing to me; it does not change me. Yesterday in Italy each grave and stream spoke of divinity: "*Non omnis moriar*," sang one in confidence, "*Non omnis moriar!*" I heard his voice, and now he is passed and gone from the world.'

'We read him still,' said Lucas Morne, with a little pride. He was not intending to take the classical tripos, but he had with the help of a translation read that ode from which she was quoting. She did not heed his interruption in the least. She went on speaking—

'And today in England there is but little which is sacred; yet here, too, my work is seen; and here, too, as they die, they cry: "I shall not die, but live!"'

'You will think me stupid,' said Lucas Morne, a little bewildered, 'but I really do not understand you. I do not follow you. I cannot see to what you refer.'

'That is because you do not know who I am. Before the end of today I think we shall understand each other well.'

There was a moment's pause, and then Lucas Morne spoke again.

'You have told me that even in the lives of commonplace people there are sometimes supreme moments. I had scarcely hoped for them, and you have bidden me not to desire them. Shall I – even I – know what ecstasy means?'

'Yes, yes; I think so.'

'Then let me see it, as I saw the rest pictured in the mirror.' He spoke with some hesitation, his eyes fixed on the tiled floor of the room.

'That need not be,' she answered, and she hardly seemed to have perfect control over the tones of her voice now. 'That need not be, Lucas Morne, for the supreme moments of your life are here, here and now.'

He looked up, suddenly and excitedly. She had flung back the grey veil over her long, dark hair, and stood revealed before him, looking ardently into his eyes. Her face was paler than that of average beauty; the lips, shapely and scarlet, were just parted; but the eyes gave the most wonderful charm. They were like flames at midnight – not the soft, grey eyes that make men better, but the passionate eyes that make men forget honour, and reason, and everything. She stretched out both hands towards him, impulsively, appealingly. He grasped them in his own. His own hands were hot, burning; every nerve in them tingled with excitement. For a moment he held her at arm's length, looking at her, and said nothing. At last he found words—

'I knew that you would be like this. I think that I have loved you all my life. I wish that I might be with you for ever.'

There was a strange expression on her face. She did not speak, but she drew him nearer to her.

'Tell me your name,' he said.

'Yesterday, where that poet lived – that confident poet – they called me Libitina; and here, today, they call me Death. My name matters not, if you love me. For to you alone have I come thus. For the rest, I have done my work unseen. Only in this hour – only in this hour – was it possible.'

He had hardly heeded what she said. He bent down over her face.

'Stay!' she said in a hurried whisper, 'if you kiss me you will die.'

He smiled triumphantly. 'But I shall die kissing you,' he said. And so their lips met. Her lips were scarlet, but they were icy cold.

The captain of the football team had just come out of evening chapel, his gown slung over his arm, his cap pulled over his eyes, looking good-tempered, and strong, and jolly, but hardly devotional. He saw the window of Morne's rooms open – they were on the ground floor – and looked in. By the glow of the failing fire he saw what he thought was Lucas Morne seated in a lounge chair. He called to him, but there was no answer. 'The old idiot's asleep,' he said to himself, as he climbed in at the window. 'Wake up, old man,' he cried, as he put his hand on the shoulder of Lucas Morne's body, and swung it forward; 'wake up, old man.'

The body rolled forward and fell sideways to the ground heavily and clumsily. It lay there motionless.

THE VENGEANCE OF THE DEAD

Robert Barr

It is a bad thing for a man to die with an unsatisfied thirst for revenge parching his soul. David Allen died, cursing Bernard Heaton and lawyer Grey; hating the lawyer who had won the case even more than the man who was to gain by the winning. Yet if cursing were to be done, David should rather have cursed his own stubbornness and stupidity.

To go back for some years, this is what had happened. Squire Heaton's only son went wrong. The squire raged, as was natural. He was one of a long line of hard-drinking, hard-riding, hard-swearing squires, and it was maddening to think that his only son should deliberately take to books and cold water, when there was manly sport in the countryside and old wine in the cellar. Yet before now such blows have descended upon deserving men, and they have to be borne as best they may. Squire Heaton bore it badly, and when his son went off on a Government scientific expedition around the world the squire drank harder and swore harder than ever, but never mentioned the boy's name.

Two years after, young Heaton returned, but the doors of the Hall were closed against him. He had no mother to plead for him, although it was not likely that would have made any difference, for the squire was not a man to be appealed to and swayed this way or that. He took his hedges, his drinks, and his course in life straight. The young man went to India, where he was drowned. As there is no mystery in this matter, it may as well be stated here that young Heaton ultimately returned to England, as drowned men have ever been in the habit of doing, when their return will mightily inconvenience innocent persons, who have taken their places. It is a disputed question whether the sudden disappearance of a man, or his reappearance after a lapse of years, is the more annoying.

If the old squire felt remorse at the supposed death of his only son he did not show it. The hatred which had been directed against his unnatural offspring redoubled itself and was bestowed on his nephew David Allen, who was now the legal heir to the estate and its income. Allen was the impecunious son of the squire's sister who had married badly. It is hard to starve when one is heir to a fine property, but that is what David did, and it soured him. The Jews would not lend on the security – the son might return – so David Allen waited for a dead man's shoes, impoverished and embittered.

At last the shoes were ready for him to step into. The old squire died as a gentleman should, of apoplexy, in his armchair, with a decanter at his elbow; David Allen entered into his belated inheritance, and his first act was to discharge every servant, male and female, about the place and engage others who owed their situations to him alone. Then were the Jews sorry they had not trusted him.

He was now rich but broken in health, with bent shoulders, without a friend on the earth. He was a man suspicious of all the world, and he had a furtive look over his shoulder as if he expected Fate to deal him a sudden blow – as indeed it did.

It was a beautiful June day, when there passed the porter's lodge and walked up the avenue to the main entrance of the Hall a man whose face was bronzed by a torrid sun. He requested speech with the master and was asked into a room to wait.

At length David Allen shuffled in, with his bent shoulders, glaring at the intruder from under his bushy eyebrows. The stranger rose as he entered and extended his hand.

'You don't know me, of course. I believe we have never met before. I am your cousin.'

Allen ignored the outstretched hand.

'I have no cousin,' he said.

'I am Bernard Heaton, the son of your uncle.'

'Bernard Heaton is dead.'

'I beg your pardon, he is not. I ought to know, for I tell you I am he.'

'You lie!'

Heaton, who had been standing since his cousin's entrance, now sat down again, Allen remaining on his feet.

'Look here,' said the newcomer. 'Civility costs nothing and—'

'I cannot be civil to an impostor.'

'Quite so. It *is* difficult. Still, if I am an impostor, civility can do no harm, while if it should turn out that I am not an impostor, then your present tone may make after arrangements all the harder upon you. Now will you oblige me by sitting down? I dislike, while sitting myself, talking to a standing man.'

'Will you oblige me by stating what you want before I order my servants to turn you out?'

'I see you are going to be hard on yourself. I will endeavour to keep my temper, and if I succeed it will be a triumph for a member of our family. I am to state what I want? I will. I want as my own the three rooms on the first floor of the south wing – the rooms communicating with each other. You perceive I at least know the house. I want my meals served there, and I wish to be undisturbed at all hours. Next, I desire that you settle upon me, say, five hundred a year – or six hundred – out of the revenues of the estate. I am engaged in scientific research of a peculiar kind. I can make money, of course, but I wish my mind left entirely free from financial worry. I shall not interfere with your enjoyment of the estate in the least.'

'I'll wager you will not. So you think I am fool enough to harbour and feed the first idle vagabond that comes along and claims to be my dead cousin. Go to the courts with your story and be imprisoned as similar perjurers have been.'

'Of course I don't expect you to take my word for it. If you were any judge of human nature you would see I am not a vagabond. Still that's neither here nor there. Choose three of your own friends. I will lay my proofs before them, and abide by their decision. Come, nothing could be fairer than that, now could it?'

'Go to the courts, I tell you.'

'Oh, certainly. But only as a last resort. No wise man goes to law if there is another course open. But what is the use of taking such an absurd position? You *know* I'm your cousin. I'll take you blindfold into every room in the place.'

'Any discharged servant could do that. I have had enough of you. I am not a man to be blackmailed. Will you leave the house yourself, or shall I call the servants to put you out?'

'I should be sorry to trouble you,' said Heaton, rising. 'That is your last word, I take it?'

'Absolutely.'

'Then goodbye. We shall meet at Philippi.'

Allen watched him disappear down the avenue, and it dimly occurred to him that he had not acted diplomatically.

Heaton went directly to lawyer Grey, and laid the case before him. He told the lawyer what his modest demands were, and gave instructions that if, at any time before the suit came off, his cousin would compromise, an arrangement avoiding publicity should be arrived at.

'Excuse me for saying that looks like weakness,' remarked the lawyer.

'I know it does,' answered Heaton. 'But my case is so strong that I can afford to have it appear weak.'

The lawyer shook his head. He knew how uncertain the law was. But he soon discovered that no compromise was possible.

The case came to trial, and the verdict was entirely in favour of Bernard Heaton.

The pallor of death spread over the sallow face of David Allen as he realized that he was once again a man without a penny or a foot of land. He left the court with a bowed head, speaking no word to those who had defended him. Heaton hurried after him, overtaking him on the pavement.

'I knew this had to be the result,' he said to the defeated man. 'No other outcome was possible. I have no desire to cast you penniless into the street. What you refused to me I shall be glad to offer you. I will make the annuity a thousand pounds.'

Allen, trembling, darted one look of malignant hate at his cousin.

'You successful scoundrel!' he cried. 'You and your villainous confederate Grey. I tell you—'

The blood rushed to his mouth; he fell upon the pavement and died. One and the same day had robbed him of his land and his life.

Bernard Heaton deeply regretted the tragic issue, but went on with his researches at the Hall, keeping much to himself. Lawyer Grey, who had won renown by his conduct of the celebrated case, was almost his only friend. To him Heaton partially disclosed his hopes, told what he had learned during those years he had been lost to the world in India, and claimed that if he succeeded in combining the occultism of the East with the science of the West, he would make for himself a name of imperishable renown.

The lawyer, a practical man of the world, tried to persuade Heaton to abandon his particular line of research, but without success.

'No good can come of it,' said Grey, 'India has spoiled you. Men who dabble too much in that sort of thing go mad. The brain is a delicate instrument. Do not trifle with it.'

'Nevertheless,' persisted Heaton, 'the great discoveries of the twentieth century are going to be in that line, just as the great discoveries of the nineteenth century have been in the direction of electricity.'

'The cases are not parallel. Electricity is a tangible substance.'

'Is it? Then tell me what it is composed of? We all know how it is generated, and we know partly what it will do, but what *is* it?'

'I shall have to charge you six-and-eightpence for answering that question,' the lawyer had said with a laugh. 'At any rate there is a good deal to be discovered about electricity yet. Turn your attention to that and leave this Indian nonsense alone.'

Yet, astonishing as it may seem, Bernard Heaton, to his undoing, succeeded, after many futile attempts – several times narrowly escaping death. Inventors and discoverers have to risk their lives as often as soldiers, with less chance of worldly glory.

First his invisible excursions were confined to the house and his own grounds, then he went further afield, and to his intense astonishment one day he met the spirit of the man who hated him.

'Ah,' said David Allen, 'you did not live long to enjoy your ill-gotten gains.'

'You are as wrong in this sphere of existence as you were in the other. I am not dead.'

'Then why are you here and in this shape?'

'I suppose there is no harm in telling *you*. What I wanted to discover, at the time you would not give me a hearing, was how to separate the spirit from its servant, the body – that is, temporarily and not finally. My body is at this moment lying apparently asleep in a locked room in my house – one of the rooms I begged from you. In an hour or two I shall return and take possession of it.'

'And how do you take possession of it and quit it?'

Heaton, pleased to notice the absence of that rancour which had formerly been Allen's most prominent characteristic, and feeling that any information given to a disembodied spirit was safe as far as the world was concerned, launched out on the subject that possessed his whole mind.

'It is very interesting,' said Allen, when he had finished.

And so they parted.

David Allen at once proceeded to the Hall, which he had not seen since the day he left it to attend the trial. He passed quickly through the familiar apartments until he entered the locked room on the first floor of the south wing. There on the bed lay the body of Heaton, most of the colour gone from the face, but breathing regularly, if almost imperceptibly, like a mechanical wax figure.

If a watcher had been in the room, he would have seen the colour slowly return to the face and the sleeper gradually awaken, at last rising from the bed.

Allen, in the body of Heaton, at first felt very uncomfortable, as a man does who puts on an ill-fitting suit of clothes. The limitations caused by the wearing of a body also discommoded him. He looked carefully around the room. It was plainly furnished. A desk in the corner he found contained the MS of a book prepared for the printer, all executed with the neat accuracy of a scientific man. Above the desk, pasted against the wall, was a sheet of paper headed:

'What to do if I am found here apparently dead.' Underneath were plainly written instructions. It was evident that Heaton had taken no one into his confidence.

It is well if you go in for revenge to make it as complete as possible. Allen gathered up the MS, placed it in the grate, and set a match to it. Thus he at once destroyed his enemy's chances of posthumous renown, and also removed evidence that might, in certain contingencies, prove Heaton's insanity.

Unlocking the door, he proceeded down the stairs, where he met a servant who told him luncheon was ready. He noticed that the servant was one whom he had discharged, so he came to the conclusion that Heaton had taken back all the old retainers who had applied to him when the result of the trial became public. Before lunch was over he saw that some of his own servants were also there still.

'Send the gamekeeper to me,' said Allen to the servant.

Brown came in, who had been on the estate for twenty years continuously, with the exception of the few months after Allen had packed him off.

'What pistols have I, Brown?'

'Well, sir, there's the old squire's duelling pistols, rather out of date, sir; then your own pair and that American revolver.'

'Is the revolver in working order?'

'Oh yes, sir.'

'Then bring it to me and some cartridges.'

When Brown returned with the revolver his master took it and examined it.

'Be careful, sir,' said Brown anxiously. 'You know it's a self-cocker, sir.'

'A what?'

'A self-cocking revolver, sir' – trying to repress his astonishment at the question his master asked about a weapon with which he should have been familiar.

'Show me what you mean,' said Allen, handing back the revolver.

Brown explained that the mere pulling of the trigger fired the weapon.

'Now shoot at the end window – never mind the glass. Don't stand gaping at me, do as I tell you.'

Brown fired the revolver, and a diamond pane snapped out of the window.

'How many times will that shoot without reloading?'

'Seven times, sir.'

'Very good. Put in a cartridge for the one you fired and leave the revolver with me. Find out when there is a train to town, and let me know.'

It will be remembered that the dining-room incident was used at the trial, but without effect, as going to show that

Bernard Heaton was insane. Brown also testified that there was something queer about his master that day.

David Allen found all the money he needed in the pockets of Bernard Heaton. He caught his train, and took a cab from the station directly to the law offices of Messrs Grey, Leason, and Grey, anxious to catch the lawyer before he left for the day.

The clerk sent up word that Mr Heaton wished to see the senior Mr Grey for a few moments. Allen was asked to walk up.

'You know the way, sir,' said the clerk.

Allen hesitated.

'Announce me, if you please.'

The clerk, being well trained, showed no surprise, but led the visitor to Mr Grey's door.

'How are you, Heaton?' said the lawyer cordially. 'Take a chair. Where have you been keeping yourself this long time? How are the Indian experiments coming on?'

'Admirably, admirably,' answered Allen.

At the sound of his voice the lawyer looked up quickly, then apparently reassured he said—

'You're not looking quite the same. Been keeping yourself too much indoors, I imagine. You ought to quit research and do some shooting this autumn.'

'I intend to, and I hope then to have your company.'

'I shall be pleased to run down, although I am no great hand at a gun.'

'I want to speak with you a few moments in private. Would you mind locking the door so that we may not be interrupted?'

'We are quite safe from interruption here,' said the lawyer, as he turned the key in the lock; then resuming his seat he added, 'Nothing serious, I hope?'

'It is rather serious. Do you mind my sitting here?' asked Allen, as he drew up his chair so that he was between Grey and the door, with the table separating them. The lawyer was watching him with anxious face, but without, as yet, serious apprehension.

'Now,' said Allen, 'will you answer me a simple question? To whom are you talking?'

'To whom—?' The lawyer in his amazement could get no further.

'Yes. To whom are you talking? Name him.'

'Heaton, what is the matter with you? Are you ill?'

'Well, you have mentioned a name, but, being a villain and a lawyer, you cannot give a direct answer to a very simple question. You think you are talking to that fool Bernard Heaton. It is true that the body you are staring at is Heaton's body, but the man you are talking to is me – David Allen – the man you swindled and then murdered. Sit down. If you move you are a dead man. Don't try to edge to the door. There are seven deaths in this revolver and the whole seven can be let loose in less than that many seconds, for this is a self-cocking instrument. Now it will take you at least ten seconds to get to the door, so remain exactly where you are. That advice will strike you as wise, even if, as you think, you have to do with a madman. You asked me a minute ago how the Indian experiments were coming on, and I answered, "Admirably". Bernard Heaton left his body this morning, and I, David Allen, am now in possession of it. Do you understand? I admit it is a little difficult for the legal mind to grasp such a situation.'

'Ah, not at all,' said Grey airily. 'I comprehend it perfectly. The man I see before me is the spirit, life, soul, whatever you like to call it – of David Allen in the body of my friend Bernard Heaton. The – ah – essence of my friend is at this moment fruitlessly searching for his missing body. Perhaps he is in this room now, not knowing how to get out a spiritual writ of ejectment against you.'

'You show more quickness that I expected of you,' said Allen.

'Thanks,' rejoined Grey, although he said to himself,

'Heaton has gone mad! stark staring mad, as I expected he would. He is armed. The situation is becoming dangerous. I must humour him.'

'Thanks. And now may I ask what you propose to do? You have not come here for legal advice. You never, unluckily for me, were a client of mine.'

'No. I did not come either to give or take advice. I am here, alone with you – you gave orders that we were not to be disturbed, remember – for the sole purpose of revenging myself on you and on Heaton. Now listen, for the scheme will commend itself to your ingenious mind. I shall murder you in this room. I shall then give myself up. I shall vacate this body in Newgate prison and your friend may then resume his tenancy or not as he chooses. He may allow the unoccupied body to lie in the cell or he may take possession of it and be hanged for murder. Do you appreciate the completeness of my vengeance on you both? Do you think your friend will care to put on his body again?'

'It is a nice question,' said the lawyer, as he edged his chair imperceptibly along and tried to grope behind himself, unperceived by his visitor, for the electric button placed against the wall. 'It is a nice question, and I would like to have time to consider it in all its bearings before I gave an answer.'

'You shall have all the time you care to allow yourself. I am in no hurry, and I wish you to realize your situation as completely as possible. Allow me to say that the electric button is a little to the left and slightly above where you are feeling for it. I merely mention this because I must add, in fairness to you, that the moment you touch it, time ends as far as you are concerned. When you press the ivory button, I fire.'

The lawyer rested his arms on the table before him, and for the first time a hunted look of alarm came into his eyes, which died out of them when, after a moment of two of intense fear, he regained possession of himself.

'I would like to ask you a question or two,' he said at last.

'As many as you choose. I am in no hurry, as I said before.'

'I am thankful for your reiteration of that. The first question is then: has a temporary residence in another sphere interfered in any way with your reasoning powers?'

'I think not.'

'Ah, I had hoped that your apprehension of logic might have improved during your – well, let us say absence; you were not very logical – not very amenable to reason, formerly.'

'I know you thought so.'

'I did; so did your own legal adviser, by the way. Well, now let me ask why you are so bitter against me? Why not murder the judge who charged against you, or the jury that unanimously gave a verdict in our favour? I was merely an instrument, as were they.'

'It was your devilish trickiness that won the case.'

'That statement is flattering but untrue. The case was its own best advocate. But you haven't answered the question. Why not murder judge and jury?'

'I would gladly do so if I had them in my power. You see, I am perfectly logical.'

'Quite, quite,' said the lawyer. 'I am encouraged to proceed. Now of what did my devilish trickiness rob you?'

'Of my property, and then of my life.'

'I deny both allegations, but will for the sake of the argument admit them for the moment. First, as to your property. It was a possession that might at any moment be jeopardized by the return of Bernard Heaton.'

'By the *real* Bernard Heaton – yes.'

'Very well then. As you are now repossessed of the property, and as you have the outward semblance of Heaton, your rights cannot be questioned. As far as property is concerned you are now in an unassailable position where formerly you were in an assailable one. Do you follow me?'

'Perfectly.'

'We come (second) to the question of life. You then

occupied a body frail, bent, and diseased, a body which, as events showed, gave way under exceptional excitement. You are now in a body strong and healthy, with apparently a long life before it. You admit the truth of all I have said on these two points?'

'I quite admit it.'

'Then to sum up, you are now in a better position – infinitely – both as regards life and property, than the one from which my malignity – ingenuity I think was your word – ah, yes – trickiness – thanks – removed you. Now why cut your career short? Why murder *me*? Why not live out your life, under better conditions, in luxury and health, and thus be completely revenged on Bernard Heaton? If you are logical, now is the time to show it.'

Allen rose slowly, holding the pistol in his right hand.

'You miserable scoundrel!' he cried. 'You pettifogging lawyer – tricky to the last! How gladly you would throw over your friend to prolong your own wretched existence! Do you think you are now talking to a biased judge and a susceptible, brainless jury? Revenged on Heaton? I *am* revenged on him already. But part of my vengeance involves your death. Are you ready for it?'

Allen pointed the revolver at Grey, who had now also risen, his face ashen. He kept his eyes fastened on the man he believed to be mad. His hand crept along the wall. There was intense silence between them. Allen did not fire. Slowly the lawyer's hand moved towards the electric button. At last he felt the ebony rim and his fingers quickly covered it. In the stillness, the vibrating ring of an electric bell somewhere below was audible. Then the sharp crack of the revolver suddenly split the silence. The lawyer dropped on one knee, holding his arm in the air as if to ward off attack. Again the revolver rang out, and Grey plunged forward on his face. The other five shots struck the lifeless body.

A stratum of blue smoke hung breast high in the room as if it were the departing soul of the man who lay motionless on the floor. Outside were excited voices, and someone flung himself ineffectually against the stout locked door.

Allen crossed the room and, turning the key, flung open the door. 'I have murdered your master,' he said, handing the revolver butt forward to the nearest man. 'I give myself up. Go and get an officer.'

SMEATH

Barry Pain

I

Percy Bellowes was not actually idle, had a good deal of ability, and wished to make money. But at the age of thirty-five he had not made it. He had been articled to a solicitor, and, in his own phrase, had turned it down. He had neglected the regular channels of education which were open to him. He could give a conjuring entertainment for an hour, and though his tricks were stock tricks, they were done in the neat professional manner.

He could play the cornet and the violin, neither of them very well. He could dance a breakdown. He had made himself useful in a touring theatrical company. But he could not spell correctly, and his grammar was not always beyond reproach. He disliked regularity. He could not go to the same office at the same time every morning. He was thriftless, and he had been, but was no longer, intemperate. He was a big man, with smooth black hair, and a heavy moustache, and he had the manners of a bully.

At the age of thirty-five he considered his position. He was at that time travelling the country as a hypnotic entertainer, under the name of Dr Sanders-Bell. At each of his entertainments he issued a Ten Thousand Pound Challenge, not having at the time ten thousand pence in the world.

He employed confederates, and he had to pay them. It was not a good business at all. His gains in one town were always being swallowed up in his losses in another. His confederates gave him constant trouble.

But though he turned things over for long in his mind, he could see nothing else to take up. There is no money nowadays for a conjurer without originality, an indifferent musician, or passable actor. His hypnotic entertainment would have been no good in London, but it did earn just enough to keep him going in the provinces.

Also, Percy Bellowes had an ordinary human weakness; he liked to be regarded with awe as a man of mystery. Even off the stage he acted his part. He had talked delirious science to agitated landladies in cheap lodgings in many towns.

Teston was a small place, and Percy Bellowes thought that he had done very well, after a one-night show, to cover his expenses and put four pounds in his pocket. He remained in the town on the following day, because he wished to see a man who had answered his advertisement for a confederate. 'Assistant to a Hypnotic Entertainer' was the phrase Mr Bellowes had used for it.

He was stopping at the Victoria Hotel. It was the only hotel in the place, and it was quite bad. But Percy Bellowes was used to that. A long course of touring had habituated him to doubtful eggs and indistinguishable coffee. This morning he faced a singularly repulsive breakfast without quailing. He was even cheerful and conversational with a slatternly maid who waited on him.

'So you saw the show last night,' he said.

'Yes, sir, I did. And very wonderful it was. There has never been anything like it in Teston, not in my memory.'

'Ah, my dear. Well, you watch this.'

He picked up the two boiled eggs which had been placed

before him. He hurled one in the air, where it vanished. He swallowed the other one whole. He then produced them both from a vase on the mantelpiece.

'Well, I never!' said the maid. 'I wonder if there's anything you can't do, sir?'

'Just one or two things,' said Mr Bellowes, sardonically. 'By the way, my dear, if a man comes here this morning and asks for me, I want to see him.' He consulted a soiled letter which he had taken from his pocket. 'The name's Smeath.'

Mr Smeath arrived, in fact, before Bellowes had finished his breakfast, and was told he could come in. He was a man of extraordinary appearance.

He was a dwarf, with a slightly hunched back. His hands were a size too large for him, and were always restless. His expression was one of snarling subservience. At first Bellowes was inclined to reject him, for a confederate should not be a man of unusual appearance, and easily recognizable. Then it struck him that, after all, this would be a very weird and impressive figure on the stage.

'Ever do anything of this kind before?' he asked.

'No, sir,' said Smeath. 'But I've seen it done and can pick it up. I think I could give you satisfaction. You see, it's not very easy for a man like me to find work.'

All the time that he was speaking, his hands were busy.

'When you've finished tearing up my newspaper,' said Bellowes.

'Sorry, sir,' said the man. He pushed the newspaper away from him, but caught up a corner of the tablecloth. It was frayed, and he began to pull the threads out of it, quickly and eagerly.

'Ever been hypnotized?' Bellowes asked.

'No, sir,' said Smeath, with a cunning smile. 'But that doesn't matter, does it? I can act the part all right.'

'It matters a devilish lot, as it happens. And you can't act the part all right, either. My assistants are always genuinely hypnotized. I employ them to save time on the stage. After I have hypnotized you a few times, I shall be able to put you into the hypnotic state in a minute or less, and to do it with certainty. I can't depend on chance people from the audience. Many of them cannot be hypnotized at all, and with most of the others it takes far too long. There are exceptional cases – I had one at my show only last night – but I don't often come across them. Come on up with me to my room.'

'You want to see if you can hypnotize me?'

'No, I don't. I know I can. I simply want to do it.'

Upstairs in the dingy bedroom Bellowes made Smeath sit down. He held the bright lid of a cigarette-tin between Smeath's eyes and slightly above the level of them.

'Look at that,' he said. 'Keep on looking at it. Keep on!'

In a few minutes Bellowes put the tin down, put his fingers on Smeath's eyes, and closed them. The eyes remained closed. The little hunchback sat tense and rigid.

An hour later, in the coffee-room downstairs, Bellowes made his definite agreement with Smeath.

'You understand?' said Bellowes. 'You'll be at the town hall at Warlow tomorrow night at seven. When I invite people to come up on the platform, you will come up. That's all you've got to do. Got any money?'

'Enough for the present.' Smeath began to pull matches from a box on the table. He broke each match into four pieces. 'But suppose that tomorrow night you can't do it?'

'There'll never be a day or night I can't do it with you now. That's definite. Now, then, leave those matches alone. I might be wanting one of them directly.'

After Smeath's departure, Percy Bellowes sat for a few minutes deep in thought. In that dingy room upstairs he had seen something of which he thought that various uses might be made. He picked up the newspaper, and was pleased to find that Smeath's busy fingers had spared the racing intelligence. Then he sought out the landlord.

'I say,' he said, 'I've got a fancy to put a few shillings on a horse. Do you know anybody here it would be safe to do it with?'

'Well,' said the landlord, 'as a matter of fact you can do it with me, if you like. I do a little in that way on the quiet.'

'The police don't bother you?'

'No; they're not a very bright lot, the police here. Besides, they're pretty busy just now. We had a murder in Teston the day before you came.'

'Who was that?'

'A Miss Samuel, daughter of some very well-to-do people here. They think it was a tramp. See that plantation up on the hill there? That was where they found her – her head all beaten to pulp and her money gone.'

'Nice set of blackguards you've got in Teston, I don't think. Well now, about this race today.'

When Percy Bellowes left the Victoria Hotel on the following morning he was not required to pay a bill. On the contrary, he had a small balance to receive from the landlord.

'Bless you, I don't mind,' said the landlord, as he paid him. 'Pretty well all my crowd were on the favourite. Queer thing that horse should have fallen.'

II

At Warlow the entertainment went very well. When it was over, Bellowes asked Smeath to come round to the hotel. They had the little smoking-room to themselves.

'You remember when I hypnotized you yesterday?'

'Yes, sir. Yes, Mr Bellowes.'

'Do you remember what you did, or said?'

Smeath shook his head.

'I went to sleep, the same as I did tonight. That was all.'

'Know anything about horse-racing?'

'Nothing. Never touched it.'

'You mean to say you've never seen a horse-race?'

'Never.'

'What did you do before you came to see me?'

'I had not been in any employment for some time. I was

once in business as a bird-fancier. I had bad luck and made no money in it. You ask me a great many questions, sir.'

'I do. That's because I've been turning things over in my mind. I want you to put your name to an agreement with me for three years. A pound a week. That's a good offer. A man who's been in business, and failed, ought to appreciate an absolute certainty like that.'

'It would be the same kind of work?' Smeath asked.

'Pretty much the same. When I've finished this tour I am thinking of settling down in London. I should employ you there.'

'No, thank you, Mr Bellowes,' said Smeath. 'I would rather not.'

'Oh, all right,' said Bellowes. 'Make an idiot of yourself, if you like. It doesn't make a pin's head of difference to me. I can easily find plenty of other men who would grab at it. I thought I was doing you a kindness. As you said yourself, chaps of your build don't find it any too easy to get work.'

'I will work for you for six months – possibly a month or two longer than that. But, afterwards, well, I wish to return to the bird-fancying again.'

'No, you don't,' said Bellowes, savagely. 'If you can't take my terms, you're not going to make your own. If you won't sign for three years, out you get! You're talking like a fool, too. How can you go back to this rotten business in six months? D'you think you're going to save the capital for it out of a pound a week?'

'I have friends who might help me.'

'Who are they?'

'They are – well, they're friends of mine. You will perhaps give me till tomorrow morning to think it over.'

'Very well. If you're not here by ten tomorrow morning to go round to the solicitor's office with me, I've finished with you. Now then, I'm going to hypnotize you again.'

'What for?'

'Practice. Now then, look at me.'

In a few moments Smeath sat with his eyes open but fixed.

'Tell me what you see?' asked Bellowes.

'Nothing,' said Smeath. 'I see nothing.'

'Yes, you do,' said Bellowes. 'There are horses with jockeys on them. They are racing, See? They get near the winning-post.'

'Yes,' said Smeath, dully. 'I see them, but it is through a mist and a long way off. Now they're gone.'

'Yesterday when I hypnotized you, you saw clearly. You actually described a race which afterwards took place. You gave me the colours. You gave me the names that the crowd shouted. You described how the favourite crossed his legs and fell. Can you do nothing of the kind today?'

'No, not today. Today I see other things.'

'What?'

'I see a street in London. There is a long row of sandwichmen. My name is on their boards. There are many fashionable people in the street. Expensive shops. Jewellers' shops, picture galleries. I can see you, too. You have just come into the street.'

'Where have I come from?'

'How can I tell? It may be your own house or offices. Your name is on a very small brass plate by the side of the door. You have got a fur coat on, and you are wearing a diamond pin. You get into a car. It is your own car, and you tell the man who opens the door for you to drive to the bank. You look very pleased and prosperous. Now the car starts. That is all. I can see no more.'

Bellowes leaned forward and blew lightly on Smeath's eyes. The tenseness of his muscles relaxed. He rubbed his eyes and stood up.

'Do you know what you've been saying?' Bellowes asked.

'I've been saying nothing,' said Smeath. 'I have been asleep, as you know. You made me go to sleep.'

Bellowes looked round the room. His eye fell on an empty cigarette-box, lying in the fender.

'Pick that up, and hold it in your hands,' he said.

Smeath looked surprised, but he did as he was told. There was a loose label on the box, and his fingers began to tear it off in small pieces.

'Now then,' said Bellowes, 'can you tell me anything about the man who had that box, and threw it down there?'

'Of course I can't. How should I be able to do that? It's not possible.'

'Very well,' said Bellowes. 'I'm going to put you to sleep once more.'

'I don't like this,' whined Smeath. 'There's too much of it. It's bad for one's health.'

'Nonsense! Look here, Smeath. I want you for three years, don't I? Then I'm not likely to do anything that will injure your health. You'll be all right.'

When Bellowes had hypnotized Smeath, he again put the cigarette-box in his hands.

'And now what do you see?' he asked.

'This is quite clear. It is a short, thick-set man who takes the last cigarette out of the box and throws it down. As he smokes it, he walks up and down the room, frowning. He is puzzled about something. He takes out his pocket-book, and as he opens it a card drops to the floor.'

'Can you see what's on the card?'

'Yes. It lies face upwards. The name is "Mr Vincent". And in the left-hand corner are the words "Criminal Investigation Department, Scotland Yard". Now he closes his note-book.'

'What was written in it?'

'I only saw one word – the name "Samuel" . . . Now a waiter comes into the room, and the man asks for a timetable.'

Once more Bellowes restored Smeath to his normal state.

'That'll do,' he said. 'That's all for tonight. You can be off now, and think over that offer of mine.'

At ten on the following morning Smeath kept his appointment. He said he would sign an agreement for two years only, and that he would want thirty shillings a week.

'What makes you suddenly think you're worth thirty shillings a week?'

'I have no idea at all, but I know you need me very much. I have that feeling.'

'It was three years I said, not two. If I pay you thirty shillings a week you can sign for three years.'

'I cannot. I want to get back to my birds. I will sign for thirty shillings a week for two years, or I will go away.'

'Oh, very well,' growled Bellowes. 'You're an obstinate little devil. Have it your own way. I hope to goodness I'm not going to lose money over you. I've never paid more than a pound to an assistant before. By the way, Smeath, were you ever in London?'

'Yes; several times.'

'Do you know Piccadilly, or Bond Street, or Regent Street?' Smeath shook his head.

'I have only passed through in going from one place to another. I know the names of those streets, but I've never been in them.'

'Very well,' said Bellowes. 'Come along with me, and we'll fix up the agreement.'

III

About a month later Mr Bellowes, who had come up to London for the purpose, called at the office of Mr Tangent's agency in Sussex Street.

'Appointment,' said Mr Bellowes, as he handed in his card, and was taken immediately into the inner office. Mr Tangent, a florid and slightly overdressed man of fifty, rose from his American desk to shake hands with him.

'Well, my dear old boy,' said Tangent, 'and how are you?'

'Fit,' said Bellowes. 'Remarkably fit.'

'And what can I do for you? I had an enquiry the other day that brought you to my mind. It's not much. A week, with a chance of an engagement if you catch on.'

'Thanks, old man, but I don't want it. I've got on to something a bit better. What I want from you is a hundred and fifty pounds.'

Tangent laughed genially.

'Long time since I've seen so much money as that. Well, well! What's it for? Tell us the story.'

'I've had a bit of luck, Tangent. I've got a man booked up to me for the next two years who is simply the most marvellous clairvoyant the world has ever seen.'

'Clairvoyants aren't going well,' said Tangent. 'Most of them don't make enough to pay for their rent and their ads in the Sunday papers. The fact is there are too many of them. I don't care what the line is – palmistry, crystal-gazing, psychometry, or what you like. There's no money in it.'

'Let's talk sense. You say there's no money in it? Do you remember when Merion fell, and a ten-to-one chance romped home?'

'Remember it? I've got good reason to. I'd backed Merion both ways, and didn't see how I was going to lose.'

'Well, I backed the winner. Not being a Croesus like yourself, I only had five bob on. I backed him, because my clairvoyant saw the whole thing, and described it to me before the race was run.'

'Can he do it again?'

'He has not been able to do it again yet. He has seen what happened in the past many times, and he has never been wrong. He is exceptional. He is only clairvoyant when he is hypnotized. In the normal state he sees nothing. He's an ugly little devil, a dwarf, and if I bring him to London he'll make a sensation. What's more, he'll make money. Pots of money. I know the crowd you've been talking about. They're a hit-or-miss lot. They're no good. This is something quite different. We shall have all the Society women paying any fee I like to consult him. There's a fortune in it.'

Tangent lit a cigarette, and pushed the box across to Bellowes. 'What is it you propose to do?' he asked.

'Rooms in Bond Street. Good furniture. Uniformed servant. Sandwichmen at first. Once the thing gets started, it will go by itself. Any woman who has consulted him once is absolutely bound to tell all her friends. The man's a miracle. I'll tell you another thing I'm going to do. When the next sensational murder turns up, and Scotland Yard can't put their hands on the man who did it, I'm going to turn my chap on to the job. I'll bet all I've got to sixpence that we find the man.'

'There was the case of that girl – Esther Samuel.'

'Yes, I remember that. But by this time most of the public have forgotten it. A better chance is bound to turn up soon.'

'I don't see how you're going to start on a hundred and fifty.'

'I'm not, my boy. I've got money of my own that I'm putting into it as well.'

'Let's see,' said Tangent, picking up a pencil. 'What did you say was this man's name and address?'

Bellowes laughed. 'Oh, no you don't,' he said. 'At present that's my business. Make it your own business as well and you shall be told everything.'

'I don't know why you should call it business at all. You ask me to lend you a hundred and fifty. You offer no security. All I've got is your story that you've found a clairvoyant who's really good.'

'Very well. If you satisfied yourself that the man was really good, would you lend the money then?'

'On terms, yes. But they'd have to be satisfactory terms.'

'They would be. Well, you shall see for yourself. The man's waiting in a cab downstairs.'

'You might have said that before.'

'Why? Anyhow, I'll go and bring him up now.'

It was a chilly morning, and Smeath shivered in a thick overcoat, which he refused to remove. No time was wasted on preliminaries. Bellowes hypnotized him at once.

'Now then, my boy,' said Bellowes. 'You shall see for

yourself. Give me any article which you or someone else has worn, or has frequently handled.'

Tangent opened a drawer in his desk, and produced a lady's glove. 'That,' he said, 'was left in my office a week ago. Let's see what he makes out of it.'

Bellowes put the glove in Smeath's hands. Smeath began to pull the buttons off it. He dragged and tore at the glove like a wild animal at its prey. Then suddenly he began to speak.

'I see a handsome woman with bright golden hair. I think the hair has been dyed. It has that appearance. She is talking with Mr What's-his-name in this room. Each is angry with the other. She is accusing him of something. Suddenly – yes – she picks up an ink-bottle and throws it at him. Ink all over the place. He bangs on a little bell, and a man comes in who looks like a clerk. That is all. I cannot see any more.'

'Wake him up and send him down to the cab again,' said Tangent. 'Then we can talk.'

'Now,' said Bellowes, when they were alone together. 'Had he got that right?'

'Absolutely. The woman was Cora Vendall. She wanted a particular berth, and thought I ought to have got it for her. She's fifty-six if she's a day, and not in any way suitable for it. If I had proposed it, the people would simply have laughed at me. She did get into a blind fury with me, and she did throw the ink at me. She's been made to pay for that, and she's been told not to show her powdered nose inside my office again. Your man is remarkable, Bellowes. There can be no two opinions about it. There is certainly money in him.'

'You will find the hundred and fifty then?'

'Yes, I'll do that. Mind, I must have a word to say in the management. The right sort of people will have to be got to see that man. Once that has been done, I do believe you're right, and the thing will go by itself.'

'What interest do you want?'

'I don't want interest. What I do is buy for a hundred and

fifty pounds a share in your profits from your agreement with the clairvoyant.'

'You shall have it. It's a jolly good thing I'm putting into your way, Tangent. I had never meant to part with a share, and I'd sooner pay you fifteen per cent on your money. However, if you insist, you can take a sixteenth.'

'Rats!' said Mr Tangent, impolitely. 'This is not everybody's business. Step across to the Bank of England, and see how much they'll advance you on it. There are three of us in it. Him and you and me. I'm going to take a third. Do just as you like about it. If I go into it I can make it a certainty. I can get the right people to see the man.'

'A third's too much. You must be reasonable, Tangent. I discovered him.'

'A man once discovered a gold-mine. He had no means of getting the gold out. He was a thousand miles from anywhere, and he was all alone. He died on the top of his blessed gold-mine. However, I'm not arguing. I'm simply telling you. Give me a third, and my cheque and the agreement will be ready this time tomorrow morning. Otherwise, no business.'

Mr Bellowes hesitated, and then gave in.

IV

At six o'clock on a summer evening, in a well-furnished room that overlooked the traffic of Bond Street, Smeath and his employer sat and quarrelled together. Both of them wore new clothes, but Bellowes had the air of prosperity, and Smeath had not.

'It's no good to talk to me,' whined Smeath. 'I know what I'm saying. Where an essential consideration has been intentionally concealed, an agreement cannot stand. You never told me I was a clairvoyant.'

'No,' said Bellowes, 'I did not. And I don't tell a man what the colour of his hair is, either, Why? Because he knows it already. You knew that you were a clairvoyant.'

'I did not. I swear I did not!' said Smeath, raising his voice.

'Now, don't get excited. Don't squeal.'

'I'm not squealing. Do you think that if I'd known, I would ever have come to you for a wage like that? We've had fourteen people here today. What did they pay?'

'Mind your own business!'

'But it is my business. And as you wouldn't tell me, I've taken my own steps to find out. Not one of them paid less than a guinea. You had as much as five guineas from some. And here am I with thirty shillings a week. I can get that agreement set aside. I can prove what I'm saying. I had never been hypnotized until I met you.'

'Look here,' said Bellowes. 'Let us get this fixed up once and for all. I don't know who's been cramming you up with these fairy-tales about my fees, but I don't get what you think, or anything like it. I get so little, that I don't want to waste any of it on lawyers. Besides, it would do the business no good, and it would do you no good. I should leave you, and then where would you be? Remember that you are not clairvoyant until I make you clairvoyant.'

'You think, perhaps, I have not read what the newspapers say about me? I can find a hundred hypnotists very easily. But there is no other man who's clairvoyant as I am.'

'And there is no other man who can run a show as I can. Who brought the newspaper men here? Who paid for the advertisements? Who did pretty well everything? However, I'm not going to argue. If you want more money, you can have it. Name your figure. If it is in any way reasonable, you shall have it, on the understanding that this is the last advance you get. If it is undesirable, you'll get nothing. You can take the thing into the courts, and I'll fight it. And, mark my words, Smeath, if I do, you might get a surprise. You know nothing at all about hypnotism. You may find yourself in the witness-box saying things that you did not intend to say. Now, then, name your figure.'

The little man took time to think it over. He rubbed his

chin with his fingers reflectively. He seemed on the point of speaking, and then stopped. Suddenly he snapped out:

'I want four pounds a week!'

'It's simply bare-faced robbery,' said Bellowes. 'But you shall have it. Mind you, you will have to sign another paper tomorrow, and this time there shall be no doubt about it.'

'If you pay me that, I'll sign anything. With four pounds a week I can keep some very good birds again. But you are right that it is bare-faced robbery, and I am the man who is being robbed.'

There had been many disputes between the two men during the six weeks that they had been associated. It was by Tangent's directions that Bellowes acted in the present quarrel.

'It would be better to pay the little devil twenty pounds a week, and keep him, than to refuse and lose him,' said Tangent. 'I believe he's right, and that your precious agreement isn't worth the paper it's written on. Anyhow, I'll get a new agreement ready. Pay him what he wants, and he'll sign it.'

'Well,' said Bellowes, doubtfully, 'if you say so you're probably right. But in that case we ought to get an extension of time out of him.'

'No,' said Tangent, 'the chap's suspicious of you. He hates you. If you try any sort of monkeying, he'll be off. Besides, with the fees you're charging, two years will about see it through. There are not such a vast number of people who can afford the game.'

'As things go at present, it looks as though it might last for ever. You should see the engagement-book. We've got appointments booked for two months ahead. It isn't only a game you see. It's not just a pastime for fashionable women. We get men from the Stock Exchange, business men of all sorts, racing-men. Yesterday morning we had the Prime Minister's private secretary. He didn't give his right name, but Smeath was on to it, and then he admitted it.'

'Hot stuff, Smeath. Do you get much out of him in the way of prophecy? Foretelling the future?'

'Not very often. He has done some wonderful things that way, but more usually he deals with something that is past.'

'Why don't you get him to foretell your own future, Percy?'

Bellowes shook his head.

'Not taking any,' he said. 'He shall have a shot with you if you like.'

But Tangent also refused.

Their business had certainly progressed very rapidly. Tangent arranged a report in a newspaper. He communicated with one or two doctors whom he knew to be interested in the subject. He sent a couple of popular actresses to Smeath. He arranged a special seance for a Cabinet Minister, whose principal interest was psychology. After the first week they no longer employed sandwichmen and advertisements. The ball had begun to roll. Everybody who came to Smeath sent somebody else. Everybody in Society was talking about the hideous little dwarf and his marvellous powers. Bellowes was regarded as a showman and a charlatan, but Smeath was clearly the genuine thing.

Despite their mutual dislike, Bellowes and Smeath both lived in the same house – the Bloomsbury lodging-house. It was Bellowes who had insisted on this. He had never felt quite safe about Smeath, and even after the new agreement had been signed he had his suspicions. He was afraid that Smeath would run away. Bellowes occupied fairly good rooms on the first floor. Smeath had one room at the top of the house, but this happened to suit him. Through his windows he could get on to a flat, leaded roof. There he made friends with the pigeons and sparrows. The maid-servant at the house, who one day saw him out on the roof with the birds all round him, said that it was witchcraft.

'They were 'opping about all over 'im. Sometimes he put

one down and called another up. I never saw anything like it in my life before.'

She had the hatred of the unusual which is prevalent among domestic servants, and gave notice at once. But before the month was up she had grown quite accustomed to seeing Smeath playing with the birds, and the notice was revoked.

V

Bellowes still used for business purposes the name of Sanders-Bell, but he no longer called himself a doctor. He was meeting too many real doctors, and Tangent had advised against it. The room in Bond Street was divided in two by a curtain. The outer part served as a waiting-room, and here, too, Bellowes had his bureau. In the inner part of the room the actual interview between the client and the clairvoyant took place. Their usual hours were only from eleven to one and two to four, but Bellowes would sometimes arrange for a special interview at an unusual hour and an increased price. On these occasions he always took care to pacify Smeath. Sometimes he gave him money, and sometimes other presents; on one occasion he gave him a big book about birds, with coloured illustrations, and Smeath remained docile and in a good temper for days afterwards.

'Yes,' said Bellowes. 'You have complained once that I was robbing you. You can't say that now. You have fixed your own salary. If there is the least little bit of extra work to be done, you always get something for it. You are not as grateful as you ought to be, Smeath. Where would you have been without me? What were you doing before you came to me?'

'Nothing. For some weeks I had been very hungry. I make no complaint against you, but when my time's up I shall stay no longer. I go back to the birds again.'

'It would be more sensible of you,' said Bellowes, 'if you banked your money. What did you want to buy that great owl for? He makes the devil of a row at night. We shall have people complaining about it.'

'She is a very good friend to me, that owl,' said Smeath. 'I am teaching her much. She will be valuable.'

At this moment there was the sound of a footstep on the stairs, and Smeath stepped behind his curtain.

The man who entered was not at all the type of client that Bellowes generally received. He was a thick-set man of common appearance, and he was unfashionably dressed. He did not look in the least as if he could afford the fee. Bellowes saluted him somewhat curtly.

'It is ten minutes to eleven, sir, and our hour for beginning is eleven. However, as you have called, if you like to pay the fee now – two guineas – I will make an appointment for you, but I'm afraid it will have to be in nine weeks' time.'

The visitor looked reflective, turning his seedy bowler hat round in his hands.

'Don't think that would do,' he said. 'Nine weeks – that's a very long time. Couldn't Mr Smeath see me today? Couldn't he make an exception?'

'Only by giving you a special appointment. And for that a very much higher fee is charged.'

'How much?' asked the man.

'He could give you ten minutes at one o'clock today. But the charge for that would be six guineas. You see, Mr Smeath is only clairvoyant while in the hypnotic state, and that cannot be repeated indefinitely.'

The visitor took an old-fashioned purse from his hip-pocket. He pulled out a five-pound note, a sovereign, and six shillings.

'There you are,' he said. 'Please book me ten minutes with Mr Smeath at one o'clock today.'

'Very good,' said Bellowes, opening the engagement-book. He looked up, with his pen in his hand. 'What name shall I put down?'

'I am Mr Vincent.'

'You'll be careful to be punctual, of course. Mr Smeath will be ready exactly at one o'clock.'

'I shall be here,' said the man.

He had no sooner gone than Smeath emerged from behind the curtain again. 'What on earth did you do that for?' he asked excitedly.

'Keep your hair on, Smeath. It's all right. I'm going to buy you a big cage for that owl of yours.'

'I do not want any cage. My birds are not kept in cages. It is not the extra work that I mind. It is that I cannot do anything for that man. I tell you he is dangerous.'

'In what way dangerous?'

'I don't know. He is dangerous to me.'

'He looked to me an honest man enough. He had the appearance of a chap up from the country. Probably wants to know what his best girl is doing. I shouldn't worry about it if I were you. Don't stand in the way of business, Smeath. You don't know what the expenses are here. I've got to pay the rent next week, and if I told you what that was, you wouldn't believe it. If you don't want the bird-cage, you shall have something else.'

But it was necessary to show Smeath a sovereign, and to present him with it before he would consent. Even then, he did so with great reluctance.

Clients with appointments came in, and the ordinary business of the morning began. Smeath no longer spoke when in the clairvoyant state, for he was often consulted upon matters requiring secrecy, and what he said might have been heard by other clients in waiting. He had a writing-block, and scribbled down on it in pencil what he saw.

At one o'clock precisely Mr Vincent returned, and was at once brought behind the curtain. Smeath sat there motionless. His eyes were open, but he did not look up at Mr Vincent.

'Now then, sir,' said Bellowes. 'What is it you want?'

Mr Vincent drew from his pocket a comb wrapped in

paper. It was of the kind that women wear in their hair, and it had been broken.

'I want him to tell me about the girl who wore this at the time when it was broken.'

Bellowes placed the comb in Smeath's hands. Smeath held it for a moment, and then the fingers relaxed, and it dropped to the floor.

Bellowes again placed it in his hand, and this time Smeath flung it from him. But immediately he began to write, Mr Vincent watching him narrowly as he did so. He wrote with an extraordinary rapidity. Presently Bellowes, who had been standing behind him, and reading what he wrote, asked Mr Vincent to wait in the outer part of the room. As soon as he was alone with Smeath, he took the writing-block out of his hands, tore the sheet from it, folded it and put it in his pocket. Then he rejoined Vincent.

'I am extremely sorry, sir,' said Bellowes, 'that the experiment has failed completely. There is perhaps some kind of antipathy between Mr Smeath and yourself. These things do occasionally happen. I find that he can tell you nothing at all, and under the circumstances, I should perhaps return your fee.'

Vincent did not seem particularly surprised.

'Very well,' he said. 'I had hardly expected to get what I wanted, but I thought I might as well try. I paid you six guineas, I think. You seem to be treating me fairly, and I have given you a certain amount of trouble. Supposing you return me five of them.'

The money was handed over, and Vincent departed. Bellowes went back to Smeath and brought him out of the trance. Smeath shivered.

'Is he here still?'

'No. Gone.'

'Was it all right?'

'It was quite all right.'

'I'm glad he's gone,' said Smeath. 'I was horribly afraid of something. Now I can go out and get my lunch, and I have to buy food for the birds too.'

'I shouldn't spend too much money on it if I were you,' said Bellowes.

Smeath laughed.

'It is not very expensive,' he said. 'And I have made one extra sovereign. Why not?'

'Because in future, Smeath, you are going to work for me for much less money – for a pound a week, to be precise.'

'I shall not,' said Smeath, loudly.

'I told you once before not to squeal. I don't like it. You will do exactly as I say, and for a very good reason. If you don't you will be taken to prison, and you will be tried before a judge, and you will be hanged, Smeath. Hanged for the murder of Esther Samuel in the woods at Teston.'

VI

'What makes you say that? How do you know it?' asked Smeath. The fingers of his big hands locked and separated and locked again. His eyes were fixed intently on Bellowes. He looked excited again, but not frightened.

'How do I know it?' echoed Bellowes. 'I have it here in your own handwriting.' He tapped his breast-pocket. 'You do not remember what happened when you were hypnotized. I put a broken comb into your hands. It was a comb which the murdered woman had worn. You began to write at once. You've put the rope around your neck, Smeath.'

'And that man – the man that I knew to be dangerous?'

'Mr Vincent? I told him that the experiment had failed, and returned his fee. He knows nothing. So long as you do exactly what I tell you, you are quite safe.'

'Who was he, this Vincent?'

Bellowes shrugged his shoulders.

'How should I know? Possibly one of the Samuel family. Possibly a 'tec. If I had given him what he had paid for, we should have had the police in here by now. I have saved your skin for you, Smeath. Don't forget it.'

'Will you read it out to me, the thing I wrote down?'

'No. It tells one everything, except the motive.'

'The motive was obvious enough. I was hungry and had no money. I had tramped to Teston and reached there two days too soon. I had nowhere to go, and I lived and slept in the woods. I begged from the girl at first, and if she had given me a few pence she might have been alive now. She was not in the least bit afraid of me. Why should she have been? I was small, misshapen, and looked weak. She was tall and strong. As she turned away from me, she said the tramps in the neighbourhood were becoming a nuisance, and she would send the police after me. Even then I only meant to hit her once, but that is a queer thing – you cannot hit a human being once. You see the body lying at your feet, and you have to go on striking and striking. When I knew she must be dead, I flung the stick down. I took nothing but the money, nothing which could be traced. Even the money made me so nervous that I hid most of it – buried it in a place where I could find it again. If the police found me, there would only have been a few coppers in my possession, and I did not look like a man who could have done it. But they never did find me.'

'I see. That was why, when I offered to advance your railway fare, you told me you had money. You had a pair of new boots on when you turned up at Warlow. I remember what an infernal squeaking row they made on the platform. Well, you've done for yourself, Smeath. You've got to work for me on very different terms now.'

'No,' said Smeath. 'That is not so.'

'Very good. I'll write my note to Mr Vincent now. He'll do the rest.'

'No you won't, and I'll tell you why. You can destroy me very likely, but if you do, you'll destroy your own livelihood. And you always take very good care for yourself, Mr Bellowes.'

'Destroy my livelihood?' said Bellowes, thumping on the table with his fist. 'That's where you make your mistake, you little devil! Because you're useful, you think you're indispensable. You're not. There's a reward of two hundred pounds out for anyone who finds the murderer of Esther Samuel. I'm a born showman. With two hundred pounds capital I can chuck this and start something else that will pay me just as well.'

'It looks as if I shall have to give in. Well, there's no help for it. I must get a much cheaper room, of course.'

'No, you won't. You'll stop in the same house as me. D'you think I haven't worked it all out? After you've paid your rent, you've a shilling a day for food, and better men have lived on less. I'm not going to give you a chance to bolt. And mark my words, Smeath, if you do bolt, the very moment I find you've gone I give you up. Don't imagine you can get away. There are not many men of your build. The police would have you for a certainty within twenty-four hours.'

'Then I become a slave; I can do nothing. There were other birds that I meant to buy. And in time I could have started a business again. That must all go.'

'Quite so. That must all go. In fact, before a fortnight is out I expect you'll sell that big white owl of yours. You'll grudge him his keep.'

'It is a she-owl, and I shall not let her go. She can do things that would surprise you.'

'Can she?' said Bellowes. 'It might be rather effective if you brought her down here. She would impress the clients.'

'I shall not. I keep her for myself!'

'Don't talk like a fool! You are forgetting that I hold you between my thumb and finger. If I tell you to wring that bird's neck you will have to do it.'

Smeath rose to his feet in fury.

'Where's my hat?' he said. 'Give me my hat!'

Bellowes stood in front of the door.

'What's the matter with you? Where are you off to?'

'Checkmate for you, Mr Bellowes. I am going now to give myself up. Where is your two hundred pounds reward, eh? Where is the money that you make out of the clairvoyant?'

'Sit down, and don't talk in that silly way. I never told you to kill the bird. I was only speaking in your interests when I said I doubted if you could afford to keep it. As a matter of fact, I don't care a pin's head about it either way. If you set so much store by it, keep it by all means.'

'In that case,' said Smeath, 'I will go on working for you and on the terms that you have said.'

'That's all right; and now you can go out to lunch. Remember that you have to be back at two o'clock. If you are not here by ten minutes past two, I shall send the police to look for you.'

'I shall be here, Mr Bellowes.'

Every Saturday morning at half-past nine Tangent called on Bellowes in Bond Street, to look over the books and to collect his share of the profits. Tangent had no great faith in Mr Bellowes. Smeath was never allowed to be present on these occasions.

On the Saturday after Mr Vincent's visit, Tangent was well pleased with the results.

'Mind you,' he said, 'the little dwarf isn't doing so badly out of it either. He gets his regular four pounds a week. This week I see he's had one pound ten in cash for extra work, and you're charging twelve-and-six for a present for him. What was the present?'

'Oh, a bird of sorts. The little beggar's simply mad about birds. That did more good than if I'd given him the actual cash.'

'Oh, I'm not grumbling, Bellowes,' said Tangent, surveying with complacency the diamond ring on his finger. 'If, by giving him a trifle extra now and then, you can keep his goodwill, it's quite worth our while to do it. No man will work for nothing, and I suppose he finds this clairvoyant game rather exhausting. Not over and above good for the health, eh?'

'He says it's exhausting. He seems to me well enough.'

When Tangent had gone Bellowes smiled. To swindle Tangent was a real pleasure to him, even apart from the profit he made for himself. He remembered the terms which Tangent had forced him to accept for the provision of capital for the enterprise.

The introduction of a large white owl into the Bloomsbury lodging-house could have but one effect. The maidservant gave notice at once on general principles. It was Smeath this time who persuaded her to remain.

'You must not be afraid of the white owl,' he said. 'Owls are wise birds. She knows who my friends are, and who my enemies are. You are my friend, and she will never hurt you. She will let you feed her and stroke her feathers. They are very, very soft, the feathers of an owl.'

In a week's time Jane was neglecting her work to play with the white owl out on the leads.

VII

For several weeks no change took place. Smeath did his work with patience and docility. He addressed Mr Bellowes with respect. He made very little objection to private engagements. As a munificent reward, on two occasions Bellowes took him out to luncheon, and once presented him with some Sunday tickets for the Zoo, which he himself did not want. Every Saturday Tangent inspected, with satisfaction, some purely fantastic accounts. Bellowes was specially careful that Smeath and Tangent should never meet, lest the discrepancy between the statements in the books and the actual facts should be discovered.

And then business began to fall off. There was no excessive drop, but the previous standard was not quite maintained. That astute showman, Mr Bellowes, decided that something would have to be done. Some new feature would have to be introduced, to set people talking again.

'Smeath,' he said one day, 'didn't you tell me something once about a white owl?'

'Yes,' said Smeath, 'I have one.'

'It does tricks, don't it?'

'It does a few things,' said Smeath, grudgingly. 'You do not want it. You said that you would leave me my owl.'

'You needn't get into a stew about it, and do for goodness sake keep those great hands of yours still. They get on my nerves. Nobody wants to take your blessed owl away from you. The only thing that I was wondering about was whether it might not be worthwhile to keep the bird here, instead of at your lodgings.'

'No, sir! No, Mr Bellowes! It is in my leisure time that I want my owl.'

'Well, I was talking to Mr Tangent about it, and he thought it was a good idea; in fact, he said I ought to have done it before. We must think about it. I have been pretty easy with you, Smeath.'

'Also, I've worked very hard for you.'

'You've done what you were told, and of late you've given me no trouble. You might let Tangent and myself have a look at the bird, anyhow. It would be effective, you know – the dwarf clairvoyant and the great white owl on the back of his chair. Tangent spoke of a poster. I'll tell him to give us a call in Bloomsbury on Sunday morning.'

'I do not want my owl to be taken away. It lives there on the leads outside my window. Here it would be unhappy. How could I leave it here all night alone?'

'Don't be unreasonable, Smeath. You will see more of the bird than you do now.'

'No,' said Smeath. 'The greater part of the time when I'm here I'm like a dead man, and know nothing.'

Bellowes had quite realized that this was the point on which Smeath would have to be handled carefully.

'Look here,' he said, 'I wouldn't do anything to hurt the bird. At any rate, let Mr Tangent and myself see it. Let us see if it can really do the things that that girl Jane jabbers so much about. If Tangent and I think it would be an asset to the show, I am prepared to go quite beyond our agreement. I'll give you two or three shillings for yourself, Smeath. You can give yourself a treat. You've not been having many treats lately; in fact, you look just about half starved.'

It was true. The little dwarf had grown very thin. His eyes seemed to have got bigger and brighter. There was a look in them now which would have made Bellowes suspicious if he had noticed it.

'Jane,' said Smeath, as he met her on the stairs that night, 'they are coming on Sunday morning to see my owl.'

'Then they'll see miracles,' said Jane, with confidence.

'And they're going to take it away.'

'If that bird goes, I goes!'

Smeath burst into a peal of mirthless laughter.

Mr Tangent arrived in a taxi-cab at the Bloomsbury lodgings at eleven on the following Sunday morning. He was in a bad temper, and swore and grumbled profusely.

'So I've got to turn out on a Sunday morning and work seven days a week, just because you're such a damn bad showman, Bellowes? You've let the thing down. The books on Saturday were perfectly awful.'

'I'm not a bad showman, and it's not my fault. The weather's been against us, for one thing. And, besides, no novelty lasts for ever. We must put something else into it to buck it up, and we must get that poster out.'

'That means more expense. I don't see why we should keep on paying Smeath four pounds a week if business is falling off. And as for that rotten old owl of his, I'm no great believer in it. It will look all right on the poster, but it will do no good in your Bond Street rooms. I know those tricks. The bird picks out cards from a pack, or shams dead, or some other nursery foolery. Stale, my boy, hopelessly stale.'

'According to what I hear, the bird does none of those things. It's a new line.'

'Is it? I'll bet a dollar it ain't. However, tell Smeath to bring it down, and let's get it over.'

'Smeath won't bring it down. We shall have to go up to it. He makes a great favour of showing it to us at all. And, if you will take my tip, you'll say nothing to Smeath beyond a good morning. I can tell you he wants devilish careful handling about this bird of his. If you interfere, you'll spoil it. All you've got to do, if you think it at all remarkable, is to say to me that it might possibly do. I shall understand. Now then, come along up!'

'All those stairs!' groaned Tangent. He was a heavy and plethoric man. When they reached Smeath's room he stood for a minute, panting.

The room was ordinarily dingy enough. It was a fine morning and the sun streamed in through the window. On the leads outside they could see the great white owl perched on the bough of a tree which had been fixed there. Smeath, with his hat off, stood beside it, and seemed to be talking to it. Around his feet were a flock of pigeons and sparrows. He nodded to the two men and then gave one wave of his hands. The pigeons and sparrows flew off and left him alone with the white owl.

'Funny sight!' grunted Tangent. 'Devilish funny sight!'

Smeath opened the window and called into the room:

'Good morning, gentlemen! Will you come out?'

'Don't much like it,' said Tangent. 'I've no head for this kind of thing.'

'Oh, you're all right!' said Bellowes. 'You needn't go anywhere near the edge.'

He placed a chair for him, and Tangent climbed out onto the roof, followed by Bellowes.

'I will leave you to look at the bird by yourselves, gentlemen,' said Smeath, and stepped down into the room.

'Then who's going to make the bird do its tricks?' asked

Tangent. 'It's a fine-looking beggar, anyhow. Seems about half asleep. Tame enough.' He passed his jewelled hand over the snowy plumage on the bird's breast. 'There's a feather-bed for you,' he said, laughing.

The bird opened its eyes, and leaped straight into the face of Bellowes. Its plumage half stifled him, its sharp claws tore his eyes. He screamed for help.

Tangent, in horror, had flung himself down flat on the leads, covering his face. Within the room Smeath stood with folded arms, watching the scene with the utmost calmness.

Bellowes tore at the bird with his hands, but step by step it forced him back. There came one final scream from him, and then two seconds of silence, and then the thud as his body struck the stones below. Up above, the white owl flew swiftly away.

The dwarf rubbed his hands and laughed. And then, changing his expression to one of extreme dismay, went to the help of the prostrate Tangent.

THE WOMAN OF THE SAETER

Jerome K. Jerome

When John Ingerfield *appeared, Jerome was in deadly earnest about the contents. 'Once upon a time, I wrote a little story of a woman who was crushed to death by a python. A day or two after its publication, a friend stopped me in the street. "Charming little story of yours," he said, "that about the woman and the snake; but it's not as funny as some of your things!" With this – and many similar experiences – in mind, I wish distinctly to state that the "The Woman of the Saeter" and "Silhouettes" are not intended to be amusing. I should be glad if they would be judged from some other standpoint than that of humour.'*

Wild reindeer stalking is hardly so exciting a sport as the evening's verandah talk in Norway hotels would lead the trustful traveller to suppose. Under the charge of your guide, a very young man with the dreamy, wistful eyes of those who live in valleys, you leave the farmstead early in the forenoon, arriving towards twilight at the desolate hut which, for so long as you remain upon the uplands, will be your somewhat cheerless headquarters.

Next morning, in the chill, mist-laden dawn, you rise; and, after a breakfast of coffee and dried fish, shoulder your

Remington, and step forth silently into the raw, damp air; the guide locking the door behind you, the key grating harshly in the rusty lock.

For hour after hour you toil over the steep stony ground, or wind through the pines, speaking in whispers, lest your voice reach the quick ears of your prey, that keeps its head ever pressed against the wind. Here and there, in the hollows of the hills lie wide fields of snow, over which you pick your steps thoughtfully, listening to the smothered thunder of the torrent, tunnelling its way beneath your feet, and wondering whether the frozen arch above it be at all points as firm as is desirable. Now and again, as in single file you walk cautiously along some jagged ridge, you catch glimpses of the green world, three thousand feet below you; though you gaze not long upon the view, for your attention is chiefly directed to watching the footprints of the guide, lest by deviating to the right or left you find yourself at one stride back in the valley – or, to be more correct, are found there.

These things you do, and as exercise they are healthy and invigorating. But a reindeer you never see, and unless, overcoming the prejudices of your British-bred conscience, you care to take an occasional pop at a fox, you had better have left your rifle at the hut, and, instead, have brought a stick which would have been helpful. Notwithstanding which the guide continues sanguine, and in broken English, helped out by stirring gesture, tells of the terrible slaughter generally done by sportsmen under his superintendence, and of the vast herds that generally infest these fjelds; and when you grow sceptical upon the subject of Reins he whispers alluringly of Bears.

Once in a way you will come across a track, and will follow it breathlessly for hours, and it will lead to a sheer precipice. Whether the explanation is suicide, or a reprehensible tendency on the part of the animal towards practical joking, you are left to decide for yourself. Then, with many rough miles between you and your rest, you abandon the chase.

But I speak from personal experience merely.

All day long we tramped through the pitiless rain, stopping only for an hour at noon to eat some dried venison and smoke a pipe beneath the shelter of an overhanging cliff. Soon afterwards Michael knocked over a ryper (a bird that will hardly take the trouble to hop out of your way) with his gun-barrel, which incident cheered us a little; and, later on, our flagging spirits were still further revived by the discovery of apparently very recent deer tracks. These we followed, forgetful, in our eagerness, of the lengthening distance back to the hut, of the fading daylight, and of the gathering mist. The track led us higher and higher, farther and farther into the mountains, until on the shores of a desolate rock-bound vand it abruptly ended, and we stood staring at one another, and the snow began to fall.

Unless in the next half-hour we could chance upon a saeter, this meant passing the night upon the mountain. Michael and I looked at the guide; but though, with characteristic Norwegian sturdiness, he put a bold face upon it, we could see that in that deepening darkness he knew no more than we did. Wasting no time on words, we made straight for the nearest point of descent, knowing that any human habitation must be far below us.

Down we scrambled, heedless of torn clothes and bleeding hands, the darkness pressing closer round us. Then suddenly it became black – black as pitch – and we could only hear each other. Another step might mean death. We stretched out our hands, and felt for each other. Why we spoke in whispers, I do not know, but we seemed afraid of our own voices. We agreed there was nothing for it but to stop where we were till morning, clinging to the short grass; so we lay there side by side, for what must have been five minutes or may have been an hour. Then, attempting to turn, I lost my grip and rolled. I made convulsive efforts to clutch the ground, but the incline was too steep. How far I fell I could not say, but at last something stopped me. I felt it cautiously with my foot: it did not yield, so I twisted myself round and touched it with my hand. It seemed planted firmly in the earth. I passed my arm along to the right, then to the left. I shouted with joy. It was a fence.

Rising and groping about me, I found an opening, and passed through, and crept forward with palms outstretched until I touched the logs of a hut; then, feeling my way round, discovered the door, and knocked. There came no response, so I knocked louder; then pushed, and the heavy woodwork yielded, groaning. But the darkness within was even darker than the darkness without. The others had contrived to crawl down and join me. Michael struck a wax vesta and held it up, and slowly the room came out of the darkness and stood round us.

Then something rather startling happened. Giving one swift glance about him our guide uttered a cry, and rushed out into the night. We followed to the door, and called after him, but only a voice came to us out of the blackness, and the only words that we could catch, shrieked back in terror, were: 'Saetervronen! Saetervronen!' ('The woman of the saeter').

'Some foolish superstition about the place, I suppose,' said Michael. 'In these mountain solitudes men breed ghosts for company. Let us make a fire. Perhaps, when he sees the light, his desire for food and shelter may get the better of his fears.'

We felt about in the small enclosure round the house, and gathered juniper and birch twigs, and kindled a fire upon the open stove built in the corner of the room. Fortunately, we had some dried reindeer and bread in our bag, and on that and the ryper and the contents of our flasks we supped. Afterwards, to while away the time, we made an inspection of the strange eyrie we had lighted on.

It was an old log-built saeter. Some of these mountain farmsteads are as old as the stone ruins of other countries. Carvings of strange beasts and demons were upon its blackened rafters, and on the lintel, in runic letters, ran this legend: 'Hund built me in the days of Haargager.' The house consisted of two large apartments. Originally, no doubt, these had been separate dwellings standing beside one another, but they were now connected by a long low gallery. Most of the scanty furniture was almost as ancient as the walls themselves, but many articles of a comparatively recent date had been added. All was now, however, rotting and falling into decay.

The place appeared to have been deserted suddenly by its last occupants. Household utensils lay as they were left, rust and dirt encrusted on them. An open book, limp and mildewed, lay face downwards on the table, while many others were scattered about both rooms, together with much paper, scored with faded ink. The curtains hung in shreds about the windows; a woman's cloak, of an antiquated fashion, drooped from a nail behind the door. In an oak chest we found a tumbled heap of yellow letters. They were of various dates, extending over a period of four months; and with them, apparently intended to receive them, lay a large envelope, inscribed with an address in London that has since disappeared.

Strong curiosity overcoming faint scruples, we read them by the dull glow of the burning juniper twigs, and, as we lay aside the last of them, there rose from the depths below us a wailing cry, and all night long it rose and died away, and rose again, and died away again; whether born of our brain or of some human thing, God knows.

And these, a little altered and shortened, are the letters:

Extract from first letter:

'I cannot tell you, my dear Joyce, what a haven of peace this place is to me after the racket and fret of town. I am almost quite recovered already, and am growing stronger every day; and joy of joys, my brain has come back to me, fresher and more vigorous, I think, for its holiday. In this silence and solitude my thoughts flow freely, and the difficulties of my task are disappearing as if by magic. We are perched upon a tiny plateau halfway up the mountain. On one side the rock rises almost perpendicularly, piercing the sky; while on the other, two thousand feet below us, the torrent hurls itself into the black waters of the fiord. The house consists of two rooms – or, rather, it is two cabins connected by a passage. The larger one we use as a living room, and the other is our sleeping apartment. We have no servant, but do everything for ourselves. I fear sometimes Muriel must find it lonely. The nearest human habitation is eight miles away, across the mountain, and not a soul comes near us. I spend as much time as I can with her, however, during the day, and make up for it by working at night after she has gone to sleep; and when I question her, she only laughs, and answers that she loves to have me to herself. (Here you will smile cynically, I know and say, "Humph, I wonder will she say the same when they have been married six years instead of six months."). At the rate I am working now I shall have finished my first volume by the spring, and then, my dear fellow, you must try and come over, and we will walk and talk together "amid these storm-reared temples of the gods." I have felt a new man since I arrived here. Instead of having to "cudgel my brains," as we say, thoughts crowd upon me. This work will make my name.'

Part of the third letter, the second being more talk about the book (a history apparently) that the man was writing:

'My dear Joyce, – I have written you two letters – this will make the third – but have been unable to post them. Every day I been expecting a visit from some farmer or villager, for the Norwegians are kindly people towards strangers – to say nothing of the inducements of trade. A fortnight having passed, however, and the commissariat question having become serious, I yesterday set out before dawn, and made my way down to the valley; and this gives me something to tell you. Nearing the village, I met a peasant woman. To my intense surprise, instead of returning my salutation, she stared at me, as if I were some wild animal, and shrank away from me as far as the width of the road would permit. In the village the same experience awaited me. The children ran from me, the people avoided me. At last a grey-haired old man appeared to take pity on me, and from him I learnt the explanation of the mystery. It seems there is a strange superstition attaching to this house in which we are living. My things were brought up here by the two men who accompanied me from Drontheim, but the natives are afraid to go near the place, and prefer to keep as far as possible from anyone connected with it.

'The story is that the house was built by one Hund, "a maker of runes" (one of the old saga writers, no doubt), who lived here with his young wife. All went peacefully until, unfortunately for him, a certain maiden stationed at a neighbouring saeter grew to love him.

'Forgive me if I am telling you what you know, but a "saeter" is the name given to the upland pastures to which, during the summer, are sent the cattle, generally under the charge of one or more of the maids. Here for three months these girls will live in their lonely huts, entirely shut off from the world. Customs change little in this land. Two or three such stations are within climbing distance of this house, at this day, looked after by the farmer's daughters, as in the days of Hund, "maker of runes".

'Every night, by devious mountain paths, the woman would come and tap lightly at Hund's door. Hund had built himself two cabins, one behind the other (these are now, as I think I have explained to you, connected by a passage); the smaller one was the homestead in the other he carved and wrote, so that while the young wife slept the "maker of runes" and the saeter woman sat whispering.

'One night, however, the wife learnt all things, but said no word. Then, as now, the ravine in front of the enclosure was crossed by a slight bridge of planks, and over this bridge the woman of the saeter passed and repassed each night. On a day when Hund had gone down to fish in the fiord, the wife took an axe, and hacked and hewed at the bridge, yet it still looked firm and solid; and that night, as Hund sat waiting in his workshop, there struck upon his ears a piercing cry, and a crashing of logs and rolling rock, and then again the dull roaring of the torrent far below.

'But the woman did not die unavenged; for that winter a man, skating far down the fiord, noticed a curious object embedded in the ice; and when, stooping, he looked closer, he saw two corpses, one gripping the other by the throat, and the bodies were the bodies of Hund and his young wife.

'Since them, they say, the woman of the saeter haunts Hund's house, and if she sees a light within she taps upon the door, and no man may keep her out. Many, at different times, have tried to occupy the house, but strange tales are told of them. "Men do not live at Hund's saeter," said my old grey-haired friend, concluding his tale, – "they die there."

'I have persuaded some of the braver of the villagers to bring what provisions and other necessaries we require up to a plateau about a mile from the house and leave them there. That is the most I have been able to do. It comes somewhat as a shock to one to find men and women – fairly educated and intelligent as many of them are – slaves to fears that one would expect a child to laugh at. But there is no reasoning with superstition.'

Extract from the same letter, but from a part seemingly written a day or two later:

'At home I should have forgotten such a tale an hour after I had heard it, but these mountain fastnesses seem strangely fit to be the last stronghold of the supernatural. The woman haunts me already. At night, instead of working, I find myself listening for her tapping at the door; and yesterday an incident occurred that makes me fear my own common sense. I had gone out for a long walk alone, and the twilight was thickening into darkness as I neared home. Suddenly looking up from my reverie, I saw, standing on a knoll the other side of the ravine, the figure of a woman. She held a cloak about her head, and I could not see her face. I took off my cap, and called out a good-night to her, but she never moved or spoke. Then – God knows why, for my brain was full of other thoughts at the time – a clammy chill crept over me, and my tongue grew dry and parched. I stood rooted to the spot, staring at her across the yawning gorge that divided us and slowly she moved away, and passed into the gloom, and I continued on my way. I have said nothing to Muriel, and shall not. The effect the story has had upon myself warns me not to do so.'

From a letter dated eleven days later:

'She has come. I have known she would, since that evening I saw her on the mountain; and last night she came, and we have sat and looked into each other's eyes. You will say, of course, that I am mad – that I have not recovered from my fever – that I have been working too hard – that I have heard a foolish tale, and that it has filled my overstrung brain with foolish fancies: I have told myself all that. But the thing came, nevertheless – a creature of flesh and blood? a creature of air? a creature of my own imagination? – what matter? it was real to me.

'It came last night, as I sat working, alone. Each night I have waited for it, listened for it, I know now. I heard the passing of its feet upon the bridge, the tapping of its hand on the door, three times – tap, tap, tap. I felt my loins grow cold, and a pricking pain about my head; and I gripped my chair with both hands, and waited, and again there came the tapping – tap, tap, tap. I rose and slipped the bolt of the door leading to the other room, and again I waited, and again there came the tapping – tap, tap, tap. Then I opened the heavy outer door, and the wind rushed past me, scattering my papers, and the woman entered in, and I closed the door behind her. She threw her hood back from her head, and unwound a kerchief from about her neck, and laid it on the table. Then she crossed and sat before the fire, and I noticed her bare feet were damp with the night dew.

'I stood over against her and gazed at her, and she smiled at me – a strange, wicked smile, but I could have laid my soul at her feet. She never spoke or moved, and neither did I feel the need of spoken words, for I understood the meaning of those upon the Mount when they said "Let us make here tabernacles: it is good for us to be here."

'How long a time passed thus I do not know, but suddenly the woman held her hand up, listening, and there came a faint sound from the other room. Then swiftly she drew her hood about her face and passed out, closing the door softly behind her; and I drew back the bolt of the inner door and waited, and hearing nothing more, sat down, and must have fallen asleep in my chair.

'I awoke, and instantly there flashed through my mind the thought of the kerchief the woman had left behind her, and I started from my chair to hide it. But the table was already laid for breakfast, and my wife sat with her elbows on the table and her head between her hands, watching me with a look in her eyes that was new to me.

'She kissed me, though her lips were cold; and I argued to myself that the whole thing must have been a dream. But later in the day, passing the open door when her back was towards me, I saw her take the kerchief from a locked chest and look at it.

'I have told myself it must have been a kerchief of her own, and that all the rest has been my imagination; that, if not, then my strange visitant was no spirit, but a woman; and that, if human thing knows human thing, it was no creature of flesh and blood that sat beside me last night.

Besides, what woman would she be? The nearest saeter is a three hour climb to a strong man, and the paths are dangerous even in daylight: what woman would have found them in the night? What woman would have chilled the air around her, and have made the blood flow cold through all my veins? Yet if she comes again I will speak to her. I will stretch out my hand and see whether she be a mortal thing or only air.'

The fifth letter:

'My dear Joyce, – Whether your eyes will ever see these letters is doubtful. From this place I shall never send them. They would read to you as the ravings of a madman. If ever I return to England I may one day show them to you, but when I do it will be when I, with you, can laugh over them. At present I write them merely to hide away, – putting the words down on paper saves my screaming them aloud.

'She comes each night now, taking the same seat beside the embers, and fixing upon me those eyes, with the hell-light in them, that burn into my brain; and at rare times she smiles, and all my being passes out of me, and is hers. I make no attempt to work. I sit listening for her footsteps on the creaking bridge, for the rustling of her feet upon the grass, for the tapping of her hand upon the door. No word is uttered between us. Each day I say: "When she comes tonight I will speak to her. I will stretch out my hand and touch her." Yet when she enters, all thought and will goes out from me.

'Last night, as I stood gazing at her, my soul filled with her wondrous beauty as a lake with moonlight, her lips parted, and she started from her chair; and turning, I thought I saw a white face pressed against the window, but as I looked it vanished. Then she drew her cloak about her, and passed out. I slid back the bolt I always draw now, and stole into the other room, and, taking down the lantern, held it above the bed. But Muriel's eyes were closed as if in sleep.'

Extract from the sixth letter:

'It is not the night I fear, but the day. I hate the sight of this woman with whom I live, whom I call "wife". I shrink from the blow of her cold lips, the curse of her stony eyes. She has seen, she has learnt; I feel it, I know it. Yet she winds her arms around my neck, and calls me sweetheart, and smooths my hair with her soft, false hands. We speak mocking words of love to one another, but I know her cruel eyes are ever following me. She is plotting her revenge, and I hate her, I hate her, I hate her!'

Part of the seventh letter:

'This morning I went down to the fiord. I told her I should not be back until the evening. She stood by the door watching me until we were mere specks to one another, and a promontory of the mountain shut me from view. Then, turning aside from the track, I made my way, running and stumbling over the jagged ground, round to the other side of the mountain, and began to climb again. It was slow, weary work. Often I had to go miles out of my way to avoid a ravine, and twice I reached a high point only to have to descend again. But at length I crossed the ridge, and crept down to a spot from where, concealed, I could spy upon my own house. She – my wife – stood by the flimsy bridge. A short hatchet, such as butchers use, was in her hand. She leant against the pine trunk, with her arm behind her, as one stands whose back aches with long stooping in some cramped position; and even at that distance I could see the cruel smile about her lips.

'Then I recrossed the ridge, and crawled down again, and, waiting until evening, walked slowly up the path. As I came in view of the house she saw me, and waved her handkerchief to me, and in answer I waved my hat, and shouted curses at her that the wind whirled away into the torrent. She met me with a kiss, and I breathed no hint to her that I had seen. Let her devil's work remain undisturbed. Let it prove to me what manner of thing this is that haunts me. If it be a spirit, then the bridge will bear it safely; if it be woman—

'But I dismiss the thought. If it be human thing, why does it sit gazing at me, never speaking? Why does my tongue refuse to question it? Why does all power forsake me in its presence, so that I stand as in a dream? Yet if it be spirit, why do I hear the passing of her feet? and why does the night-rain glisten in her hair?

'I force myself back into my chair. It is far into the night, and I am alone, waiting, listening. If it be spirit, she will come to me; and if it be woman, I shall hear her cry above the storm – unless it be a demon mocking me.

'I have heard the cry. It rose, piercing and shrill, above the storm, above the riving and rending of the bridge, above the downward crashing of the logs and loosening stones. I hear it as I listen now. It is cleaving its way upward from the depths below. It is wailing through the room as I sit writing.

'I have crawled upon my belly to the utmost edge of the still standing pier, until I could feel with my hand the jagged splinters left by the falling planks, and have looked down. But the chasm was full to the brim with darkness. I shouted, but the wind shook my voice into mocking laughter. I sit here, feebly striking at the madness that is creeping nearer and nearer to me. I tell myself the whole thing is a fever in my brain. The bridge was rotten. The storm was strong. The cry is but a single one among the many voices of the mountain. Yet still I listen; and it rises, clear and shrill, above the moaning of the pines, above the sobbing of the waters. It beats like blows upon my skull, and I know that she will never come again.'

Extract from the last letter:

'I shall address an envelope to you, and leave it among these letters. Then should I never come back, some chance wanderer may one day find and post them to you, and you will know.

'My books and writings remain untouched. We sit together of a night – this woman I call "wife" and I – she holding in her hands some knitting thing that never grows longer by a single stitch, and I with a volume before me that is ever open at the same page. And day and night we watch each other stealthily, moving too and fro about the silent house; and at times, looking round swiftly, I catch the smile upon her lips before she has time to smooth it away.

'We speak like strangers about this and that, making talk to hide our thoughts. We make a pretence of busying ourselves about whatever will help us to keep apart from one another.

'At night, sitting here between the shadows and the dull glow of the smouldering twigs, I sometimes think I hear the tapping I have learnt to listen for, and I start from my seat, and softly open the door and look out. But only the Night stands there. Then I close-to the latch, and she – the living woman – asks me in her purring voice what sound I heard, hiding a smile as she stoops low over her work; and I answer lightly, and, moving towards her, put my arm about her, feeling her softness and her suppleness, and wondering, supposing I held her close to me with one arm while pushing me from her with the other, how long before I should hear the cracking of her bones.

'For here, amid these savage solitudes, I also am grown savage. The old primeval passions of love and hate stir within me, and they are fierce and cruel and strong, beyond what you men of the later ages could understand. The culture of the centuries has fallen from me as a flimsy garment whirled away by the mountain wind; the old savage instincts of the race lie bare. One day I shall twine my fingers about her full white throat, and her eyes will slowly come towards me, and her lips will part, and the red tongue creep out; and backwards, step by step, I shall push her before me, gazing the while upon her bloodless face, and it will be my turn to smile. Backwards through the open door, backwards along the garden path between the juniper bushes, backwards until her heels are overhanging the ravine, and she grips her life with nothing but her little toes, I shall force her, step by step, before me. Then I shall lean forward, closer, closer, till I kiss her purple lips, and down, down, down, past the startled sea-birds, past the white spray of the foss, past the downward peeping pines, down, down, down, we will go together, till we find the thing that lies sleeping beneath the waters of the fiord.'

With these words ended the last letter, unsigned. At the first streak of dawn we left the house, and, after much wandering, found our way back to the valley. But of our guide we heard no news. Whether he remained still upon the mountain, or whether by some false step he had perished upon that night, we never learnt.

THE GREEN LIGHT

Barry Pain

The man looked down at the figure of the woman on the couch. The little silver clock on the mantelpiece began to chime; he could not bear the sound of it. He flew at the clock like a madman, and dashed it on the ground, and stamped on it. Then he drew down the blind, and opened the door and listened; there was no one on the staircase. Silence seemed now as intolerable to him as sound had been a moment before. He tried to whistle, but his lips were too dry and made only a ridiculous hissing sound. Closing the door behind him, he ran down the staircase and out into the street. The woman on the couch never moved or spoke. It was late in the afternoon; the light from the low sun penetrated the green blind and took from it a horrible colour that seemed to tint the face of the woman on the couch. Flies came out of the dark corners of the room, sulkily busy, crawling and buzzing. One very little fly passed backwards and forwards over the woman's white ringed hand; it moved rapidly, a black speck.

Outside in the street, the man stepped from the pavement into the roadway; a cabman shouted and swore at him, and someone dragged him back by the arm, and told him roughly to look where he was going. He stood still for a minute, and rubbed his forehead with his hand. This would not do. The critical moment had come, the moment when, above all things, it was necessary that his nerve should be perfect and his thoughts clear; and now, when he tried to think, a picture came before the thought and filled his mind – the picture of the white face with the green light upon it. And his heart was beating too fast, and, it seemed to him, almost audibly. He begun to feel his pulse, counting the strokes out loud as he stood on the kerb; then he was conscious that two or three boys and loafers were standing in a little group watching him and laughing at him. One of the loafers handed him his hat; it had fallen off when he dodged back on the pavement, and he had not noticed it. He took the hat, and felt for some coins to give the man. He found a half-crown and a half-penny; he held them in his hand, and stared at them, and forgot why he wanted them. Then he suddenly remembered and gave them. There was a loud yell of laughter; the boys and loafers were running away, and he heard one of them shouting, 'Let the old stinker out a bit too soon, ain't they?' and another, 'Garn! 'E's tight – that's all's wrong with 'im.'

Again he told himself that this would not do. He must not think of the past – the awful past. He must not think of the future – of his schemes for escape. He must concentrate his thoughts on the present moment, until he could get to some place where he could be alone. Yes, Regent's Park would do well, and it was near. He brushed his hat with his coat-sleeve, put it on, and walked. He thought about the movement of his feet, and the best way to cross the road, and how to avoid running into people, and how to behave as other people in the street behaved. All the things that one generally does unconsciously and automatically required now for their conduct a distinct mental effort.

As he walked on, his mind seemed to clear a little. He reached a spot in Regent's Park where he could lie down in the grass with no one near him, out of sight. 'Now,' he said to himself, 'I need concentrate my thoughts no longer – I can let them go.' In a second he had gone rapidly through the past

– the jealousy that had burned in his heart, and the way that he had quieted himself and made his scheme, and carried it out slowly. It had been finished that afternoon, when he had lost control over himself, and—

Through the transparent leaves of the tree near him the sun came with a greenish glare. He shuddered and turned away, so that he could not see it.

Yes, he was to escape – he had made all the arrangements for that. He drew from his side-pocket a roll of notes, and counted them, and entered the numbers in his pocket-book. He had changed a cheque for fifty pounds at the bank that morning. The police would find that out, and endeavour to trace him by discovering where the notes with those numbers were changed. That was one of his means of escape. He would see to it that the notes were never changed by himself, or in any town where he had been or was likely to be. He was going to sacrifice those ten bank-notes to put the police on a wrong scent. He had plenty of money ready in gold – in gold that could not be traced – for his own needs. He chuckled to himself. It was brilliant, this scheme for providing a wrong scent, for making the very carefulness and astuteness of the detectives the stumbling-block in their way; and it would be so easy to get the notes changed by others – the dishonesty of ordinary human beings would serve his purpose.

His mood had changed now to one of exultation. He told himself time after time that he was right. The law would condemn him, but morally he was right, and had only punished the woman as she deserved to be punished. Only, he must escape. And – yes – he must not forget.

He looked round. There was still no one near; but his position did not satisfy him. Not a person must see what he was going to do next. He went on and found a spot near the canal, where he seemed to be out of sight, and more secure from interruption. Then he took from his pocket a little looking-glass and a pair of scissors. Very carefully he cut away his beard and moustache, that hid the thin-lipped, wide mouth, and the small weak chin. He cut as close as he could, and when he had finished he looked like a man who had neglected to shave for a day or two. A barber would shave him now without suspicion. He was satisfied with the operation. The glass showed him a face so changed that it startled him to look at it. He glanced at his watch – it was time to start for the station, where his luggage had been waiting since the day before, if he meant to get shaved on the way there.

He walked a little way, and sat down again. 'How well everything has been thought out!' he said to himself. All would succeed. With a new name, and in another country, without that drunken, faithless, beautiful woman, he would grow happy again. He had only meant to sit down for a minute or two, but his thoughts rambled and became nonsense, and suddenly he fell into a deep sleep. He had been over-taxed.

An hour passed. The train that he had intended to take steamed out of the station, and still he slept. It grew dusk, and still he slept. When the park-keeper touched him on the shoulder, he half woke, and spoke querulously. Then consciousness came back, and slowly he realized what had happened.

As he walked slowly out of the park, his mind refreshed with sleep, he for the first time realized something else. In the awful moment when he had left the woman, he had broken down, and forgotten everything. The bag of gold was still lying on the table of the room with the green blind. He must go back and get it. It would be horrible to re-enter that room, but it could not be helped. He dared not change the notes himself, and in any case that amount would be insufficient. He must have the gold.

It added, he told himself, slightly to the risk of discovery, but only slightly. His servants had all been sent out and were not to return until half-past nine. No one else could have entered the house. He would find everything as he left it –

the gold on the table and the figure of the woman on the couch. He would let himself in with his latch-key. No passer-by would take any notice of so ordinary an incident. He had no occasion to hurry now, and he turned into the first barber's shop that he saw. His mind was as alert now as it had been when he first formed his scheme.

'Let me have your best razor,' he said; 'my skin's tender; in fact, for the last two or three days I haven't been able to shave at all.'

He chatted with the barber about horse-racing, and said that he himself had a couple of horses in training. Then he enquired the way to Piccadilly, saying that he was a stranger in London, and seemed to take careful note of the barber's directions.

He walked briskly away from the shop towards his own house. A comfortable-looking ruddy-faced woman was coming towards him. A shaft of green light from a chemist's shop-window fell full on her face as she passed, and the horror came back upon him. It was with difficulty that he checked himself from crying out. He hurried on, but that hideous light seemed to linger in his eyes and to haunt him.

'Keep quiet!' he kept saying to himself under his breath. 'Steady yourself; don't be a fool!'

There was an Italian restaurant near, and he went in and drank a couple of glasses of cognac. Then only was he able to go on.

As he turned the corner where his house came into sight he looked up. All the house was dark but for one green eye in the centre that looked at him. There were lights in that room.

He stood still close to a lamp-post, just touching it to keep his balance. He spoke to himself aloud:

'It's green . . . it's green . . . someone's there!'

A working man passed him, heard him mumbling, looked at him curiously, and went on.

The great green eye stared at him and fascinated him.

Then other lights darted about, red lights, white lights. Someone must be going up and down the staircase and passages. Had she got off the couch? Was the dead woman walking? How his head throbbed! There were two nerves that seemed to sound like two consecutive notes on a piano, struck in slow alternation, then quickening to a rapid shake – whirr! whirr! Now the two notes were struck together, a repeated discord, thumped out – clatter! clatter! No, the sound was outside in the street, and it was the sound of people running. There were boys with excited eyes and white faces, and blowsy, laughing women, and a little old ferret-faced man who coughed as he ran. A police-whistle screamed.

In front of the door of the house a black mass grew up, getting quickly bigger. It was a crowd of people swaying backwards and forwards, kept back by the police.

The police! He was discovered, then. He must get away at once, not wait another moment. Only the green light was looking at him.

'Stop that light!' he called.

No one noticed him. The green light went on glimmering, and drew him nearer. He had to get there. He was on the outskirts of the crowd now.

Why would not the crowd let him pass? Could not they hear that he was being called? He pushed his way, struggling, dragging people on one side. There were angry voices, a hum growing louder and louder. He caught a woman by the neck and flung her aside. She screamed. Someone struck him in the face, and he tried to strike back. Down! He was down on the road. The air was stifling and stinking there. He tried to get up, and was forced back again, his coat torn off his back, muddy, bleeding, fighting, spitting, howling like a madman.

'Damn you! damn you all!'

The crowd was a storm all round him, tossing him here and there. Again and again he was struck. There was blood streaming over his eyes, and through the blood and mingled with blood he saw the green light looking.

There came a sudden lull. A couple of policemen stood by him, and one of them had him by the arm, and asked him what he was doing. He began to cry, sobbing like a child.

'Take me up there,' he said, panting, 'where the green light is; it's the dead woman calling.'

The policeman stood for a moment hesitating. For a moment the crowd was motionless and silent. Then one of the white-faced boys shrank further back whispering:

'It's the man!'

THE SNAKE

Jerome K. Jerome

After a particularly interesting tale, Brown turned to Jephson and asked: 'Did you ever know a man's character to change?'

'Yes,' he answered, 'I did know a man whose character seemed to me to be completely changed by an experience that happened to him. It may, as you say, only have been that he was shattered, or that the lesson may have taught him to keep his natural disposition ever under control. The result, in any case, was striking.'

We asked him to give us the history of the case, and he did so.

'He was a friend of some cousins of mine,' Jephson began, 'people I used to see a good deal of in my undergraduate days. When I met him first he was a young fellow of twenty-six, strong mentally and physically, and of a stern and stubborn nature that those who liked him called masterful, and that those who disliked him – a more numerous body – termed tyrannical. When I saw him three years later, he was an old man of twenty-nine, gentle and yielding beyond the borderline of weakness, mistrustful of himself and considerate of others to a degree that was often unwise. Formerly, his anger had been a thing very easily and frequently aroused. Since the change of which I speak, I have never known the shade of anger to cross his face but once. In the course of a walk, one day, we came upon a young rough terrifying a small child by pretending to set a dog at her. He seized the boy with a grip that almost choked him, and administered to him a punishment that seemed to me altogether out of proportion to the crime, brutal though it was.

'I remonstrated with him when he rejoined me.

'"Yes," he replied apologetically; "I suppose I'm a hard judge of some follies." And, knowing what his haunted eyes were looking at, I said no more.

'He was junior partner in a large firm of tea brokers in the City. There was not much for him to do in the London office, and when, therefore, as the result of some mortgage transactions, a South Indian tea plantation fell into the hands of the firm, it was suggested that he should go out and take the management of it. The plan suited him admirably. He was a man in every way qualified to lead a rough life; to face a by no means contemptible amount of difficulty and danger, to govern a small army of native workers more amenable to fear than affection. Such a life, demanding thought and action, would afford his strong nature greater interest and enjoyment than he could ever hope to obtain amid the cramped surroundings of civilization.

'Only one thing could in reason have been urged against the arrangement, that thing was his wife. She was a fragile, delicate girl, whom he had married in obedience to that instinct of attraction towards the opposite which Nature, for the purpose of maintaining her average, has implanted in our breasts – a timid, meek-eyed creature, one of those women to whom death is less terrible than danger, and fate easier to face than fear. Such women have been known to run screaming from a mouse and to meet martyrdom with heroism. They can no more keep their nerves from trembling than an aspen tree can stay the quivering of its leaves.

'That she was totally unfitted for, and would be made wretched by the life to which his acceptance of the post would condemn her might have readily occurred to him, had he stopped to consider for a moment her feelings in the matter. But to view a question from any other standpoint than his own was not his habit. That he loved her passionately, in his way, as a thing belonging to himself, there can be no doubt, but it was with the love that such men have for the dog they will thrash, the horse they will spur to a broken back. To consult her on the subject never entered his head. He informed her one day of his decision and of the date of their sailing, and, handing her a handsome cheque, told her to purchase all things necessary to her, and to let him know if she needed more; and she, loving him with a dog-like devotion that was not good for him, opened her big eyes a little wider, but said nothing. She thought much about the coming change to herself, however, and, when nobody was by, she would cry softly; then hearing his footsteps, would hastily wipe away the traces of her tears, and go to meet him with a smile.

'Now, her timidity and nervousness, which at home had been a butt for mere chaff, became, under the new circumstances of their life, a serious annoyance to the man. A woman who seemed unable to repress a scream whenever she turned and saw in the gloom a pair of piercing eyes looking at her from a dusky face, who was liable to drop off her horse with fear at the sound of a wild beast's roar a mile off, and who would turn white and limp with horror at the mere sight of a snake, was not a companionable person to live with in the neighbourhood of Indian jungles.

'He himself was entirely without fear, and could not understand it. To him it was pure affectation. He had a muddled idea, common to men of his stamp, that women assume nervousness because they think it pretty and becoming to them, and that if one could only convince them of the folly of it they might be induced to lay it aside, in the same way that they lay aside mincing steps and simpering voices. A man who prided himself, as he did, upon his knowledge of horses, might, one would think, have grasped a truer notion of the nature of nervousness, which is a mere matter of temperament. But the man was a fool.

'The thing that vexed him most was her horror of snakes. He was unblessed – or uncursed, whichever you may prefer – with imagination of any kind. There was no special enmity between him and the seed of the serpent. A creature that crawled upon its belly was no more terrible to him than a creature that walked upon its legs; indeed, less so, for he knew that, as a rule, there was less danger to be apprehended from them. A reptile is only too eager at all times to escape from man. Unless attacked or frightened, it will make no onset. Most people are content to acquire their knowledge of this fact from the natural history books. He had proved it for himself. His servant, an old sergeant of dragoons, has told me that he has seen him stop with his face six inches from the head of a hooded cobra, and stand watching it through his eye-glass as it crawled away from him, knowing that one touch of its fangs would mean death from which there could be no possible escape. That any reasoning being should be inspired with terror – sickening, deadly terror – by such pitifully harmless things, seemed to him monstrous; and he determined to try to cure her of her fear of them.

'He succeeded in doing this eventually somewhat more thoroughly than he had anticipated, but it left a terror in his own eyes that has not gone out of them to this day, and that never will.

'One evening, riding home through a part of the jungle not far from his bungalow, he heard a soft, low hiss close to his ear, and looking up, saw a python swing itself from the branch of a tree and make off through the long grass. He had been out antelope-shooting, and his loaded rifle hung by his stirrup. Springing from the frightened horse, he was just in time to get a shot at the creature before it disappeared. He had hardly expected, under the circumstances, to even hit it. By chance the bullet struck it at the junction of the vertebrae with the head, and killed it instantly. It was a well-marked specimen, and, except for the small wound the bullet had made, quite uninjured. He picked it up, and hung it across the saddle, intending to take it home and preserve it.

'Galloping along, glancing down every now and again at the huge, hideous thing swaying and writhing in front of him almost as if still alive, a brilliant idea occurred to him. He would use this dead reptile to cure his wife of her fear of living ones. He would fix matters so that she should see it, and think it was alive, and be terrified by it; then he would show her that she had been frightened by a mere dead thing, and she would feel ashamed of herself and be healed of her folly. It was the sort of idea that would occur to a fool.

'When he reached home, he took the dead snake into his smoking room; then, locking the door, the idiot set out his prescription. He arranged the monster in a very natural and life-like position. It appeared to be crawling from the open window across the floor, and anyone coming into the room suddenly could hardly avoid treading on it. It was very cleverly done.

'That finished, he picked out a book from the shelves, opened it, and laid it face downward upon the couch. When he had completed all things to his satisfaction he unlocked the door and came out, very pleased with himself.

'After dinner he lit a cigar and sat smoking a while in silence.

'"Are you feeling tired?" he said to her at length, with a smile.

'She laughed, and, calling him a lazy old thing, asked what it was he wanted.

'"Only my novel that I was reading. I left it in my den. Do you mind? You will find it open on the couch."

'She sprang up and ran lightly to the door.

'As she paused there for a moment to look back at him and ask the name of the book, he thought how pretty and how sweet she was; and for the first time a faint glimmer of the true nature of the thing he was doing forced itself into his brain.

'"Never mind," he said, half rising, "I'll—"; then, enamoured of the brilliancy of his plan, checked himself; and she was gone.

'He heard her footsteps passing along the matted passage, and smiled to himself. He thought the affair was going to be rather amusing. One finds it difficult to pity him even now when one thinks of it.

'The smoking-room door opened and closed, and he still sat gazing dreamily at the ash of his cigar, and smiling.

'One moment, perhaps two passed, but the time seemed much longer. The man blew the grey cloud from before his eyes and waited. Then he heard what he had been expecting to hear – a piercing shriek. Then another, which, expecting to hear the clanging of the distant door and the scurrying back of her footsteps along the passage, puzzled him, so that the smile died away from his lips.

'Then another, and another, and another, shriek after shriek.

'The native servant, gliding noiselessly about the room, laid down the thing that was in his hand and moved instinctively towards the door. The man started up and held him back.

'"Keep where you are," he said hoarsely. "It is nothing. Your mistress is frightened, that is all. She must learn to get over this folly." Then he listened again, and the shrieks ended with what sounded curiously like a smothered laugh; and there came a sudden silence.

'And out of that bottomless silence, Fear for the first time in his life came to the man, and he and the dusky servant looked at each other with eyes in which there was a strange likeness; and by a common instinct moved together towards the place where the silence came from.

'When the man opened the door he saw three things: one was the dead python, lying where he had left it; the second was a live python, its comrade apparently, slowly crawling round it; the third a crushed, bloody heap in the middle of the floor.

'He himself remembered nothing more until, weeks afterwards, he opened his eyes in a darkened, unfamiliar place, but the native servant, before he fled screaming from the house, saw his master fling himself upon the living serpent and grasp it with his hands, and when, later on, others burst into the room and caught him staggering in their arms, they found the second python with its head torn off.

'That is the incident that changed the character of my man – if it be changed,' concluded Jephson. 'He told it me one night as we sat on the deck of the steamer, returning from Bombay. He did not spare himself. He told me the story, much as I have told it to you, but in an even, monotonous tone, free from emotion of any kind. I asked him, when he had finished, how he could bear to recall it.

'"Recall it!" he replied, with a slight accent of surprise; "it is always with me."'

THE HOUR AND THE MAN

Robert Barr

Prince Lotarno rose slowly to his feet, casting one malignant glance at the prisoner before him.

'You have heard,' he said, 'what is alleged against you. Have you anything to say in your defence?'

The captured brigand laughed.

'The time for talk is past,' he cried. 'This has been a fine farce of a fair trial. You need not have wasted so much time over what you call evidence. I knew my doom when I fell into your hands. I killed your brother; you will kill me. You have proven that I am a murderer and a robber; I could prove the same of you if you were bound hand and foot in my camp as I am bound in your castle. It is useless for me to tell you that I did not know he was your brother, else it would not have happened, for the small robber always respects the larger and more powerful thief. When a wolf is down, the other wolves devour him. I am down, and you will have my head cut off, or my body drawn asunder in your courtyard, whichever pleases your Excellency best. It is the fortune of war, and I do not complain. When I say that I am sorry I killed your brother, I merely mean I am sorry you were not the man who stood in his shoes when the shot was fired. You, having more men than I had, have scattered my followers and captured me. You may do with me what you please. My consolation is that killing me will not bring to life the man who is shot; therefore conclude the farce that has dragged through so many weary hours. Pronounce my sentence. I am ready.'

There was a moment's silence after the brigand had ceased speaking. Then the Prince said, in low tones, but in a voice that made itself heard in every part of the judgement-hall—

'Your sentence is that on the fifteenth of January you shall be taken from your cell at four o'clock, conducted to the room of execution, and there beheaded.'

The Prince hesitated for a moment as he concluded the sentence, and seemed about to add something more, but apparently he remembered that a report of the trial was to go before the King, whose representative was present, and he was particularly desirous that nothing should go on the records which savoured of old-time malignity; for it was well known that his Majesty had a particular aversion to the ancient forms of torture that had obtained heretofore in his kingdom. Recollecting this, the Prince sat down.

The brigand laughed again. His sentence was evidently not so gruesome as he had expected. He was a man who had lived all his life in the mountains, and he had had no means of knowing that more merciful measures had been introduced into the policy of the Government.

'I will keep the appointment,' he said jauntily, 'unless I have a more pressing engagement.'

The brigand was led away to his cell. 'I hope,' said the Prince, 'that you noted the defiant attitude of the prisoner.'

'I have not failed to do so, your Excellency,' replied the ambassador.

'I think,' said the Prince, 'that under the circumstances, his treatment has been most merciful.'

'I am certain, your Excellency,' said the ambassador, 'that his Majesty will be of the same opinion. For such a miscreant beheading is too easy a death.'

The Prince was pleased to know that the opinion of the ambassador coincided so entirely with his own.

The brigand Toza was taken to a cell in the northern tower, where, by climbing on a bench, he could get a view of the profound valley at the mouth of which the castle was situated. He well knew its impregnable position commanding, as it did, the entrance to the valley. He knew also that if he succeeded in escaping from the castle he was hemmed in by mountains practically unscalable, while the mouth of the gorge was so well guarded by the castle that it was impossible to get to the outer world through that gateway. Although he knew the mountains well, he realized that, with his band scattered, many killed, and the others fugitives, he would have a better chance of starving to death in the valley than of escaping out of it. He sat on the bench and thought over the situation. Why had the Prince been so merciful? He had expected torture, whereas he was to meet the easiest death that a man could die. He felt satisfied there was something in this that he could not understand. Perhaps they intended to starve him to death, now that the appearance of a fair trial was over. Things could be done in the dungeon of a castle that the outside world knew nothing of. His fears of starvation were speedily put to an end by the appearance of his gaoler with a better meal than he had had for some time; for during the last week he had wandered a fugitive in the mountains until captured by the Prince's men, who evidently had orders to bring him in alive. Why then were they so anxious not to kill him in a fair fight if he were now to be merely beheaded?

'What is your name?' asked Toza of his gaoler.

'I am called Paulo,' was the answer.

'Do you know that I am to be beheaded on the fifteenth of the month?'

'I have heard so,' answered the man.

'And do you attend me until that time?'

'I attend you while I am ordered to do so. If you talk much I may be replaced.'

'That, then, is a tip for silence, good Paulo,' said the brigand. 'I always treat well those who serve me well; I regret, therefore, that I have no money with me, and so cannot recompense you for good service.'

'That is not necessary,' answered Paulo. 'I receive my recompense from the steward.'

'Ah, but the recompense of the steward and the recompense of a brigand chief are two very different things. Are there so many pickings in your position that you are rich, Paulo?'

'No; I am a poor man.'

'Well, under certain circumstances, I could make you rich.'

Paulo's eyes glistened, but he made no direct reply. Finally he said in a frightened whisper, 'I have tarried too long, I am watched. By-and-by the vigilance will be relaxed, and then we may perhaps talk of riches.'

With that the gaoler took his departure. The brigand laughed softly to himself. 'Evidently,' he said, 'Paulo is not above the reach of a bribe. We will have further talk on the subject when the watchfulness is relaxed.'

And so it grew to be a question of which should trust the other. The brigand asserted that hidden in the mountains he had gold and jewels, and these he would give to Paulo if he could contrive his escape from the castle.

'Once free of the castle, I can soon make my way out of the valley,' said the brigand.

'I am not so sure of that,' answered Paulo. 'The castle is well guarded, and when it is discovered that you have escaped, the alarm-bell will be rung, and after that not a mouse can leave the valley without the soldiers knowing it.'

The brigand pondered on the situation for some time, and at last said, 'I know the mountains well.'

'Yes,' said Paulo; 'but you are one man, and the soldiers of the Prince are many. Perhaps,' he added, 'if it were made worth my while, I could show you that I know the mountains even better than you do.'

'What do you mean?' asked the brigand, in an excited whisper.

'Do you know the tunnel?' inquired Paulo, with an anxious glance towards the door.

'What tunnel? I never heard of any.'

'But it exists, nevertheless; a tunnel through the mountains to the world outside.'

'A tunnel through the mountains? Nonsense!' cried the brigand. 'I should have known of it if one existed. The work would be too great to accomplish.'

'It was made long before your day, or mine either. If the castle had fallen, then those who were inside could escape through the tunnel. Few knew of the entrance; it is near the waterfall up the valley, and is covered with brushwood. What will you give me to place you at the entrance of that tunnel?'

The brigand looked at Paulo sternly for a few moments, then he answered slowly, 'Everything I possess.'

'And how much is that?' asked Paulo.

'It is more than you will ever earn by serving the Prince.'

'Will you tell me where it is before I help you to escape from the castle and lead you to the tunnel?'

'Yes,' said Toza.

'Will you tell me now?'

'No; bring me a paper tomorrow, and I will draw a plan showing you how to get it.'

When his gaoler appeared, the day after Toza had given the plan, the brigand asked eagerly, 'Did you find the treasure?'

'I did,' said Paulo quietly.

'And will you keep your word? – will you get me out of the castle?'

'I will get you out of the castle and lead you to the entrance of the tunnel, but after that you must look to yourself.'

'Certainly,' said Toza, 'that was the bargain. Once out of this accursed valley, I can defy all the princes in Christendom. Have you a rope?'

'We shall need none,' said the gaoler. 'I will come for you at midnight, and take you out of the castle by the secret passage; then your escape will not be noticed until morning.'

At midnight his gaoler came and led Toza through many a tortuous passage, the two men pausing now and then, holding their breaths anxiously as they came to an open court through which a guard paced. At last they were outside of the castle at one hour past midnight.

The brigand drew a long breath of relief when he was once again out in the free air.

'Where is your tunnel?' he asked, in a somewhat distrustful whisper of his guide.

'Hush!' was the low answer. 'It is only a short distance from the castle, but every inch is guarded, and we cannot go direct; we must make for the other side of the valley and come to it from the north.'

'What!' cried Toza in amazement, 'traverse the whole valley for a tunnel a few yards away?'

'It is the only safe plan,' said Paulo. 'If you wish to go by the direct way, I must leave you to your own devices.'

'I am in your hands,' said the brigand with a sigh. 'Take me where you will, so long as you lead me to the entrance of the tunnel.'

They passed down and down around the heights on which the castle stood, and crossed the purling little river by means of stepping-stones. Once Toza fell into the water, but was rescued by his guide. There was still no alarm from the castle as daylight began to break. As it grew more light they both crawled into a cave which had a low opening difficult to find, and there Paulo gave the brigand his breakfast, which he took from a little bag slung by a strap across his shoulder.

'What are we going to do for food if we are to be days between here and the tunnel?' asked Toza.

'Oh, I have arranged for that, and a quantity of food has been placed where we are most likely to want it. I will get it while you sleep.'

'But if you are captured, what am I to do?' asked Toza. 'Can you not tell me now how to find the tunnel, as I told you how to find my treasure?'

Paulo pondered over this for a moment, and then said, 'Yes: I think it would be the safer way. You must follow the stream until you reach the place where the torrent from the east joins it. Among the hills there is a waterfall, and halfway up the precipice on a shelf of rock there are sticks and bushes. Clear them away, and you will find the entrance to the tunnel. Go through the tunnel until you come to a door which is bolted on this side. When you have passed through, you will see the end of your journey.'

Shortly after daybreak the big bell of the castle began to toll, and before noon the soldiers were beating the bushes all around them. They were so close that the two men could hear their voices from their hiding-place, where they lay in their wet clothes, breathlessly expecting every moment to be discovered.

The conversation of two soldiers, who were nearest them, nearly caused the hearts of the hiding listeners to stop beating.

'Is there not a cave near here?' asked one. 'Let us search for it!'

'Nonsense,' said the other. 'I tell you that they could not have come this far already.'

'Why could they not have escaped when the guard changed at midnight?' insisted the first speaker.

'Because Paulo was seen crossing the courtyard at midnight, and they could have had no other chance of getting away until just before daybreak.'

This answer seemed to satisfy his comrade, and the search was given up just as they were about to come upon the fugitives. It was a narrow escape, and, brave as the robber was, he looked pale, while Paulo was in a state of collapse.

Many times during the nights and days that followed, the brigand and his guide almost fell into the hands of the minions of the Prince. Exposure, privation, semi-starvation, and, worse than all, the alternate wrenchings of hope and fear, began to tell upon the stalwart frame of the brigand. Some days and nights of cold winter rain added to their misery. They dare not seek shelter, for every habitable place was watched.

When daylight overtook them on their last night's crawl through the valley, they were within a short distance of the waterfall, whose low roar now came soothingly down to them.

'Never mind the daylight,' said Toza; 'let us push on and reach the tunnel.'

'I can go no farther,' moaned Paulo; 'I am exhausted.'

'Nonsense,' cried Toza; 'it is but a short distance.'

'The distance is greater than you think; besides, we are in full view of the castle. Would you risk everything now that the game is nearly won? You must not forget that the stake is your head; and remember what day this is.'

'What day is it?' asked the brigand, turning on his guide.

'It is the fifteenth of January, the day on which you were to be executed.'

Toza caught his breath sharply. Danger and want had made a coward of him, and he shuddered now, which he had not done when he was on his trial and condemned to death.

'How do you know it is the fifteenth?' he asked at last.

Paulo held up his stick, notched after the method of Robinson Crusoe.

'I am not so strong as you are, and if you will let me rest here until the afternoon, I am willing to make a last effort, and try to reach the entrance of the tunnel.'

'Very well,' said Toza shortly.

As they lay there that morning neither could sleep. The noise of the waterfall was music to the ears of them both; their long toilsome journey was almost over.

'What did you do with the gold that you found in the mountains?' asked Toza suddenly.

Paulo was taken unawares, and answered, without thinking, 'I left it where it was. I will get it after.'

The brigand said nothing, but that remark condemned Paulo to death. Toza resolved to murder him as soon as they were well out of the tunnel, and get the gold himself.

They left their hiding-place shortly before twelve o'clock, but their progress was so slow, crawling, as they had to, up the steep side of the mountain, under cover of bushes and trees, that it was well after three when they came to the waterfall, which they crossed, as best they could, on stones and logs.

'There,' said Toza, shaking himself, 'that is our last wetting. Now for the tunnel!'

The rocky sides of the waterfall hid them from view of the castle, but Paulo called the brigand's attention to the fact that they could be easily seen from the other side of the valley.

'It doesn't matter now,' said Toza; 'lead the way as quickly as you can to the mouth of the cavern.'

Paulo scrambled on until he reached a shelf about halfway up the cataract; he threw aside bushes, brambles, and logs, speedily disclosing a hole large enough to admit a man.

'You go first,' said Paulo, standing aside.

'No,' answered Toza; 'you know the way, and must go first. You cannot think that I wish to harm you – I am completely unarmed.'

'Nevertheless,' said Paulo, 'I shall not go first. I did not like the way you looked at me when I told you the gold was still in the hills. I admit I distrust you.'

'Oh, very well,' laughed Toza, 'it doesn't really matter.' And he crawled into the hole in the rock, Paulo following him.

Before long the tunnel enlarged so that a man could stand upright.

'Stop!' said Paulo; 'there is the door near here.'

'Yes,' said the robber, 'I remember that you spoke of a door,' adding, however, 'What is it for, and why is it locked?'

'It is bolted on this side,' answered Paulo, 'and we shall have no difficulty in opening it.'

'What is it for?' repeated the brigand.

'It is to prevent the current of air running through the tunnel and blowing away the obstruction at this end,' said the guide.

'Here it is,' said Toza, as he felt down its edge for the bolt.

The bolt drew back easily, and the door opened. The next instant the brigand was pushed rudely into a room, and he heard the bolt thrust back into its place almost simultaneously with the noise of the closing door. For a moment his eyes were dazzled by the light. He was in an apartment blazing with torches held by a dozen men standing about.

In the centre of the room was a block covered with black cloth, and beside it stood a masked executioner, resting the corner of a gleaming axe on the black draped block, with his hands crossed over the end of the axe's handle.

The Prince stood there surrounded by his ministers. Above his head was a clock, with the minute hand pointed to the hour of four.

'You are just in time!' said the Prince grimly; 'we are waiting for you!'

THE CASE OF VINCENT PYRWHIT

Barry Pain

The death of Vincent Pyrwhit, JP, of Ellerdon House, Ellerdon, in the county of Buckinghamshire, would in the ordinary way have received no more attention than the death of any other simple country gentleman. The circumstances of his death, however, though now long since forgotten, were sensational, and attracted some notice at the time. It was one of those cases which is easily forgotten within a year, except just in the locality where it occurred. The most sensational circumstances of the case never came before the public at all. I give them here simply and plainly. The psychical people may make what they like of them.

Pyrwhit himself was a very ordinary country gentleman, a good fellow, but in no way brilliant. He was devoted to his wife, who was some fifteen years younger than himself, and remarkably beautiful. She was quite a good woman, but she had her faults. She was fond of admiration, and she was an abominable flirt. She misled men very cleverly, and was then sincerely angry with them for having been misled. Her husband never troubled his head about these flirtations, being assured quite rightly that she was a good woman. He was not jealous; she, on the other hand was possessed of a jealousy amounting almost to insanity. This might have caused trouble if he had ever provided her with the slightest basis on which her jealousy could work, but he never did. With the exception of his wife, women bored him. I believe she did once or twice try to make a scene for some preposterous reason which was no reason at all; but nothing serious came of it, and there was never a real quarrel between them.

On the death of his wife, after a prolonged illness, Pyrwhit wrote and asked me to come down to Ellerdon for the funeral, and to remain at least a few days with him. He would be quite alone, and I was his oldest friend. I hate attending funerals, but I *was* his oldest friend, and I was, moreover, a distant relation of his wife. I had no choice and I went down.

There were many visitors in the house for the funeral, which took place in the village churchyard, but they left immediately afterwards. The air of heavy gloom which had hung over the house seemed to lift a little. The servants (servants are always emotional) continued to break down at intervals, noticeably Pyrwhit's man, Williams, but Pyrwhit himself was self-possessed. He spoke of his wife with great affection and regret, but still he could speak of her and not unsteadily. At dinner he also spoke of one or two other subjects, of politics and of his duties as a magistrate, and of course he made the requisite fuss about his gratitude to me for coming down to Ellerdon at that time. After dinner we sat in the library, a room well and expensively furnished, but without the least attempt at taste. There were a few oil paintings on the walls, a presentation portrait of himself, and a landscape or two – all more or less bad, as far as I remember. He had eaten next to nothing at dinner, but he had drunk a good deal; the wine, however, did not seem to have the least effect upon him. I had got the conversation definitely off the subject of his wife when I made a blunder. I noticed an Erichsen's extension standing on his writing-table. I said:

'I didn't know that telephones had penetrated into the villages yet.'

'Yes,' he said, 'I believe they are common enough now. I had that one fitted up during my wife's illness to communicate with her bedroom on the floor above us on the other side of the house.'

At that moment the bell of the telephone rang sharply.

We both looked at each other. I said with the stupid affectation of calmness one always puts on when one is a little bit frightened:

'Probably a servant in that room wishes to speak to you.'

He got up, walked over the the machine, and swung the green cord towards me. The end of it was loose.

'I had it disconnected this morning,' he said; 'also the door of that room is locked, and no one can possibly be in it.'

He had turned the colour of grey blotting-paper; so probably had I.

The bell rang again – a prolonged, rattling ring.

'Are you going to answer it?' I said.

'I am not,' he answered firmly.

'Then,' I said, 'I shall answer it myself. It is some stupid trick, a joke not in the best of taste, for which you will probably have to sack one or other of your domestics.'

'My servants,' he answered, 'would not have done that. Besides, don't you see it is impossible? The instrument is disconnected.'

'The bell rang all the same. I shall try it.'

I picked up the receiver.

'Are you there?' I called.

The voice which answered me was unmistakably the rather high staccato voice of Mrs Pyrwhit.

'I want you,' it said, 'to tell my husband that he will be with me tomorrow.'

I still listened. Nothing more was said.

I repeated, 'Are you there?' and still there was no answer.

I turned to Pyrwhit.

'There is no one there,' I said. 'Possibly there is thunder in the air affecting the bell in some mysterious way. There

must be some simple explanation, and I'll find it all out
tomorrow.'

He went to bed early that night. All the following day I was
with him. We rode together, and I expected an accident every
minute, but none happened. All the evening I expected him
to turn suddenly faint and ill, but that also did not happen.
When at about ten o'clock he excused himself and said good-
night, I felt distinctly relieved. He went up to his room and
rang for Williams.

The rest is, of course, well known. The servant's reason
had broken down, possibly the immediate cause being the
death of Mrs Pyrwhit. On entering his master's bedroom,
without the least hesitation, he raised a loaded revolver
which he carried in his hand, and shot Pyrwhit through the
heart. I believe the case is mentioned in some of the textbooks
on homicidal mania.

NOT ACCORDING TO THE CODE

Robert Barr

Even a stranger to the big town walking for the first time through London, sees on the sides of the houses many names with which he has long been familiar. His precognition has cost the firms those names represent much money in advertising. The stranger has had the names before him for years in newspapers and magazines, on the hoardings and boards by the railway side, paying little heed to them at the time; yet they have been indelibly impressed on his brain, and when he wishes soap or pills his lips almost automatically frame the words most familiar to them. Thus are the lavish sums spent in advertising justified, and thus are many excellent publications made possible.

When you come to ponder over the matter, it seems strange that there should ever be any real man behind the names so lavishly advertised; that there should be a genuine Smith or Jones whose justly celebrated medicines work such wonders, or whose soap will clean even a guilty conscience. Granting the actual existence of these persons and probing still further into the mystery, can anyone imagine that the excellent Smith to whom thousands of former sufferers send entirely unsolicited testimonials, or the admirable Jones whom prima donnas love because his soap preserves their dainty complexions – can anyone credit the fact that Smith and Jones have passions like other men, have hatreds, likes and dislikes?

Such a condition of things, incredible as it may appear, exists in London. There are men in the metropolis, utterly unknown personally, whose names are more widely spread over the earth than the names of the greatest novelists, living or dead, and these men have feeling and form like ourselves.

There was the firm of Danby and Strong, for instance. The name may mean nothing to any reader of these pages, but there was a time when it was well known and widely advertised, not only in England but over the greater part of the world as well. They did a great business, as every firm that spends a fortune every year in advertising is bound to do. It was in the old paper-collar days. There actually was a time when the majority of men wore paper collars, and, when you come to think of it, the wonder is that the paper-collar trade ever fell away as it did, when you consider with what vile laundries London is and always had been cursed. Take the Danby and Strong collars, for instance, advertised as being so similar to linen that only an expert could tell the difference. That was Strong's invention. Before he invented the Piccadilly collar so called, paper collars had a brilliant glaze that would not have deceived the most recent arrival from the most remote shire in the country. Strong devised some method by which a slight linen film was put on the paper, adding strength to the collar and giving it the appearance of the genuine article. You bought a pasteboard box containing a dozen of these collars for something like the price you paid for the washing of half a dozen linen ones. The Danby and Strong Piccadilly collar jumped at once into great popularity, and the wonder is that the linen collar ever recovered from the blow dealt by this ingenious invention.

Curiously enough, during the time the firm was struggling to establish itself, the two members of it were the best of friends, but when prosperity came to them, causes of difference arose, and their relations, as the papers say of war-like nations, became strained. Whether the fault lay with John Danby or with William Strong no one has ever been able to find out. They had mutual friends who claimed that each one of them was a good fellow, but those friends always added that Strong and Danby did not 'hit it off'.

Strong was a bitter man when aroused, and could generally be counted upon to use harsh language. Danby was quieter, but there was a sullen streak of stubbornness in him that did not tend to the making up of a quarrel. They had been past the speaking point for more than a year when there came a crisis in their relations with each other that ended in disaster to the business carried on under the title of Danby and Strong. Neither man would budge, and between them the business sank to ruin. Where competition is fierce no firm can stand against it if there is internal dissension. Danby held his ground quietly but firmly, Strong raged and cursed, but was equally steadfast in not yielding a point. Each hated the other so bitterly that each was willing to lose his own share in a profitable business, if by doing so he could bring ruin on his partner.

We are all rather prone to be misled by appearances. As one walks down Piccadilly, or the Strand, or Fleet Street, and meets numerous irreproachably dressed men with glossy tall hats and polished boots, with affable manners and a courteous way of deporting themselves toward their fellows, one is apt to fall into the fallacy of believing that these gentlemen are civilized. We fail to realize that if you probe in the right direction you will come upon possibilities of savagery that would draw forth the warmest commendation from a Pawnee Indian. There are reputable business men in London who would, if they dared, tie an enemy to a stake and roast him over a slow fire, and these men have succeeded so well, not only in deceiving their neighbours, but also themselves, that they would actually be offended if you told them so. If law were suspended in London for one day, during which time none of us would be held answerable for any deed then done, how many of us would be alive next morning? Most of us would go out to pot some favourite enemy, and would doubtless be potted ourselves before we got safely home again.

The law, however, is a great restrainer, and helps to keep the death-rate from reaching excessive proportions. One department of the law crushed out the remnant of this business of Messrs Danby and Strong, leaving the firm bankrupt, while another department of the law prevented either of the partners taking the life of the other.

When Strong found himself penniless, he cursed, as was his habit, and wrote to a friend in Texas asking if he could get anything to do over there. He was tired of a country of law and order, he said – which was not as complimentary to Texas as it might have been. But his remark only goes to show what extraordinary ideas Englishmen have of foreign parts. The friend's answer was not very encouraging, but, nevertheless, Strong got himself out there somehow, and in course of time became a cowboy. He grew reasonably expert with his revolver and rode a mustang as well as could be expected, considering that he had never seen such an animal in London, even at the Zoo. The life of a cowboy on a Texas ranch leads to the forgetting of such things as linen shirts and paper collars.

Strong's hatred of Danby never ceased, but he began to think of him less often.

One day when he least expected it, the subject was brought to his mind in a manner that startled him. He was in Galveston ordering supplies for the ranch, when in passing a shop which he would have called a draper's, but which was there designated as dealing in dry goods, he was amazed to see the name 'Danby and Strong' in big letters at the bottom of a huge pile of small cardboard boxes that filled the whole window. At first the name merely struck him as familiar, and he came near asking himself 'Where have I seen that before?'

It was some moments before he realized that the Strong stood for the man gazing stupidly in at the plate-glass window. Then he noticed that the boxes were all guaranteed to contain the famous Piccadilly collar. He read in a dazed manner a large printed bill which stood beside the pile of boxes. These collars, it seemed, were warranted to be the genuine Danby and Strong collar, and the public was warned against imitations. They were asserted to be London made and linen faced, and the gratifying information was added that once a person wore the D and S collar he never afterwards relapsed into wearing any inferior brand. The price of each box was fifteen cents, or two boxes for a quarter. Strong found himself making a mental calculation which resulted in turning this notation into English money.

As he stood there a new interest began to fill his mind. Was the firm being carried on under the old name by someone else, or did this lot of collars represent part of the old stock? He had had no news from home since he left, and the bitter thought occurred to him that perhaps Danby had got somebody with capital to aid him in resuscitating the business. He resolved to go inside and get some information.

'You seem to have a very large stock of those collars on hand,' he said to the man who was evidently the proprietor.

'Yes,' was the answer. 'You see, we are the State agents for this make. We supply the country dealers.'

'Oh, do you? Is the firm of Danby and Strong still in existence? I understood it had suspended.'

'I guess not,' said the man. 'They supply us all right enough. Still, I really know nothing about the firm, except that they turn out a first-class article. We're not in any way responsible for Danby and Strong; we're merely agents for the State of Texas, you know,' the man added, with sudden caution.

'I have nothing against the firm,' said Strong. 'I asked because I once knew some members of it, and was wondering how it was getting along.'

'Well, in that case you ought to see the American representative. He was here this week . . . that's why we make such a display in the window, it always pleases the agent . . . he's now working up the State and will be back in Galveston before the month is out.'

'What's his name? Do you remember?'

'Danby. George Danby, I think. Here's his card. No, John Danby is the name. I thought it was George. Most Englishmen are George, you know.'

Strong looked at the card, but the lettering seemed to waver before his eyes. He made out, however, that Mr John Danby had an address in New York, and that he was the American representative of the firm of Danby and Strong, London. Strong placed the card on the counter before him.

'I used to know Mr Danby, and I would like to meet him. Where do you think I could find him?'

'Well, as I said before, you could see him right here in Galveston if you wait a month, but if you are in a hurry you might catch him at Broncho Junction on Thursday night.'

'He is travelling by rail then?'

'No, he is not. He went by rail as far as Felixopolis. There he takes a horse, and goes across the prairies to Broncho Junction; a three-day journey. I told him he wouldn't do much business on that route, but he said he was going partly for his health and partly to see the country. He expected to reach Broncho Thursday night.' The dry goods merchant laughed as one who suddenly remembers a pleasant circumstance. 'You're an Englishman, I take it.'

Strong nodded.

'Well, I must say you folks have queer notions about this country. Danby, who was going for a three-day journey across the plains, bought himself two Colt revolvers, and a knife half as long as my arm. Now I've travelled all over this State, and never carried a gun, but I couldn't get Danby to believe his route was as safe as a church. Of course, now and then in Texas a cowboy shoots off his gun, but it's more often his mouth, and I don't believe there's more killing done in Texas than in any other bit of land the same size. But you can't get an Englishman to believe that. You folks are an awful law-abiding crowd. For my part I would sooner stand my chance with a revolver than a lawsuit any day.' Then the good-natured Texan told the story of the pistol in Texas; of the general lack of demand for it, but the great necessity of having it handy when it was called for.

A man with murder in his heart should not hold a conversation like this, but William Strong was too full of one idea to think of prudence. Such a talk sets the hounds of justice on the right trail, with unpleasant results for the criminal.

On Thursday morning Strong set out on horseback from Broncho Junction with his face towards Felixopolis. By noon he said to himself he ought to meet his former partner with nothing but the horizon around them. Besides the revolvers in his belt, Strong had a Winchester rifle in front of him. He did not know but he might have to shoot at long range, and it was always well to prepare for eventualities. Twelve o'clock came, but he met no one, and there was nothing in sight around the empty circle of the horizon. It was nearly two before he saw a moving dot ahead of him. Danby was evidently unused to riding and had come leisurely. Some time before they met, Strong recognized his former partner and he got his rifle ready.

'Throw up your hands!' he shouted, bringing his rifle butt to his shoulder.

Danby instantly raised his hands above his head. 'I have no money on me,' he cried, evidently not recognizing his opponent. 'You may search me if you like.'

'Get down off your horse; don't lower your hands, or I fire.'

Danby got down, as well as he could, with his hands above his head. Strong had thrown his right leg over to the left side of the horse, and, as his enemy got down, he also slid to the ground, keeping Danby covered with the rifle.

'I assure you I have only a few dollars with me, which you are quite welcome to,' said Danby.

Strong did not answer. Seeing that the firing was to be at short range, he took a six-shooter from his belt, and, cocking it, covered his man, throwing the rifle on the grass. He walked up to his enemy, placed the muzzle of the revolver against his rapidly beating heart, and leisurely disarmed him, throwing Danby's weapons on the ground out of reach. Then he stood back a few paces and looked at the trembling man. His face seemed to have already taken on the hue of death and his lips were bloodless.

'I see you recognize me at last, Mr Danby. This is an unexpected meeting, is it not? You realize, I hope, that there are no judges, juries, nor lawyers, no mandamuses and no appeals. Nothing but a writ of ejectment from the barrel of a pistol and no legal way of staying the proceedings. In other words, no cursed quibbles and no damned law.'

Danby, after several times moistening his pallid lips, found his voice.

'Do you mean to give me a chance, or are you going to murder me?'

'I am going to murder you.'

Danby closed his eyes, let his hands drop to his sides, and swayed gently from side to side as a man does on the scaffold just before the bolt is drawn. Strong lowered his revolver and fired, shattering one knee of the doomed man. Danby dropped with a cry that was drowned by the second report. The second bullet put out his left eye, and the murdered man lay with his mutilated face turned up to the blue sky.

A revolver report on the prairies is short, sharp, and echoless. The silence that followed seemed intense and boundless, as if nowhere on earth was there such a thing as sound. The man on his back gave an awesome touch of the eternal to the stillness.

Strong, now that it was all over, began to realize his position. Texas, perhaps, paid too little heed to life lost in fair fight, but she had an uncomfortable habit of putting a rope round the neck of a cowardly murderer. Strong was an inventor by nature. He proceeded to invent his justification. He took one of Danby's revolvers and fired two shots out of it into the empty air. This would show that the dead man had defended himself at least, and it would be difficult to prove that he had not been the first to fire. He placed the other pistol and the knife in their places in Danby's belt. He took Danby's right hand while it was still warm and closed the fingers around the butt of the revolver from which he had fired, placing the forefinger on the trigger of the cocked six-shooter. To give effect and naturalness to the tableau he was arranging for the benefit of the next traveller by that trail, he drew up the right knee and put revolver and closed hand on it as if Danby had been killed while just about to fire his third shot.

Strong, with the pride of a true artist in his work, stepped back a pace or two for the purpose of seeing the effect of his work as a whole. As Danby fell, the back of his head had struck a lump of soil or a tuft of grass which threw the chin forward on the breast. As Strong looked at his victim his heart jumped, and a sort of hypnotic fear took possession of him and paralysed action at its source. Danby was not yet dead. His right eye was open, and it glared at Strong with a malice and hatred that mesmerized the murderer and held him there, although he felt rather than knew he was covered by the cocked revolver he had placed in what he thought was a dead hand. Danby's lips moved but no sound came from them. Strong could not take his fascinated gaze from the open eye. He knew he was a dead man if Danby had the strength to crook his finger, yet he could not take the leap that would bring him out of range. The fifth pistol-shot rang out and Strong pitched forward on his face.

The firm of Danby and Strong was dissolved.

LINDA

Barry Pain

My elder brother, Lorrimer, married ten years ago the daughter of a tenant farmer. I was at that time a boy at school, already interested in the work which has since made me fairly well known, and I took very little interest in Lorrimer or my sister-in-law. From time to time I saw her, of course, when I paid brief visits to their farm in Dorset during the holidays. But I did not greatly enjoy these visits. Lorrimer seemed to me to become daily more morose and taciturn. His wife had the mind of a heavy peasant, deeply interested in her farm and in little else, and only redeemed from the commonplace by her face. I have heard men speak of her as being very beautiful and as being hideous. Already an artist, I saw the point of it all at once: her eyes were not quite human. Sometimes when she was angry with a servant over some trivial piece of neglect, they looked like the eyes of a devil. She was exceedingly superstitious and had little education.

Our guardian had the good sense to send me to Paris to complete my art education, and one snowy March I was recalled suddenly from Paris to his death-bed. I was at this time twenty-two years of age, and of course the technical guardianship had ceased. Accounts had been rendered,

Lorrimer had taken his share of my father's small fortune and I had taken mine. But we both felt a great regard for this uncle who, during so many years, had been in the place of a father to us. I found Lorrimer at the house when I arrived, and learned then, for the first time, that our uncle had strongly disapproved of his marriage. He spoke of it in the partially conscious moments which preceded his end, and he said some queer things. I heard little, because Lorrimer asked me to go out. After my guardian's death Lorrimer returned to his farm and I to my studies in Paris. A few months later I had a brief letter from Lorrimer announcing the death of his wife. He asked me, and, indeed, urged me not to return to England for her funeral, and he added that she would not be buried in consecrated ground. Of the details of her death he said nothing, and I have heard nothing to this day. That was five years ago, and from that time until this last winter I saw nothing of my brother. Our tastes were widely different – we drifted apart.

During those five years I made great progress and a considerable sum of money. After my first Academy success I never wanted commissions. I had sitters all the year round all the day while the light lasted. I worked very hard, and, possibly, a little too hard. Of my engagement with Lady Adela I will say nothing, except that it came about while I was painting her portrait, and that the engagement was broken off in consequence of the circumstances I am about to relate.

It was then one day last winter that a letter was brought to me in my studio in Tite Street from my brother Lorrimer. He complained slightly of his health, and said that his nerves had gone all wrong. He complained that there some curious matters on which he wished to take advice, and that he had no one to whom he could speak on those subjects. He urged me to come down and stay for some time. If there were no room in the farmhouse that suited me for painting he would have a studio built for me. This was put in his usual formal and business-like language, but there was a brief postscript – 'For Heaven's sake come soon!' The letter puzzled me.

Lorrimer, as I knew him, had always been a remarkably independent man, reserved, taking no one into his confidence, resenting interference. His manner towards me had been slightly patronizing, and his attitude toward my painting frankly contemptuous. This letter was of a man disturbed, seeking help, ready to make any concessions.

As I have already said, I had been working far too hard, and wanted a rest. During the last year I had made twenty times the sum that I had spent. There was no reason why I should not take a holiday. The country around my brother's place is very beautiful. If I did work there at all, I thought it might amuse me to drop portraits for a while and to take up with my first love – landscape. There had never been any affection between Lorrimer and myself, but neither had there been any quarrel; there was just the steady and unsentimental family tie. I wrote to him briefly that I would come on the following day, and I hoped he had, or could get, some shooting for me. I told him that I should do little or no work, and he need not bother about a studio for me. I added: 'Your letter leaves me quite in the dark, and I can't make out what the deuce is the matter with you. Why don't you see a doctor if you're ill?'

It was a tedious journey down. One gets off the main line onto an insignificant local branch. People on the platform stare at the stranger and know when he comes from London. In order to be certain where he is going, they read with great care and no sense of shame the labels on his luggage. There are frowsy little refreshment rooms, tended by frowsy old women, who could never at any period of their past have been barmaids, and you can never get anything that you want. If you turn in despair from these homes of the fly-blown bun and the doubtful milk, to the platforms, you may amuse yourself by noting that the farther one gets from civilization, the greater is the importance of the railway porter. Some of them quite resent being sworn at. I got out at the least important station on this unimportant line, and as I gave up my ticket, asked the man if Mr Estcourt was waiting for me.

'If,' said the man slowly, 'you mean Mr Lorrimer Estcourt, of the Dyke Farm, he is outside in his dogcart.'

'What's the sense of talking like that, you fool?' I asked. 'Have you got twenty different Estcourts about here?'

'No,' he replied gravely, 'we have not, and I don't know that we want them.'

I explained to him that I was not interested in what he wanted or didn't want, and that he could go to the devil. He mumbled some angry reply as I went out of the station. Lorrimer leant down from the dogcart and shook hands with me impassively. He is a big man, with a stern, thin-lipped, clean-shaven face. I noted that his hair had gone very grey, though at this time he was not more than thirty-six years of age. He shouted a direction that my luggage was to come up in the farm cart that stood just behind, bade me rather impatiently to climb up, and brought his whip sharply across his mare's shoulder. There was no necessity to have touched her at all, and, as she happened to be a good one, she resented it. Once outside the station yard, we went like the wind. So far as driving was concerned, his nerves seemed to me to be right enough. The road got worse and worse, and the cart jolted and swayed.

'Steady, you idiot!' I shouted to him. 'I don't want my neck broken.'

'All right,' he said. He pulled the mare in, spoke to her and quieted her. Then he turned to me. 'If this makes you nervous,' he said, 'I'd better turn round and drive you back. A man who is easily frightened wouldn't be of much use to me at Dyke Farm just now.'

'When a man drives like a fool, I suppose it's always a consolation to call the man a funk who tells him so. You can go on to your farm, and I'll promise you one thing – when I am frightened I will tell you.'

He became more civil at once. He said that was better. As for the driving, he had merely amused himself by trying to take a rise out of a Londoner. His house was six miles from the

station, and for the rest of the way we chatted amicably
enough. He told me that he was his own bailiff and his own
housekeeper – managed the farm like a man and the house
like a woman. He said that hard work suited him.

'You must find it pretty lonely,' I said.

'I do,' he answered. 'Lately I have been wishing that I
could find it still lonelier.'

'Look here,' I said, 'do you mind telling me plainly what
on earth is the matter?'

'You shall see for yourself,' he said.

The farmhouse had begun by being a couple of cottages
and two or three considerable additions had been made to it
at different times; consequently, the internal architecture
was somewhat puzzling. The hall and two of the living-rooms
were fairly large, but the rooms upstairs were small and
detestably arranged. Often one room opened into another
and sometimes into two or three others. The floor was of
different heights, and one was always going up or down a
step or two. Three staircases in different parts of the house
led from the ground floor to the upper storey. The old moss-
grown tiles of the roof were pleasing, and the whole place
was rather a picturesque jumble. But we only stopped in the
house for the time of a whisky-and-soda. Lorrimer took me
round the garden almost immediately. It was a walled garden
and good as only an old garden can be. Lorrimer was fond of
it. His spirits seemed to improve, and at the moment I could
find nothing abnormal in him. The farm cart, with my
luggage, lumbered slowly up, and presently a gong inside the
house rang loudly.

'Ah!' said Lorrimer, pulling out his watch, 'time to dress.
I'll show you your room if you like.'

My room consisted really of two rooms, opening into one
another. They seemed comfortable enough, and there were
beautiful views from the windows of both of them. Lorrimer
left me, and I began, in a leisurely way, to dress for dinner. As
I was dressing I heard a queer little laugh coming apparently

from one of the upper rooms in the passage. I took little notice of it at first; I supposed it was due to one of the neat and rosy-cheeked maids who were busy about the house. Then I heard it again, and this time it puzzled me. I knew that laugh, knew it perfectly well, but could not place it. Then, suddenly, it came to me. It was exactly like the laugh of my sister-in-law who had died in this house. It struck me as a queer coincidence.

Naturally enough, I blundered on coming downstairs and first opened the door of the dining-room. I noticed that the table was laid for three people, and supposed that Lorrimer had asked some neighbour to meet me, possibly a man over whose land I was to shoot. One of the maids directed me to the drawing-room, and I went in. At one end of the room a log fire flickered and hissed, and the smell of the wood was pleasant. The room was lit by two large ground-glass lamps, relics of my dead sister-in-law's execrable taste. I had at once the feeling that I was not alone in the room, and almost instantly a girl who had been kneeling on the rug in front of the fire got up and came towards me with hands outstretched.

Her age seemed to be about sixteen or seventeen. She had red hair, perhaps the most perfect red that I have ever seen. Her face was beautiful. Her eyes were large and grey, but there was something queer about those eyes. I noticed it immediately. She was dressed in the simplest manner in white. As she came towards me she gave that little laugh which I had heard upstairs. And then I knew what was strange in her eyes. They also at moments did not look quite human.

'You look surprised,' she said. 'Did not Mr Estcourt tell you that I should be here? I am Linda, you know.' Linda was the name of my dead sister-in-law. The name, the laugh, the eyes – all suggested that this was the daughter of Linda Estcourt. But this was a girl of sixteen or seventeen, and my brother's marriage had taken place only nine years before. Besides, she spoke of him as 'Mr Estcourt'. I was making some amiable and some more or less confused reply when Lorrimer entered.

'Ah!' he said. 'I see you have already made Miss Marston's acquaintance. I had hoped to be in time to introduce you.'

We began to chat about my journey down, the beauty of the country, all sorts of commonplace things. I was struck greatly by her air, at once mysterious and contemptuous. It irritated, and yet it fascinated me. At dinner she said laughingly that it would really be rather confusing now; there would be two Mr Estcourts – Mr Lorrimer Estcourt and Mr Hubert Estcourt. She would have to think of some way of making a distinction.

'I think,' she said, turning to my brother, 'I shall go on calling you Mr Estcourt, and I shall call your brother Hubert.'

I said that I should be greatly flattered, and her grey eyes showed me that I had no need to be. From this time onward she called me Hubert, as though she had known me and despised me all my life. I noticed that two or three times at dinner she seemed to fall into fits of abstraction, in which she was hardly conscious that one had spoken to her; I noticed, moreover, that these fits of abstraction irritated my brother immensely. She rose at the end of dinner, and said she would see if the billiard-room was lit up. We could come and smoke in there as soon as we liked. I gave a sigh of relief as I closed the door behind her.

'At last!' I said 'Now, then, Lorrimer, perhaps you will tell me who this Miss Marston is?'

'Tell me who you think she is – no, don't. She is my dead wife's younger sister, younger by many years. Her father took the name of Marston shortly before his death. I am her guardian. My wife's dying words were occupied entirely with this sister, about whom she told me much that would seem to you strange beyond belief; and at that time she gave me injunctions, wrested promises from me which, under certain conditions, I shall have to carry out. The conditions may arise; I think they will. I don't mind saying that I'm afraid they will.'

'Why does she bear her sister's name? Why does she

address you as "Mr Estcourt"? And why do you address her as "Miss Marston," when she introduces herself to me simply as "Linda"?'

'Her mother had three daughters. The eldest was called Linda. When she died, the second, who was my wife, took that name. When my wife died the name descended to the third of them. There has always been a Linda in the family. The rest is simply Miss Marston's own whim. She has several.'

'Who chaperones her here?' I asked.

He smiled. 'That question is typical of you. She is little more than a child, and she has an almost excessively respectable governess living here to look after her. Only I can't be bothered with the governess at dinner quite every night. Does that satisfy you?'

'No; well, perhaps yes. I suppose so.'

'It may make your rigid mind a little easier if I tell you – and it is the truth – that if I had my own way I would turn Miss Marston out of this house tomorrow, and I would never set eyes on her again; that I have a horror of her, and she has a contempt of me.'

'And of most other people, I fancy. Well, anyhow, what's the trouble?'

'I haven't the time to tell you a long story now; she will be waiting for us. Besides, you would merely laugh at me. You have not yet seen for yourself. What would you say if I told you of a compact made years and years ago with some power of evil, and that this girl was concerned in the fulfilment of it?'

'What should I say? Very little. I should get a couple of doctors to sign you up at once.'

'Naturally. You would think me mad. Well, wait here for a few weeks, and see what you make of things. In the meantime, come along to the billiard-room.'

The billiard-room was an addition that Lorrimer himself had made to the house. We found Linda crouched on the rug in front of the blazing fire; I soon found that this was a favourite attitude with her. Her coffee cup was balanced on her knees. Her eyes stared into the flames. She did not seem to notice our entrance.

'Miss Marston,' said my brother. There was a shade of annoyance in his voice. She looked up at him with a disdainful smile. 'Do you care to give Hubert a game?' he asked.

'Not yet. I want to watch a game first. You two play, and I'll mark.'

'What am I to give you, Lorrimer?' I asked. 'Thirty?' He was not even a moderate player. I had always been able to give him at least that.

'You had better play even,' said Linda. 'And I think you will be beaten, Hubert.'

I looked at Lorrimer in astonishment. 'Very well, Miss Marston,' he said, as he took down his cue. I could only suppose that during the last few years his play had improved considerably. And even then I did not see why Linda had interfered. How on earth could she know what my game was like?'

'This is your evening,' I said to Lorrimer after his first outrageous fluke.

'It would seem so,' he answered, and fluked again. And this went on. His game had not improved; he did the wrong things and did them badly, and they turned out all right. Now and again, I heard Linda's brief laugh, and looked up at her. Her eyes seemed to have power to coax a lagging ball into a pocket; one had a curious feeling that she was controlling the game. I did my best with all the luck dead against me. It was a close finish, but I was beaten, as Linda said I should be.

Linda would not play. She said she was too tired, and suddenly she looked tired. The light went out of her eyes. She lit a cigarette, and went back to her place on the rug before the fire. Lorrimer talked about his farm with me. The quiet of the place seemed almost ghastly to a man who was used to London. Presently Linda got up to go to bed. 'Good-night, Mr Estcourt,' she said, as she shook hands with my brother. Then she turned to me: 'Good-night, Hubert. You shouldn't quarrel with ticket-collectors about nothing. It's silly, isn't it?' She kissed me on the cheek, and ran off laughing. She left me astounded by her words and insulted by her kiss.

Lorrimer turned out the lights over the billiard-table, and we sat down again by the fire.

'What did you think of that game?' he asked.

'It was remarkable.'

'Nothing more?'

'I never saw a game like it before. But there was nothing impossible about it.'

'Very well. And did you have a row with that ticket-collector?'

'Not a row exactly. He annoyed me, and I may have called him a fool. I suppose you overheard and told her about it.'

'I could not have overheard. I was outside the station buildings and you were on the farther platform.'

'Yes, that's true. It's a queer coincidence.'

'I tried that, too, at first – the belief that things were remarkable, but not impossible, and that queer coincidences happen. Personally I can't keep it up any more.'

'Look here,' I said. 'We may as well go to the point at once. Why do you want me here? Why did you send for me?'

'Suppose I said that I wanted you to marry Miss Marston?'

'I thought at the time of my engagement with Adela I wrote and gave you the news.'

'You did. The artistic temperament does sometimes do a brilliant business thing for itself. Lady Adela Marys—'

'We won't discuss her.'

'Then suppose we discuss you. You are half in love with Linda already.'

'Very well,' I said, 'let us carry the supposition a little further. Suppose that I or anybody else was entirely in love with her, what on earth would be the use? The one thing that one can feel absolutely certain about in her is that she has amused contempt for the rest of her species, male or female. It's not affected, it's perfectly genuine. Even if I wished to marry her, she would not look at me.'

'Really?' said Lorrimer, with a sneer. 'She seemed fond enough of you when she said good-night.'

'That,' I said meditatively, 'was the cleverest kiss that ever was kissed. It finished what the interchange of Christian names began. It settled the situation exactly – that I was the fool of a brother, and she the good-natured, though contemptuous sister.'

'You needn't look at it like that. It is important, exceedingly important that she should be married.'

'Marry her yourself – it won't be legal in this country, but it will in others, and I don't know that it matters.'

'No, I don't know that it matters. On the day I wrote to you I did ask her to be my wife. She replied that it was disagreeable to have to speak of such things, and that they need not be allowed to come to the surface again, but that, as a matter of fact, *au fond* we hated one another. It was true. I do hate her. What I do for her is for my dead wife's sake, for the promises I made, and perhaps, a little for common humanity. There are others who would marry her. The man whose pheasants you will be shooting next week would give his soul for her cheerfully, and it's no use. Very likely it will be of no use in your case.'

'What was the story that you had not time to tell me after dinner?'

The door opened, and a servant brought in the decanters and soda-water and arranged them on the table by Lorrimer's side. He did not speak until the servant had gone out of the room, and then he seemed to be talking almost more to himself than to me.

'At night, when one wakes up in the small hours, after a bad dream or hearing some sudden noise in the house, one believes things of which one is a little ashamed next morning.'

He paused, and then leant forward, addressing me directly.

'Look here; I'll say it in a few words. You won't believe it, and that doesn't matter a tinker's curse to me. You'll believe it a little later if you stop here. Generations ago, in the time of witches, a woman who was to have been burned as a witch escaped miraculously from the hands of the officers. It was said that she had a compact with the devil; that at some future time he should take a living maiden of her line. Death and marriage are the two ways of safety for any woman of that family. The compact has not yet been carried out, and Linda is the last of the line. She bears the signs of which my wife told me. One by one I watch them coming out in her. Her power over inanimate objects, her mysterious knowledge of things which have happened elsewhere, the terror which all animals have of her. A year or two ago she was always about the farm on the best of terms with every dog and horse in the place. Now they will not let her come near them. Well, it is my business to save Linda. I have given my promise. I wish her to be married. If that is not possible, and the moment arrives, I must kill her.'

'Why talk like a fool?' I said. 'Come and live in London for a week. It strikes me that both Linda and yourself might perhaps be benefited by being put into the hands of a specialist. In any case, don't tell these fairy stories to a sane man like myself.'

'Very well,' he said, getting up. 'I must be going to bed. I am out on the farm before six every morning, and I shall probably have breakfasted before you are up. Miss Marston and Mrs Dennison – that's her old governess – breakfast at nine. You can join them if you like, or breakfast by yourself later.'

Long after my brother had gone to bed I sat in the billiard-room thinking the thing over, angry with myself, and, indeed, ashamed, that I could not disbelieve quite as certainly as I wished. At breakfast next morning I asked Linda to sit to me for her portrait, and she consented. We found a room with a good light. Mrs Dennison remained with us during the sitting.

This went on for days. The portrait was a failure. I have the best of several attempts that I made still. The painting's all right. But the likeness is not there; there is something missing in the eyes. I saw a great deal of Linda, and I came at last to this conclusion, that I had no explanation whatever of the powers which she undoubtedly possessed. I also learned that she herself was well acquainted with the story of her house. She alluded to the fact that neither of her sisters was buried in consecrated ground; no woman of her family would ever be.

'And you?' I asked.

'I am not sure that I shall be buried at all. To me strange things will happen.'

I had letters occasionally from Lady Adela. I was glad to see that she was getting tired of the whole thing. My conduct had not been so calculating and ignoble as Lorrimer had supposed. She was a very beautiful woman. It was easy enough to suppose that one was in love with her – until one happened to fall in love. I determined to go to London to see Lady Adela, and to give her the chance, which I was sure she wanted, to throw me over. I promised Lorrimer that I would only be away for one night. Lady Adela missed her appointment with me at her mother's house, and left a note of excuse. Something serious had happened, I believe, with regard to a dress that she was going to wear that night. But, really, I do not remember what her excuse was. I went back to my rooms in Tite Street, and there I found a telegram from Mrs Dennison. It told me in plain language, and with due regard to the fact that each word cost a halfpenny, that my brother, in a fit of madness, had murdered Linda Marston and taken his own life. I got back to my brother's farm late that night.

The evidence at the inquest was simple enough. Linda had three rooms, opening into one another, the one farthest from the passage being her bedroom. At the time of the murder Mrs Dennison was in the second room, reading, and Linda was playing the piano in the room which opened into the passage. Mrs Dennison heard the music stop suddenly. Linda was whimsical in her playing, as in everything else. There was a pause, during which the governess was absorbed in her book. Then she heard in the next room Lorrimer say distinctly: 'It is all right, Linda. I have come to save you.' This was followed by three shots in succession. Mrs Dennison rushed in and found the two lying dead. She was greatly affected at the inquest, and as few questions as possible were put to her.

Some time afterwards Mrs Dennison told me a thing which she did not mention at the inquest. Shortly after the music had stopped, and before Lorrimer entered the room, she had heard another voice, as though someone were speaking with Linda. This third voice, and Linda's own, were in low tones, and no words could be heard. I thought this over, and I remembered that Lorrimer fired three times, and that the third bullet was found in another part of the room.

Lady Adela was certainly quite right to give me up, which she did in a most tactful and sympathetic letter.

SILHOUETTES

Jerome K. Jerome

I fear I must be of a somewhat gruesome turn of mind. My sympathies are always with the melancholy side of life and nature. I love the chill October days, when the brown leaves lie thick and sodden underneath your feet, and a low sound as of stifled sobbing is heard in the damp woods – the evenings in late autumn time, when the white mist creeps across the fields, making it seem as though old Earth, feeling the night air cold to its poor bones, were drawing ghostly bedclothes round its withered limbs. I like the twilight of the long grey street, sad with the wailing cry of the distant muffin man. One thinks of him as, strangely mitred, he glides by through the gloom, jangling his harsh bell, as the High Priest of the pale spirit of Indigestion, summoning the devout to come forth and worship. I find a sweetness in the aching dreariness of Sabbath afternoons in genteel suburbs – in the evil-laden desolateness of waste places by the river, when the yellow fog is stealing inland across the ooze and mud, and the black tide gurgles softly round worm-eaten piles.

I love the bleak moor, when the thin long line of the winding road lies white on the darkening heath, while overhead some belated bird, vexed with itself for being out so late, scurries across the dusky sky, screaming angrily. I love the lonely, sullen lake, hidden away in mountain solitudes.

I suppose it was my childhood's surroundings that instilled in me this affection for sombre hues. One of my earliest recollections is of a dreary marshland by the sea. By day, the water stood there in wide, shallow pools. But when one looked in the evening they were pools of blood that lay there.

It was a wild, dismal stretch of coast. One day, I found myself there all alone – I forget how it came about – and, oh, how small I felt amid the sky and the sea and the sandhills! I ran, and ran, and ran, but I never seemed to move; and then I cried, and screamed, louder and louder, and the circling seagulls screamed back mockingly at me. It was an 'unken' spot, as they say up North.

In the far back days of the building of the world, a long, high ridge of stones had been reared up by the sea, dividing the swampy grassland from the sand. Some of these stones – 'pebbles', so they called them round about – were as big as a man, and many as big as a fair-sized house; and when the sea was angry – and very prone he was to anger by that lonely shore, and very quick to wrath; often have I known him sink to sleep with a peaceful smile on his rippling waves, to wake in fierce fury before the night was spent – he would snatch up giant handfuls of these pebbles and fling and toss them here and there, till the noise of their rolling and crashing could be heard by the watchers in the village afar off.

'Old Nick's playing at marbles tonight,' they would say to one another, pausing to listen. And then the women would close tight their doors, and try not to hear the sound.

Far out to sea, by where the muddy mouth of the river yawned wide, there rose ever a thin white line of surf, and underneath those crested waves there dwelt a very fearsome thing, called the Bar. I grew to hate and be afraid of this mysterious Bar, for I heard it spoken of always with bated breath, and I knew that it was very cruel to fisher folk, and hurt them so sometimes that they would cry whole days and nights together with the pain or would sit with white scared faces, rocking themselves to and fro.

Once when I was playing among the sandhills, there came by a tall, grey woman, bending beneath a load of driftwood. She paused when nearly opposite to me, and, facing seaward, fixed her eyes upon the breaking surf above the Bar. 'Ah, how I hate the sight of your white teeth!' she muttered; then turned and passed on.

Another morning, walking through the village, I heard a low wailing come from one of the cottages, while a little farther on a group of women were gathered in the roadway, talking. 'Ay,' said one of them, 'I thought the Bar was looking hungry last night.'

So, putting one and the other together, I concluded that the 'Bar' must be an ogre, such as a body reads of in books, who lived in a coral castle deep below the river's mouth, and fed upon the fishermen as he caught them going down to the sea or coming home.

From my bedroom window, on moonlit nights, I could watch the silvery foam, marking the spot beneath where he lay hid; and I would stand on tiptoe, peering out, until at length I would come to fancy I could see his hideous form floating below the waters. Then, as the little white-sailed boats stole by him, tremblingly, I used to tremble too, lest he should suddenly open his grim jaws and gulp them down; and when they had all safely reached the dark, soft sea beyond, I would steal back to the bedside, and pray to God to make the Bar good, so that he would give up killing and eating the poor fishermen.

Another incident connected with that coast lives in my mind. It was the morning after a great storm – great even for that stormy coast – and the passion-worn waters were still heaving with the memory of a fury that was dead. Old Nick had scattered his marbles far and wide, and there were rents and fissures in the pebbly wall such as the oldest fisherman had never known before. Some of the hugest stones lay tossed a hundred yards away, and the waters had dug pits here and there along the ridge so deep that a tall man might stand in some of them, and yet his head not reach the level of the sand.

Round one of these holes a small crowd was pressing eagerly, while one man, standing in the hollow, was lifting the few remaining stones off something that lay there at the bottom. I pushed my way between the straggling legs of a big fisher lad, and peered over with the rest. A ray of sunlight streamed down into the pit, and the thing at the bottom gleamed white. Sprawling there among the black pebbles it looked like a huge spider. One by one the last stones were lifted away, and the thing was left bare, and then the crowd looked at one another and shivered.

'Wonder how he got there,' said a woman at length; 'somebody must ha' helped him.'

'Some foreign chap, no doubt,' said the man who had lifted off the stones; 'washed ashore and buried here by the sea.'

'What, six foot below the water-mark, wi' all they stones atop of him?' said another.

'That's no foreign chap,' cried a grizzled old woman, pressing forward. 'What's that that's aside him?'

Someone jumped down and took it from the stone where it lay glistening, and handed it up to her, and she clutched it in her skinny hand. It was a gold earring, such as fishermen sometimes wear. But this was a somewhat large one, and of rather unusual shape.

'That's young Abram Parsons, I tell 'ee, as lies down there,' cried the old creature, wildly. 'I ought to know. I gave him the pair o' these forty year ago.'

It may be only an idea of mine, born of after brooding upon the scene. I am inclined to think it must be so, for I was only a child at the time, and would hardly have noticed such a thing. But it seems to my remembrance that as the old crone ceased, another woman in the crowd raised her eyes slowly, and fixed them on a withered, ancient man, who leant upon a stick, and that for a moment, unnoticed by the rest, these two stood looking strangely at each other.

From these sea-scented scenes, my memory travels to a weary land where dead ashes lie, and there is blackness – blackness everywhere. Black rivers flow between black banks; black, stunted trees grow in black fields; black withered flowers by black wayside. Black roads lead from blackness past blackness to blackness; and along them trudge black, savage-looking men and women; and by them black, old-looking children play grim, unchildish games.

When the sun shines on this black land, it glitters black and hard; and when the rain falls a black mist rises towards heaven, like the hopeless prayer of a hopeless soul.

By night it is less dreary, for then the sky gleams with a lurid light, and out of the darkness the red flames leap, and high up in the air they gambol and writhe – the demon spawn of that evil land, they seem.

Visitors who came to our house would tell strange tales of this black land, and some of the stories I am inclined to think were true. One man said he saw a young bulldog fly at a boy and pin him by the throat. The lad jumped about with much sprightliness, and tried to knock the dog away. Whereupon the boy's father rushed out of the house, hard by, and caught his son and heir roughly by the shoulder. 'Keep still, thee young—, can't 'ee!' shouted the man angrily; 'let 'un taste blood.'

Another time, I heard a lady tell how she had visited a cottage during a strike, to find the baby, together with the other children, almost dying for want of food. 'Dear, dear me!' she cried, taking the wee wizened mite from the mother's arms, 'but I sent you down a quart of milk, yesterday. Hasn't the child had it?'

'Theer weer a little coom, thank 'ee kindly, ma'am,' the father took upon himself to answer; 'but thee see it weer only just enough for the poops.'

We lived in a big lonely house on the edge of a wide common. One night, I remember, just as I was reluctantly preparing to climb into bed, there came a wild ringing at the gate, followed by a hoarse, shrieking cry, and then a frenzied shaking of the iron bars.

Then hurrying footsteps sounded through the house, and the swift opening and closing of doors; and I slipped back hastily into my knickerbockers and ran out. The women folk were gathered on the stairs, while my father stood in the hall, calling to them to be quiet. And still the wild ringing of the bell continued, and, above it, the hoarse, shrieking cry.

My father opened the door and went out, and we could hear him striding down the gravel path, and we clung to one another and waited.

After what seemed an endless time, we heard the heavy gate unbarred, and quickly clanged to, and footsteps returning on the gravel. Then the door opened again, and my father entered, and behind him a crouching figure that felt its way with its hands as it crept along, as a blind man might. The figure stood up when it reached the middle of the hall, and mopped its eyes with a dirty rag that it carried in its hand; after which it held the rag over the umbrella-stand and wrung it out, as washerwomen wring out clothes, and the dark drippings fell into the tray with a dull, heavy splut.

My father whispered something to my mother, and she went out towards the back; and, in a little while, we heard the stamping of hoofs – the angry plunge of a spur-startled horse – the rhythmic throb of the long, straight gallop, dying away into the distance.

My mother returned and spoke some reassuring words to the servants. My father, having made fast the door and extinguished all but one or two of the lights, had gone into a small room on the right side of the hall; the crouching figure, still mopping that moisture from its eyes, following him. We could hear them talking there in low tones, my father questioning, the other voice thick and interspersed with short panting grunts.

We on the stairs huddled closer together, and, in the darkness, I felt my mother's arm steal round me and encompass me; so that I was not afraid. Then we waited, while the silence round our frightened whispers thickened and grew heavy till the weight of it seemed to hurt us.

At length, out of its depths, there crept to our ears a faint murmur. It gathered strength like the sound of the oncoming of a wave upon a stony shore, until it broke in a Babel of vehement voices just outside. After a few moments, the hubbub ceased, and there came a furious ringing – then angry shouts demanding admittance.

Some of the women began to cry. My father came out into the hall, closing the room door behind him, and ordered them to be quiet, so sternly that they were stunned into silence. The furious ringing was repeated; and, this time, threats mingled among the hoarse shouts. My mother's arm tightened around me, and I could hear the beating of her heart.

The voices outside the gate sank into a low confused mumbling. Soon they died away altogether, and the silence flowed back.

My father turned up the hall lamp, and stood listening.

Suddenly, from the back of the house, rose the noise of a great crashing, followed by oaths and savage laughter.

My father rushed forward, but was borne back; and, in an instant the hall was full of grim, ferocious faces. My father, trembling a little (or else it was the shadow cast by the flickering lamp), and with lips tight pressed, stood confronting them; while we women and children, too scared to even cry, shrank back up the stairs.

What followed during the next few moments is, in my memory, only a confused tumult, above which my father's high, clear tones rise every now and again, entreating, arguing, commanding. I see nothing distinctly until one of the grimmest of the faces thrusts itself before the others, and a voice which, like Aaron's rod, swallows up all its fellows, says in deep, determined bass, 'Coom, we've had enow chatter, master. Thee mun give 'un up, or thee mun get out o' th' way an' we'll search th' house for oursel'.'

Then a light flashed into my father's eyes that kindled something inside me, so that the fear went out of me, and I struggled to free myself from my mother's arm, for the desire stirred me to fling myself down upon the grimy faces below, and beat and stamp upon them with my fists. Springing across the hall, he snatched from the wall where it hung an ancient club, part of a trophy of old armour, and planting his back against the door through which they would have to pass, he shouted, 'Then be damned to you all, he's in this room! Come and fetch him out.'

(I recollect that speech well. I puzzled over it, even at that time, excited though I was. I had always been told that only low, wicked people ever used the word 'damn', and I tried to reconcile things, and failed.)

The men drew back and muttered among themselves. It was an ugly-looking weapon, studded with iron spikes. My father held it secured to his hand by a chain, and there was an ugly look about him also, now, that gave his face a strange likeness to the dark faces round him.

But my mother grew very white and cold, and underneath her breath she kept crying, 'Oh, will they never come – will they never come?' and a cricket somewhere about the house began to chirp.

Then all at once, without a word, my mother flew down the stairs, and passed like a flash of light through the crowd of dusky figures. How she did it I could never understand, for the two heavy bolts had both been drawn, but the next moment the door stood wide open; and a hum of voices, cheery with the anticipation of a period of perfect bliss, was borne in upon the cool night air.

My mother was always very quick of hearing.

Again, I see a wild crowd of grim faces, and my father's, very pale, amongst them. But this time the faces are very many, and they come and go like faces in a dream. The ground beneath my feet is wet and sloppy, and a black rain is falling.

There are women's faces in the crowd, wild and haggard, and long skinny arms stretch out threateningly towards my father, and shrill, frenzied voices call out curses on him. Boys' faces also pass me in the grey light, and on some of them there is an impish grin.

I seem to be everybody's way; and to get out of it, I crawl into a dark, draughty corner and crouch there among cinders. Around me, great engines fiercely strain and pant like living things fighting beyond their strength. Their gaunt arms whirl madly above me, and the ground rocks with their throbbing. Dark figures flit to and fro, pausing from time to time to wipe the black sweat from their faces.

The pale light fades, and the flame-lit night lies red upon the land. The flitting figures take strange shapes. I hear the hissing of wheels, the furious clanking of iron chains, the hoarse shouting of many voices, the hurrying tread of many feet; and, through all, the wailing and weeping and cursing that never seem to cease. I drop into a restless sleep, and dream that I have broken a chapel window, stone-throwing, and have died and gone to hell.

At length, a cold hand is laid upon my shoulder, and I awake. The wild faces have vanished, and all is silent now, and I wonder if the whole thing has been a dream. My father lifts me into the dog-cart, and we drive home through the chill dawn.

My mother opens the door softly as we alight. She does not speak, only looks her question. 'It's all over, Maggie,' answers my father very quietly, as he takes off his coat and lays it across a chair; 'we've got to begin the world afresh.'

My mother's arms steal up about his neck; and I, feeling heavy with a trouble I do not understand, creep off to bed.

THE TOWER

Barry Pain

In the billiard-room of the Cabinet Club, shortly after midnight, two men had just finished a game. A third had been watching it from the lounge at the end of the room. The winner put up his cue, slipped on his coat, and with a brief 'Good-night' passed out of the room. He was tall, dark, clean-shaven and foreign in appearance. It would not have been easy to guess his nationality, but he did not look English.

The loser, a fair-haired boy of twenty-five, came over to the lounge and dropped down by the side of the elderly man who had been watching the billiards.

'Silly game, ain't it, doctor?' he said cheerfully. The doctor smiled.

'Yes,' he said, 'Vyse is a bit too hot for you, Bill.'

'A bit too hot for anything,' said the boy. 'He never takes any trouble; he never hesitates; he never thinks; he never takes an easy shot when there's a brilliant one to be pulled off. It's almost uncanny.'

'Ah,' said the doctor, reflectively, 'it's a queer thing. You're the third man whom I have heard say that about Vyse within the last week.'

'I believe he's quite all right – good sort of chap, you know.

He's frightfully clever too – speaks a lot of beastly difficult Oriental languages – does well at any game he takes up.'

'Yes,' said the doctor, 'he is clever; and he is also a fool.'

'What do you mean? He's eccentric, of course. Fancy his buying that rotten tower – a sweet place to spend Christmas in all alone, I don't think.'

'Why does he say he's going there?'

'Says he hates the conventional Christmas, and wants to be out of it; says also that he wants to shoot duck.'

'That won't do,' said the doctor. 'He may hate the conventional Christmas. He may, and he probably will, shoot duck. But that's not his reason for going there.'

'Then what is it?' asked the boy.

'Nothing that would interest you much, Bill. Vyse is one of the chaps that want to know too much. He's playing about in a way that every medical man knows to be a rotten, dangerous way. Mind, he may get at something; if the stories are true he has already got at a good deal. I believe it is possible for a man to develop in himself certain powers at a certain price.'

'What's the price?'

'Insanity, as often as not. Here, let's talk about something pleasanter. Where are you yourself going this Christmas, by the way?'

'My sister has taken compassion upon this lone bachelor. And you?'

'I shall be out of England,' said the doctor. 'Cairo, probably.'

The two men passed out into the hall of the club.

'Has Mr Vyse gone yet?' the boy asked the porter.

'Not yet, Sir William. Mr Vyse is changing in one of the dressing-rooms. His car is outside.'

The two men passed the car in the street, and noticed the luggage in the tonneau. The driver, in his long leather coat, stood motionless beside it, waiting for his master. The powerful headlight raked the dusk of the street; you could see the paint on a tired woman's cheek as she passed through it on her way home at last.

'See his game?' said Bill.

'Of course,' said the doctor. 'He's off to the marshes and that blessed tower of his tonight.'

'Well, I don't envy him – holy sort of amusement it must be driving all that way on a cold night like this. I wonder if the beggar ever goes to sleep at all?'

They had reached Bill's chambers in Jermyn Street.

'You must come in and have a drink,' said Bill.

'Don't think so, thanks,' said the doctor; 'it's late, you know.'

'You'd better,' said Bill, and the doctor followed him in.

A letter and a telegram were lying on the table in the diminutive hall. The letter had been sent by messenger, and was addressed to Sir William Orlsey, Bart., in a remarkably small handwriting. Bill picked it up, and thrust it into his pocket at once, unopened. He took the telegram with him into the room where the drinks had been put out, and opened it as he sipped his whisky-and-soda.

'Great Scot!' he exclaimed.

'Nothing serious, I hope,' said the doctor.

'I hope not. I suppose all children have got to have the measles some time or another; but it's a bit unlucky that my sister's three should all go down with it just now. That does for her house-party at Christmas, of course.'

A few minutes later, when the doctor had gone, Bill took the letter from his pocket and tore it open. A cheque fell from the envelope and fluttered to the ground. The letter ran as follows:

'Dear Bill, – I could not talk to you tonight, as the doctor, who happens to disapprove of me, was in the billiard-room. Of course, I can let you have the hundred you want, and enclose it herewith with the utmost pleasure. The time you mention for repayment would suit me all right, and so would any other time. Suit your own convenience entirely.

'I have a favour to ask of you. I know you are intending to go down to the Leylands' for Christmas. I think you will be prevented from doing so. If that is the case, and you have no better engagement, would you hold yourself at my disposal for a week? It is just possible that I may want a man like you pretty badly. There ought to be plenty of duck this weather, but I don't know that I can offer any other attraction – Very sincerely yours,

'Edward Vyse.'

Bill picked up the cheque, and thrust it into the drawer with a feeling of relief. It was a queer invitation, he thought – funnily worded, with the usual intimations of time and place missing. He switched off the electric lights and went into his bedroom. As he was undressing a thought struck him suddenly.

'How the deuce,' he said aloud, 'did he know that I should be prevented from going to Polly's place?' Then he looked round quickly. He thought that he had heard a faint laugh just behind him. No one was there, and Bill's nerves were good enough. In twenty minutes he was fast asleep.

The cottage, built of grey stone, stood some thirty yards back from the road, from which it was screened by a shrubbery. It was an ordinary eight-roomed cottage, and it did well enough for Vyse and his servants and one guest – if Vyse happened to want a guest. There was a pleasant little walled garden of a couple of acres behind the cottage. Through a doorway in the further wall one passed into a stunted and dismal plantation, and in the middle of this rose the tower, far higher than any of the trees that surrounded it.

Sir William Orlsey had arrived just in time to change before dinner. Talk at dinner had been of indifferent subjects – the queer characters of the village and the chances of sport on the morrow. Bill had mentioned the tower, and his host had hastened to talk of other things. But now that dinner was over, and the man who had waited on them had left the room, Vyse of his own accord returned to the subject.

'Danvers is a superstitious ass,' he observed, 'and he's in quite enough of a funk about that tower as it is; that's why I wouldn't give you the story of it while he was in the room. According to the village tradition, a witch was burned on the site where the tower now stands, and she declared that where she burned the devil should have his house. The lord of the manor at that time, hearing what the old lady had said, and wishing to discourage house-building on that particular site, had it covered with a plantation, and made it a condition of his will that this plantation should be kept up.'

Bill lit a cigar. 'Looks like checkmate,' he said. 'However, seeing that the tower is actually there—'

'Quite so. This man's son came no end of a cropper, and the property changed hands several times. It was divided and sub-divided. I, for instance, only own about twenty acres of it. Presently there came along a scientific old gentleman and bought the piece that I now have. Whether he knew of the story, or whether he didn't, I cannot say, but he set to work to build the tower that is now standing in the middle of the plantation. He may have intended it as an observatory. He got the stone for it on the spot from his own quarry, but he had to import his labour, as the people in these parts didn't think the work healthy. Then one fine morning before the tower was finished they found the old gentleman at the bottom of his quarry with his neck broken.'

'So,' said Bill, 'they say of course that the tower is haunted. What is it that they think they see?'

'Nothing. You can't see it. But there are people who think they have touched it and have heard it.'

'Rot, ain't it?'

'I don't know exactly. You see, I happen to be one of those people.'

'Then, if you think so, there's something in it. This is interesting. I say, can't we go across there now?'

'Certainly, if you like. Sure you won't have any more wine? Come along, then.'

The two men slipped on their coats and caps. Vyse carried a lighted stable-lantern. It was a frosty moonlit night, and the path was crisp and hard beneath their feet. As Vyse slid back the bolts of the gate in the garden wall, Bill said suddenly, 'By the way, Vyse, how did you know that I shouldn't be at the Leylands' this Christmas? I told you I was going there.'

'I don't know. I had a feeling that you were going to be with me. It might have been wrong. Anyhow, I'm very glad you're here. You are just exactly the man I want. We've only a few steps to go now. This path is ours. That cart-track leads away to the quarry where the scientific gentleman took the short cut to further knowledge. And here is the door of the tower.'

They walked round the tower before entering. The night was so still that, unconsciously, they spoke in lowered voices and trod as softly as possible. The lock of the heavy door groaned and screeched as the key turned. The light of the lantern fell now on the white sand of the floor and on a broken spiral staircase on the further side. Far up above one saw a tangle of beams and the stars beyond them. Bill heard Vyse saying that it was left like that after the death in the quarry.

'It's a good solid bit of masonry,' said Bill, 'but it ain't a cheerful spot exactly. And, by Jove! it smells like a menagerie.'

'It does,' said Vyse, who was examining the sand on the floor.

Bill also looked down at the prints in the sand. 'Some dog's been in here.'

'No,' said Vyse, thoughtfully. 'Dogs won't come in here, and you can't make them. Also, there were no marks on the sand when I left the place and locked the door this afternoon. Queer, isn't it?'

'But the thing's a blank impossibility. Unless, of course, we are to suppose that—'

He did not finish his sentence, and, if he had finished it, it would not have been audible. A chorus of grunting, growling and squealing broke out almost from under his feet, and he sprang backwards. It lasted for a few seconds, and then died slowly away.

'Did you hear that?' Vyse asked quietly.

'I should rather think so.'

'Good; then it was not subjective. What was it?'

'Only one kind of beast makes that row. Pigs, of course – a whole drove of them. It sounded as if they were in here, close to us. But as they obviously are not, they must be outside.'

'But they are not outside,' said Vyse. 'Come and see.'

They hunted the plantation through and through with no result, and then locked the tower door and went back to the cottage. Bill said very little. He was not capable of much self-analysis, but he was conscious of a sudden dislike of Vyse. He was angry that he had ever put himself under an obligation to this man. He had wanted the money for a gambling debt, and he had already repaid it. Now he saw Vyse in the light of a man with whom one should have no dealings, and the last man from whom one should accept a kindness. The strange experience that he had just been through filled him with loathing far more than with fear or wonder. There was something unclean and diabolical about the whole thing that made a decent man reluctant to question or to investigate. The filthy smell of the brutes seemed still to linger in his nostrils. He was determined that on no account would he enter the tower again, and that as soon as he could find a decent excuse he would leave the place altogether.

A little later, as he sat before the log fire and filled his pipe, he turned to his host with a sudden question: 'I say, Vyse, why did you want me to come down here? What's the meaning of it all?'

'My dear fellow,' said Vyse, 'I wanted you for the pleasure of your society. Now, don't get impatient. I also wanted you because you are the most normal man I know. Your confirmation of my experiences in the tower is most valuable to me. Also, you have good nerves, and, if you will forgive me for saying so, no imagination. I may want help that only a man with good nerves would be able to give.'

'Why don't you leave the thing alone? It's too beastly.'

Vyse laughed. 'I'm afraid my hobby bores you. We won't talk about it. After all, there's no reason why you should help me?'

'Tell me just what it is that you wanted.'

'I wanted you if you heard this whistle' – he took an ordinary police whistle down from the mantelpiece – 'any time tonight or tomorrow night, to come over to the tower at once and bring a revolver with you. The whistle would be a sign that I was in a tight place – that my life, in fact, was in danger. You see, we are dealing here with something preternatural, but it is also something material; in addition to other risks, one risks ordinary physical destruction. However, I could see that you were repelled by the sight and the sound of those beasts, whatever they may be; and I can tell you from my own experience that the touch of them is even worse. There is no reason why you should bother yourself any further about the thing.'

'You can take the whistle with you,' said Bill. 'If I hear it I will come.'

'Thanks,' said Vyse, and immediately changed the subject. He did not say why he was spending the night in the tower, or what it was he proposed to do there.

It was three in the morning when Bill was suddenly startled out of his sleep. He heard the whistle being blown repeatedly. He hurried on some clothes and dashed down into the hall, where his lantern lay all ready for him. He ran along the garden path and through the door in the wall until he got to the tower. The sound of the whistle had ceased now, and everything was horribly still. The door of the tower stood wide open, and without hesitation Bill entered, holding his lantern high.

The tower was absolutely empty. Not a sound was to be heard. Bill called Vyse by name twice loudly, and then again the awful silence spread over the place.

Then, as if guided by some unseen hand, he took the track that led to the quarry, well knowing what he would find at the bottom of it.

The jury assigned the death of Vyse as an accident, and said that the quarry should be fenced in. They had no explanation to offer of the mutilation of the face, as if by the teeth of some savage beast.

THE FOUR-FINGERED HAND

Barry Pain

Charles Yarrow held fours, but as he had come up against Brackley's straight flush they only did him harm, leading him to remark – by no means for the first time – that it did not matter what cards one held, but only when one held them. 'I get out here,' he remarked, with resignation. No one else seemed to care for further play. The two other men left at once, and shortly afterwards Yarrow and Brackley sauntered out of the club together.

'The night's young,' said Brackley; 'if you're doing nothing you may as well come round to me.'

'Thanks, I will. I'll talk, or smoke, or go so far as to drink; but I don't play poker. It's not my night.'

'I didn't know,' said Brackley, 'that you had any superstitions.'

'Haven't. I've only noticed that, as a rule, my luck goes in runs, and that a good run or a bad run usually lasts the length of a night's play. There is probably some simple reason for it, if I were enough of a mathematician to worry it out. In luck as distinct from arithmetic I have no belief at all.'

'I wish you could bring me to that happy condition. The hard-headed man of the world, without a superstition or a belief of any kind, has the best time of it.'

They reached Brackley's chambers, lit pipes, and mixed drinks. Yarrow stretched himself in a lounge chair, and took up the subject again, speaking lazily and meditatively. He was a man of thirty-eight, with a clean shaven face; he looked, as indeed he was, travelled and experienced.

'I don't read any books,' he remarked, 'but I've been twice round the world, and am just about to leave England again. I've been alive for thirty-eight years and during most of them I have been living. Consequently, I've formed opinions, and one of my opinions is that it is better to dispense with superfluous luggage. Prejudices, superstitions, beliefs of any kind that are not capable of easy and immediate proof are superfluous luggage; one goes more easily without them. You implied just now that you had a certain amount of this superfluous luggage, Brackley. What form does it take? Do you turn your chair – are you afraid of thirteen at dinner?'

'No, nothing of that sort. I'll tell you about it. You've heard of my grandfather – who made the money?'

'Heard of him? Had him rubbed into me in my childhood. He's in *Smiles* or one of those books, isn't he? Started life as a navvy, educated himself, invented things, made a fortune, gave vast sums in charity.'

'That is the man. Well, he lived to be a fair age, but he was dead before I was born. What I know of him I know from my father, and some of it is not included in those improving books for the young. For instance, there is no mention in the printed biography of his curious belief in the four-fingered hand. His belief was that from time to time he saw a phantom hand. Sometimes it appeared to him in the daytime, and sometimes at night. It was a right hand with the second finger missing. He always regarded the appearance of the hand as a warning. It meant, he supposed, that he was to stop anything on which he was engaged; if he was about to let a house, buy a horse, go on a journey, or whatever it was, he stopped if he saw the four-fingered hand.'

'Now, look here,' said Yarrow, 'we'll examine this thing

rationally. Can you quote one special instance in which your grandfather saw this maimed hand, broke off a particular project, and found himself benefited?'

'No. In telling my father about it he spoke quite generally.'

'Oh, yes,' said Yarrow, drily. 'The people who see these things do speak quite generally as a rule.'

'But wait a moment. This vision of the four-fingered hand appears to have been hereditary. My father also saw it from time to time. And here I can give you the special circumstances. Do you remember the Crewe disaster some years ago? Well, my father had intended to travel by the train that was wrecked. Just as he was getting into the carriage he saw the four-fingered hand. He at once got out and postponed his journey until later in the day. Another occasion was two months before the failure of Varings'. My father banked there. As a rule he kept a comparatively small balance at the bank, but on this occasion he had just realized an investment, and was about to place the result – six thousand pounds – in the bank, pending re-investment. He was on the point of sending off his confidential clerk with the money, when once more he saw the four-fingered hand. Now at that time Varings' was considered to be as safe as a church. Possibly a few people with special means of information may have had some slight suspicion at the time, but my father certainly had none. He had always banked with Varings', as his father had done before him. However, his faith in the warning hand was so great that instead of paying in the six thousand he withdrew his balance that day. Is that good enough for you?'

'Not entirely. Mind, I don't dispute your facts, but I doubt if it requires the supernatural to explain them. You say that the vision appears to be hereditary. Does that mean that you yourself have ever seen it?'

'I have seen it once.'

'When?'

'I saw it tonight.' Brackley spoke like a man suppressing some strong excitement. 'It was just as you got up from the card-table after losing on your fours. I was on the point of urging you and the other two men to go on playing. I saw the hand distinctly. It seemed to be floating in the air about a couple of yards away from me. It was a small white hand, like a lady's hand, cut short off at the wrist. For a second it moved slowly towards me, and then vanished. Nothing would have induced me to go on playing poker tonight.'

'You are – excuse me for mentioning it – not in the least degree under the influence of drink. Further, you are by habit an almost absurdly temperate man. I mention these things because they have to be taken into consideration. They show that you were not at any rate the victim of a common and disreputable form of illusion. But what service has the hand done you? We play a regular point at the club. We are not the excited gamblers of fiction. We don't increase the points, and we never play after one in the morning. At the moment when the hand appeared to you, how much had you won?'

'Twenty-five pounds – an exceptionally large amount.'

'Very well. You're a careful player. You play best when your luck's worst. We stopped play at half-past eleven. If we had gone on playing till one, and your luck had been of the worst possible description all the time, we will say that you might have lost that twenty-five and twenty-five more. To me it is inconceivable, but with the worst luck and the worst play it is perhaps possible. Now then, do you mean to tell me that the loss of twenty-five pounds is a matter of such importance to a man with your income as to require a supernatural intervention to prevent you from losing it?'

'Of course it isn't.'

'Well, then, the four-fingered hand has not accomplished its mission. It has not saved you from anything. It might even have been inconvenient. If you had been playing with strangers and winning, and they had wished to go on playing, you could hardly have refused. Of course, it did not matter with us – we play with you constantly, and can have our revenge at any time. The four-fingered hand is proved in this instance to have been useless and inept. Therefore, I am inclined to believe that the appearances when it really did some good were coincidences. Doubtless your grandfather and father and yourself have seen the hand, but surely that may be due to some slight hereditary defect in the seeing apparatus, which, under certain conditions, say, of the light and of your own health creates the illusion. The four-fingered hand is natural and not supernatural, subjective and not objective.'

'It sounds plausible,' remarked Brackley. He got up, crossed the room, and began to open the card-table. 'Practical tests are always the most satisfactory, and we can soon have a practical test.' As he put the candles on the table he started a little and nearly dropped one of them. He laughed drily. 'I saw the four-fingered hand again just then,' he said. 'But no matter – come – let us play.'

'Oh, the two game isn't funny enough.'

'Then I'll fetch up Blake from downstairs; you know him. He never goes to bed, and he plays the game.'

Blake, who was a youngish man, had chambers downstairs. Brackley easily persuaded him to join the party. It was decided that they should play for exactly an hour. It was a poor game; the cards ran low, and there was very little betting. At the end of the hour Brackley had lost a sovereign, and Yarrow had lost five pounds.

'I don't like to get up a winner, like this,' said Blake. 'Let's go on.'

But Yarrow was not to be persuaded. He said that he was going off to bed. No allusion to the four-fingered hand was made in speaking in the presence of Blake, but Yarrow's smile of conscious superiority had its meaning for Brackley. It meant that Yarrow had overthrown a superstition, and was consequently pleased with himself. After a few minutes' chat Yarrow and Blake said good-night to Brackley, and went downstairs together.

Just as they reached the ground floor they heard, from far up the staircase, a short cry, followed a moment afterwards by the sound of a heavy fall.

'What's that?' Blake exclaimed.

'I'm just going to see,' said Yarrow, quietly. 'It seemed to me to come from Brackley's rooms. Let's go up again.'

They hurried up the staircase and knocked at Brackley's door. There was no answer. The whole place was absolutely silent. The door was ajar; Yarrow pushed it open, and the two men went in.

The candles on the card-table were still burning. At some distance from them, in a dark corner of the room, lay Brackley, face downwards, with one arm folded under him and the other stretched wide.

Blake stood in the doorway. Yarrow went quickly over to Brackley, and turned the body partially over.

'What is it?' asked Blake, excitedly. 'Is the man ill? Has he fainted?'

'Run downstairs,' said Yarrow, curtly. 'Rouse the porter and get a doctor at once.'

The moment Blake had gone, Yarrow took a candle from the card-table, and by the light of it examined once more the body of the dead man. On the throat there was the imprint of a hand – a right hand with the second finger missing. The marks, which were crimson at first, grew gradually fainter.

Some years afterwards, in Yarrow's presence, a man happened to tell some story of a warning apparition that he himself had investigated.

'And do you believe that?' Yarrow asked.

'The evidence that the apparition was seen – and seen by more than one person – seems to me fairly conclusive in this case.'

'That is all very well. I will grant you the apparition if you like. But why speak of it as a warning? If such appearances take place, it still seems to me absurd and disproportionate to suppose that they do so in order to warn us, or help us, or hinder us, or anything of the kind. They appear for their own unfathomable reasons only. If they seem to forbid one thing or command another, that also is for their own purpose. I have an experience of my own which would tend to show that.'

TRANSFORMATION

Robert Barr

If you grind castor sugar with an equal quantity of chlorate of
potash, the result is an innocent-looking white compound,
sweet to the taste, and sometimes beneficial in the case of a
sore throat. But if you dip a glass rod into a small quantity of
sulphuric acid, and merely touch the harmless-appearing
mixture with the wet end of the rod, the dish which contains
it becomes instantly a roaring furnace of fire, vomiting forth
a fountain of burning balls, and filling the room with a dense,
black, suffocating cloud of smoke.

So strange a combination is that mystery which we term
Human Nature, that a touch of adverse circumstance may
transform a quiet, peaceable, law-abiding citizen into a
malefactor whose heart is filled with a desire for vengeance,
stopping at nothing to accomplish it.

In a little narrow street off the broad Rue de Rennes, near
the great terminus of Mont-Parnasse, stood the clock-making
shop of the brothers Delore. The window was filled with
cheap clocks, and depending from a steel spring attached to
the top of the door was a bell, which rang when anyone
entered, for the brothers were working clockmakers,
continually busy in the room at the back of the shop, and
trade in the neighbourhood was not brisk enough to allow

them to keep an assistant. The brothers had worked amicably in this small room for twenty years, and were reported by the denizens of that quarter of Paris to be enormously rich. They were certainly contented enough, and had plenty of money for their frugal wants, as well as for their occasional exceedingly mild dissipations at the neighbouring café. They had always a little money for the church, and a little money for charity, and no one had ever heard either of them speak a harsh word to any living soul, and least of all to each other. When the sensitively adjusted bell at the door announced the arrival of a possible customer, Adolph left his work and attended to the shop, while Alphonse continued his task without interruption. The former was supposed to be the better business man of the two, while the latter was admittedly the better workman. They had a room over the shop, and a small kitchen over the workroom at the back; but only one occupied the bedroom above, the other sleeping in the shop, as it was supposed that the wares there displayed must have formed an almost irresistible temptation to any thief desirous of accumulating a quantity of timepieces. The brothers took weekly turns at guarding the treasures below, but in all the twenty years no thief had yet disturbed their slumbers.

One evening, just as they were about to close the shop and adjourn together to the café, the bell rang, and Adolph went forward to learn what was wanted. He found waiting for him an unkempt individual of appearance so disreputable, that he at once made up his mind that here at last was the thief for whom they had waited so long in vain. The man's wild, roving eye, that seemed to search out every corner and cranny in the place and rest nowhere for longer than a second at a time, added to Delore's suspicions. The unsavoury visitor was evidently spying out the land, and Adolph felt certain he would do no business with him at that particular hour, whatever might happen later.

The customer took from under his coat, after a furtive glance at the door of the back room, a small paper-covered parcel, and untying the string somewhat hurriedly, displayed a crude piece of clockwork made of brass. Handing it to Adolph, he said, 'How much would it cost to make a dozen like that?'

Adolph took the piece of machinery in his hand and examined it. It was slightly concave in shape, and among the wheels was a strong spring. Adolph wound up this spring, but so loosely was the machinery put together that when he let go the key, the spring quickly uncoiled itself with a whirring noise of the wheels.

'This is very bad workmanship,' said Adolph.

'It is,' replied the man, who, notwithstanding his poverty-stricken appearance, spoke like a person of education. 'That is why I come to you for better workmanship.'

'What is it used for?'

The man hesitated for a moment. 'It is part of a clock,' he said at last.

'I don't understand it. I never saw a clock made like this.'

'It is an alarm attachment,' replied the visitor, with some impatience. 'It is not necessary that you should understand it. All I ask is, can you duplicate it and at what price?'

'But why not make the alarm machinery part of the clock? It would be much cheaper than to make this and then attach it to a clock.'

The man made a gesture of annoyance.

'Will you answer my question?' he said gruffly.

'I don't believe you want this as part of a clock. In fact, I think I can guess why you came in here,' replied Adolph, as innocent as a child of any correct suspicion of what the man was, thinking him merely a thief, and hoping to frighten him by this hint of his own shrewdness.

His visitor looked loweringly at him, and then, with a quick eye, seemed to measure the distance from where he stood to the pavement, evidently meditating flight.

'I will see what my brother says about this,' said Adolph. But before Adolph could call his brother, the man bolted and was gone in an instant, leaving the mechanism in the hands of the bewildered clockmaker.

Alphonse, when he heard the story of their belated customer, was even more convinced than his brother of the danger of the situation. The man was undoubtedly a thief, and the bit of clockwork merely an excuse for getting inside the fortress. The brothers, with much perturbation, locked up the establishment, and instead of going to their usual café, they betook themselves as speedily as possible to the office of the police, where they told their suspicions and gave a description of the supposed culprit. The officer seemed much impressed by their story.

'Have you brought with you the machine he showed you?'

'No. It is at the shop,' said Adolph. 'It was merely an excuse to get inside, I am sure of that, for no clockmaker ever made it.'

'Perhaps,' replied the officer. 'Will you go and bring it? Say nothing of this to anyone you meet, but wrap the machine in paper and bring it as quickly and as quietly as you can. I would send a man with you, only I do not wish to attract attention.'

Before morning the man, who gave his name as Jacques Picard, was arrested, but the authorities made little by their zeal. Adolph Delore swore positively that Picard and his visitor were the same person, but the prisoner had no difficulty in proving that he was in a café two miles away at the time the visitor was in Delore's shop, while Adolph had to admit that the shop was rather dark when the conversation about the clockwork took place. Picard was ably defended, and his advocate submitted that, even if he had been in the shop as stated by Delore, and had bargained as alleged for the mechanism, there was nothing criminal in that, unless the prosecution could show that he intended to put what he bought to improper uses. As well arrest a man who entered to buy a key for his watch. So Picard was released, although the police, certain he was one of the men they wanted, resolved to keep a close watch on his future movements. But the suspected man, as if to save them unnecessary trouble, left two days later for London, and there remained.

For a week Adolph slept badly in the shop, for although he hoped the thief had been frightened away by the proceedings taken against him, still, whenever he fell asleep, he dreamt of burglars, and so awoke himself many times during the long nights.

When it came the turn of Alphonse to sleep in the shop, Adolph hoped for an undisturbed night's rest in the room above, but the Fates were against him. Shortly after midnight he was flung from his bed to the floor, and he felt the house rocking as if an earthquake had passed under Paris. He got on his hands and knees in a dazed condition, with a roar as of thunder in his ears, mingled with the sharp crackle of breaking glass. He made his way to the window, wondering whether he was asleep or awake, and found the window shattered. The moonlight poured into the deserted street, and he noticed a cloud of dust and smoke rising from the front of the shop. He groped his way through the darkness towards the stairway and went down, calling his brother's name; but the lower part of the stair had been blown away, and he fell upon the debris below, lying there half-stunned, enveloped in suffocating smoke.

When Adolph partially recovered consciousness, he became aware that two men were helping him out over the ruins of the shattered shop. He was still murmuring the name of his brother, and they were telling him, in a reassuring tone, that everything was all right, although he vaguely felt that what they said was not true. They had their arms linked in his, and he stumbled helplessly among the wreckage, seeming to have lost control over his limbs. He saw that the whole of the front of the shop was gone, and noticed through the wide opening that a crowd stood in the street, kept back by the police. He wondered why he had not seen all these people when he looked out of the shattered window. When they brought him to the ambulance, he resisted slightly, saying he wanted to go to his brother's assistance, who was sleeping in the shop, but with gentle force they placed him in the vehicle, and he was driven away to the hospital.

For several days Adolph fancied that he was dreaming, that he would soon awake and take up again the old pleasant, industrious life. It was the nurse who told him he would never see his brother again, adding by way of consolation that death had been painless and instant, that the funeral had been one of the grandest that quarter of Paris had ever seen, naming many high and important officials who had attended it. Adolph turned his face to the wall and groaned. His frightful dream was to last him his life.

When he trod the streets of Paris a week later, he was but a shadow of his former portly self. He was gaunt and haggard, his clothes hanging on him as if they had been made for some other man, a fortnight's stubby beard on the face which had always heretofore been smoothly shaven. He sat silently at the café, and few of his friends recognized him at first. They heard he had received ample compensation from the Government, and now would have money enough to suffice him all his life, without the necessity of working for it, and they looked on him as a fortunate man. But he sat there listlessly, receiving their congratulations or condolences with equal apathy. Once he walked past the shop. The front was boarded up, and glass had been put in the upper windows.

He wandered aimlessly through the streets of Paris, some saying he was insane, and that he was looking for his brother; others, that he was searching for the murderer. One day he entered the police station where he had first made his unlucky complaint.

'Have you arrested him yet?' he asked of the officer in charge.

'Whom?' inquired the officer, not recognizing his visitor.

'Picard. I am Adolph Delore.'

'It was not Picard who committed the crime. He was in London at the time, and is there still.'

'Ah! He said he was in the north of Paris when he was with me in the south. He is a liar. He blew up the shop.'

'I quite believe he planned it, but the deed was done by another. It was done by Lamoine, who left for Brussels next morning and went to London by way of Antwerp. He is living with Picard in London at this moment.'

'If you know that, why has neither of them been taken?'

'To know is one thing; to be able to prove quite another. We cannot get these rascals from England merely on suspicion, and they will take good care not to set foot in France for some time to come.'

'You are waiting for evidence, then?'

'We are waiting for evidence.'

'How do you expect to get it?'

'We are having them watched. They are very quiet just now, but it won't be for long. Picard is too restless. Then we may arrest someone soon who will confess.'

'Perhaps I could help. I am going to London. Will you give me Picard's address?'

'Here is his address, but I think you had better leave the case alone. You do not know the language, and you may merely arouse his suspicions if you interfere. Still, if you learn anything, communicate with me.'

The former frank, honest expression in Adolph's eyes had given place to a look of cunning, that appealed to the instincts of a French police officer. He thought something might come of this, and his instincts did not mislead him.

Delore with great craftiness watched the door of the house in London, taking care that no one should suspect his purpose. He saw Picard come out alone on several occasions, and once with another of his own stripe, whom he took to be Lamoine.

One evening, when crossing Leicester Square, Picard was accosted by a stranger in his own language. Looking round with a start, he saw at his side a cringing tramp, worse than shabbily dressed.

'What did you say?' asked Picard, with a tremor in his voice.

'Could you assist a poor countryman?' whined Delore.

'I have no money.'

'Perhaps you could help me to get work. I don't know the language, but I am a good workman.'

'How can I help you to work? I have no work myself.'

'I would be willing to work for nothing, if I could get a place to sleep in and something to eat.'

'Why don't you steal? I would if I were hungry. What are you afraid of? Prison? It is no worse than tramping the streets hungry; I know, for I have tried both. What is your trade?'

'I am a watchmaker and a first-class workman, but I have pawned all my tools. I have tramped from Lyons, but there is nothing doing in my trade.'

Picard looked at him suspiciously for a few moments.

'Why did you accost me?' he asked at last.

'I saw you were a fellow-countryman; Frenchmen have helped me from time to time.'

'Let us sit down on this bench. What is your name, and how long have you been in England?'

'My name is Adolph Carrier, and I have been in London three months.'

'So long as that? How have you lived all that time?'

'Very poorly, as you may see. I sometimes get scraps from the French restaurants, and I sleep where I can.'

'Well, I think I can do better than that for you. Come with me.'

Picard took Delore to his house, letting himself in with a latchkey. Nobody seemed to occupy the place but himself and Lamoine. He led the way to the top storey, and opened a door that communicated with a room entirely bare of furniture. Leaving Adolph there, Picard went downstairs again and came up shortly after with a lighted candle in his hand, followed by Lamoine, who carried a mattress.

'This will do for you for tonight,' said Picard, 'and tomorrow we will see if we can get you any work. Can you make clocks?'

'Oh yes, and good ones.'

'Very well. Give me a list of the tools and materials you need, and I will get them for you.'

Picard wrote in a notebook the items Adolph recited to him, Lamoine watching their new employee closely, but saying nothing. Next day a table and chair were put into the room, and in the afternoon Picard brought in the tools and some sheets of brass.

Picard and Lamoine were somewhat suspicious of their recruit at first, but he went on industriously with his task, and made no attempt to communicate with anybody. They soon saw that he was an expert workman, and a quiet, innocent, half-daft, harmless creature, so he was given other things to do, such as cleaning up their rooms and going errands for beer and other necessities of life.

When Adolph finished his first machine, he took it down to them and exhibited it with pardonable pride. There was a dial on it exactly like a clock, although it had but one hand.

'Let us see it work,' said Picard; 'set it so that the bell will ring in three minutes.'

Adolph did as requested, and stood back when the machine began to work with a scarcely audible tick-tick. Picard pulled out his watch, and exactly at the third minute the hammer fell on the bell. 'That is very satisfactory,' said Picard; 'now, can you make the next one slightly concave, so that a man may strap it under his coat without attracting attention? Such a shape is useful when passing the Customs.'

'I can make it any shape you like, and thinner than this one if you wish it.'

'Very well. Go out and get us a quart of beer, and we will drink to your success. Here is the money.'

Adolph obeyed with his usual docility, staying out, however, somewhat longer than usual. Picard, impatient at the delay, spoke roughly to him when he returned, and ordered him to go upstairs to his work. Adolph departed meekly, leaving them to their beer.

'See that you understand that machine, Lamoine,' said Picard. 'Set it at half an hour.'

Lamoine, turning the hand to the figure VI on the dial, set the works in motion, and to the accompaniment of its quiet tick-tick they drank their beer.

'He seems to understand his business,' said Lamoine.

'Yes,' answered Picard. 'What heady stuff this English beer is. I wish we had some good French hock; this makes me drowsy.'

Lamoine did not answer; he was nodding in his chair. Picard threw himself down on his mattress in one corner of the room; Lamoine, when he slipped from his chair, muttered an oath, and lay where he fell.

Twenty minutes later the door stealthily opened, and Adolph's head cautiously reconnoitred the situation, coming into the silent apartment inch by inch, his crafty eyes rapidly searching the room and filling with malicious glee when he saw that everything was as he had planned. He entered quietly and closed the door softly behind him. He had a great coil of thin strong cord in his hand. Approaching the sleeping men on tiptoe, he looked down on them for a moment, wondering whether the drug had done its work sufficiently well for him to proceed. The question was settled for him with a suddenness that nearly unnerved him. An appalling clang of the bell, a startling sound that seemed loud enough to wake the dead, made him spring nearly to the ceiling. He dropped his rope and clung to the door in a panic of dread, his palpitating heart nearly suffocating him with its wild beating, staring with affrighted eyes at the machine which had given such an unexpected alarm. Slowly recovering command over himself, he turned his gaze on the sleepers: neither had moved; both were breathing as heavily as ever.

Pulling himself together, he turned his attention first to Picard, as the more dangerous man of the two, should an awakening come before he was ready for it. He bound Picard's wrists tightly together; then his ankles, his knees, and his elbows. He next did the same for Lamoine. With great effort he got Picard in a seated position on his chair, tying him there with a coil of cord. So anxious was he to make everything secure, that he somewhat overdid the business, making the two seem like seated mummies swathed in cord. The chairs he fastened immovably to the floor, then he stood back and gazed with a sigh at the two grim seated figures, with their heads drooping helplessly forward on their corded breasts, looking like silent effigies of the dead.

Mopping his perspiring brow, Adolph now turned his attention to the machine that had startled him so when he first came in. He examined minutely its mechanism to see that everything was right. Going to the cupboard, he took up a false bottom and lifted carefully out a number of dynamite cartridges that the two sleepers had stolen from a French mine. These he arranged in a battery, tying them together. He raised the hammer of the machine, and set the hand so that the blow would fall in sixty minutes after the machinery was set in motion. The whole deadly combination he placed on a small table, which he shoved close in front of the two sleeping men. This done, he sat down on a chair patiently to await the awakening. The room was situated at the back of the house, and was almost painfully still, not a sound from the street penetrating to it. The candle burnt low, guttered and went out, but Adolph sat there and did not light another. The room was still only half in darkness, for the moon shone brightly in at the window, reminding Adolph that it was just a month since he had looked out on a moonlit street in Paris, while his brother lay murdered in the room below. The hours dragged along, and Adolph sat as immovable as the two figures before him. The square of moonlight, slowly moving, at last illuminated the seated form of Picard, imperceptibly climbing up, as the moon sank, until it touched his face. He threw his head first to one side, then back, yawned, drew a deep breath, and tried to struggle.

'Lamoine!' he cried, 'Adolph! What the devil is this? I say, here. Help! I am betrayed.'

'Hush,' said Adolph quietly. 'Do not cry so loud. You will wake Lamoine, who is beside you. I am here; wait till I light a candle, the moonlight is waning.'

'Adolph, you fiend, you are in league with the police.'

'No, I am not. I will explain everything in a moment. Have patience.' Adolph lit a candle, and Picard, rolling his eyes, saw that the slowly awakening Lamoine was bound like himself.

Lamoine, glaring at his partner and not understanding what had happened, hissed—

'You have turned traitor, Picard; you have informed, curse you!'

'Keep quiet, you fool. Don't you see I am bound as tightly as you.'

'There has been no traitor and no informing, nor need of any. A month ago tonight, Picard, there was blown into eternity a good and honest man, who never harmed you or anyone. I am his brother. I am Adolph Delore, who refused to make your infernal machine for you. I am much changed since then; but perhaps now you recognize me?'

'I swear to God,' cried Picard, 'that I did not do it. I was in London at the time. I can prove it. There is no use in handing me over to the police, even though, perhaps, you think you can terrorize this poor wretch into lying against me.'

'Pray to the God, whose name you so lightly use, that the police you fear may get you before I have done with you. In the police, strange as it may sound to you, is your only hope; but they will have to come quickly if they are to save you. Picard, you have lived, perhaps, thirty-five years on this earth. The next hour of your life will be longer than all these years.'

Adolph put the percussion cap in its place and started the mechanism. For a few moments its quiet tick-tick was the only sound in the room, the two bound men staring with wide-open eyes at the dial of the clock, while the whole horror of their position slowly broke upon them.

Tick-tick, tick-tick, tick-tick, tick-tick, tick-tick, tick-tick. Each man's face paled, and rivulets of sweat ran down from their brows. Suddenly Picard raised his voice in an unearthly shriek.

'I expected that,' said Adolph quietly. 'I don't think anyone can hear, but I will gag you both, so that no risks may be run.' When this was done, he said: 'I have set the clockwork at sixty minutes; seven of those are already spent. There is still time enough left for meditation and repentance. I place the candle here so that its rays will shine upon the dial. When you have made your own peace, pray for the souls of any you have sent into eternity without time for preparation.'

Delore left the room as softly as he had entered it, and the doomed men tried ineffectually to cry out as they heard the key turning in the door.

The authorities knew that someone had perished in that explosion, but whether it was one man or two they could not tell.

THE GRAY CAT

Barry Pain

I heard this story from Archdeacon M—. I should imagine that it would not be very difficult, by trimming it a little and altering the facts here and there, to make it capable of some simple explanation; but I have preferred to tell it as it was told to me.

After all, there is some explanation possible, even if there is not one definite and simple explanation clearly indicated. It must rest with the reader whether he will prefer to believe that some of the so-called uncivilized races may possess occult powers transcending anything of which the so-called civilized are capable, or whether he will consider that a series of coincidences is sufficient to account for the extraordinary incidents which, in a plain brief way, I am about to relate. It does not seem to me essential to state which view I hold myself, or if I hold neither, and have reasons for not stating a third possible explanation.

I must add a word or two with regard to Archdeacon M—. At the time of this story he was in his fiftieth year. He was a fine scholar, a man of considerable learning. His religious views were remarkably broad; his enemies said remarkably thin. In his younger days he had been something of an athlete, but owing to age, sedentary habits, and some amount of self-indulgence, he had grown stout, and no longer took exercise in any form. He had no nervous trouble of any kind. His death, from heart disease, took place about three years ago. He told me the story twice, at my request; there was an interval of about six weeks between the two narrations; some of the details were elicited by questions of my own. With this preliminary note, we may proceed to the story.

In January, 1881, Archdeacon M——, who was a great admirer of Tennyson's poetry, came up to London for a few days, chiefly in order to witness the performance of *The Cup*, at the Lyceum. He was not present on the first night (Monday, 3 January), but on a later night in the same week. At that time, of course, the poet had not received his peerage, nor the actor his knighthood.

On leaving the theatre, less satisfied with the play than with the magnificence of the setting, the Archdeacon found some slight difficulty in getting a cab. He walked a little way down the Strand to find one, when he encountered unexpectedly his old friend, Guy Breddon.

Breddon (that was not his real name) was a man of considerable fortune, and devoted to Central African exploration. He was two or three years younger than the Archdeacon, and a man of tremendous physique.

Breddon was surprised to find the Archdeacon in London, and the Archdeacon was equally surprised to find Breddon in England at all. Breddon carried off the Archdeacon with him to his rooms, and sent a servant in a cab to the Langham to pay the Archdeacon's bill and fetch his luggage. The Archdeacon protested, but faintly, and Breddon would not hear of his hospitality being refused.

Breddon's rooms were an expensive suite immediately over a ruinous upholsterer's in a street off Berkeley Square. There was a private street-door, and from it a private staircase to the first and second floors.

The suite of rooms on the first floor, occupied by Breddon, was entirely shut off from the staircase by a door. The second floor suite, tenanted by an Irish MP, was similarly shut off, and at that time was unoccupied.

Breddon and the Archdeacon passed through the street-door and up the stairs to the first landing, from whence, by the staircase-door, they entered the flat. Breddon had only recently taken the flat, and the Archdeacon had never been there before. It consisted of a broad L-shaped passage with rooms opening into it. There were many trophies on the walls. Horned heads glared at them; stealthy but stuffed beasts watched them furtively from under tables. There was a perfect arsenal of murderous weapons gleaming brightly under the shaded gaslights.

Breddon's servant prepared supper for them before leaving for the Langham, and soon the two men were discussing Mr Tennyson, Mr Irving, and a parody of the *Queen of the May* which had recently appeared in *Punch,* and doing justice to some oysters, a cold pheasant with an excellent salad, and a bottle of '74 Pommery. It was characteristic of the Archdeacon that he remembered exactly the items of the supper, and that Breddon rather neglected the wine.

After supper they passed into the library, where a bright fire was burning. The Archdeacon walked towards the fire, rubbing his plump hands together. As he did so, a portion of the great rug of gray fur on which he was standing seemed to rise up. It was a gray cat of enormous size, larger than any that the Archdeacon had ever seen before, and of the same colour as the rug on which it had been sleeping. It rubbed itself affectionately against the Archdeacon's leg, and purred as he bent down to stroke it.

'What an extraordinary animal!' said the Archdeacon. 'I had no idea cats could grow to this size. Its head's queer too – so much too small for the body.'

'Yes,' said Breddon, 'and his feet are just as much too big.'

The gray cat stretched himself voluptuously under the Archdeacon's caressing hand, and the feet could be seen plainly. They were very broad, and the claws, which shot out, seemed unusually powerful and well developed. The beast's coat was short, thick and wiry.

'Most extraordinary!' the Archdeacon repeated.

He lowered himself into a comfortable chair by the fire. He was still bending over the cat and playing with it when a slight chink made him look. Breddon was putting something down on the table behind the liquor decanters.

'Any particular breed?' the Archdeacon asked.

'Not that I know of. Freakish, I should say. We found him on board the boat when I left for home – may have come there after mice. He'd have been thrown overboard but for me. I got rather interested in him. Smoke?'

'Oh, thank you.'

Outside a cold north wind screamed in quick gusts. Within came the sharp scratch of the match on the ribbed glass as the Archdeacon lit his cigar, the bubble of the rose-water in Breddon's hookah, the soft step of Breddon's man carrying the Archdeacon's luggage into the bedroom at the end of the L-shaped passage, and the constant purring of the big gray cat.

'And what's the cat's name?' the Archdeacon asked.

Breddon laughed.

'Well, if you must have the plain truth, he's called Gray Devil – or, more frequently, Devil *tout court*.'

'Really, now, really, you can't expect an Archdeacon to use such abominable language. I shall call him Gray – or perhaps Mr Gray would be more respectful, seeing the shortness of our acquaintance. Do you object to the smell of smoke, Mr Gray? The intelligent beast does not object. Probably you've accustomed him to it.'

'Well, seeing what his name is, he could hardly object to smoke, could he?'

Breddon's servant entered. As the door opened and shut, one heard for a moment the crackle of the newly lit fire in the room that awaited the Archdeacon. The servant swept up the hearth, and, under Archidiaconal direction, mixed a lengthy brandy-and-soda. He retired with the information that he would not be wanted again that night.

'Did you notice,' asked the Archdeacon, 'the way Mr Gray followed your man about?' I never saw a more affectionate cat.'

'Think so?' said Breddon. 'Watch this time.'

For the first time he approached the gray cat, and stretched out his hand as if to pet him. In an instant the cat seemed to have gone mad. Its claws shot out, its back hooped, its coat bristled, its tail stood erect; it cursed and spat, and its small green eyes glared. But a close observer would have noticed that all the time it watched not only Breddon, but also that object which had chinked as Breddon had put it down behind the decanters.

The Archdeacon lay back in his chair and laughed heartily.

'What funny creatures they are, and never so funny as when they lose their tempers! Really, Mr Gray, out of respect to my cloth, you might have refrained from swearing like that. Poor Mr Gray! Poor puss!'

Breddon resumed his seat with a grim smile. The gray cat slowly subsided, and then thrust its head, as though demanding sympathy, into the fat palm of the Archdeacon's dependent hand.

Suddenly the Archdeacon's eye lighted on the object which the cat had been watching, visible now that the servant had displaced the decanters.

'Goodness me!' he exclaimed, 'you've got a revolver there.'

'That is so,' said Breddon.

'Not loaded, I trust?'

'Oh yes, fully loaded.'

'But isn't that very dangerous?'

'Well, no; I'm used to these things, and I'm not careless with them. I should have thought it more dangerous to have introduced Gray Devil to you without it. He's much more powerful than an ordinary cat, and I fancy there's something beside cat in his pedigree. When I bring a stranger to see him I keep the cat covered with the revolver until I see how the land lies. To do the brute justice, he has always been most friendly with everybody except myself. I'm his only antipathy. He'd have gone for me just now but that he's smart enough to be afraid of this.'

He tapped the revolver.

'I see,' said the Archdeacon seriously, 'and can guess how it happened. You scared him one day by firing the revolver for joke; the report frightened him, and he's never forgiven you or forgotten the revolver. Wonderful memory some of these animals have!'

'Yes,' said Breddon, 'but that guess won't do. I have never, intentionally or by chance, given the "Devil" any reason for his enmity. So far as I know he has never heard a firearm, and certainly he has never heard one since I made his acquaintance. Somebody may have scared him before, and I'm inclined to think that somebody did, for there can be no doubt that the brute knows all that a cat needs know about a revolver, and that he's scared of it.

'The first time we met was almost in darkness. I'd got some cases that I was particular about, and the captain had said I could go down to look after them. Well, this beast suddenly came out of a lump of black and flew at me. I didn't even recognize that it was a cat, because he's so mighty big. I fetched him a clip on the side of the head that knocked him off, and whipped out my iron. He was away in a streak. He knew. And I've had plenty of proof since that he knows. He'd bite me now if he had the chance, but he understands that he hasn't got the chance. I'm often half inclined to take him on plain – shooting barred – and to feel my own hands breaking his damned neck!'

'Really, old man, really!' said the Archdeacon in perfunctory protest, as he rose and mixed himself another drink.

'Sorry to use strong language, but I don't love that cat, you know.'

The Archdeacon expressed his surprise that in that case Breddon did not get rid of the brute.

'You come across him on board ship and he flies at you. You save his life, give him board and lodging, and he still hates you so much that he won't let you touch him, and you are no fonder of him than he is of you. Why don't you part company?'

'As for his board, I've rarely known him to eat anything except his own kill. He goes out hunting every night. I keep him simply and solely because I'm afraid of him. As long as I can keep him I know my nerves are all right. If I let my funk of him make any difference – well, I shouldn't be much good in a Central African forest. At first I had some idea of taming him – and, besides, there was a queer coincidence.'

He rose and opened the window, and Gray Devil slowly slunk up to it. He paused a few moments on the window-sill and then suddenly sprang and vanished.

'What was the coincidence?'

'What do you think of that?'

Breddon handed the Archdeacon a figure of a cat which he had taken from the mantelpiece. It was a little thing about three inches high. In colour, in the small head, enormous feet, and curiously human eyes, it seemed an exact reproduction of Gray Devil.

'A perfect likeness. How did you get it made?'

'I got the likeness before I got the original. A little Jew dealer sold it to me the night before I left for England. He thought it was Egyptian, and described it as an idol. Anyhow, it was a niceish piece of jade.'

'I always thought jade was bright green.'

'It may be – or white – or brown. It varies. I don't think there can be any doubt that this little figure is old, thought I doubt if it's Egyptian.'

Breddon put it back in its place.

'By the way, that same night the little Jew came to try and buy it back again. He offered me twice what I had given for it. I said he must have found somebody who was pretty keen on it. I asked if it was a collector. The Jew thought not; said it was a coloured gentleman. Well, that finished it. I wasn't going to do anything to oblige a negro. The Jew pleaded that it was a particularly fine negro, with mountains of money, who'd been tracking the thing for years, and hinted at all manner of mumbo-jumbo business – to scare me, I suppose. However, I wouldn't listen, and kicked him out. Then came the coincidence. Having bought the likeness, next day I found the living original. Rum, wasn't it?'

At this moment the clock struck, and the Archdeacon recognized with horror that it was very, very much past the time when respectable Archdeacons should be in bed and asleep. He rose and said good-night, observing that he'd like to hear more about it on the morrow.

This was extremely unfortunate, for it will be seen it is just at this part of the story that one wants full details, and on the morrow it became impossible to elicit them.

Before leaving the library Breddon closed the window, and the Archdeacon asked how 'Mr Gray,' as he called him, would get back.

'Very likely he's back already. He's got a special window in the kitchen, made on purpose, just big enough to let him get in and out as he likes.'

'But don't other cats get in, too?'

'No,' said Breddon, 'Other cats avoid Gray Devil.'

The Archdeacon found himself unaccountably nervous when he got to his room. He owned to me that he had to satisfy himself that there was no one concealed under the bed or in the wardrobe. However, he got into bed, and after a little while fell into a deep sleep; his fire was burning brightly, and the room was quite light.

Shortly after four he was awaken by a loud scream. Still sleepy, he did not for the moment locate the sound, thinking that it must have come from the street outside. But almost immediately afterwards he heard the report of a revolver fired twice in quick succession, and then, after a short pause, a third time.

The Archdeacon was terribly frightened. He did not know what had happened, and thought of armed burglars. For a time – he did not think it could have been more than a minute – fear held him motionless. Then with an effort he rose, lit the gas, and hurried on his clothes. As he was dressing, he heard a step down the passage and a knock at his door.

He opened it, and found Breddon's servant. The man had put on a blue overcoat over his night-things, and wore slippers. He was shivering with cold and terror.

'Oh, my God, sir!' he exclaimed, 'Mr Breddon's shot himself. Would you come, sir?'

The Archdeacon followed the man to Breddon's bedroom. The smoke still hung thickly in the room. A mirror had been smashed, and lay in fragments on the floor. On the bed, with his back to the Archdeacon, lay Breddon, dead. His right hand still grasped the revolver, and there was a blackened wound behind his right ear.

When the Archdeacon came round to look at the face he turned faint, and the servant took him out into the library and gave him brandy, the glasses and decanters still standing there. Breddon's face certainly had looked very ghastly; it had been scratched, torn and bitten; one eye was gone, and the whole face was covered with blood.

'Do you think it was that brute did it?'

'Sure of it, sir; sprang on his face while he was asleep. I knew it would happen one of these nights. He knew it too; always slept with the revolver by his side. He fired twice at the brute, but couldn't see for the blood. Then he killed himself.'

It seemed likely enough, with his eyesight gone, horribly mauled, in an agony of pain, possibly believing that he was saving himself from a death still more horrible, Breddon might very well have turned the weapon on himself.

'What do we do now?' the man asked.

'We must get a doctor and fetch the police at once. Come on.'

As they turned the corner of the passage, they saw that the door communicating with the staircase was open.

'Did you open that door?' asked the Archdeacon.

'No,' said the man, aghast.

'Then who did?'

'Don't know, sir. Looks as if we aren't at the end of this yet.'

They passed down the stairs together, and found the street-door also ajar. On the pavement outside lay a policeman slowly recovering consciousness. Breddon's man took the policeman's whistle and blew it. A passing hansom, going back to the mews, slowed up; the cab was sent to fetch a doctor, and communication with the police station rapidly followed.

The injured policeman told a curious story. He was passing the house when he heard shots fired. Almost immediately afterwards he heard the bolts of the front-door being drawn, and stepped back into the neighbouring doorway. The front-door opened, and a negro emerged clad in a gray tweed suit with a gray overcoat. The policeman jumped out, and without a second's hesitation the black man felled him. 'It was all done before you could think,' was the policeman's phrase.

'What kind of negro?' asked the Archdeacon.

'A big man – stood over six foot, and black as coal. He never waited to be challenged; the moment he knew that he was seen he hit out.'

The policeman was not a very intelligent fellow, and there was little more to be got out of him. He had heard the shots, seen the street-door open and the man in gray appear, and had been felled by a lightning blow before he had time to do anything.

The doctor, a plain, matter-of-fact little man, had no hesitation in saying that Breddon was dead, and must have died immediately. After the injuries received, respiration and heart-action must have ceased at once. He was explaining something which oozed from the dead man's ear, when the

Archdeacon could stand it no longer, and staggered out into the library. There he found Breddon's servant, still in the blue overcoat, explaining to a policeman with a notebook that as far as he knew nothing was missing except a jade image or idol of a cat which formerly stood on the mantelpiece.

The cat known as 'Gray Devil' was also missing, and, although a description of it was circulated in the public press, nothing was ever heard of it again. But gray fur was found in the clenched left hand of the dead man.

The inquest resulted in the customary verdict, and brought to light no new facts. But it may be as well to give what the police theory of the case was. According to the police the suicide took place much as Breddon's servant had supposed. Mad with pain and unable to bear the thought of his awful mutilation, Breddon had shot himself.

The story of the jade image, as far as it was known, was told at the inquest. The police held that this image was an idol, that some uncivilized tribe was much perturbed by the theft of it, and was ready to pay an enormously high price for its recovery. The negro was assumed to be aware of this, and to have determined to obtain possession of the idol by fair means or foul. Fair means failing, it was suggested that the negro followed Breddon to England, tracked him out, and on the night in question found some means to conceal himself in Breddon's flat. There it was assumed that he fell asleep, was awakened by the screams and the sound of the firing, being scared, caught up the jade image and made off. Realizing that the shots would have been heard outside, and that his departure at that moment would be considered extremely suspicious, he was ready as he opened the street-door to fell the first man that he saw. The temporary unconsciousness of the policeman gave him time to get away.

The theory sounds at first sight like the only possible theory. When the Archdeacon first told me the story I tried to find out indirectly whether he accepted it. Finding him rather disposed to fence with my hints and suggestions, I put the question to him plainly and bluntly:

'Do you believe in the police theory?'

He hesitated, and then answered with complete frankness:

'No, most emphatically not.'

'Why?' I asked; and he went over the evidence with me.

'In the first place, I do not believe that Breddon, in the ordinary sense, committed suicide. No amount of physical pain would have made him even think of it. He had unending pluck. He would have taken the facial disfigurement and loss of sight as the chances of war, and would have done the best that could be done by a man with such awful disabilities. One must admit that he fired the fatal shot – the medical evidence on that point is too strong to be gainsaid – but he fired it under circumstances of supernatural horror of which we, thank God! know nothing.'

'I'm naturally slow to admit supernatural explanation.'

'Well, let's go on. What's this mysterious tribe the police talk about? I want to know where it lives and what its name is. It's wealthy enough to offer a huge reward; it must be of some importance. The negro managed to get in and secrete himself. How? Where? I know the flat, and that theory won't do. We don't even know that it was the negro who took that little image, though I believe it was. Anyhow, how did the negro get away at that hour of the morning absolutely unobserved? Negroes are not so common in London that they can walk about without being noticed; yet not one trace of him was ever found, and equally mysterious is the disappearance of the Gray Cat. It was such an extraordinary brute, and the description of it was so widely circulated that it would have seemed almost certain we should hear of it again. Well, we've not heard.'

We discussed the police theory for some little time, and something which he happened to say led me to exclaim:

'Really! Do you mean to say that the Gray Cat actually was the negro?'

'No,' he replied, 'not exactly that, but something near it. Cats are strange animals, anyhow. I needn't remind you of their connection with certain old religions or with that witchcraft in which even in England today some still believe, and not so long ago almost all believed. I have never, by the way, seen a good explanation of the fact that there are people who cannot bear to be in the room with a cat, and are aware of its presence as if by some mysterious extra sense. Let me remind you of the belief which undoubtedly exists both in China and Japan, that evil spirits may enter into certain of the lower animals, the fox and badger especially. Every student of demonology knows about these things.'

'But that idea of evil spirits taking possession of cats or foxes is surely a heathen superstition which you cannot hold.'

'Well, I have read of the evil spirits that entered into the swine. Think it over, and keep an open mind.'

The unusual spelling of 'gray' (with an 'a') is as the story was first published and has been retained here. H.L.

THE DANCING PARTNER

Jerome K. Jerome

'This story,' commenced MacShaugnassy, 'comes from Furtwangen, a small town in the Black Forest. There lived there a very wonderful old fellow named Nicholaus Geibel. His business was the making of mechanical toys, at which work he had acquired an almost European reputation. He made rabbits that would emerge from the heart of a cabbage, flop their ears, smooth their whiskers, and disappear again; cats that would wash their faces, and mew so naturally that dogs would mistake them for real cats, and fly at them; dolls, with phonographs concealed within them, that would raise their hats and say, "Good morning; how do you do?" and some that would even sing a song.

'But he was something more than a mere mechanic; he was an artist. His work was with him a hobby, almost a passion. His shop was filled with all manner of strange things that never would, or could, be sold – things he had made for the pure love of making them. He had contrived a mechanical donkey that would trot for two hours by means of stored electricity, and trot, too, much faster than the live article, and with less need for exertion on the part of the driver; a bird that would shoot up into the air, fly round and round in a circle, and drop to earth at the exact spot from where it started; a skeleton that, supported by an upright iron bar, would dance a hornpipe; a life-size lady doll that could play the fiddle; and a gentleman with a hollow inside who could smoke a pipe and drink more lager beer that any three average German students put together, which is saying much.

'Indeed, it was the belief of the town that old Geibel could make a man capable of doing everything that a respectable man need want to do. One day he made a man who did too much, and it came about this way:

'Young Doctor Follen had a baby, and the baby had a birthday. Its first birthday put Doctor Follen's household into somewhat of a flurry, but on the occasion of its second birthday, Mrs Doctor Follen gave a ball in honour of the event. Old Geibel and his daughter Olga were among the guests.

'During the afternoon of the next day some three or four of Olga's bosom friends, who had also been present at the ball, dropped in to have a chat about it. They naturally fell to discussing the men, and to criticizing their dancing. Old Geibel was in the room, but he appeared to be absorbed in his newspaper, and the girls took no notice of him.

'"There seem to be fewer men who can dance at every ball you go to," said one of the girls.

'"Yes, and don't the one's who can give themselves airs," said another; "they make quite a favour of asking you."

'"And how stupidly they talk," added a third, "They always say exactly the same things: 'How charming you are looking tonight.' 'Do you often go to Vienna? Oh, you should, it's delightful.' 'What a charming dress you have on.' 'What a warm day it has been.' 'Do you like Wagner?' I do wish they'd think of something new."

'"Oh, I never mind how they talk," said a fourth. "If a man dances well he may be a fool for all I care."

'"He generally is," slipped in a thin girl, rather spitefully.

'"I go to a ball to dance," continued the previous speaker, not noticing the interruption. "All I ask of a partner is that he shall hold me firmly, take me round steadily, and not get tired before I do."

'"A clockwork figure would be the thing for you," said the girl who had interrupted.

'"Bravo!" cried one of the others, clapping her hands, "what a capital idea!"

'"What's a capital idea?" they asked.

'"Why, a clockwork dancer, or, better still, one that would go by electricity and never run down."

'The girls took up the idea with enthusiasm.

'"Oh, what a lovely partner he would make," said one; "he would never kick you, or tread on your toes."

'"Or tear your dress," said another.

'"Or get out of step."

'"Or get giddy and lean on you."

'"And he would never want to mop his face with his handkerchief. I do hate to see a man do that after every dance."

'"And wouldn't want to spend the whole evening in the supper room."

'"Why, with a phonograph inside him to grind out all the stock remarks, you would not be able to tell him from a real man," said the girl who had suggested the idea.

'"Oh, yes, you would," said the thin girl, "he would be so much nicer."

'Old Geibel had laid down his paper, and was listening with both his ears. On one of the girls glancing in his direction, however, he hurriedly hid himself again behind it.

'After the girls were gone, he went to his workshop, where Olga heard him walking up and down, and every now and then chuckling to himself; and that night he talked to her a good deal about dancing men – asked what they usually said and did – what dances were most popular – what steps were gone through, with many other questions bearing on the subject.

'Then for a couple of weeks he kept much to his factory, and was very thoughtful and busy, though prone at unexpected moments to break into a quiet low laugh, as if enjoying a joke that nobody else knew of.

'A month later another ball took place in Furtwangen. On this occasion it was given by old Wenzel, the wealthy timber merchant, to celebrate his niece's betrothal, and Geibel and his daughter were again among the invited.

'When the hour arrived to set out, Olga sought her father. Not finding him in the house, she tapped at the door of his workshop. He appeared in his shirt-sleeves, looking hot but radiant.

'"Don't wait for me," he said, "you go on, I'll follow you. I've got something to finish."

'As she turned to obey he called after her "Tell them I'm going to bring a young man with me – such a nice young man, and an excellent dancer. All the girls will like him." Then he laughed and closed the door.

'Her father generally kept his doings secret from everybody, but she had a pretty shrewd suspicion of what he had been planning, and so, to a certain extent, was able to prepare the guests for what was coming. Anticipation ran high, and the arrival of the famous mechanist was eagerly awaited.

'At length the sound of wheels was heard outside, followed by a great commotion in the passage, and old Wenzel himself burst into the room and announced in stentorian tones:

'"Herr Geibel – and a friend."

'Herr Geibel and his "friend" entered, greeted with shouts of laughter and applause, and advanced to the centre of the room.

'"Allow me, ladies and gentlemen," said Herr Geibel, "to introduce you to my friend, Lieutenant Fritz. Fritz, my dear fellow, bow to the ladies and gentlemen."

'Geibel placed his hand encouragingly on Fritz's shoulder, and the lieutenant bowed low, accompanying the action with a harsh clicking noise in his throat, unpleasantly suggestive of a death rattle. But that was only a detail.

'"He walks a little stiffly," (old Geibel took his arm and

walked him forward a few steps. He certainly did walk stiffly),
"but then, walking is not his forte. He is essentially a dancing
man. I have only been able to teach him the waltz as yet, but
at that he is faultless. Come, which of you ladies may I
introduce him to as a partner? He keeps perfect time; he
never gets tired; he won't kick you or tread on your dress; he
will hold you as firmly as you like, and go as quickly or as
slowly as you please; he never gets giddy; and he is full of
conversation. Come, speak up for yourself, my boy."

'The old gentleman twisted one of the buttons at the back
of his coat, and immediately Fritz opened his mouth, and in
thin tones that appeared to proceed from the back of his
head, remarked suddenly, "May I have the pleasure?" and
then shut his mouth again with a snap.

'That Lieutenant Fritz made a strong impression on the
company was undoubted, yet none of the girls seemed
inclined to dance with him. They looked askance at his
waxen face, with its staring eyes and fixed smile, and
shuddered. At last old Geibel came to Annette, the girl who
had conceived the idea.

'"It is your own suggestion, carried out to the letter," said
Geibel, "an electric dancer. You owe it the the gentleman to
give him a trial."

'She was a bright, saucy little girl, fond of a frolic. Her host
added his entreaties, and she consented.

'Herr Geibel fixed the figure to her. Its right arm was
screwed round her waist, and held her firmly: its delicately
jointed left hand was made to fasten itself upon her right.
The old toymaker showed her how to regulate its speed, and
how to stop it, and release herself.

'"It will take you round in a complete circle," he explained;
"be careful that no one knocks against you, and alters its
course."

'The music struck up. Old Geibel put the current in motion,
and Annette and her strange partner began to dance.

'For a while everyone stood watching them. The figure

performed its purpose admirably. Keeping perfect time and step, and holding its little partner tight clasped in an unyielding embrace, it revolved steadily, pouring forth at the same time a constant flow of squeaky conversation, broken by brief intervals of grinding silence.

'"How charming you are looking tonight," it remarked in its thin, far-away voice. "What a lovely day it has been. Do you like dancing? How well our steps agree. You will give me another, won't you? Oh, don't be so cruel. What a charming gown you have on. Isn't waltzing delightful? I could go on dancing for ever – with you. Have you had supper?"

'As she grew more familiar with the uncanny creature, the girl's nervousness wore off, and she entered into the fun of the thing.

'"Oh, he's just lovely," she cried, laughing, "I could go on dancing with him all my life."

'Couple after couple now joined them, and soon all the dancers in the room were whirling round behind them. Nicholaus Geibel stood looking on, beaming with childish delight at his success.

'Old Wenzel approached him, and whispered something in his ear. Geibel laughed and nodded, and the two worked their way quietly towards the door.

'"This is the young people's house tonight." said Wenzel, as soon as they were outside; "you and I will have a quiet pipe and a glass of hock, over in the counting house."

'Meanwhile the dancing grew more fast and furious. Little Annette loosened the screw regulating her partner's rate of progress, and the figure flew round with her swifter and swifter. Couple after couple dropped out exhausted, but they only went the faster, till at length they remained dancing alone.

'Madder and madder became the waltz. The music lagged behind: the musicians, unable to keep pace, ceased and sat staring. The younger guests applauded, but the older faces began to grow anxious.

'"Hadn't you better stop, dear," said one of the women, "you'll make yourself so tired."

'But Annette did not answer.

'"I believe she's fainted," cried out a girl who had caught sight of her face as it was swept by.

'One of the men sprang forward and clutched at the figure, but its impetus threw him down on to the floor, where its steel-cased feet laid bare his cheek. The thing evidently did not intend to part with its prize easily.

'Had anyone retained a cool head, the figure, one cannot help thinking, might easily have been stopped. Two or three men acting in concert might have lifted it bodily off the floor, or have jammed it into a corner. But few human heads are capable of remaining cool under excitement. Those who are not present think how stupid must have been those who were; those who are reflect afterwards how simple it would have been to do this, that, or the other, if only they had thought of it at the time.

'The women grew hysterical. The men shouted contradictory directions to one another. Two of them made a bungling rush at the figure, which had the result of forcing it out of its orbit in the centre of the room, and sending it crashing against the walls and furniture. A stream of blood showed itself down the girl's white frock, and followed her along the floor. The affair was becoming horrible. The women rushed screaming from the room. The men followed them.

'One sensible suggestion was made; "Find Geibel – fetch Geibel."

'No one had noticed him leave the room, no one knew where he was. A party went in search of him. The others, too unnerved to go back into the ballroom, crowded outside the door and listened. They could hear the steady whir of the wheels upon the polished floor as the thing spun round and round; the dull thud as every now and again it dashed itself and its burden against some opposing object and ricocheted off in a new direction.

'And everlastingly it talked in that thin ghostly voice, repeating over and over the same formula: "How charming you are looking tonight. What a lovely day it has been. Oh, don't be so cruel. I could go on dancing for ever – with you. Have you had supper?"

'Of course they sought for Geibel everywhere but where he was. They looked in every room in the house, then they rushed off in a body to his own place, and spent precious minutes in waking up his deaf old housekeeper. At last it occurred to one of the party that Wenzel was missing also, and then the idea of the counting-house across the yard presented itself to them, and there they found him.

'He rose up, very pale, and followed them; and he and old Wenzel forced their way through the crowd of guests gathered outside, and entered the room, and locked the door behind them.

'From within there came the muffled sound of low voices and quick steps, followed by a confused scuffling noise, then silence, then the low voices again.

'After a time the door opened, and those near it pressed forward to enter, but old Wenzel's broad shoulders barred the way.

'"I want you – and you, Bekler," he said addressing a couple of the elder men. His voice was calm, but his face was deadly white. "The rest of you, please go – get the women away as quickly as you can."

'From that day old Nicholaus Geibel confined himself to the making of mechanical rabbits, and cats that mewed and washed their faces.'

AN ALPINE DIVORCE

Robert Barr

In some natures there are no half-tones; nothing but raw primary colours. John Bodman was a man who was always at one extreme or the other. This probably would have mattered little had he not married a wife whose nature was an exact duplicate of his own.

Doubtless there exists in this world precisely the right woman for any given man to marry, and vice versa; but when you consider that a human being has the opportunity of being acquainted with only a few hundred people, and out of the few hundred that there are but a dozen or less whom he knows intimately, and out of the dozen, one or two friends at most, it will easily be seen, when we remember the number of millions who inhabit this world, that probably, since the earth was created, the right man has never yet met the right woman. The mathematical chances are all against such a meeting, and this is the reason that divorce courts exist. Marriage at best is but a compromise, and if two people happen to be united who are of an uncompromising nature there is trouble.

In the lives of these two young people there was no middle distance. The result was bound to be either love or hate, and in the case of Mr and Mrs Bodman it was hate of the most bitter and arrogant kind.

In some parts of the world incompatibility of temper is considered a just cause for obtaining a divorce, but in England no such subtle distinction is made, and so, until the wife became criminal, or the man became both criminal and cruel, these two were linked together by a bond that only death could sever. Nothing can be worse than this state of things, and the matter was only made the more hopeless by the fact that Mrs Bodman lived a blameless life, and her husband was no worse, but rather better, than the majority of men. Perhaps, however, that statement held only up to a certain point, for John Bodman had reached a state of mind in which he resolved to get rid of his wife at all hazards. If he had been a poor man he would probably have deserted her, but he was rich, and a man cannot freely leave a prospering business because his domestic life happens not to be happy.

When a man's mind dwells too much on any one subject, no one can tell just how far he will go. The mind is a delicate instrument, and even the law recognizes that it is easily thrown from its balance. Bodman's friends – for he had friends – claim that his mind was unhinged; but neither his friends nor his enemies suspected the truth of the episode, which turned out to be the most important, as it was the most ominous, event in his life.

Whether John Bodman was sane or insane at the time he made up his mind to murder his wife will never be known, but there was certainly craftiness in the method he devised to make the crime appear the result of an accident. Nevertheless, cunning is often a quality in a mind that has gone wrong.

Mrs Bodman well knew how much her presence afflicted her husband, but her nature was as relentless as his, and her hatred of him was, if possible, more bitter than his hatred of her. Wherever he went she accompanied him, and perhaps the idea of murder would never have occurred to him if she had not been so persistent in forcing her presence upon him at all times and on all occasions. So, when he announced to her that he intended to spend the month of July in

Switzerland, she said nothing, but made her preparations for the journey. On this occasion he did not protest, as was usual with him, and so to Switzerland this silent couple departed.

There is an hotel near the mountain-tops which stands on a ledge over one of the great glaciers. It is a mile and a half above the level of the sea, and it stands alone, reached by a toilsome road that zigzags up the mountain for six miles. There is a wonderful view of snow-peaks and glaciers from the verandahs of this hotel, and in the neighbourhood are many picturesque walks to points more or less dangerous.

John Bodman knew the hotel well, and in happier days he had been intimately acquainted with the vicinity. Now that the thought of murder arose in his mind, a certain spot two miles distant from this inn continually haunted him. It was a point of view overlooking everything, and its extremity was protected by a low and crumbling wall. He arose one morning at four o'clock, slipped unnoticed out of the hotel, and went to this point, which was locally named the Hanging Outlook. His memory had served him well. It was exactly the spot, he said to himself. The mountain which rose up behind it was wild and precipitous. There were no inhabitants near to overlook the place. The distant hotel was hidden by the shoulder of rock. The mountains on the other side of the valley were too far away to make it possible for any casual tourist or native to see what was going on on the Hanging Outlook. Far down in the valley the only town in view seemed like a collection of little toy houses.

One glance over the crumbling wall at the edge was generally sufficient for a visitor of even the strongest nerves. There was a sheer drop of more than a mile straight down, and at the distant bottom were jagged rocks and stunted trees that looked, in the blue haze, like shrubbery.

'This is the spot,' said the man to himself, 'and tomorrow morning is the time.'

John Bodman had planned his crime as grimly and relentlessly, and as coolly, as ever he had concocted a deal on the Stock Exchange. There was no thought in his mind of mercy for his unconscious victim. His hatred had carried him far.

The next morning after breakfast, he said to his wife: 'I intend to take a walk in the mountains. Do you wish to come with me?'

'Yes,' she answered briefly.

'Very well, then,' he said; 'I shall be ready at nine o'clock.'

'I shall be ready at nine o'clock,' she repeated after him.

At that hour they left the hotel together, to which he was shortly to return alone. They spoke no word to each other on their way to the Hanging Outlook. The path was practically level, skirting the mountains, for the Hanging Outlook was not much higher above the sea than the hotel.

John Bodman had formed no fixed plan for his procedure when the place was reached. He resolved to be guided by circumstances. Now and then a strange fear arose in his mind that she might cling to him and possibly drag him over the precipice with her. He found himself wondering whether she had any premonition of her fate, and one of his reasons for not speaking was the fear that a tremor in his voice might possibly arouse her suspicions. He resolved that his action should be sharp and sudden, that she might have no chance either to help herself, or to drag him with her. Of her screams in that desolate region he had no fear. No one could reach the spot except from the hotel, and no one that morning had left the house, even for an expedition to the glacier – one of the easiest and most popular trips from the place.

Curiously enough, when they came within the sight of the Hanging Outlook, Mrs Bodman stopped and shuddered. Bodman looked at her through the narrow slits of his veiled eyes, and wondered again if she had any suspicion. No one can tell, when two people walk closely together, what unconscious communication one mind may have with another.

'What is the matter?' he asked gruffly. 'Are you tired?'

'John,' she cried, with a gasp in her voice, calling him by his Christian name for the first time in years, 'don't you think that if you had been kinder to me at first, things might have been different?'

'It seems to me,' he answered, not looking at her, 'that it is rather late in the day for discussing that question.'

'I have much to regret,' she said quaveringly. 'Have you nothing?'

'No,' he answered.

'Very well,' replied his wife, with the usual hardness returning to her voice. 'I was merely giving you a chance. Remember that.'

Her husband looked at her suspiciously.

'What do you mean?' he asked, 'giving me a chance? I want no chance nor anything else from you. A man accepts nothing from one he hates. My feeling towards you is, I imagine, no secret to you. We are tied together, and you have done your best to make the bondage insupportable.'

'Yes,' she answered, with her eyes on the ground, 'we are tied together – we are tied together!'

She repeated these words under her breath as they walked the few remaining steps to the Outlook. Bodman sat down upon the crumbling wall. The woman dropped her alpenstock on the rock, and walked nervously to and fro, clasping and unclasping her hands. Her husband caught his breath as the terrible moment drew near.

'Why do you walk about like a wild animal?' he cried. 'Come here and sit down beside me, and be still.'

She faced him with a light he had never before seen in her eyes – a light of insanity and of hatred.

'I walk like a wild animal,' she said, 'because I am one. You spoke a moment ago of your hatred of me; but you are a man, and your hatred is nothing to mine. Bad as you are, much as you wish to break the bond which ties us together, there are still things which I know you would not stoop to. I know there is no thought of murder in your heart, but there is in mine. I will show you, John Bodman, how much I hate you.'

The man nervously clutched the stone beside him, and gave a guilty start as she mentioned murder.

'Yes,' she continued, 'I have told all my friends in England that I believed you intended to murder me in Switzerland.'

'Good God!' he cried. 'How could you say such a thing?'

'I say it to show how much I hate you – how much I am prepared to give for revenge. I have warned the people at the hotel, and when we left two men followed us. The proprietor tried to persuade me not to accompany you. In a few moments those two men will come in sight of the Outlook. Tell them, if you think they will believe you, that it was an accident.'

The mad woman tore from the front of her dress shreds of lace and scattered them around.

Bodman started up to his feet, crying, 'What are you about?' But before he could move toward her she precipitated herself over the wall, and went shrieking and whirling down the awful abyss.

The next moment two men came hurriedly round the edge of the rock, and found the man standing alone. Even in his bewilderment he realized that if he told the truth he would not be believed.

THE MYSTERY OF
BLACK ROCK CREEK

INTRODUCTION

To round off the book, here is a long lost Idler *classic, making its first appearance in book form after 123 years.*

'The Mystery of Black Rock Creek', from the October 1894 issue of The Idler, *is a narrative in sequence, a literary exercise not seen very often nowadays, but well known in Victorian times.*

One author starts the story, another writes the next chapter and so on, until the poor writer at the end has to clear it all up. Perhaps they drew lots to establish the order – if so, Barry Pain drew the short straw but he coped manfully.

Jerome K. Jerome starts off (editor's privilege?) and then future famous thriller and fantasy writer Eden Phillpotts takes over. Next is E.F. Benson, who had just published his first novel, followed by Frank Frankfort Moore (Bram Stoker's brother-in-law and enjoying great success that year). Finally, Barry Pain gets to sort it all out, with a gruesome flourish at the end.

'The Mystery of Black Rock Creek' is a splendid coda to this collection. I hope you enjoy it.

CHAPTER I

Jerome K. Jerome

'How did he come here?'

'By the coach this evening. They found him lying in the road by Jenkins' Claim, and brought him on.'

'And you don't know who he is, nor anything about him?'

'Nothing. He was quite unconscious when they picked him up, and has remained so ever since.'

The Doctor thrust his hands into his trousers-pockets, and stood regarding the unconscious heap of humanity before him with an expression of profound thought. He was puzzling out to himself what answers to make should the Barkeeper become inquisitive as to details, and clamour to know what was the particular ailment that made the stranger so curiously silent. The medical fraternity found practising in the Australian bush are not as a rule the pick of the profession.

'Do you think there's any hope for him?' asked the Barkeeper, at last.

'Difficult to say,' was the diplomatic, but, so far as 'Doctor' Millett himself was personally concerned, most truthful reply. 'If he has a good constitution he may pull through. Or,' added the prudent Doctor, feeling the necessity of not committing himself to a one-sided opinion, 'he may die tonight.'

'Not very pleasant for me if he dies here,' grumbled the

Barkeeper, with a comprehensive glance round the dismal shanty, that served himself for living room and sleeping apartment, and the scattered miners of Black Rock Creek for their one centre of social entertainment.

The silent stranger by a convulsive shiver slipped the pillows from beneath him, so that his head fell with a bump upon the rude bench where he lay stretched. The Doctor raised him in his arms.

'I'll call at the hut as I pass,' he said quietly, as he withdrew his arm from around the man's waist, 'and send the Inspector down. Meanwhile I'll get you to take this to my place. My man will make it up for you. Get back as quickly as you can.'

He scribbled, while speaking, a prescription, and, tearing out the leaf from his pocket-book, held it out to the Barkeeper.

The man took it but stood hesitating.

'Who's to look after him?' he asked, jerking his thumb in the direction of the sick man.

The Doctor pushed a couple of the heavy chairs against the bench, and arranged the pillows to slightly better advantage.

'You'll find him here when you return,' he answered. 'No possible change can take place in him.'

'Yes, but there can in my bar,' returned the other sulkily; 'somebody will be walking in and helping himself.'

The Doctor laughed. 'To your whiskey, Raynham! He won't take a second dose. Beside, who's likely to walk in? The boys are gone, and there aren't many chance customers knocking about Black Rock Creek of a night, are there?'

The man seemed but half persuaded.

'Well, you can never tell, and—'

'Ah, well, it must be done,' was the impatient interruption; 'I wouldn't ask you if I could go myself, but I can't. Pat Joyce's wife is dying the other side of the Creek and I must run over there. You can take the mare, I'll walk. You'll be back before I am if you're quick.'

As the simplest way to end the argument, the Doctor picked up his hat and went out. The Barkeeper, left alone, stood thinking.

Suddenly his lips parted with an exclamation.

'Why the devil didn't I think of it before,' he muttered; 'no wonder he's in such a hurry to have the police here.'

Taking the dirt-encrusted lantern from the shelf, he bent down above the prostrate form upon the bench; but at that moment the Doctor's figure reappeared in the open doorway, and the Doctor's voice cried angrily to him to make haste.

'Damn him,' growled the man; 'I suppose he'll watch till I'm off.'

He seized an old shawl, which he wrapped about his shoulders, for the night was cold, and plunged into the darkness.

It was well for man and beast that the Doctor's mare knew every hole and boulder of the ill-laid road, for the Barkeeper rode hard through the black night.

'Gentleman Jock,' ex-financier, ex-miner, ex-jockey, ex-dead-beat, who now served the Doctor in the mixed capacity of medical assistant, groom, and cook, remarked upon the ill-concealed impatience with which he paced the verandah while the simple prescription of quinine and brandy, ventured upon by the bewildered Doctor, was being prepared, and was irritated by the same.

'It won't kill him, and it won't cure him,' he grunted as he rammed the cork down. 'One would fancy you were a young woman with your baby sick for the first time in its life.'

'I've took an interest in him,' answered the Barkeeper, dryly, as, pocketing the bottle, he flung himself back into the saddle.

'Well, I guess he ain't worth breaking the mare's neck over, whoever he may be, though your own mayn't much matter,' shouted Gentleman Jock after him, as in response to a vicious cut, the animal dashed down the steep incline. A long experience of both had given Gentleman Jock a higher opinion of horses than of men. He objected to the nobler animal being sacrificed to the exigencies of the less.

A hundred yards from his own door, the Barkeeper pulled up and dismounted. Throwing the bridle over his arm, he moved cautiously forward till close to the door of the hut, then paused and listened. No sound came from within. A feeble ray of light stole from the chink beneath the door, and struggled half-way across the road. The Barkeeper raised his head. The troubled panting of the horse, the whispering of the pines, were the only sounds that reached him. Fastening the mare, he raised the latch noiselessly, and peered in. A stranger watching him from the shadow of the pines beyond, would have taken him for a thief rather than for a man crossing his own threshold.

The sick man lay on the bench between the high-backed chairs and the wall. The Barkeeper could hear his steady breathing. It sounded easier and more regular. Closing the door behind him, he drew the bolt across softly, and, taking the lantern in his hand, crept up and passed its light backwards and forwards above the closed eyes.

The examination seemed to satisfy him, for, replacing the lantern on the table, he returned, and, moving the chairs out of his way, felt round the sick man's waist for the leathern belt that during the last half hour had been ceaselessly pirouetting and twirling in devilish dances before his eager eyes.

As his hands touched it, however, he paused. Hastily crossing to the window he drew carefully the tattered curtains over every inch of pane, then resumed with feverish haste his task. The sick man lay heavily, and it was necessary to move him to draw the belt away. Once a smothered sound escaped his lips, as if, in spite of the unconsciousness of his body, some watchful corner of his brain were protesting against the robbery. The Barkeeper waited with the sweat upon his hands and face, expecting the white eyelids to open, but no movement followed, and with a little more manœuvring, the belt fell heavily to the floor and lay coiled about the Barkeeper's feet.

He picked it up, and, taking it to the table, examined it by the dim light of the lantern. From every pocket as he opened it there poured forth gold. It made a glittering pile upon the rude table. The Barkeeper's hands caressed it lovingly, lingeringly. The yellow light from the lantern close to his cheek showed a gaping mouth wreathed round with fatuous smiles. In his utterly bestial excitement the saliva trickled down unheeded from his mouth on to the table.

Suddenly from the shadows behind him arose a hoarse, croaking cry as of some inarticulate thing struggling for a voice. The coins in his hand fell with a rattle on the floor and rolled away, and the cry crept round him again freezing his face into terror.

Slowly he turned his head to see a figure with two claw-like hands stretched out against him, to hear a voice he thought at first came from the dead, crying, 'Mine, mine.'

He remained spell-bound to his chair, and the figure tottered forward step by step, till with one out-thrust arm it touched his glittering heap.

The action roused the Barkeeper from his stupor. With a snarl as of an angry animal he flung himself upon the weak swaying thing. Seizing the shawl he had hastily unwrapped from his shoulders, he held it pressed against the sick man's face, stifling the thin cries. Slowly he forced him back to the bench still holding the shawl tight pressed about his head, till the feeble struggles ceased and the long arms fell listless to the floor. Then the Barkeeper unwound the shawl and looked at the dead face.

To hide the belt and gold, to replace the body naturally upon the bench was his next care. This done, he drew back the curtains from the window, and opening the door leant idly against it waiting.

He had completed his labour none too soon, for as he threw away the match that lighted his cigar the sound of footsteps reached him, and the figures of the Doctor and the Inspector drew away from the gloom and became distinct.

The Barkeeper was the first to speak.

'Dead,' he said curtly, as the Doctor stepped into the framework of the door.

'Dead! already?'

'I found him dead when I got back; I thought 't warn't the thing to leave him.'

The Doctor made no reply, but passed straight over to where the dead man lay. The Inspector closed the door.

The Doctor seemed strangely interested in his case, and it was some minutes before he spoke. Then he said quietly,—

'This man never died. He has been murdered.'

'It's a lie!' cried the Barkeeper. 'I tell you he was dead when I got back.'

'I tell you,' repeated the Doctor quietly, 'he has been murdered – poisoned.'

He took a glass from the shelf above the dead man's head – 'Poisoned with henbane. His whole body stinks of it. Why, there's enough left in the glass to have killed a dozen men.'

And the Barkeeper stood staring from the Doctor to the Inspector; and the Inspector, who was an officer of wide experience, said to himself, 'This man knows nothing of it, anyhow.'

CHAPTER II

Eden Phillpotts

The Barkeeper was the first to speak. He saw Fate had played into his hand and felt that the least he could do was to score the trick at once. So he spoke politely to the Inspector.

'I reckon it's one of two things, 'Spec. Either there came along somebody and done this devil's job while I was fetchin' the poor toad his physic, or else he done it himself. You see the shelf's within reach of his 'and. And if he woke up torn with thirst, and got his paw on a glass with liquid in it, maybe, in his mazed state, he'd a' sopped it up and never stopped to think.'

'What's the action of this 'ere stuff, Doctor?' asked the Inspector, not paying much attention to Raynham.

'Depends on how much he was given—'

'Or took,' suggested Raynham. 'Maybe, Doctor Millett,' he continued, 'you'll haul him over now, poor devil, and me an' 'Spec 'll bear witness of what you find. All that's known 'pears to be that the cove come by coach, that he told the driver to drop him by Flying Fox Corner, and that two hours later he was found insensible not a hundred yards from where he got off the coach by Jenkins' Claim.'

Doctor Millett had already begun to assist Inspector Mark. They removed the dead man's coat and waistcoat and, as they did so, from the pocket of the former dropped a letter.

This the Doctor took to the light and read, while Inspector Mark continued to strip the corpse.

'Listen,' said Millett presently, after reading the communication. 'Here's a mighty strange story. Blest if we ain't up to our necks in the tidiest mystery that ever made men scratch their heads in Black Rock Creek. Listen to this.' And he read the following communication:—

'Dear Ned, you'd better watch it pretty sharp and keep your weather eye lifting, for young Peterkin *hasn't panned out after all*. In fact the cuss is on his damned legs again and hopping round lively as a grig. Of course he don't know what you're playing at – not yet. But Sally's hardly to be trusted. Half a word from her and he'd be on your track like a bloodhound. Get rid of the stone at all costs. The dibs is your own and mine – you can just shovel them into the bank when you get to Sydney; but the stone's different. You'll have to take that to Europe. He looks at the quartz in the case and doesn't see the difference. But any day the cat may be out of the bag.

'Yours,

'T. F.'

'Not much light in that, I'm thinking,' commented Millett.

'Here's one glimmer of light, maybe, and only one,' said Inspector Mark. 'Look at this. 'Twas round his neck.'

He showed them a little bag made of soft chamois leather with a receptacle of about an inch in depth. It was hung upon a very delicate gold chain, next his skin; and it was empty. The Inspector said, 'That's about all I find. There ain't no big hunk of money as that letter alludes to, but there's a gold pencil-case in the waistcoat pocket, and a pipe and baccy and a few stray shillings and some cards done up in a bit of paper. The cards has "The Honble. Ralph Peterkin' on 'em."

'And yet if the letter is to be believed, this is one Ned or

Edward; the envelope is addressed certainly to the Honble. Ralph Peterkin. Moreover the letter is a month old.'

Doctor Millett turned to look at the dead man. He had been handsome in life and, whether blue-blooded or not, certainly showed an almost patrician cast of features.

'Shall you want to cut the cove up, Doctor?' asked Inspector Mark calmly.

'I think not. There is no need. But, of course, an official inquiry must be held. It is a difficult matter. We find him first insensible. Then he is left here by himself about an hour or more—'

'More,' said the Barkeeper.

'More. And Raynham comes back and finds him poisoned. You see, Raynham, a good deal depends on you. Mark must decide as to whether you're to be locked up or not. You say he was dead when you came back. I don't doubt it, but the law's bound to doubt everybody in a fix like this. It's clear this man was personating some chap called Ralph Peterkin. It's also clear, from the letter, that he had money of his own and a diamond or some precious stone stolen from somebody else. But neither gold nor diamond are on him now, though we can guess he had a diamond or something in that chamois leather bag.'

'We can't say as he 'ad them things on him when he come to my bar,' declared Raynham.

'No – so far as the diamond was concerned. But I'll swear he wore a heavy belt, for I felt it when I lifted him and put my arm round him. Where's that belt? Who took it off?' asked the Doctor.

'It's a mighty tangle, sure enough. I'll have to search the bar anyhow, Raynham,' said Mark. 'And I'll ask you to help me if it's all the same to you. There's a missing belt – see? Well, if I don't find that here it proves you honest anyway.'

'Or else deeper than we think you,' said Doctor Millett calmly. He did not trust Mr Raynham far.

Raynham scowled, but felt pretty comfortable and triumphant. He had hidden the belt and its contents under the floor of the room in which they stood. The rough board was nailed back in its place. Twenty detectives would hardly have pulled up the floor planking.

'Look in welcome, and I'll 'elp with all my 'eart,' said the Barkeeper. 'But if you asks me, I reckon belt and gold and diamond's all a-making tracks and leaving more space 'twixt them and this poor clay every minute of the night. It's twelve now. Him as broke in while I was away might be twenty mile off by this if he had a tidy horse.'

Inspector Mark made a thorough search by lantern light, but nothing rewarded it until its conclusion. Then he returned to the room in which the dead man lay.

'We've found nothing, Doc,' he said to Millett, who was still bending over the corpse.

'But I have, Mark. I was wrong. Henbane never killed this man. See, it is the bottle of the stuff that fell and broke and saturated his coat and shirt. The bottle was knocked from the shelf. It might have been by one of the rats that swarm here. The glass is dry at the rim and sides. It has not been moved. The henbane in it was poured out long ago. Why did not you mention that, Raynham?'

'I didn't think of it. I poured the stuff out, as you say, and soaked cheese in it for them same rats.'

'Well, it was not poison killed this man. An autopsy will be necessary now. I shall . . .'

He was interrupted in a manner very startling. Mark, still pursuing his search, had reached a tall cupboard at one corner of the room in which they were assembled. He threw it open and started violently back as he did so, for within it stood a woman – a pale, wild-eyed creature dressed in black – a stranger to them all.

'Who in God's name are you, and how did you get here?' asked Raynham, who first found his tongue.

'I can explain if you will listen,' she answered. 'I came by the coach which brought this unhappy man today. My name is Sarah Peterkin.'

CHAPTER III

E. F. Benson

Sarah Peterkin paused dramatically for a moment on the threshold of the high dark cupboard. She had not played leading lady in melodramatic tragedy on the boards of third-rate provincial theatres for nothing. Unexpected entrances into rooms where strangers were wrangling over dead bodies were in fact her *forte*, and had earned her the title of 'the divine Sarah' from more than one ingenious admirer.

The pause reached its artistic climax, and Sarah spoke again.

'I'll be stepping down,' she said.

The Inspector extended a somewhat grimy hand, and Sarah descended into the room.

'It was mighty stuffy in there,' she said, 'and I'll take a drink.'

Certainly the divine Sarah was in no hurry. She moved leisurely over to the bar and Raynham poured her out a glass of the maligned whiskey. Whether the fact that Raynham had not offered the Doctor any led to that gentleman's disparaging remark about it, or whether the divine Sarah's taste was less educated than his is doubtful; it is, however, perfectly certain that she drank it with gusto. It is also certain that she said a couple of words to Raynham as he qualified it for her, that a smile of intelligence crossed his usually unilluminated face, and that he nodded to her.

The Doctor threw a rug over the half-naked body, and waited patiently for the divine Sarah to finish her refection. That lady wiped her mouth with an exceedingly tidy lace-edged handkerchief, and turned to the company.

'Who stands treat?' she remarked.

The Doctor and Inspector made a show of feeling in their pockets, but Raynham interrupted.

'The loss is the bank's,' he said.

Sarah crossed the room and seated herself on the end of the bench where the corpse lay. The others felt that she was mistress of the situation, and waited for her to develop it.

'Seems to me,' she said, denuding herself, figuratively speaking, of the burden, 'that we'd just better have a talk over this matter. If this gentleman' – indicating the Inspector – 'would assume the part of High Jury, the witnesses – which is chiefly me – will lay the case before him. The Judge—'

The Doctor was considered a humorist of the first water by the higher circles in Black Rock Creek, and he decided to make a joke.

'Our unknown friend here will be the judge,' said he, pointing to the corpse.

Sarah did not laugh, but gave him a look out of the third act of 'La Tosca.'

'Exactly,' she said. 'Ned shall be the judge.'

There was a pause, and Sarah shifted her seat slightly and looked straight at the Doctor.

'The Honourable Edward Peterkin has taken his seat,' she remarked. 'The trial will now be commencing.'

For the second time that evening a gleam of intelligence shot across Raynham's face, but, ashamed of exhibiting such weakness, he instantly repressed it.

Sarah, who seemed to be doubling the parts of witness and judge, in the indisposition of the latter, turned and addressed, the jury, who was sitting cross-legged on a two-legged stool, and balancing it with much accuracy.

'I'm the wife of the judge's brother,' she said, 'and my name is the Honourable Sarah Peterkin, usually known as Sally. He married me last July; and as times were bad I remained behind in Dunkeld followin' the histrionic profession, and he went up to Broken Hill. He an' his brother – the Honourable Edward Peterkin, whom the jury sees his lordship before him – had a claim together. There was another woman up there, and I guess Ralph, that's my husband, felt lonesome without me, so he took up with her, which proceedin' was in bad taste.'

The Doctor here interpolated a remark.

'Dam' bad taste,' he said.

'You've not seen the other woman,' remarked Sarah, 'so not knowin' you can't say. Then Ralph and Ned between them got hold of Black Jack.'

'Who was Black Jack?' demanded the jury.

'Black Jack was a big diamond, comin' from up country, being white by nature. Ned and Ralph quarrelled over Black Jack, and what between Black Jack and the other woman, there was, you may say, bad blood between them, as Ned said Ralph was a married man, an' ought to know better, whereas he was untrammelled, an' was lookin' out for a wife himself. An' so they parted, Ned having got hold of Black Jack by fair means or foul – knowin' Ned well, I should say foul – and Ralph followed him down to Dunkeld, swearin' and ragin' round. Then he lost sight of him, an' here Ned lies. An' the question before the jury is who killed Ned, and where's Black Jack? I've been in that black bathing machine in the corner an hour or more, and kin form a guess or two about it. An' now the other witnesses will say what they know. Also there was a belt of dibs round Ned's waist. That's a matter of less importance, there bein' only a hundred or so of them, and Black Jack was worth fifty of these belts. Black Jack, I may say, was on Ned when he was brought into this house.'

'How do you know?' asked the jury.

''Cause I saw it.'

The humorous Doctor found it hard to break himself of a habit which had become inveterate.

'Them as sees believes,' he remarked, jocosely.

The divine Sarah favoured him with another look.

'Give your evidence,' she said, 'an' don't scatter insperions over others. Wait till the jury an' the judge has had an opportunity of scatterin' insperions over your remarks.'

The Doctor spat thoughtfully on the floor.

'I was coming up from Jenkins' claim this evening,' he said, 'and was told there was a man lyin' here deadly sick. I saw him, and sent Raynham to my house with a prescription, while I went to see another case over the creek. I came back here, with the jury, and found the corpse lying dead. Raynham had already returned and was alone in the house.'

Sarah looked impartially at all the witnesses in turn.

'You forget the lady in the cupboard,' she said.

The Doctor disregarded the interruption, and went on.

'I have since learned there was a lady in the cupboard,' he said. 'The corpse had a belt on when I left the house, and the belt was missing when I came back. The lady assures me also that he had a diamond on him when he was brought here, and that also is missing now. And that,' he remarked gaily, 'closes the case for the prosecution.'

'For the defence,' said the divine Sarah.

'How do you make out that?' asked the last witness.

Sarah stood up.

'You've given your defence very well,' she said, 'but it's a little incomplete in detail. The third witness, Mr Raynham, will now give his evidence, which no doubt will supply some little deficiencies in yours, an' I shall have the pleasure of collaboratin' him.'

'Corroborate,' suggested the jury, tentatively.

'Corroborate or collaborate, it's all one,' said Sarah.

But before Mr Raynham had time to get on his feet the door opened, and the divine Sarah emitted a sound which partook of the nature of a gurgle, a scream, and a gasp, and which if she had produced it on the stage would have made her ingenious admirers think her even diviner than ever.

CHAPTER IV

F. Frankfort Moore

The door had opened slowly. It remained ajar for the few seconds during which that singularly complex vocal effort was made by the woman, and then it closed quickly. But Sarah's eyes continued glaring at the roughly-planed boards that constituted the panels of the door. She glared, then gave a gasp – such a glare and such a gasp would have made her fortune on the boards of those theatres in England which make a speciality of those potent elements of histrionic art, the glare and the gasp. Then she staggered back a step or two, and in another instant she had snatched the covering from the face of the corpse. She bent her face down to that face – the Inspector could not at that moment have said which of the two was the more ghastly – scrutinising it eagerly. Still keeping her eyes fixed upon the eyes that stared glassily up from the bench to the rough beams of the roof, she put out her arm and felt along the wall until she had grasped the tin lantern with the guttering candle inside it – the sole illumination of the place. She swung it down to the dead face, so that a wave of sickly light swept over the pallid, rigid features.

A crash, and then darkness followed.

She had let the lantern fall, and she herself had dropped upon the end of the bench, without a cry.

'What the blazes!' shouted the Inspector, leaping to his feet and striking a match, which he sheltered from the many draughts of the 'shanty' with his capacious hands, while the Doctor groped for the lantern and endeavoured to set up the candle once more. 'What the blazes do you mean by dropping the glim?'

'Isn't it something like contempt of Court, my lass?' said the facetious physician, replacing the freshly-lighted lantern.

The Barkeeper said nothing. He shifted a foot or two in the direction of the door.

'Heavens above!' muttered the woman. 'Oh, heavens above! What does this mean?'

'That's just what we want to know, my fine lady,' said the Inspector. 'What did you see at the door?'

The three men had been so seated that the door had opened upon them, thus preventing them from seeing through the entrance. The woman alone had been in a position to see by whom the door had been opened.

'Come, madam,' said the Doctor; 'Remember the important official position you occupy – remember what's due to the honourable Court. What the Lord Chancellor did you see at the door?'

Sarah looked at the speaker, then at the Inspector, and lastly at Raynham.

'What did I see? – what did I see? Is that what you ask me?' she said.

'That was the inquiry of the Court, madam,' said the Doctor, with a very humorous bow.

'I'll tell you what I saw, though you'll call me a liar,' said she.

'Very probably,' remarked the Inspector dryly.

'Oh, no, no; couldn't think of such unpoliteness,' said the Doctor.

The Barkeeper said nothing; only he got a foot nearer to the door.

'The door opened – you saw it; though, being on the off side, you couldn't see out,' said she.

'That's true, any way,' acquiesced the Inspector.

'Inspector Mark couldn't inspect or mark anything,' said the facetious physician.

'What did you see?' cried the Inspector.

'Him!' cried the woman, starting to her feet and pointing to the corpse. 'I saw him at the door.'

'The dead man? I reckon that's a whopper,' said the Inspector. 'He didn't budge.'

'I saw him – him!' cried the woman. 'He opened the door and stood there for a moment – long enough! – the light shone upon his face. He gave me a look – a look that I understood well – too well – a look that said, "Denounce my murderer! Denounce my murderer!" I obey that voice. Dick Raynham, I denounce you in the presence of witnesses as the murderer of this man!'

She swept round and pointed a melodramatic finger at the Barkeeper.

In a second he was pointing something at her – not a finger, but the barrel of a revolver. The flash of the light on the steel, the sound of the shot, the shriek of the woman, and the crash of the bullet into the centre of the tin lantern, occupied but one second. The next, the Inspector and the Doctor had fired their revolvers on chance in the direction of the door.

The bullets went into the open air.

The door was open and Dick Raynham had escaped.

'Follow him – follow him, if you are men!' yelled the woman. 'You cowards! give me a shootin' iron and I'll follow him myself.'

'Keep your back hair on,' said the Inspector. 'The troopers will have heard the shootin', and if we don't have our hands on him in half-an-hour they'll do for him. Come along, Doc. He's sure to make for the gulch.'

The two men hurried out into the starlit night, the Inspector mounting his horse, which he had hitched outside, and the Doctor getting astride his wiry little mare.

They galloped across the cleared scrub in the direction of

the notorious Choke-neck Gulch – a wild gully just above Black Rock Creek, which had for years constituted a place of refuge for such members of the criminal population of the neighbourhood as had overstepped the boundary of discretion in some moment of excitement.

The entrance to the gulch was by a narrow path, and on this path the two horsemen pulled up.

'We're here a bit ahead of him,' remarked the Inspector. 'There's no way that he could reach here sooner, unless he flew, and that's not Dick's form.'

'No; he's a good liar but a bad flyer,' said the humorous medico.

'He'll have to fly if he wants to escape our revolvers,' said the Inspector. 'He'll walk into our arms. Eh, what's that? Listen. By the Lord Harry, he has got a horse and is coming straight for us! Keep well in cover, Doc, and we'll cry "Bail up!" before he can whip out his iron.'

This programme was rigidly carried out. The horses were backed among the rocks, and each of the men cocked his revolver and waited silently, while the sound of galloping hoofs became more distinct. In a few minutes the horseman was within twenty yards of the entrance, and then the Inspector and the Doctor forced their horses out, shouting 'Bail up! my lad!' as they covered the newcomer with their revolvers.

He threw his horse on its haunches.

'Hallo, Inspector; what's all this?' he cried.

The man was one of the Inspector's troopers.

'What, Stanley? Good!' said the Inspector. 'Man, we took you for the fellow we're in search of.'

'I heard the shots,' said the trooper, 'and I guessed that there was something bright going on. I looked in at the saloon and saw Raynham.'

'Saw whom?' the Inspector shouted.

'Raynham. Was it a murder do you think?'

'You mean to say that you saw Raynham in the shanty?'

'Of course I did.'

Without another word the Inspector sent his horse forward with a bound. He galloped back to the shanty that passed by the name of the saloon, the other two following him. They all dismounted at the open door, the Inspector entering with his revolver in his hand.

A candle was burning, stuck in the neck of a bottle, and its light showed that the place was empty; only along the bench the body was lying.

'Now where's the man you said you left here?' the Inspector asked of the trooper.

'Where? Why there, to be sure; where else would he be?' said the trooper.

He jerked his thumb in the direction of the body on the bench.

'You're a fool,' said the Inspector. 'That's Great Lord Harry! What's this, anyway?'

He snatched up the bottle and held the light close to the dead man's face.

'Great Lord! great Lord!' he said.

It was the Barkeeper, Dick Raynham, who was lying dead on the bench in the very place that had been occupied by the man whom he had robbed and murdered.

CHAPTER V

Barry Pain

The Doctor examined carefully the body of the dead man. The face of the corpse was distorted and looked horrible in the candle-light.

'Shot?' said the Inspector laconically.

'No,' replied the Doctor.

'Then how?'

'I can't say yet. It's a queer case – looks to me as if he'd died from some shock – from a fright.'

'Where's the other corpse?' said the Inspector. 'And where's the woman? She was a clever 'un that woman was.' He took up the candle and walked to the cupboard. It was empty. In returning to the bench, he stumbled and fell; his foot had caught in a hole in the flooring, a board had been up and not replaced. 'See that!' said the Inspector as he re-lit the candle.

'Yes; what does it mean?'

'It means that *pro tem* we've been done. That was where the bilk was hidden, and I don't like being done, even *pro tem*. Stanley, be off, and bring a couple of men to watch here. Then when you come back, you and I will go and search for that woman in the gulch. We must get her – she's at the bottom of this. Will you come with us, Doctor?'

The Doctor shook his head. 'No,' he said. 'I've had enough of this, I'm off home.' After a little more talk with the Inspector, he mounted his horse and rode off. About a couple of hundred yards away he thought that he heard voices in the brushwood by the side of the road. He pulled up short. All was silent, and he rode on again.

If he had pursued his investigations further he would have found something. He would have found the dead body of Ned Peterkin, and on one side of it, seated with her knees drawn up to her chin, the Hon. Mrs Ralph Peterkin, and on the other side of it, Ralph Peterkin himself.

Even in the dim starlight the remarkable likeness which Ralph bore to his dead brother was noticeable. He, also, was seated on the ground, and beside him lay a spade, a clasp-knife open, and the dead man's belt.

'Curious,' said Sarah, in a low voice, 'that we two should be in partnership again.'

'Husband and wife,' said Ralph, shrugging his shoulders.

'You can stow that,' she retorted dryly.

'It's a bond between us,' said the man. 'You can't get over it. Why did you send me word that Ned had played me false while I was down with the fever, unless it was because you were my wife?'

'I wanted you to get back the stone because of Ida.'

'What the devil had she to do with it? She went off in the end with Ned's pal, Tom Ferris, the same that gave him the tip that I had got the better of the fever, and was likely to be suspicious. Ida wasn't for Ned; no, and she wasn't for me either.'

'That's true, but you were both after the woman. You quarrelled about her as you quarrelled about what share each was to hold in the diamond. If Ida had been good enough to go off with you, I had a notion that you would both die – to prevent any accidents, I would have seen that you both died myself. Well then, I should have been left a widow, and, as I thought you should leave your widow properly provided for, I was anxious that you should get back the stone. You managed your part of the business badly. You made a great noise and foamed at the mouth, and did nothing. It was a good idea of his to pass himself off as you. You missed the track of him at Dunkeld.'

'Did I?' said the man in a surly voice.

'Yes, you did, and I took it up. It was your notion, I believe, that I wasn't going to be on in this act, but I was. I came here by coach expecting to find Ned here; instead of that we found him lying in the road by Jenkin's Claim. I didn't let on that I knew anything about him. He had been drugged – that was what was the matter with him. Doctor was a fool, or he'd have seen it. When the Doctor took him on to Raynham's I followed at a bit of a distance behind. The Doctor and Raynham went out, and I slipped in; I'd noticed the chain round his neck and guessed he had the diamond there, undoing his collar brought him round for a minute and I couldn't do anything.'

'You told the Inspector that you'd seen the diamond tonight.'

'So I did. And I tell you that I couldn't do anything. If you want to see that stone again you'll take your orders from me, tell the truth, and ask no questions. To proceed. Just then Raynham came back with the medicine for Ned, and I hid myself in the cupboard. Ned seemed to have dropped off again. I saw Raynham steal the belt and murder Ned. I saw him hide the money where we took it from just now. Then the Inspector and the Doctor came in, and found me in the cupboard ; you were listening outside and heard all I said then, I suppose.'

The man nodded.

'And you were fool enough to push the door open. I saw you, and it scared me. I was afraid they'd take the light and look for you; so I dropped it, to create a diversion; and when they'd lit it again, I began a bit of melodramatic business that I had seen in the door the ghost of Ned calling on me to denounce his murderer.'

'Yes, yes. I saw all that,' said Ralph impatiently. 'Then the shootin' began. The Inspector went off to the gulch.'

'Yes, he's a one-idea man, that Inspector. He's probably looking for me there now. Raynham went round to the back of his shanty without seeing me and dropped there, waiting. I came in then, and we lit the candle.'

'But why was it that when Raynham came back – to get the belt and make off with it, I suppose – and saw me standing in the doorway, he just gasped and dropped dead like that?'

'Simple enough. Raynham drank too much, and his heart had gone. He was already scared, and when he saw you he thought you were the ghost of the man he had murdered. He died of fright.'

'Why did you leave him there, and make me carry Ned here?'

'Don't ask questions. When the dawn comes, you'll know – and, if you do as you're told, you'll have the diamond back again. To speak more accurately, you'll have a half-share in the diamond.'

'That's not fair.'

'Very well; without me you'll get nothing.'

'All right,' said the man, 'I go under – always have.'

'Now then, I'll put a question to you. Who drugged Ned?'

'Don't know.'

'That's a lie. How came you here tonight at all?'

'Don't know. I was tramping about, miscellaneously.'

'That also is a lie.' Sarah smiled sweetly; she was playing the part of the person who, in a difficult situation has the whip-hand, and she enjoyed it. 'And,' she added, 'you'd much better tell me the truth.'

The man pulled out his revolver. 'Now then, you devil, I'll have my turn. Tell me who took that diamond, or I'll blow your brains out.'

Sarah laughed pleasantly. 'This ain't an enjoyable world,' she said. 'I'd think no more about leaving it than you would about puttin' me out of it. You'll get nothing from me that way. If you want a half share in that diamond you will hand me your revolver and tell me the truth.'

The man glared at her sullenly for a minute, and then handed her his revolver. 'I lighted by chance,' he said, 'on Ned's track two nights ago. I daren't track him in the ordinary way, and I got a chap to give him drugged baccy. I was just coming up to him when that damned coach picked him up, and by the time that I got to Raynham's shanty, the diamond was gone.'

'That will do,' said Sarah. 'I'm going to sleep till dawn.'

'I can't sleep alongside of that,' said Ralph, with a glance towards the corpse. 'I'll dig a hole and bury him first.'

'No, you won't. If you can't sleep you may keep awake. It will only be for an hour. What are you frightened of? Dead men do no harm.'

In the end Peterkin did drop off to sleep. He was waked by Sarah touching him on the shoulder.

'Get up,' she said. 'It's time to get back the diamond. Ned swallowed it when he thought I was going to take it from him, and it's there,' she touched the body with her foot.

Ralph shuddered, picked up the clasp-knife, and threw it down again.

'I can't do that,' he said. 'I can't hack open—'

'You fool, don't talk about it. That's what makes it worse. I tried to do. it and couldn't. You *must*. Here – I brought this from Raynham's when we skedaddled last night.'

It was a bottle of whiskey. Ralph took a deep draught at it, drew a long breath, and then suddenly knelt down beside his dead brother with the clasp-knife open in his hand. Sally stood at a little distance, covering him with the revolver.

There was no necessity for it. In a few minutes Ralph rose and came towards her, rubbing something with a rag of the clothes that the dead man had worn. His knees were shaking; even if he had meant treachery, he would have been physically incapable of running away with the diamond. The body was buried and the spade and knife hidden in the brushwood. Then the two moved away together.

'It's halves, then?' said Ralph.

'In the stone and the belt – yes.'

'If we get to England – that is.'

'We shall,' said Sarah confidently.

ACKNOWLEDGEMENTS

Three Men in the Dark would not have happened without the late Michael Cox, who published its original version, *Stories in the Dark*, in 1989. Nor would it be here now without the enthusiasm and generosity of David Brawn and Georgie Cauthery at HarperCollins. For her kindness and help with photocopying at a crucial stage, Judy Buckfield deserves a medal. Thank you all.

BIBLIOGRAPHY

Jerome K. Jerome

He did not produce many books of short stories, but all can be recommended. Stories included here come from these sources:

Told After Supper (Leadenhall Press, 1891)
The Haunted Mill

Novel Notes (Leadenhall Press, 1893)
The Dancing Partner
The Skeleton
The Snake

John Ingerfield (McClure, 1894)
The Woman of the Saeter
Silhouettes

I can also recommend:

The Passing of the Third Floor Back (Hurst & Blackett, 1907)

Barry Pain

The most prolific short story writer of the three. Stories included here come from these sources:

Stories and Interludes (Henry & Co., 1892)
The Glass of Supreme Moments

Stories in the Dark (Grant Richards, 1901)
The Undying Thing
The Moon-slave
The Green Light
The Case of Vincent Pyrwhit
The Gray Cat
The End of a Show

Stories in Grey (T. Werner Laurie, 1911)
Smeath
Linda

Here and Hereafter (Methuen, 1911)
The Tower
The Four-fingered Hand
The Unfinished Game

I can also recommend:

In a Canadian Canoe (Henry & Co., 1891)
Nothing Serious (Black & White, 1901)
Deals (Hodder & Stoughton, 1904)
The Kindness of the Celestial (Henry & Co., 1904)
Three Fantasies (Methuen, 1904)
The Shadow of the Unseen (Chapman & Hall, 1907)

(in collaboration with James Blythe – a fine witchcraft novel)
The New Gulliver (T. Werner Laurie, 1912)
Stories Without Tears (Mills & Boon, 1912)

Robert Barr

His crime fiction is worth finding but is really outside the scope of this book. All the stories included here come from:

Revenge! (Chatto & Windus, 1896)

ALSO AVAILABLE

Edith Nesbit's natural gift for storytelling, exemplified by *The Railway Children* and *Five Children and It*, has brought her worldwide renown as a classic children's author. But beyond her beloved children's stories lay a darker side to her imagination, revealed here in her chilling tales of the supernatural. Haunted by lifelong phobias which provoked, in her own words, 'nights and nights of anguish and horror, long years of bitterest fear and dread', Nesbit was inspired to pen terrifying stories of a twilight world where the dead walked the earth.

All but forgotten for almost a hundred years until *In the Dark* was first published 30 years ago, this collection finally restored Nesbit's reputation as one of the most accomplished and entertaining ghost-story writers of the Victorian age. With seven extra newly-discovered stories now appearing for the first time in paperback, this revised edition includes a new introduction by Hugh Lamb exploring the life of the woman behind these tales and the events and experiences that contributed to her fascination with the macabre.

ISBN: 978-0-00-